Maisey Yates is a *New York Times* bestselling author of over one hundred romance novels. Whether she's writing stories about strong, hard-working cowboys, dissolute princes or multigenerational families, she loves getting lost in fictional worlds. An avid knitter, with a dangerous yarn addiction and an aversion to housework, Maisey lives with her husband and three kids in rural Oregon. Check out her website: maiseyyates.com

New York Times and *USA TODAY* bestselling author **Barbara Dunlop** has written more than forty novels for Mills & Boon, including the acclaimed Chicago Sons series. Her sexy, lighthearted stories regularly hit bestseller lists. Barbara is a three-time finalist for the Romance Writers of America's *RITA®* Award.

Also by Maisey Yates

Rancher's Wild Secret
Claiming the Rancher's Heir
The Rancher's Wager
Take Me, Cowboy
Hold Me, Cowboy
Seduce Me, Cowboy
Claim Me, Cowboy
Want Me, Cowboy
Need Me, Cowboy

Also by Barbara Dunlop

Sex, Lies and the CEO
Seduced by the CEO
A Bargain with the Boss
His Stolen Bride
The Twin Switch
The Dating Dare

Discover more at millsandboon.co.uk

RANCHER'S CHRISTMAS STORM

MAISEY YATES

BIDDING ON A TEXAN

BARBARA DUNLOP

MILLS & BOON

First Published in Great Britain 2021
by Mills & Boon, an imprint of HarperCollins*Publishers* Ltd
1 London Bridge Street, London, SE1 9GF

www.harpercollins.co.uk

HarperCollins*Publishers*
1st Floor, Watermarque Building,
Ringsend Road, Dublin 4, Ireland

Rancher's Christmas Storm © 2021 Maisey Yates
Bidding On A Texan © 2021 Harlequin Books S.A.

Special thanks and acknowledgement are given to Barbara Dunlop for her contribution to the *Texas Cattleman's Club: Heir Apparent* series.

ISBN: 978-0-263-28304-4

0921

RANCHER'S CHRISTMAS STORM

MAISEY YATES

One

As Honey Cooper looked around the beautiful tasting room that—other than the vineyards themselves—was the crown jewel of Cowboy Wines—she thought to herself that if she had a book of matches and just a tiny bit more moxie, she might've burned the entire place to the ground.

Not that it could ever be said that she was lacking in moxie—maybe it was just the desire to avoid prison. Perhaps not the best reason to avoid engaging in the torching of her family winery. Scratch that, her family's *former* winery.

Until it had been sold to Jericho Smith. Jericho Smith, who was the most infuriating, obnoxious, sexy man she had ever known.

He made her itch. Down beneath her skin where she couldn't scratch it. It drove her crazy. And now he had

her legacy. Just because her brothers were no longer interested in the day-to-day running of Cowboy Wines
and her father wanted to retire, Jericho had offered to
buy and her father had sold. Sure, she had a tidy sum
of money sitting in her bank account that her father
had felt was her due post sale, but that didn't matter. It
wasn't the point.

Maybe she should go find a matchbook.

Instead, she looked down at her phone—she had
bought herself a smartphone with her ill-gotten rage
money—and saw that it had lit up again. She had a
message.

It was from Donovan. Which thrilled her a little bit.

Donovan ran an equine facility up north, on the outskirts of Portland. She had met him on a dating app.
A dating app. Yes, Honey Cooper had signed up for a
dating app.

But the thing was, she was really sick of the pickings
down in Gold Valley. She was sick of cowboys. She was
sick of everybody knowing her brothers. Her father.

Jericho.

She was untouchable here. They might as well up
and put her in a glass case. Everybody acted like they
were afraid of getting punched in the face if they came
within thirty yards of her. In fairness, they probably
were in danger of getting punched in the face. Jackson
and Creed weren't exactly known for their measured
temperaments, and when it came to Jericho… Well, he
was the older brother that she absolutely didn't need.

He twisted her up in ways she hated, and had for as
long as she'd noticed that boys were different from girls.
Of course, the problem with knowing a man that long
was that he could only see you as the pigtail-wearing

brat you'd once been and would never really see you as a woman.

There was also the fact she knew all too well that Jericho's personal policy when it came to relationships was that they were best as a good time, not a long time.

But he was just so hot.

So was Donavan though. You know, if the pictures that she had gotten from him weren't a lie. No, they weren't those kind of pictures. He had not sent her his nudes. She wasn't sure if she was offended by that or not, as she had it on very good authority—TV—that men often sent women their anatomy when they wanted to hook up.

Not that they physically sent their anatomy, but pictures of them.

Still, she was on the road to getting out of Gold Valley, to getting away from the winery—without setting it on fire—and getting away from Jericho once and for all.

That was part of the problem. The proximity was killing her. She still lived at Cowboy Wines. And she felt surrounded—absolutely surrounded—by her father's perfidy.

So she was going to run away to Portland. Take a job at a different ranch. Maybe lose her virginity to Donovan.

No, she was *definitely* going to lose her virginity to Donovan.

For Christmas.

And she would forget all about Jericho and the fact that she thought he was hot. And the fact that he had devastated her by buying the winery. The winery that had been her only dream, her only goal for as long as she could remember. She'd knuckled down and worked the land, worked it till her knuckles bled, the same as the rest of them, for years. And now it was gone.

To add insult to injury, she still thought he was hot. Even while furious with him. Even while he took a new woman into his bed practically every night. Which didn't matter.

She didn't care about that. She didn't care. Because she didn't actually want to date him. She just wanted to climb him like a tree.

And who didn't? Honestly. He was incredibly beautiful. Tall, broad and well muscled. Sin in cowboy boots. And in a cowboy hat. And a tight T-shirt. And as much as she would like to actually be sick of cowboys, it was kind of her aesthetic.

She'd lost her mother when she was only thirteen, and it had stuck with her. There was something about the loss that was a lot like the bottom of the world had fallen out, and she'd done her best to cling to what she could.

She had her dad, she had her brothers and the most important thing to her had been to fit in with them.

She knew that dealing with her in her grief had been hard for her dad so she'd done her best to be more stoic. She'd pushed off her desire to experiment with makeup or clothes or anything like that.

She'd become the cowgirl she needed to be.

But it hadn't gotten her anywhere. Now she was ready for something else.

To see what else she could do and be.

Donovan was different. He was sophisticated. The place he ran was an *equine facility.* It wasn't a *ranch.* She wouldn't be a ranch hand. She would be a horse trainer. She would be fancy. She would be free.

She would not be a virgin.

If her father didn't think that she needed a winery, then she didn't need to be around them.

That made her heart clench tight. She wasn't… She wasn't going to fall out with her family. Not entirely. Her mother had died when she was so young, and her father had taken good care of her. But he just didn't understand having a daughter. He loved her. She knew that—no matter how difficult things had been around the time of her mother's death, she did know that. But it didn't occur to him that she might want a piece of this place. Even though she had worked it most of her life.

And her brothers… They were pains in the butt. They really were. But they loved her. She needed distance though.

She so badly needed distance.

And she had a plan to get it.

She picked up her phone and looked at the message.

What's your estimated date of arrival?

I was thinking the week of Christmas.

She was actually thinking she'd leave tomorrow. That was what she was thinking. Leaving tomorrow. Getting out. Getting gone. Pulling off the Band-Aid.

She had never missed Christmas with her family before. But this was part of her defiance. She wasn't going to consult them on her leaving. She was going to just… She was going to go. She was going to do whatever she wanted.

She didn't need to ask their permission, and she hadn't. She hadn't told them any of what she was thinking, or let them know how furious she was, because why would she?

Her dad didn't want to deal with her emotions anyway.

Plus he was rarely around anymore. She had no idea what was going on with him, but he was never home. Her brothers were married now—and to the Maxfields at that. Which meant they would be off doing things at their fancy winery. Or worse. Expecting her to join them.

It wasn't that she didn't like her sisters-in-law. They were just…a lot. A whole lot. Cricket was her age—she supposed they ought to be friends. It was just… She had a difficult time thinking about how she was going to cozy up to a girl who was sleeping with her brother. *Ew.*

That would work just fine. I'll have a room ready for you.

She hoped that it would be a room *with* him.

She had to do something. To erase this place, her pain, her stupid, pointless attraction to Jericho, the man who had stolen her whole future from her. The man who owned way too much space in her head.

Her stomach twisted in defiance of that thought.

She did hope there was a room ready for the two of them to share. She *did.* She was ready. She was ready for this. For a change. For something new. For a chance to be different.

She was going to make her way in the world. And she did not need Cowboy Wines to do it.

Jericho was tired. Down to his bones. And he only had a day or so before he had to leave for the Dalton family Christmas.

He would love to resist it. Hell, he would love to be an asshole and just stay away entirely no matter how many times the Daltons reached out. But two months ago, he was contacted by West Caldwell, who was apparently his half brother, telling him about his connection to the Dalton family.

Apparently Hank had expected Jericho would be too mad to speak to him, considering it had come out that his various half children were under the impression he'd known about them and denied them, even though that wasn't true.

West had been the voluntary envoy, meeting him down at the Gold Valley Saloon, explaining the situation and how he himself had come to be in Gold Valley and come to be part of the Dalton clan.

The thing was, Jericho had already known about his connection to the Daltons. He'd known about it from the time he was old enough to understand that everyone had a father—it was just that his own didn't give a fuck.

But it turned out he'd gotten that wrong.

Hank Dalton hadn't known. The infamous retired rodeo cowboy was apparently the father to a whole passel of kids he didn't know he had. Owing to his wild years, when he had been philandering and cheating on his wife—and apparently not understanding condom usage—he had a spread of kids in their thirties. Some of whom were with his wife, Tammy, others of whom were not.

Apparently, he was the last one who hadn't been tracked down, owed to the fact that Hank hadn't known his first name, and his last name was so common.

Hank was infamous in Gold Valley, and his mother had made no secret of the fact that he was his father.

But then, his mother had died when Jericho was only sixteen, and it had been the Cooper family that had taken him in. Finished raising him. Made sure that he never wanted for much of anything.

Cancer was a bitch and it had taken his strong, caring mother from him far too soon. A pain he had in common with the Coopers. They didn't talk about it—feelings weren't high on their list of things to deal with—but they all just…knew. That was enough.

They'd been enough.

And he had just never… Hank had rejected her as far as she was concerned, and Jericho had never wanted to take a damn thing from Hank.

But the story was more complicated than that. It turned out it was Hank's wife, Tammy, who had dealt with the former mistresses who'd all had his children. Hank himself had never really known.

And so he was… He was doing this. He was heading up to this family Christmas thing. And he didn't know what the hell was in store for him. But he'd spent his life without any real family. He was curious, frankly. To see this whole big family that was his.

Thankfully, Honey would be around to see to the running of the winery. Plus, Jackson and Creed could get their asses in gear to give them some help. They were like brothers to him.

And Honey was…

Under his skin in ways he didn't like to acknowledge. He'd known her since she was a scrappy, spiky kid, and now she was a scrappy, spiky woman who ignited his blood and made him question if hell was really all that hot, or if it was something he should risk.

Lord knew, if he ever touched her, Jackson and Creed would have his head on a pike. And if he were the kind of man who could offer something extra, it might be different.

But in his mind, love was a sacrifice. And he'd bled out all that he could on that score.

So he kept his fly up and his hands to himself. Around her anyway.

Unwanted attraction aside, she was a good worker, and she would be more than up to the task of seeing to the place around the holidays. In fact, since he'd bought the place, he swore she'd been working two times as hard.

Being here without him wouldn't be that difficult either, especially because it wasn't exactly prime wine tasting time. They had a couple of private parties, but otherwise, people were getting together and sitting outdoors and watching music every week during this time of the year. Maybe his success in life was part of the reason he'd agreed to meet with the Daltons.

Because hell, he'd gotten pretty far in life without Hank.

He pulled himself up from nothing with bloody knuckles. Bought his first ranch after years of working it. Bought another one. Expanded. Made profits. Got to the point where he could buy the winery. And now he had several different business ventures relating to ranching and agriculture.

And he was successful. No matter how you looked at it.

He didn't need the Daltons' pity or their money. There had been a time when his mother really could've used it. They had gotten a single settlement from Hank, but her cancer had bankrupted them.

He'd been a kid left with nothing in the end. And yeah, he'd spent some time being bitter about it. Until he'd decided the best revenge could only ever be living well, and he'd done whatever the hell he could to make sure he was living as well as any man could be.

He worked hard, he played harder. Family, marriage… That shit wasn't in the cards for him.

He walked into the winery tasting room, to see Honey leaning over the table on her phone. She was wearing a pair of blue jeans that seemed on a mission to hug her ass as tightly as possible.

No. Honey was not his sister. She was also barely over the age of twenty-two, too damned young, too damned earnest and more likely to bite him on the wrist than kiss him. She was like a wild mink.

And damn if it didn't appeal.

He knew exactly when the switch had flipped, and he did his best to never think about it. It had been back last November when Creed had announced he was marrying his rival—because she was pregnant.

Honey had been incensed, a furious little ball of rage.

"You don't marry somebody just because you lust after them. That's silly."

"Fine. The pregnancy."

"I still don't understand how you could be so stupid. You're not a kid."

"Honey, I pray that you always keep your head when it comes to situations of physical desire."

"I would never get that stupid over a man."

She'd said that with total and certain confidence and

something had broken inside him. Shattered. She was a woman.

And he wondered what sort of man could make her that stupid.

His immediate, gut response had been...

Him.

He'd wanted to run out of there like his pants were on fire and his ass was catching. Instead he'd stayed—like it was nothing—and tamped it all down to a manageable burn.

It was what he'd been doing ever since.

"Afternoon."

She lifted her head slowly, then turned to look at him, her expression cool. "Jericho."

"Did you practice that face in the mirror?"

"What face?" she said, the coolness evaporating immediately, her eyebrows locking together.

"There you go. Now you look like you. I'm going to need you to oversee things while I'm gone over Christmas."

"Excuse me?"

"You heard me."

She blinked wide, whiskey eyes. "Do you think that you're my... Do you think you're my boss, Jericho?"

"Honey," he said, realizing that he was tempting fate. And her temper. "I own the winery now. You do work for me." He was the one that would be signing the checks once that first pay cycle ended. So maybe she hadn't realized it. But it was true.

"I... I quit," she said.

"Excuse me?"

"I quit. I'm leaving, actually. I'm leaving."

"You're leaving?"

"Jericho, do you always just repeat what women say? Because if so, I find it hard to believe that you have such good luck with them."

"Women don't gravitate to me for my conversational skills," he said.

A streak of color flooded her cheeks. And he would be a fool to read anything into that.

"I don't really care why women seek out your…company. I'm not seeking your company out. I'm leaving. I got a job."

"You…" He realized he was about to say *you got a job*. "Where?"

"Up near Portland."

"What are you going to do? Work at one of those assy coffee shops that only serves drinks in one size? And sells more macho than coffee?"

"It's not in the city. It's a ranch on the outskirts. An equine facility. I got a job there as a trainer."

"Sight unseen?"

"Yes."

"What the hell is this place called?"

"None of your business."

"Does your father know?"

"My father is too busy with… Well, he seems to have taken to my brothers marrying into the Maxfield family with a lot of enthusiasm."

"What's that supposed to mean?"

He knew what it was supposed to mean. Cash Cooper had carried on a youthful affair with Lucinda Maxfield years ago. Time and misunderstandings had separated them. But since her marriage to James had fallen apart, and Cash's wife had passed, he suspected the two of them had rekindled things.

And it seemed Honey suspected it too.

"Apparently the Maxfield women are universally irresistible to the men in my family." She shook her head. "But I don't want to spend my Christmas at Maxfield Vineyards. I don't want to be part of their fancy ass… whatever. I don't want you to own Cowboy Wines. I want everything to go back to the way it was. But it isn't going to. Which means I'm going to take myself off. I got a place. And I really like… I really like Donovan."

"Who's Donovan?" he asked, eyes narrowing. Jackson and Creed weren't currently in residence, which meant that it was up to him to make sure she wasn't doing anything dumbass.

Honey was open; she was honest to a near fault. If the thought was in her head, it was out of her mouth just as quick.

The fact that she'd been keeping secrets set off big loud alarm bells.

"He owns the equine facility that I'm going to," she said, sniffing loudly. "And I've been talking with him on an app."

His stomach went tight. "Explain."

"Well, if you must know, I met him on a dating app."

"You met a guy that you're going to go work for *on a dating app*?"

"Yes."

"This is an HR violation waiting to happen."

"I think he might be HR."

"All the more reason for you to turn tail and run. This doesn't sound like a safe situation at all."

"I'm not a *child*, Jericho. And anyway, I'm going up there with the express intention of violating HR mandates."

"Hell no." Anger burned in his gut. Honey might not be for him. He knew she wasn't. But even so, he was not going to let Honey Cooper run off up north to shack up with some guy who owned an equine facility—that was the most pretentious little bullshit he'd ever heard—and…start sleeping with him immediately. The very idea made him see red.

"No," he said. "You are not doing that. You are staying here."

"It may shock you to learn, Jericho, that you don't get to control my life. You don't get to tell me what to do. You don't even get the tiniest say in what I do with my time. Because it isn't your business."

"You are my business, Honey Cooper, whether you like it or not."

She rounded on him, her expression a fury. "You're not my brother, asshole. You're not my boss, and it isn't your decision. I'm leaving. I'm leaving tomorrow. I've got everything packed up."

"That's a problem, because I'm also leaving tomorrow."

"Sounds like a you problem."

"Honey…"

"No," she said. "I'm out. I should've been the first in line to buy the winery. My father never consulted me. You never considered it. You never considered my feelings at all. Acting concerned for me now, when you bought out my family's winery without thinking that I might want to…"

"I didn't realize Cash didn't consult you." He felt slightly guilty about saying that, because Jackson had basically told him that Honey wouldn't be happy about the decision. And he'd chosen to ignore that. He'd chosen to go ahead with it, because it was what he wanted. There wasn't a whole lot in this world that he could claim as a legacy. His mother was dead; his father had never wanted much of anything to do with him—so he'd thought. Cowboy Wines was the closest thing he had to a family anything. The Coopers were the closest thing he had to a family.

Which meant that getting a piece of it had mattered to him. And when Cash had wanted out...

He never mentioned the possibility of selling it to Honey. It wasn't like he had taken it out from under her deliberately. And she hadn't said anything, not a damn thing, in the time since.

But Honey's happiness meant something to him. The Coopers meant something to him. Which was why, no matter how nice Honey's ass looked in a pair of jeans, he'd never do anything about it. There were plenty of women out there. More than willing to warm his bed for a few hours. He wasn't going to mess with his friends' sister. He also wasn't going to let her go off half-cocked to warm some other dude's bed just because she was mad.

Not that he didn't figure she'd be warming beds, or that she hadn't. It was just that this was a bad idea. Clearly, up front from the start. And there was no point doing something that was so clearly this dumbass right from step one.

"It doesn't matter whether you knew or not. You should talk to me. You all should talk to me."

"The thing is, I wanted it." He figured honesty was the best policy here. "Whatever was going to get it. Whether you're happy about it or not."

"Well, I'm not happy. But it doesn't matter, because I won't be around to be unhappy anymore. Fuck you."

She turned around and stalked out of the room, and he resisted the urge to go after her. Honey and her tantrums weren't his problem. He had bigger issues. Like making sure everything was covered before he went up to deal with the Daltons. Of course, if he called Creed and Jackson about it, he would blow Honey's operation. Which was probably for the best.

He took his phone out of his pocket and dialed Jackson. "Hey. I'm going to need your help with the winery for the next week."

"All right."

"I'm going to meet my family."

"Your family?"

"Yeah. My father. Hank Dalton."

"Well, hell."

"Don't say it like that. It's not that big of a deal."

"It *is* a big deal," Jackson insisted. "He finally acknowledged your existence?"

He didn't particularly want to talk about this. But it was reality right now, so he supposed there was no avoiding it. "He didn't know about my existence. Apparently."

"Hell."

"I don't see it as that big of a deal. So I don't see why you should."

"Because it's a big fucking deal."

"Only if you think I'm going to make a big, happy family out of it. I'm going up for some big Christmas thing. That's it."

"Well, I don't mind helping out." And he thought about selling Honey out just then. But he didn't.

"Thanks."

He might pay for that later. But he would deal with her. No point sending Jackson off after her.

She was already angry enough. He wouldn't make it worse. And hell, she would see reason. He couldn't actually imagine Honey taking off and moving up north. She wouldn't do it.

No. She would come to her senses and see reason.

She had to. He didn't want to think too deep about the alternative.

Two

Honey flung a suitcase into the bed of her truck and slapped her hands together. She had every box in her bedroom all packed up. And she was ready to go. She had left a note for her dad.

The boxes would be picked up by a moving company—she was really enjoying the fact that she'd gotten a bit of money from the sale of the winery—and driven up separately.

She would be taking her truck and an overnight bag. Traveling light. And she was ready. Especially after that discussion with Jericho yesterday. Which couldn't even be called a discussion. He was such a high-handed dick. And she was over it. Honestly, completely and utterly over men acting like they thought they knew what was best for her life. *If it was only acting like they knew what was best for my life, it wouldn't be that bad.* But they actually made decisions that impacted her life and didn't seem to get it when it infuriated her. More than infuriated. She was so… She was just so hurt by the whole thing with the vineyard.

She didn't know that she would ever really get over it.

Getting ready to leave this place now… She wished that it felt more triumphant. Instead, it felt sad. This place housed the few memories that she had of her mother. And so many happy ones with her father and her brothers. And yes, even Jericho.

They were a close family, and they always had been. But this move by her dad had driven such a wedge between them.

A wedge she hadn't told anyone about. But she didn't know how. Didn't know how to do it without flying off the handle, and after a decade of keeping it all to herself, the idea of letting it all out terrified her.

And her brothers had gone off and got married… It was just that everything was different. She didn't think it could ever go back to the way it was. No, she knew it couldn't. So she might as well start over. She might as well.

She put her hands on her hips and looked back at the room that was neatly stacked with boxes and then looked at her truck. There was no point delaying it now. She was on her way.

She walked around to the other side of her truck and started when she saw Jericho standing back next to a tree, his arms crossed over his broad chest.

His black hat was pulled low over his face, his dark eyes glittering. "And where exactly do you think you're going?"

"Lake Oswego," she said.

"Oh please," he said. "You're going to last about five minutes there. You're going to die of hipster."

"I don't think Lake Oswego is renowned for its hipsterdom."

He arched a dark brow and it made her stomach feel funny. "You're really leaving?"

She frowned deeply. "My shit is packed. What do you think?"

"Stay," he said, the word low and rumbling, and it tugged at her and she hated it. She had to get away from here. From him. She'd wanted a whole bunch of things for years. To be an equal to her brothers, to work this winery as they'd done and be able to have a piece of it someday. For Jericho to look at her with heat in his eyes. She wasn't going to be able to find new patterns if she didn't change things. Everything. "Don't be rash about it."

She really wanted to punch him for that. He had no idea. This wasn't rash. It was the culmination of so much stuff. Of realizing that she was going to be treading water in Gold Valley for the rest of her life.

She had no career here. Not like she'd believed.

Her crush—toxic attraction sprinkled with a dash of irritation… Whatever you wanted to call it, it was on him.

"I'm going to go."

"Look. I asked your brother to come here and handle things while I was away, and I did not blow your cover. So now I want you to be reasonable."

"*Reasonable* meaning do exactly what you want me to do?"

He lifted a brow, which she had privately deemed his most arrogant eyebrow some years ago. "Hell yeah."

She huffed. "Jericho, I don't owe you the reality that you want. You sure as hell didn't care about what I wanted when you bought the winery."

"It wasn't that I didn't care."

"It was. You didn't talk to me about it. Nothing. My entire world felt like it had been pulled out from under my feet."

"How is it different? You didn't own the place when your dad ran it. Why is it so different working for me?"

"Because I…" It hurt, this admission. But she was going to have to practice it because she was going to have to tell her dad eventually. Tell him without dissolving. She might as well practice on Jericho. "Because I expected someday that maybe my father would leave this to me. To us. I don't have any problem with you having a piece of it. You've been part of us from… For a long time. But me being cut out of it…that's what I can't understand."

"You got some money."

"I did. But it's not the same as getting this land. I can go earn money anywhere. Which is what I'm going to do."

"And you're going to sleep with this guy?"

That spiked a wave of fury in her blood. He had her vineyard. He had her desire. He didn't deserve to be spared her honesty. "Yep. Lots of times."

"Honey…"

Her eyes collided with his, and there was something about the look on his face that made a reckless heat careen through her blood. Because while she was talking about sleeping with Donovan, she couldn't actively picture it. Yes, she'd seen photographs of him, but they couldn't compare to Jericho standing in front of her in the angry, hard, hot flesh.

His mouth firmed into a grim line.

"What?"

"It's a bad idea," he said, his voice hard.

"So what?" she asked. "Has every one of your ideas been good?"

He cleared his throat. "Well, no."

"Why do I have to make good decisions all the time? I want to make a bad decision. I want to try something. I don't think it's up to you to decide whether or not I get to do something crazy. So, I'm off."

"Dammit, Honey."

"Damn *you*, Jericho." She walked past him, and then he grabbed her by the arm, whirling her to face him. She felt like all the breath had been sucked out of her body as she stared into his thunderous face.

She took stock of him. Of his beautiful features. His dark brown eyes and skin, the black stubble that covered his square jaw. And she felt like he was taking up all the space. In addition to having taken this winery from her, he had stolen her ability to breathe. Her ability to think. And right now it just enraged her.

"Let go of me."

She wouldn't allow him to steal this from her too. He had been her most secret, most shameful fantasy for far too long, and she was on her way to make something new, to get something new. She was going to have what she wanted. And she did want Donovan. Or at least, she really wanted to want Donovan. And that was going to have to be enough, because she couldn't have Jericho.

Ever.

He was now the emblem of everything ruinous.

And she had called her brothers out for being dumbasses more than once, too many times to ever let herself be a dumbass over a man.

You don't think that you're being dumb about Donovan?

No. She wasn't. Because the simple truth was... He was handsome, and maybe having a fling with him would be fun. But it wouldn't devastate her. There was no way that it could. Because the ranch wasn't the family winery.

And he wasn't a man that was so close to her brothers he was practically family.

And he didn't... He didn't make her itch under her skin.

He didn't get to places that she couldn't reach.

So there was no risk involved. Jericho represented too much risk. Every risk. Every risk she couldn't take.

So yes, she could run away to Lake Oswego. She could hook up with a guy who may or may not be permanent. But she could never... She could never.

She jerked away from him and climbed up into the cab of her truck, defiant. Then she slammed the heavy door and unrolled her window. "I'm leaving."

"Yeah, you're doing a real convincing job of it too."

"I'll run your ass over if you get in my way."

"Honey..."

"Look, Merry Christmas and whatever. And good luck with your family. I don't hate you." Her throat suddenly got tight. "I just can't be here."

She started the engine, and before she could think better of it, she put the truck in Drive and punched the gas. And then she was leaving. Driving away from the little house she had called her own for years. From the winery that had always been her home. From the man who had given her butterflies in her stomach since before she knew what it meant.

This was better. Because she couldn't stay here. Held back, held in place, not anymore. Everyone else had moved on. And she would have to watch Jericho bring an endless succession of women to the winery for sex for the rest of her life. And never resolve the feelings that she had… Never move on. She hated how much this was about that. How much it was about him.

So she drove away, and she challenged herself not to look back. She was not going to look back.

And pretty soon the road became less familiar, winding and lined with trees. And as she went up in elevation, what had started as a light dusting of the snow turned into big banks of it piled up on the sides of the road.

Luckily, it wasn't cold enough right now to turn anything to ice.

She was on her way. She was on her way. She had quite a few miles of the middle of nowhere before she hit the interstate, and so she plugged her new phone in and cranked some country music, singing along with Luke Bryan, but pretty soon the lyrics of the song made her too sad. And she couldn't even say why, because it was a party tune about someone being excited to hear her song playing on the radio. Maybe it was because it reminded her of warm nights at the winery and sitting around with her family. Sitting with Jericho. Making s'mores and dancing up on the tailgate.

But the problem was, somewhere deep in her soul, that it always felt a little bit electric because he was there. And she just couldn't…

Why are you really mad?

She didn't want to think about that. She did not want to think about why she was really upset. Why she really needed to leave. Because him buying the vineyard had shown her something. That he really didn't think about her. And that she thought about him far too much. Way more than a woman should think about a man who had never showed any interest in her at all.

The road wound along the river, and she took in the beautiful scene. The rapids rolling over big smooth rocks, pine trees lining the banks and even a bald eagle giving her a patriotic show as he went fishing in the water.

And you're moving to the city.

It was not the city. It was the outskirts of the city, and she would be at an equine facility. Really, it was completely up her alley. It was great. It was going to be fine.

Better than fine. Better than fine.

She was really full of affirmations today.

Sadly, she did not feel all that affirmed.

Suddenly, her truck sputtered slightly and gave a jolt. She startled, looking around as if there would be answers for what the hell was going on out there in nature.

It sputtered again, and she pulled over to the side of the road, letting it idle as she started breathing hard.

It would be fine. It was fine.

She put it in Drive and started to maneuver back out onto the road, and it made a horrible grinding sound and then stopped.

Well. Shit.

She grabbed her phone to call her brothers and saw that she didn't have any bars.

What the hell? Had she driven back into 1996?

She got out of the truck and looked around. It was freezing. The wind whipped up, the sky going gray.

It felt ominous.

She couldn't walk back to Gold Valley. She had driven more than an hour, and it would take her all day. On the route that she had driven, there was no town back or forward for at least fifteen miles.

This was…terrible.

Horrible.

No one knew where she'd gone, that she'd left, that she was coming…

Only Jericho knew and he wasn't expecting her to get in touch anytime soon. Donavan didn't even know to be expecting her.

Someone would happen down the road, she was certain of that.

She was not going to panic. There was no point panicking. She just had to deal. She had protein bars in the glove box. She reached over and opened it, grabbed one and opened it immediately, suddenly feeling ravenous. Because, of course, the prospect of being stuck here did not agree with her at all.

Someone would come by. It wasn't like she was in the middle of nowhere.

She tore open the bar and shoved the food into her mouth.

She was fine. It was fine. Forty-five minutes into sitting there, she felt much less fine. Especially when the first light snowflake tumbled from the sky.

Great. She was going to freeze to death on the side of the road. A frozen pathetic virgin, whose last thought wouldn't be the man she was going to have sex with, but her older brothers' best friend, whom she had left behind.

She laid her head back against the seat and groaned.

And instantly, her mind conjured up summer. Summer, and Jericho half naked at the ocean. Wearing nothing but a pair of swim shorts, low on his hips. She could still remember the way that line cut right there, lowering her IQ by several points. His washboard abs, his chest, with just the right amount of dark hair.

And his skin… She wanted to lick it. And she had never licked another person in her life, but she was absolutely confident she wanted to lick him.

And punch him. In fairly equal measure most of the time. And what the hell was that?

She pounded her head against the back of the seat now.

"And here you are, just beginning to be responsible and take control of yourself. Here is your reward."

Freezing in her truck.

She heard a truck engine before she saw one. She turned sharply, opening the driver's-side door and stumbling out of the cab of the truck quickly. She didn't even bother to put her coat and mittens on.

She just started to wave.

She was a motorist, and she was in distress. And she was going to make sure this person knew that she was distressed.

She hopped up and down, feeling ridiculous, but her desperation outweighed the ridiculousness by a fair amount.

It was a red truck, sort of a rusty red. And it did not take her long to realize…

No.

Of course.

The bane of her existence. The object of her desire.

That damn pain in the ass.

He turned his blinker on, and she took a step back, and then he pulled right into the outcropping where she had parked her truck.

"What the hell?"

She looked into Jericho's stormy face.

"Well," she said. "I am having some car trouble. And I have no cell service."

"Shit," he said.

"What are you doing?"

"I told you that I was leaving. I'm heading up north to go to this… Big Dalton family shindig. They rented some complex up in the mountains."

"Oh really?"

"In Washington."

"In Washington?"

"Yeah."

"Can you drop me off?"

"Drop you off?"

"We're repeating again. And yes," she said. "In Lake Oswego. That would be perfect. I could have a tow truck bring my truck up there. But then I don't have to delay anything."

She really badly needed to get there. She needed to see Donovan in person. She needed to get this all taken care of. She just really needed it.

"You want me to drive you up to your fancy equine facility booty call?"

"How many times have I watched you pick up squealing, giggling bridesmaids at bachelorette parties?"

It was a fair question. Because she had watched him.

A lot. In fact, she had something of a running tally in her head. And she didn't like it. It made her want to vomit her guts out every time.

She hated the idea of a woman touching him. She hated it.

Some woman running her hands over those abs. The ones that she wanted to lick.

The ones that she hated herself for wanting to lick.

Because there was just no point to it. He was Creed and Jackson's best friend. He was basically a surrogate son to her father, and try as she might, she genuinely could not see Jericho as a brother. She just couldn't.

And he wasn't… He was never going to marry her.

She didn't want to marry him anyway. She wasn't even sure she wanted to get married. She didn't know what she wanted. She had been certain that it was the winery, but now that wasn't going to happen and she had to reevaluate things. Wanting to lick somebody's abs did not equate to wanting to marry them.

But they couldn't just… They couldn't do anything. Not given the proximity of their lives. Not given just how enmeshed they were.

But that did not mean that she liked knowing that he was off fucking some other girl.

"It will be a few," he said.

"How many times have you watched me pick up a guy?"

She could practically hear him grinding his teeth together. "I haven't."

Her cheeks were hot, but she was determined to be bold in this. Her brothers had never been discreet about their sex lives, and Jericho certainly hadn't been. Why should she? "Drive me to my booty call," she said.

It was poetic in a way.

She would use Jericho as a vehicle to get rid of her virginity. Not… Just in the way that he was going to actually drive the vehicle that would lead her up to the guy that was going to take her virginity. And that would be perfect.

"Your brothers…"

"Can hardly expect that I don't have a sex life," she said, lying, since she clearly did not have a sex life, but she hoped that Jericho didn't know that.

"They probably aren't going to want to know about you having a sex life with some guy who's going to be signing your paychecks."

"Right. Like you've never had an ill-advised love affair."

He huffed a laugh. "I wouldn't call anything that I've ever had 'a love affair.'"

"We can stand around debating the semantics of where you had your dick, Jericho, or we can get out of the cold. I would like to get out of the cold. Can you give me a damned ride or not?"

She was incredibly proud of herself for not falling apart completely for saying the word *dick* in his presence, especially not when she meant his actual dick, which made her feel sweaty and hot and more than a little bit excited. She wasn't going to think about his dick. No. She was not.

She really needed to take care of her virginity.

Not in the way she had been taking care of it, which had been like a preservation project. This was eradication.

"Yeah, I'll give you a ride."

"Brilliant," she said. She took a photo of exactly

where the truck was and the mile marker it was by, grabbed her suitcase and hefted it out of the bed, slinging it over into Jericho's.

Then she climbed up into the passenger side.

Thankfully, the truck was warm. And she buckled up, snuggling into the much more comfortable seats.

"Your truck's fancy ass," she said.

"I'm rich as fuck," he said.

She raised her brows. "Must be nice."

"Didn't you get a bit of money from the sale?"

"Yeah," she said, idly adjusting the heater knob on the truck.

"So, why don't you buy yourself a new truck?"

"Well, I don't really want a new truck. I mean I don't really need one. I mean, I don't really know what I want. It'll take some trying to figure it out."

"Right. Hence the taking the new job with the guy that you're…"

"I like him," she said.

"Great," he said. "Happy for you."

"You don't seem happy for me."

"Did you want me to throw you a party? A 'Honey is going to get laid' party?"

"That's all you're thinking in terms of. Maybe I really like him."

"Sorry. But you don't seem like you do."

"You don't…" She sputtered. "You don't get to decide what I sound like."

They drove down the road, fat flakes building as they hit the windshield.

"Is this four-wheel drive?" she asked.

He shot her a sideways look. It clearly said: *What do you think?*

She continued, "I do like him."

"You have shown a lot more emotion over generally being pissed off with me than you have over being with him. Being horny for somebody is not the same as being into them. Like into them completely."

"Excuse me," she said. "I'm not horny for him. I am not a fourteen-year-old boy."

"If you're not horny, what's the point?"

"I oppose the terminology," she said.

"Oh, I'm sorry. Did you want to split hairs about your sex language?"

"I would rather not get into sex language with you. How about that?"

"Suit yourself."

She cleared her throat. "It doesn't bother you to use it with me?"

"Hell no. I say it to anybody. I'd say it to your brothers."

"So I am…the same as my brothers to you."

"Yeah," he said.

"Bullshit," she practically screamed, but she was losing her mind here. He was not one of her brothers. He was being a possessive, demanding jerk, and he wasn't even one of her brothers. But worse, he was a man she wanted to be possessive of for all the wrong reasons. Still wrong. Still not what she wanted. Never what she wanted.

"You would not want Jackson or Creed to go sleep with somebody that they were working with. Hell, Jackson was working with Cricket when he started to have sex with her. She's my age. Also, Creed was working in opposition to Wren when he had unprotected sex with her in a wine cellar. He got her pregnant. They're ridiculous. They are so irresponsible with sex that even I know all about their sex lives, and I really shouldn't. I am their sister, and I oppose that I know so much about it. But because they've been such idiots, the entire town is aware of it. So the fact that you're trying to warn me off sleeping with somebody just because I'm going to work at his ranch proves definitively that you don't actually think of me the way that you do Jackson and Creed."

He looked at her for a moment, lifting a brow. "Who said I didn't tell them they were being dumbasses?"

"Did you?" she pressed.

"Not in so many words, no, but I didn't really want to get punched in the face."

She turned, balled her hand into a fist and slugged his shoulder. He was so muscular his flesh didn't even budge. It was like punching a granite wall.

"You tool," she said, shaking her hand.

"Honestly, language. And you were upset about *horny*."

"And fuck you," she said.

"All right, I don't think of you as your brothers," he said. The windshield wipers on his truck were moving faster now. Working overtime. Trying to keep up with the snowfall.

"You wouldn't want me to anyway."

"You don't get to say what I want," she said.

"You're awfully spiky," he said.

"I have a right to be spiky," she returned. "You're being patronizing."

"I'm not intending to be patronizing. But the fact of

the matter is, you are younger than us. And I worry a little bit about you."

That last comment made her feel like she was on uneven ground. But her fury still lingered, even while his concern wound its way around her heart. "You worry about me so much that you took my livelihood out from under me without a second thought."

"I didn't the hell know you wanted the winery, Honey, and I'm not invested in you not having it. We should've talked about this before you went off half-cocked."

"I'm about to go get a whole cock, thank you very much."

"I'm sorry, but *horny* was offensive?"

She chewed the inside of her cheek, feeling red and embarrassed and mad. She was just so… It wasn't fair. None of it was fair.

"This weather is getting intense," she said.

"Yeah," he said.

But something about the way he said that made her think that he wasn't really thinking of the weather.

They ended up not talking for a while, and she fiddled with the radio until she eventually gave up and just plugged her phone into his cable, firing up her country playlist. But he didn't complain.

It transitioned from Luke Bryan to Mickey Guyton, and she tried to focus on the song lyrics and not on the fact that the cab of the truck suddenly felt too small.

But about fifteen minutes into their determined silence, making commentary on the weather wasn't just to deal with awkwardness. It actually really merited a comment.

"This is crazy," she said.

The snow was beginning to truly pile up on the side of the road and starting to actually cover the road in earnest.

"It's fine," he said.

"I'm glad that you have so much confidence in your truck. That seems just like a man."

"No, it's spoken like a woman whose truck gave out a few miles back in good weather. I have a decent vehicle. It's going to be fine."

But the snow escalated until they couldn't see in front of them. Jericho slowed his truck to a crawl, maneuvering over the road as best he could.

"Shit," he said. "I might have to pull off. I can't see a damn thing." Just then, a big truck hauling logs came by in the oncoming lane. They didn't see it until it was right on top of them. It breezed by them so close, hugging the yellow line and making Honey jump.

She put her hand on his forearm, breathing hard.

"Good Lord," she said.

"Yeah," he said. "I'm going to have to pull off till it eases up. Assuming I can find a spot. See a spot."

"Where the hell are we?"

"Somewhere between Gold Valley and Lake Oswego," he said.

She thought she should probably laugh at that comment, because obviously… But her heart was still beating too quickly.

He took his phone out, and she could see that he didn't have any bars. She didn't hold out any hope that it meant she would either. He pulled off slowly, and she could feel the truck slide, then sink.

"Oh…" she said. "We're not going to be able to get back out."

"We'll be able to get back out."

Not today.

Not soon.

He didn't say that but she knew it. So did he.

The snow didn't ease.

They sat there, the engine idling, the heater doing its best to keep them from freezing.

"I thought I was going to die in my truck all alone. But it turns out I'm going to die in your truck sitting next to you. I have to tell you, it is not an infinitely more cheering prospect."

"We're not going to die," he said.

"You don't know that."

"No," he said. "I don't know that on any given day. But I don't figure as a matter of course that I'm going to die, and I don't really figure it now."

"But again," she said. "You don't know."

"For the love of God, Honey."

He didn't say anything after that. He was just breathing in irritation.

Hard and heavy, and she became very aware of her own breathing. Of her heart beating. She turned to look at him, suddenly afraid.

"What are we going to do?"

"Not panic," he said.

"This is how people die," she said.

"Yeah," he said. "It is. But I'm not going to let anything happen to you. You understand?"

His brown eyes were sincere, and that was so unusual that it twisted up her insides. Plus she was afraid.

And for some reason, it was stirring deep truths and longings inside her. Making her feel shaken.

She suddenly felt very aware of how close they were.

Of the heat coming off his body. Especially as things outside began to cool.

"I'm not going to let anything happen to you," he said. He moved his hand across the empty space on the truck seat and placed it over hers. "I swear."

She shivered, looking away. "Okay."

"It's going to be all right."

"I believe you," she said.

She jerked her hand away, feeling suddenly beset by his touch.

It didn't mean anything to him. He was comforting her like he would a child. But it made her too hot. Even in all this cold. They both knew that no one was going to happen by. Because everybody was getting off the road. There was not going to be any help coming for them unless it was somebody specifically looking for people who were stuck.

And neither of them were relishing the prospect of sleeping outside, she was sure.

"I'm going to get out and take a look around."

"No," she said, leaping forward, grabbing onto his hand. "People do that and they don't come back."

"I'm going to come back."

"They always think they will."

"I will not get away from the view of the truck. I promise you."

"Promise," she said. "You know… You know that happened to that man… The family got stuck and he walked away and…"

"I know," he said. "But I'm not going to lose sight of the truck. I just need to see if there's anyone else around here. Or if there's a house even."

"This is the middle of nowhere."

"It's the middle of we don't know where. That's a fact. So I'm just going to see."

And then Jericho opened up his truck door and stepped out into the snow.

Three

The weather outside made a witch's tit look like Hawaii. It was cold. And he was not prepared for a blizzard. But then, he didn't figure there was going to be a blizzard. Sure, there had been a forecast for snow, but it was Oregon. The much talked about snow apocalypse was always only ever a few flakes. If anything, you might get a foot, but nothing like this. Nothing like this. This was unprecedented. And crazy.

He kept his word to Honey, keeping one eye on the truck as he walked up and down the side of the road, then took a step into the woods to see if he could see houses.

Under the cover of the trees there was less snowfall, and there was better visibility. That was good.

His hand burned. From where he had covered hers with his. Ill-advised. But she had been afraid. And he'd have been a bigger jerk if he hadn't tried to comfort her.

There was something about the fact she was telling him all this when she'd told no one else that made it feel different.

There was also something about being away from the vineyard, sitting with her in his truck, that made her feel different. It made things between them feel different, and he couldn't say that he liked it overly much.

It was just… Not what it was supposed to be.

Right, and you need to be thinking about this while you're in a survival situation?

He kept thinking of the way she'd said *dick. His* dick, in fact.

Honey used vulgar language all the time. It was kind of her thing. She was surrounded by men, and he kind of assumed that she tended to overdo it a little bit to prove that she was one of them.

But that was different. It felt different.

He felt it right on the aforementioned body part.

Just find some shelter, asshole.

All right, so he'd lied to Honey a little bit. He took hold of his scarf, unwrapped it from his neck and set it right next to a tree that was parallel to the car. As long as he kept a visual on that, he would be fine. The visibility was just so much better in the woods.

He pushed forward, always keeping the scarlet red of that scarf in his view.

He was looking for a house. Someplace that would have a phone so that they could call.

Anybody out here would have a landline. Or a phone that managed to get service somehow.

And then he saw it, just barely visible under the cover of the trees. A cabin. It was huge, but there were no lights on. It didn't look like anyone was there.

Well. He was not sitting on the side of the road with Honey. And… Hell. If he had to break into the place to use a landline, he would.

He crossed the expansive trees and went up through the back of the house. He knocked just in case. But there was nothing. No one.

There was a lockbox on the door, like it was something that was for sale. He checked every window and found one in the back ajar. He pushed it up, popped the screen out and climbed in.

And he really the hell hoped that he didn't trip a burglar alarm, or anything of the kind, because he didn't especially want to get shot, either by a homeowner or a cop, in the pursuit of shelter. But this was an emergency. He laughed, because no cop was going to come out here even if a burglar alarm was tripped.

So there was that. The weather had caused the problem, but at least it was helping with this part.

He walked through toward the front door and saw a big basket sitting there. There were bottles of wine in it, and there was a piece of paper sitting in a plastic sleeve.

He looked down at it. Welcome to Pineview. There were instructions for everything in the house, plus a list of amenities.

A vacation rental. He'd stumbled on a vacation rental. Hell.

He went to flip on some lights, and realized there weren't any. Then he looked down at the paper again.

In this off-grid retreat…

Well. Shit. However, he could see from the amenities paper that there should be a way to start a fire. A way to get lights going. And there were generators. For the hot water and for the toilets. All in all, it could be worse.

The paper also had a code to access the lockbox, and he did so, taking the keys out with him, before going back and replacing the screen on the window and closing it.

Wine in hand, he walked out the front door and back toward where he left the scarf.

From there, he made his way to the truck.

The visibility was so poor. He could hardly see.

He jerked the door open on the passenger side of the truck, and Honey jumped. "Oh," she said. "I did not see you."

"This is ridiculous," he said, pulling the door open with great effort. The snow was up to the bottom of it, piling higher and higher.

"Come on out," he said.

She did, as best she could. But there was a fair amount of wrestling with the snow in trying to get the door to open.

"Crazy," she said.

"I know it."

They both had suitcases in the back that were now covered with snow.

"What exactly are we doing?"

"I found a house."

"And they're letting us come inside?"

"Kind of."

He hefted her suitcase out of the back of the truck and handed it to her. Then he took her free hand with his and led her into the woods. She was wearing gloves, which offered a barrier to their touch. But he still felt the fact that he was holding Honey Cooper's hand.

She dropped hold of it when they were beneath the trees. He stopped and gathered his scarf.

"What was that?"

"A marker. I didn't keep the truck in sight. But I kept that in sight, and I knew that the truck was just parallel to it."

"Of course you couldn't just be safe," she said.

"Hey, I found a house," he said. "You should just be thankful."

"That's a very male thing to say," she said.

"I'm a man," he responded.

"Sure," she said.

He gestured in front of them. "It's just through here." They went through the trees, and the house was still there, standing dark.

"I thought you said…"

"I didn't say anything. It's a vacation rental."

"A vacation rental."

"Handily, with a list of amenities right inside."

He pushed open the door, and she followed behind him.

"Damn," she said. "It's as cold in here as it is out there."

"But dry," he said. "It's off-grid."

"Off-grid," she squeaked.

She looked so distressed it might have been funny if there was anything funny about it. "Yeah," he said. "But there's fire starter. And it's designed to be this way. So, if the power goes out in the broader world everywhere, we'll be just fine here."

"Because the power's already out," she said.

"But again," he said. "Set up for it." He gestured around. "Lanterns."

"Seems a fire hazard," she said.

"Are you going to get overly excited and knock any of the lanterns down?"

"No," she sniffed.

"Well then, I expect it's fine."

He watched as Honey wandered around the room, setting her suitcase down and ferreting about.

He looked down at the paper. "So if we get the generators to fire up, you can use the bathrooms."

"Well, thank God for that. I wouldn't have relished going outside to take care of things."

"No," he said.

"What else have we got?"

"There's a store of food. A root cellar and some evaporative cooling. Apparently. The off-grid experience is enhanced by the foods that they stock and provide. There is salted meat."

She looked around as if everything in the room might be a potential threat. And damned if he didn't find it... cute.

What the hell. He didn't do cute.

"Well," she said. "I feel like a pioneer."

"You don't sound thrilled about it."

"In fourth grade we had to spend an entire year playing *Oregon Trail*. I had enough party members die of dysentery to be cured of this fantasy."

"I always liked *Oregon Trail*."

"Sure. As a game. Less so as something I actually have to experience. I do not have an endless supply of bullets with which to go hunt buffalo."

He leaned into the humor of the moment because it was that or lean into the tension, and he didn't want to do that. "You wouldn't be able to find any buffalo in this weather anyway."

"Maybe they have some of the salted meat," she said.

"I guess we'll have to find out."

"Right now I'm more cold than I am hungry. I stuffed a protein bar in my face before you came to pick me up."

"Why?"

"I felt imperiled. Which made me feel hungry."

"Right. Well. Fair enough."

She scampered into the living room and he followed behind her. And saw that she was already taking out the fire starting gear from the basket near the hearth.

"Looks pretty good."

In this room there was a large fireplace. And he had noticed that there was a den off to the side where there was a woodstove.

That would actually likely produce more effective heat.

He assumed that whatever they cooked on in the kitchen also ran on wood heat. And it might benefit them to fire everything up.

"You got this?"

"Of course I've got this," she said. "I'm a country girl."

He chuckled. It was getting dark outside, and he took one of the lighters and a little lantern and decided to carry it with him.

The cabin was cavernous, massive, but it was also solid and sturdy and fairly well insulated from the cold outside. Rustic, but comfortable.

The furniture was expensive, very nice. There was a big bedroom with a large king-size bed. And furs covering what looked like a pretty plush mattress.

And instantly, he pictured laying Honey down on those furs.

The image was so stark, so clear, that it made him jerk back. Shit. He could not be having thoughts like that. That just wasn't going to fly.

There was a big fireplace in there, which was good. The other two bedrooms did not have a heat source.

He assumed that this place was mostly for rent during the summer. He couldn't imagine people going to the trouble of trying to rent it this time of year. And with weather like this it was basically a liability. He went back down the stairs, and there was a raging fire going in the living room.

"Well done," he said.

"I'm not entirely useless," she said.

"You're not even a little bit useless. I'm pretty damn sure you know that." Their eyes met and held for a long moment.

And it made him conscious of how alone they were.

And how beautiful she was.

He looked away.

"I don't know. Sometimes I feel a little bit like I might be useless."

"Is this about the winery again?"

"It's hard for things not to be about the winery right now."

"I get that. I really do. I get it. But I don't think it was actually a commentary on you. Your dad wanted out from under it. He told me...he hasn't really been happy there for a long time. You may not believe this, but he approached me about it. I'm not sure that he's thinking any deeper than that. He's not capable of seeing the winery as a dream right now."

"Well, but..."

"He cautioned me plenty, even as he offered it. But the thing is, it's in a much different state now than it was all those years ago when he first started. It's profitable, it's got a full staff. Asking Jackson to look after things is kind of a formality. I think your dad sees a younger person wanting to take over the winery and remembers himself at my age…"

Honey snickered.

"What's so funny?" he asked.

"A younger person."

"I'm young," he said.

This was just insulting. He was in his midthirties, for heaven's sake, and this child, who was not a child at all, but a woman he found incredibly attractive, was laughing at him.

"Not really."

"Wow."

"Well. I'm just saying. You're not as young as I am."

Damned if he didn't know that.

"No," he said. "I'm not."

"Just making sure you remember."

Suddenly, that statement took on an edge, and it sliced through his gut like a knife.

"All right," he said. "Quit mouthing off and let's figure out something to eat."

"I hope that nobody's going to show up," she said.

"I don't think anyone's showing up. Even if they had a reservation… If we can't get out, people sure can't get in."

"Fair. This is so wild."

She stood and looked out the window, and he gazed at her, silhouetted by the waning light. The snow was beginning to pile up in earnest, even with the cover of the trees.

"There's no internet. Obviously. And there's no service. So until we are able to get out of here… We're not going to be able to get in touch with anyone."

"Great. So my truck is just going to be sitting up where we left it. Good thing I brought my stuff."

"Good thing."

"What are the Daltons going to think when you don't show up?"

He laughed. Hard and without humor. "Probably that I had second thoughts. About joining that circus."

"Well, I guess that would be fair."

"Yeah. Definitely."

"You never seem to be really affected by anything, and I guess I didn't really appreciate how weird it must be to find out you have this whole big family."

"I've known," he said.

"Oh," she said. "Well, I guess it must be weird to get an invitation to join it then."

"It's all weird. But… On the scale of things I've been through in my life, it doesn't really register. I felt like why not go." But even to his own ears that sounded hollow. If he didn't care, he wouldn't be going. But the truth of the matter was, he wasn't entirely certain why he was going. He just didn't have a good answer. Not for himself. Not at all. He didn't know what he wanted to prove, though he would like to think that he wanted to prove nothing. That he literally didn't care at all about Hank Dalton or what he thought. That he didn't have any desire to get to know his half siblings.

But there were a lot of them. And nieces and nephews too. And… Yeah, all right. Once you had an invitation to join in with the big family, it just seemed… He just wanted to see. He wanted to see what they were like. He wanted to see if he was like them.

Hardheaded and stubborn and determined.

He knew that Hank and Tammy Dalton were white

trash from way back, and then Hank had done good in the rodeo and gotten a lot of money. That the money had managed to buy them class.

He knew they were hardscrabble and determined people, whose fights had always been legendary in town.

Jericho himself had a hot temper, he was more determined than most and he had been certain that he was meant for better things than what he was born to. And he had done all that he could to make that possible. He'd worked with his hands and used his brain to figure out the best usage of his work ethic. Basically, he had to wonder if he got some of that from Hank.

Granted, he knew he got plenty of spirit from his mom, who had been a beautiful woman, and a fighter. All the way to the end.

"Sorry," she said.

"No need to apologize. It's a weird situation. But it is what it is."

"You know," Honey said, wrinkling her nose. "For a while there, Cricket thought that she might be our half sister."

Jericho sputtered. "Really?"

"Yeah. She's not."

"Yeah, judging by the fact that she is now engaged to your brother, and they're having a baby, I figured."

Honey shrugged. "Well. It's just… Families are complicated. Is my point."

"Yeah. I know. Though I've always been kind of short on family."

She looked away. "You've always been like family to us."

He arched a brow. "Right. You just love me."

"Well, when you're not being annoying."

"Why don't you make yourself useful and start a fire in the woodstove. I'll go dig around for food?"

And then Honey left him sitting there, pondering the moment. And pondering the strange interruption to his life that this was. He been on his way to deal with this family stuff, and now he was here.

With her.

Far too much temptation for him to consider.

He didn't know what the hell any of it meant. And he had to wonder if by the end of it he would have a better idea, or if it would just be one of those things.

Not everything in life means something. Sometimes it's just a shitty detour.

Yeah. Well. He just hoped the shitty detour had decent food.

Four

Honey managed to find the root cellar, and in it the evaporative coolers. There were vegetables in there, remarkably well-preserved. Which only reinforced her theory that the house had been intended to receive visitors.

She hummed as she dug around for food, trying not to overthink the moment that had happened in the living room.

She really hadn't given a lot of thought to this whole situation with Jericho and the Daltons.

But then, she didn't know what to make of it. And they didn't exactly confide in each other. Mostly they just…bickered.

Because he made her feel strange, and if she wasn't saying something, they were sitting in silence, and she didn't like sitting in silence with him.

She found bacon and eggs, and some potatoes, and

decided to go with breakfast for dinner. Unfortunately there was no pop can of biscuits, which would've made everything complete, and she wasn't about to go scrounging around for baking supplies.

There was a basket sitting by the door of the root cellar, and she grabbed hold of it, put her spoils inside and walked back up the stairs to the main level of the house.

The whole place was beautiful. High-gloss logs that built a sturdy, impressive-looking house. She just couldn't understand why anybody would choose to put a house this beautiful right out in the middle of nowhere with no amenities. Though, she supposed these were amenities. They were just a lot more work than the amenities she was used to.

She walked into the kitchen, and he was standing there, stripped down to a T-shirt, stoking the fire underneath the woodstove. His brown skin gleamed in the light, his muscles shifting with each movement.

He took her breath away.

And that was silly. She really needed to get a hold of herself.

"Breakfast for dinner," she said, lifting the basket.

"Perfect," he said.

"I did find ketchup."

"Well, that is the important thing."

"Absolutely. You can't have eggs or hash browns without a whole bunch of ketchup."

"On that we agree."

"Well, glad to know there's something. Maybe the secret to world peace is ketchup."

"Somehow I doubt it."

"What would it be then?"

He frowned. "Ranch dressing?"

"They don't have ranch dressing everywhere."

"All the more reason to use it as an agent of world change. People just need to know about ranch dressing," he said.

"Also true."

His dark brows shot up. "Two agreements in under a minute. We may survive this."

"Yeah, and I have bacon in this basket. So…" He chuckled. He straightened and crossed his forearms over his broad chest.

Her heart thundered.

"I turned on the generator. For the bathroom. So, all that's functional. And if you want to shower…"

"Oh," she said, suddenly feeling a little bit fluttery. "Thank you. That's great."

"As far as I can tell, it's got enough gasoline to run for a bit. But we probably don't want to run it constantly."

"The appeal of off-grid living escapes me," she said. "I have to say, I like a modern amenity."

"Careful, I'm going to start thinking we're friends."

"Oh, God forbid."

She forced a smile, then started to root around through the cabinets, producing a frying pan, some cooking oil and the cheese grater. She found a potato peeler and stuck it in Jericho's hand. "Care to make yourself useful?"

"Amend that," he said. "I have been very useful this entire time."

She rolled her eyes. "Oh certainly," she said.

He moved alongside of her, grabbing the potatoes and starting to peel them into the trash. His muscular forearms flexed and shifted, and she did her best not to be distracted by it. And she did her best to ignore it while she sliced the bacon off the slab—which she had never done before—and cracked the eggs into a bowl, whisking them around.

It was a little bit of a learning curve, figuring out how to get everything onto the stove without burning it or causing huge drama, but owing to the basic nature of the meal, she managed to put together something nice. The dishes were camp plates. Blue tin with white speckles, and she found herself overwhelmed by nostalgia holding on to them. She couldn't even quite say why.

Until an image came into her head of her mother sitting at the table in the kitchen, holding a mug made of the same material. She smiled. "My mom used to like this kind of thing."

"Living off-grid?"

"No, these camp dishes." Her heart squeezed, and the image in her head got fuzzy around the edges. "My memories of her are so thin. I wish there were more. I wish I'd understood I was losing her so I would have held on to every memory more than I did."

"I'm sorry. From what I remember of her, she was great," he said. "I... I was glad I got to know her even if it was for a short amount of time."

She cleared her throat. "Yeah. I'm glad too. She really loved you, you know."

"That's how I met your brothers, you know."

"How?"

"Because both of our moms were sick. That sucked. And of course at school... That was something people talked about. Then I lost my mom. I related to what they were going through with your mom's illness... It's not a great thing to be bonded over, that's for sure. Because it just kind of sucks."

"Yeah," she said. "It does."

"But your dad… He found out about my living situation, and he took me in. I don't know if you realize just how much I depended on your family."

She frowned. "No. I didn't. I didn't think about it. It was just that one day you didn't really leave."

"Well, if not for your dad, I was either going to have to figure out becoming an emancipated minor or possibly going into the system. And I didn't really relish that. He became my legal guardian… He made sure that I had everything I wanted. He did what Hank Dalton never did. He was like a father to me."

"Jericho…" Guilt twisted her. Because she hadn't realized all this. She'd been a kid, and she'd been consumed with the changes in her own family, and of course consumed with the fact that she thought he was handsome. And the associated torture therein.

She had never really thought about his losses. About the strangeness of his relationship to Hank Dalton. About…

You've never thought about him as a person. He's been an object. There to be good-looking to you, irritating to you…

Yeah. Well, turns out he wasn't exactly the crappiest person in their relationship. It was her. It left her feeling rocked. Because she had spent so much time absolutely certain no one understood her. But how much of an effort had she ever made to really understand the people around her?

She was sure she was stoic because they all simply were.

Were they also trying to protect her? Protect themselves?

"I'm sorry that I never thought about that," she whispered, the words coming out raspy. "It's pretty much inexcusable."

"It's fine, Honey."

Her chest felt sore, and her heart was beating hard. She didn't like it. "No. I've been a brat to you. Always."

He stared at her, long and hard. "You know I never forgot. That you are just a little girl who lost her mom the way that I did. I didn't forget. Because I'm older than you. Because I got to have some perspective along with my grief. You were a kid. And..."

"I'm not a kid now. And it seems that I haven't done a very good job of recognizing...the full picture of things."

"I think that's pretty normal."

"Stop absolving me for being a jerk. I don't deserve it."

"Since when is any of this about what we deserve."

"I don't know. I just know that... I should've been a better friend."

"You're a pretty good friend. You made some bacon."

"Yeah, well you saved my life. What if you hadn't of happened by? I would be completely stuck in my truck in this blizzard. Nowhere to go. No cell service, no hope of rescue. Because at a certain point people that were smarter than us got off the road."

"Well, I did happen by. And here we are."

She looked around. "Yeah. Here we are."

"I guess there's not really much to do up here."

"There's some bookshelves."

"Yeah, I noticed that. Maybe I'll finally get around to reading *Lord of the Rings*."

She wrinkled her nose. "I think I'll stick with the field guide of birds that I saw earlier."

"Birds, huh?"

Why couldn't he just let her find a thing to do to distract herself so they didn't have to talk?

She sniffed. "I like birds, Jericho."

"Like *particularly*, or in comparison to how much you like hobbits?"

She huffed a laugh. "No. *I like birds.*"

"What's to like about birds?"

"They're...cute. Or majestic. Or *menacing*. Birds can be all three. I admire it." Then she added, "I aspire to it."

"They're also good fried," he said.

She scowled. "Yes. But that isn't... I'm not reading a recipe book. I am reading a *field guide*."

"Well, enjoy your field guide."

"Perhaps I will."

They finished eating, and she gave thanks for the running water, rinsing off all the plates while Jericho dried and put them away. Then they retreated to the living room, where they had built a big fire, and she pretended to peruse the illustrated guide to birds while he did a good impression of somebody reading a thick fantasy novel.

And really, she was just suddenly overwhelmed. By the isolation. By his proximity.

By the fact that she had intended to be with another man tonight. Losing her virginity.

And suddenly the idea made her feel strung out. On edge.

Suddenly it made her feel... Way too much of everything. She also thought of her suitcase, which was currently full of lingerie.

And she swallowed hard.

She turned her focus to the Mott Mott. Which was an interesting enough bird. But not half as interesting as the intrusive thoughts swirling around in her head. Which should not be interesting, but problematic. Very, very problematic.

"Well," she said. "I'm sleepy."

"It's probably about that time," he said.

"We'll let the fire die out."

"Oh."

"I started one upstairs a bit ago."

"Oh good."

Except her throat was dry, and it didn't particularly feel good. It felt…like something, and it shouldn't feel like something. They were just out here surviving together. There was nothing happening. No undertone to the offer of preparing beds and fireplaces.

She followed him upstairs, and it took a moment for things to begin to dawn on her fully.

"Wait… You started one?"

"The other bedrooms don't have fireplaces," he said. "If you want to stay warm… This is the room."

He pushed the door open and revealed a master bedroom, with a roaring fire and a massive bed covered in blankets and furs.

"Oh but…"

"It's not a big deal," he said. "It's a huge bed."

"But…"

"Is it a problem?"

A thousand thoughts cascaded through her head. Yes, it was a problem. She had never shared a bed with a man in her life, and now she was supposed to sleep next to the most beautiful man she'd ever known. Now she was supposed to… What the hell? How was she going to survive this? How was she going to survive this?

"You seem bothered," he said.

She did her best not to sputter outrageously. "I am *unbothered*."

"I brought your suitcase up too. If you want to get in some pajamas."

She thought about the pajamas she had brought. All of a rather lacy nature. Because she had been planning on…

She swallowed hard.

"You know. I think I'm just going to sleep in this. For warmth."

"Suit yourself."

"Do you need to… You need to change into…pajamas?"

He fixed her with a hard stare, his dark eyebrows lifted. "No. I think I'll stick with this."

"It's okay…"

"I don't wear pajamas, Honey."

"You don't…"

He slept naked.

The truth slammed into her hard. And she felt it between her legs. Oh gosh. She was failing at not making this sexual. This thing that would never be sexual to him because of course he didn't feel that way about her at all.

"Well, then." She coughed. "Stay in your jeans."

"Somehow I thought that might be your stance."

She decided she just better rip the Band-Aid off. She got into the bed quickly, lifting at the edge of one of the furs and sliding beneath it, huddling on one edge of the bed.

It was so warm. It was luxurious. There had been a

slight chill to everything, and the quilt, combined with the furs, took the edge off.

She was far enough on one side of the king-size bed that she didn't even feel it when Jericho got in.

She gave thanks for that. If she stayed on her edge, she should be all right.

She closed her eyes and tried to make her breathing sound normal. Tried not to sound like somebody who was faking being asleep.

"I'll tend the fire."

She opened one eye. "You don't have to do that by yourself."

"It's no big deal."

"But it's not… I mean…"

"Honey, don't worry about it. Get some sleep. If this turns into a multiday thing, then we may have to have conversations about who's manning the fire and who's not. But right now… We don't need to make a big deal out of it."

"Oh. Okay."

"Get some sleep. Because tomorrow is going to be a full-time job to keep ourselves warm. And fed."

"Hopefully the snow will have stopped by then." How long could it possibly do this? It had to stop. Tomorrow it would warm up and things would melt.

It had to.

"Hopefully. But I don't have any way to check the forecast. So I've a feeling we'll be walking down to check the road intermittently."

"Yeah." She sighed. "You know, nobody's even going to realize that we are missing except for the Daltons. And since they're just going to think that you blew them off…"

"I know. Thankfully your truck is sitting there closer to town than mine. So, it's possible that somebody will realize."

She blinked. "Right."

But neither of them said what they were both thinking, which was that they might be stuck here for a pretty long time. And that if they were, there wasn't going to be a whole hell of a lot that they could do about it.

They were just going to have to be very comfortable with each other.

And on that note, she curled up as close to the edge of the mattress as she possibly could. And closed her eyes tight.

Five

Jericho woke up and realized that the room was cold. And that he was *very* warm.

She wasn't touching him, but there was only a scant foot between the two of them, and he could feel the heat radiating off her body. He had tried initially to get under only one layer of the blankets, but it had just gotten so damned cold, that he had ended up surrendering to the need to get beneath them. And that put them far too close for his comfort.

And he needed to get that fire going again.

He stood up and looked out the window, pulling the curtains back. It was gray, early. The sun would probably be up in another half hour or so. But he wasn't quite ready to face the day. Not considering what they had ahead of them.

Because the snow had piled up impossibly high underneath the trees, and one thing was certain, even if the snowplow had been out this far, his truck was stuck on the side of the road. And he was going to have to get to a space where he could get a tow truck.

And right now, none of that was looking likely.

So he got the fire going again, and eyed the bed. And the space Honey had crowded into.

He lay back down, one layer beneath the blankets, and stared directly up at the ceiling, trying to ignore the way her breath fanned over his neck.

She was Jackson and Creed's little sister. She was practically a sister to him. And what he'd said to her last night had been true. He had always known that she was just a kid grieving her mom.

And it had never really bothered him that she didn't treat him like there was something grieving and broken in him. It was funny to see her distress over it. Like she thought she should've been sweeter and kinder for some damned reason.

As if he was suddenly breakable, because she realized they shared a common grief.

He'd always known that.

The fact that she was such a determined person. The kind of person who did just sort of get along with things… That was one reason he… Well, he recognized it. Because life was hard, and somehow you had to keep going. She was good at that. And he admired it.

Gradually, he realized that he wasn't going to be getting back to sleep. And he decided the better part of virtue would be getting the downstairs warmed up and figuring out some breakfast. And most especially coffee. He figured round two of bacon and eggs wasn't the worst thing in the world, and did that up quickly, and then gave up a prayer of thanks when he found a percolator and some coffee.

He set that on to steep and then decided to go back to the bedroom.

He didn't grab a lantern because the light was gray, and he could see more or less, and he'd taken decent note of the layout of the place the night before.

He pushed the bedroom door open and saw Honey, now curled up firmly in the middle of the bed.

He started to cross the space, but bumped against the dresser and knocked her suitcase down. It popped open, landing on its end, the contents spilling out.

"Shit," he muttered, bending down to pick it up. He reached down to begin to shove the items back inside and recognized the texture of the handful of things that he grabbed.

Lace.

He had an entire handful of lingerie. Because the suitcase was… Well, hell, it appeared to be 90 percent see-through underwear.

He was frozen. Completely and totally frozen, and grateful for the fact that he couldn't see all that well, because if he had too much of a sense of the kind of panties Honey was into, he might just die of a heart attack. And he didn't need that kind of drama, not on everything else.

He didn't have that kind of restraint; he damn well did not.

But it was too late. Because he was already figuring out exactly what these panties consisted of from just a casual touch, and his mind was constructing highly visual fantasies.

He heard a squeaking sound, and then she sat up, just in time to see him crouched there, holding on to her clothes.

"What the hell are you doing?"

"I knocked your shit over," he said. And he shoved it back into the suitcase as quickly as possible and turned the thing flat.

"Don't go through my things," she said, climbing out of the bed and scrambling over to the suitcase, viciously pushing the clips back down.

"Sorry," he said. "I didn't mean to. I just came to tell you that I made coffee. And bacon and eggs."

"Well, fine," she said.

"I'd suggest you get changed, but I don't think you have a change of clothes in there."

"Oh, you had to say something."

"Yeah. Apparently I did." He had meant to say something, because at the end of the day, it was his bad that he knocked the suitcase over and it wasn't really his business what was in it. But he had seen it. He couldn't unsee it. Not even a little bit.

"A gentleman wouldn't comment."

"I never said that I was a gentleman."

"Well, that is… That is very clear and obviously true."

"Settle down, Honey."

"Do not tell me to settle down. Do not tell me to settle down when you're the person who…who has been manhandling my things."

"Were you planning on actually working up there?"

"I was going to have the rest of my things sent. But in point of fact, I was intent on launching a seduction."

"Hell. I need coffee."

He turned and stomped out of the room, went down the stairs.

And he heard her furious footsteps behind him.

"Not that it's any of your business," she said. "I was on a mission to lose my virginity."

Everything in him went quiet. Still.

He turned, and he couldn't really make out her face in the dim light. Couldn't tell if she was angry or horrified that she let that slip. Couldn't tell what she'd been thinking by doing it.

Virginity.

She had been going up there to lose her virginity to… To some random dude.

And he would never, ever, be able to get that image out of his head. That Honey Cooper was a virgin.

That she was ready to lose it. That she had a whole bunch of lingerie designed for that very thing in that suitcase up there.

He was only a man. And what really worried him was that he might have more in common with Hank Dalton than he had previously realized. Because he was a little bit of a womanizer and always had been, but this was something else. This felt like a compulsion. A tug.

And he didn't want to think about it. But it was there. And it was driving him.

And he felt…

It was deeper than the attraction he'd felt before.

Something in him felt like he would never really be satisfied if he didn't strip her naked right then and there, kiss her lips and…

Coffee.

"I am getting coffee," he said.

"Does that bother you? Does it bother you to know that I was taking control of my life and my sexuality?"

"I was happy to previously have never thought about your sexuality," he said through gritted teeth.

Such a damned lie.

But a virgin? A virgin. He had not considered that. Not ever.

"Well. How nice for me. That's the problem, Jericho. I could stay in Gold Valley and remain a sexless, boring object that just sits around the winery, not seen as somebody who could take over, not seen as somebody capable of being the boss, not seen as an actual woman, or I could go off and make a life for myself.

"So maybe you don't understand why I might want to get a new job, or sleep with the man who gave me that job. Honestly, those things are accidentally linked. I met him on a dating site. I wasn't going to take work from him, but the offer came up. And it…it seemed infinitely better to what I had. Seemed infinitely better than dying on the vine out in Gold Valley."

"Let me tell you something," he said, breaking his own rule and mandate about going to get the coffee. "There's a whole lot out there in this world, good sex and bad sex, and none of it makes you who you are. You make you who you are, and there should be no reason to go out and fling your virginity at the nearest person you can find just because you're unsatisfied with the state of things."

"It doesn't matter, and yet you are lecturing me on the fact that I shouldn't throw my virginity away? Can you see how those two things conflict with each other?"

"Dammit," he said. "That's not the point of anything.

Just sit… You don't need to find the first guy you're remotely interested in and…"

He didn't like any scenario, but for some reason he extra hated Donavan.

"You don't know who I'm interested in. You don't know who I have been interested in. And who I haven't been. You don't know as much about me as you think. Look, I admitted that I don't know as much about you as I should. That I kind of just saw you as… It doesn't matter. But the fact that you knew that I was a grieving little girl doesn't mean that you know me now."

"No. It doesn't. And if I'm honest… I figured that you… I mean… You're twenty-two."

"I know how old I am," she said.

"I figured you had." He gritted his teeth. "You know. If pressed to think about it."

"Well, I know you have, because you flaunted all over the place. And that's what I don't understand. How is it okay for you to do that, but you're all up in arms about me."

"I don't want you to get hurt," he said.

"Why do you think I would get hurt?"

"Because women *do*," he said. "They end up making rash choices about sex and they get hurt."

"Wow. That is the most… You are infuriating. And you have no right to comment on anything. None at all. I didn't want you to see that suitcase, I didn't want you to know about any of this."

"Why did you tell me?"

She sputtered. "I need coffee."

She brushed past him and went into the kitchen, grabbing hold of the percolator and the camp mug— that was identical to the plate she'd used last night—and pouring an amount in. "I guess it would be too much to hope that they had half-and-half."

"Sorry. Nothing quite so civilized."

"Well, that's just terrible."

She just served herself up a heaping portion of eggs and bacon, then retreated into the living room, where there was a fire going. He stayed in the kitchen, stood while he ate.

This was fine. It was early, and the situation they were in was weird. They didn't need to carry on talking about her hymen, or whatever. He didn't care about things like that. He never had.

So why his brain should be stuck on Honey and her sexual status, he didn't know.

Maybe because he'd been too damned fascinated by her to begin with, and now that he knew for a fact no man had ever touched her...

The idea of being the first one to do it...

Hell.

And no.

As if she hadn't been off-limits to begin with.

After he got the coffee into him, he felt a little more balanced. And he took himself into the living room, where Honey was sitting, her giant bird book on her lap, her empty plate beside her. She was studying the birds.

"How are the birds?"

"Much the same as I left them," she said, sniffing.

"Good. Good." He looked at her. "You know speaking of birds. And bees..."

"No," she said, holding up her hand. "I could happily never have this discussion with you, Jericho."

"Why not?"

"Because it's awkward. Because I'm going to die of being awkward."

"It's just…" He didn't know why he couldn't leave this alone.

He had to…deal with it. Talk about it until he wasn't so preoccupied with it. Make it feel like something normal and not taboo and definitely not the source of a host of new fantasies surrounding a woman he never should have had any fantasies about in the first place.

Let alone fantasies about being her first.

"Look," he said. "It's just that… Women get a lot of feelings around sex."

"Oh," she said. "*Women.* Women get a lot of feelings around sex. Which is why you are prowling around like an angry cat unable to drop the subject."

"I'm not prowling. Most especially not like a cat."

"Panther."

"Not less offensive."

"Why?"

He knew why. Because he felt like a predator all of a sudden. Stuck in the house with her. Like a fox in the henhouse, if he had to choose. No. He had control over himself. He was not Hank Dalton.

He looked at Honey, who was staring yet more resolutely at the birds.

"Are there new birds?"

She didn't look up. "I can report that there are no new birds since yesterday."

"But you seem very committed to the book."

"Just let me deal with the awkward situation by pretending to be engrossed. I think we both know that's what I'm doing. Why can't you do the same?"

He didn't know.

"Because. Ignoring stuff doesn't make it go away."

And that was the biggest load of bullshit he ever spewed in his life, because if he was good at one thing, it was ignoring feelings until they went away. Because he had been a lonely, sad kid who had just pushed those feelings aside and made himself tough. Because he had been forced to be grown before he ever should've been, taking care of his mother and missing so very much being the one that was taken care of. Because he had developed resentment heaped upon resentment at the father who wasn't there.

Who hadn't given them enough money to survive the medical bills that were piling up. Because his mother—because of her pride—refused to accept any money from Hank, or to allow Jericho to ask for any. Yeah. He was a champion at ignoring emotions. A damned *king*.

And he flashed back to the moment in the winery before he found out that Honey was leaving. Before she yelled at him. And he suddenly had an inkling as to what was going on here. It was an excuse. An excuse that his body was latching onto like a champion. She had introduced something interesting, and he had taken that as an opportunity to swing wide the door on the attraction that had been building there for longer than he cared to admit.

It was harder right now to deny how attracted to her he was than it ever had been. His blood felt hot with it.

It had become harder and harder to think of her as the little girl she'd once been.

The image of her now had fully replaced the one of the past, and it was even hard for him to think of her solely as Jackson and Creed's little sister. They worked together. They spent a lot of time at the winery together. And he saw her, her moods, her work ethic. Her strength. She was snappy and feisty and every inch the kind of woman he'd love to tangle with if she weren't…

No. That was a lie. She was not the kind of woman he'd want to tangle with if she weren't Honey Cooper. Because she was too… She was too earnest. Everything that she felt and did came from a very real place. Including all the anger she'd spewed at him back at Cowboy Wines, and…even her running up north to go sleep with some guy. Because she was put out about the situation at the winery.

Like she was trying to shed her skin, shed her expectations. And he didn't do earnest. He didn't, because there was nothing he could do in the face of it. Because he had spent so many years deadening his own feelings. And he didn't know what to do with the person who simply…hadn't.

"Isn't there something to do? Like some manly homesteading thing? That will get you out of my grill."

"I made you breakfast," he pointed out.

"And it was appreciated. The coffee was good. But… Isn't it a full-time job survivaling?"

"*Survivaling* isn't a word."

"It is. It's what we're doing. We are survivaling."

"We're *surviving.*"

"No. Because it's like—" she waved a hand "— survivalist stuff. It's not just like surviving."

He huffed out a laugh. "Has anyone ever told you that you're ridiculous?"

But the ridiculousness didn't ease the tension. She was too cute, sitting there on the overstuffed couch by the fire, woolly socks on her feet, her brown hair in a loose knot on her head. As she held a giant book that opened across her whole lap and pretended to read it.

She looked up at him. "Oh. All the time."

"So, you want me to go survivaling. And what are you going to do? Sit here reading about birds? How is that useful?"

"A solid database of avian knowledge can always be useful, Jericho."

He stared at her for a long moment. At the way the sun glowed on her skin. The curve of her cheekbones, her round, pink mouth. Her whiskey-colored eyes.

She was a pretty creature. No doubt about that.

The kind of pretty, delicate thing his hands could easily spoil. And he would do well to remember that.

"For what?"

"For example, I will know which birds we can cook and eat if it comes down to it."

"You know, I think I'm going to go ahead and hope we skip that part. There's no way the weather's going to keep up like this."

"I wouldn't have thought it would have kept up overnight," she said, putting the book down and scrambling to the window, looking outside. "I've never seen anything like this."

He didn't want to say that he hadn't either. Didn't want to acknowledge that this was outside of his scope of experience. "It'll be fine. We are really very okay with our setup."

"Yeah. Except for the whole being out of touch with civilization."

"We don't need civilization. We have each other." He paused for a moment. "And bacon."

"The bacon won't last forever." Her voice sounded thin and it made his gut tighten.

They were talking about bacon.

"No." And he was a little afraid of what might happen if the two of them kept on in close quarters. But no, there was no reason to be afraid. He was in control of himself. In control of his body. Brief flashes of attraction, and a newfound fascination with her sexual status did not get to dictate what he did next.

And what he would do, was go chop wood.

Because that was useful. And it was not sitting here ruminating on things that he shouldn't.

"I'm going to go chop some wood. Best make me some bread."

"Bread?"

"Yeah, that's your women's work. For the survivaling."

That earned him her anger and damned it if didn't ignite a fire in his blood. He needed to go jump in a snowbank.

Good thing there were so many handy.

"*Really*," she said.

"Well, once I'm done chopping wood I'm going to have expended a lot of calories."

"All right," she said. "I'll make you something. I can't promise it'll be bread. I don't have… Anything. And I'm not good at that stuff anyway. I know just enough to keep myself fed."

"Well, maybe it's your chance to expand your skills."

That hit. And it hit hard. And in spite of himself, he caught himself holding her gaze. Lingering.

It hit him deeper than it should.

Made him think of all kinds of skills he could help her expand.

His hands on her skin. Her body against his. He'd denied it for so long now it was second nature. Wanting what he couldn't have was his natural state.

As a boy he'd wanted a father. He hadn't had one.

He'd wanted his mother to be well. He'd wanted to not be a caregiver, and he hadn't gotten that either.

Wanting Honey was just a piece of all that same longing he'd lived with his whole life.

No.

"Wood," he bit out.

And then he strode out, like the fire had leaped out of the fireplace and was chasing at his heels.

Six

Honey felt prickly and perturbed. As she had, ever since this morning's explosion with Jericho. She had not meant to tell him about her virginity. But then, he shouldn't have looked at all of her lingerie.

Still, the lingerie had not necessitated her confession. She didn't really know why she'd done it.

Maybe wanted to see what he'd do…

That made her breath quicken.

It was a strange thing, being trapped here with him. It was a lot like being in the den with a lion. And the problem with that was, she kept getting tempted to… feed herself to him.

The problem was, in close proximity like this it was difficult for her to forget that she was attracted to him. Wildly. But what had started as a fluttery sort of teenage feeling had lately become extremely adult and quite *imagination after dark.*

But she…

The fact was, she wanted him, and Donovan had only ever been a surrogate for that. Because she felt like her attraction to Jericho was emblematic of the fact that she had held on to her virginity for too long. But she had convinced herself that she could rid herself of her issues by just losing it to anybody. And now she was beginning to wonder.

It was a really distressing thing to have to admit to herself. Especially while she was trapped here with him.

Especially while it felt a lot like the universe was giving her an opportunity to exorcise the actual demon that was hounding her.

The problem was that she had a job lined up with a man who certainly thought that she was coming to also have a physical relationship with him. And that, she supposed, was where Jericho's concern for her well-being in that regard had come from. She could suddenly see how very sticky it all was. Because if she slept with Jericho now…

Well, she wouldn't expect them to have a relationship. No. Far from that.

They could barely be in the same room without bickering. They were a very bad match, actually. It was just that she happened to be very particularly attracted to him. It was just that she couldn't imagine touching him and then… And then touching someone else.

Well, he has given no real indication that he wants to touch you, barring his strange and deep fascination with your virginal status.

It was true. He had not given a real indication that he wanted to touch her. Everything that she was thinking was based firmly in the realm of fantasy. Firmly in her head.

She started to open up the pantry doors and search around for dry ingredients. She found a cookbook and was successful at finding the ingredients necessary for a quick bread. There was no yeast. And she supposed that was a gift. The Irish soda bread would be quick. And the odds of her screwing it up, even with the woodstove were low.

She was thankful now that her father had made her learn basic survival skills. And that he had made sure she knew how to keep a fire going.

And she just had to wonder…if what Jericho said was true. If what was happening with the winery didn't have anything to do with the fact that she was a girl, or the fact that her father doubted her competence. But everything to do with the fact that he was simply done. That it had become an albatross to him, and he had nothing left to prove.

She knew that the reason that he'd started the winery in the first place had been to get at James Maxfield, her sister-in-law's father, who had stolen the love of her father's life away from him many years ago.

Her father's obsession with proving that he was good enough had driven a wedge between her parents; at least, that was something that her father had been talking about lately. His own shortcomings. The ways that he hadn't managed to be the husband that he wanted to be because he was so lost in what could've been. The way that he had never really appreciated what he'd had.

He had the woman he'd always loved now, but she knew that getting there hadn't been the easiest of journeys.

So maybe that was it. Maybe he just couldn't separate his own feelings from the equation.

She mixed together all the dough, which in her opinion formed kind of an unattractive lump, and put it in a cast-iron skillet, which she then slipped into the oven.

She had no idea how to gauge the heat or the doneness in a wood fire oven, so she kept a continual eye on it. But much to her gratification, the smell that filled the kitchen was lovely.

By the time lunch rolled around she had a beautiful-looking round of bread that she was ready to slather in butter.

But Jericho hadn't returned.

She felt the prickle of worry.

The snow was still coming down pretty hard outside, and while she didn't think he could've gotten lost, she didn't really know.

Neither of them knew this area, and the visibility was poor. She had no idea where the wood was that he was supposed to go chop. And he might've injured himself. It was icy outside. Him walking in the ice with an ax was a whole different thing to concern herself with.

And it just didn't matter how fine everything seemed. She knew that better than most.

Good people were taken away for no reason. All the time.

No one was safe. Nothing was truly protected from harm.

With a bit of panic building in her breast, she grabbed her coat and slipped out the front door.

The silence was eerie. All noise insulated by the dense cover of snow all around. It was still falling, and every so often she would hear a tree groan beneath the weight of it.

That was another thing to worry about. Falling trees and limbs. The snow here was so wet that it fell heavy and thick on the branches. And could easily create a disaster. Downed power lines and trees, mudslides...

She sucked in a sharp breath and regretted it, when the cold touched the back of her throat and made her cough.

It was so cold.

Snow like this was such a rarity that she really wasn't used to it. They got a light dusting now and again down in Gold Valley, but anything thicker and heavier typically fell up in the mountains, where she did not live. So it was just all very unusual.

She would like to enjoy the novelty a little bit, but it was essentially impossible, given that the novelty was pretty well stripped away by the reality of the situation.

She paused for a moment and heard a loud crack. One that she hoped was the sound of Jericho chopping wood, and not the sound of a tree limb giving way.

She scrambled that direction, slipping and sliding in the slushy snow that went past her knees.

Her boots were insufficient, and snow went over the edges, down into her feet.

She shivered. But she kept on going.

She heard the crack again and was reasonably certain that it had to be Jericho. But she pressed on anyway.

She came up over a snowy ridge and saw him, swinging the ax and bringing it down unerringly on the log piece, splitting it in two.

Then he dropped the ax, and picked up the stack of wood that he had produced, lifting it easily and beginning to walk up the hill. He stopped when he saw her.

"What the hell are you doing?"

"I came looking for you."

"It's freezing," he said.

"Yes, I know. It's why I was worried about you. I'm fine." Except for the snow in her boots.

"You don't look fine."

"I am." But her teeth began to chatter.

"March yourself back to the house."

"I was worried about you," she said. He walked up the hill, and she waited for him to reach her. He was laden with wood.

"I can take some of that."

"No, you can't. Go on."

"I could," she insisted.

"Your feet are about to fall off. Don't tell me those boots are waterproof."

"Fine. They're not. But my feet are not going to fall off."

"Go."

"There are fires and everything back at the house," she protested. "I'll be fine."

"This isn't a joke," he said. "I understand that we landed ourselves in a really cushy situation, but this is the kind of weather that kills people, Honey, and you were worried about that when we were stuck by the side of the road, but I feel like you're not as worried about as you should be now."

"Oh no, that's not fair. Because I went out looking for you because I was afraid that something happened to you. Because I know that this is the kind of weather that kills people."

"And if you found me, what were you going to do? Were you going to carry me back to the cabin?"

She looked up, all the way up, so she could meet his gaze. "Yeah. I think I could have."

"You think that you could've carried me back. Through the snow."

"Women lift cars and stuff when their children are in trouble. I'm pretty sure that I could drag you if I had the kind of adrenaline that… Well, I'm sure it's less adrenaline than a woman needing to lift the car off her child. But I bet it's an appropriate amount to move you."

"You're infuriating."

"How am I infuriating?"

"Because you keep overestimating yourself. You keep acting like you know the way of the world when you damn well don't. You don't know the state of anything, Honey. You just don't. You don't know as much as you think you do, you don't…"

"I'm fine. I made bread."

"No. You're acting like a child. Because why? Because you're mad that I have the winery?"

"Because I am furious," she said. "Because I'm furious that you have the winery, and that I had been fixated on your ass for at least ten years. It is ridiculous, and I'm over it. How can I… How can I want you when you are such a jerk, and I don't even like you."

He looked like she had picked up a ball of that wet snow and hit him in the face with it.

And she realized that she'd said it. She had actually said it. And it was more awful and horrible than the revelation of her virginity ever could have been.

"Oh…"

"What do you mean you want me?"

"It's just that…" She stopped.

"Don't stop," he said. "Your feet are wet. Explain yourself."

She felt she was being frog-marched through the snow, and she had gone and embarrassed herself so deeply that she was sweaty along with freezing. Which was just a terrible combination. And it couldn't get any worse.

So some small part of her felt compelled to try to *make it worse.*

"I'll explain myself… It's just… I wanted to sleep with somebody else to get away from you. And to get away from the way that you make me feel. And to get away from…everything."

They arrived back at the house and he opened the door, propelling her inside. "Go take your clothes off."

"What?" It came out as a squeak.

"You heard me."

"I… I said that I… I didn't say that I wanted to…"

"We'll deal with that later. Right now you need to get warm. There's a sauna outside. Get those boots off, strip yourself down and put on the robe in the bathroom. I'll start the sauna."

"Oh… But don't you want to…"

"What I want is for your feet to not fall off," he said. "That's what I want. The rest of all this running off at the mouth you're doing we'll deal with later. But right now, you keeping your feet is the important thing."

Shivering, she shut herself in the bathroom and looked at the shower. She knew that it theoretically had hot water. She could just refuse to do what he said and get in the shower. But instead, she found herself stripping down and putting on the thick robe that was hung there. There were a pair of boots that looked soft and fuzzy, and the label over the top said sauna slippers.

She slipped her feet into them. They were lined with wool, and appeared to have a treated, waterproof exterior.

When she exited the bathroom, Jericho was nowhere to be seen, and it was probably all for the best, because she was naked beneath the robe and it made her feel uncomfortable, even though she was naked beneath all of her clothes, if she thought too deeply about it.

She picked up the paper that had all the directions for the house and saw that it stated there was a map on the back. She flipped it over and saw a hand-drawn guide to how to get to the sauna.

She shuffled out into the snow, thankfully not into any parts that were as deep as where she'd been a little earlier. So her feet stayed dry.

She saw smoke coming out of the top and was curious. She did not know how an off-grid sauna worked.

She opened up the door and Jericho was inside, his jacket cast to the side, his shirtsleeves rolled up as he fed wood chips into the fire. Then he took a ladle and poured water over the hot rocks at the top of the stove, steam coming off them in waves.

"This is how you do it," he said, pouring more water over it.

It was already toasty inside.

"And you need it."

"Thanks," she said.

She had closed the door behind her, because leaving it open seemed... Well, it seemed counter to the point of getting the sauna warm. But now she realized that she had gone and enclosed herself in a very tight space with the very man she was feeling completely self-conscious about.

And also that she was wearing only a robe.

"If you're in here for longer than twenty minutes, I'm going to come looking for you."

"Right."

Wherein she would be naked.

She shifted uncomfortably, heat building between her legs. Why was it like this? Why was it so...

It wasn't inevitable. She wanted it to be. And that was the problem. She was so hung up on him that she was pushing in a direction that she probably shouldn't go.

But all this... All this blurting she was doing, she didn't actually think that it was organic. She was obviously pushing the conversation. Holding herself back from saying the thing that she actually wanted, but saying everything but.

The fact of the matter was, what she really wanted was for him to be her first. What she really wanted was for him to be the one to introduce her to...to sex.

Because for all that he infuriated her, he was the only man that she had practically ever really wanted. He was the only man that she could really imagine herself being with. And imagine it she had. Repeatedly. In vivid detail.

Her chest felt tight, and her whole body flushed.

And then suddenly, she realized. She was going to do it. She was going to do it, become it, because she had already embarrassed herself. She had already told him that she was a virgin. She had already told him that she wanted him. She was just going to do this.

So she reached down to the belt of the robe and undid it. Then she let it drop to the floor. And she was standing before him, wearing nothing other than ridiculous shearling boots and a smile.

"Maybe you could stay." Her voice felt scratchy; she

felt scratchy. Her heart was pounding so hard she could barely hear, and the steam filling up the room seemed to swallow her voice.

But she could see his face. She could see the tightness there. The intensity.

"Honey…"

"No. I just… Maybe this is the time to have a conversation, actually. The one that we decided to have later. Because I'm getting warm. I'm very warm."

"Put your robe back on."

"What if I don't want to?"

"Why not?"

"Because I want you. I already admitted to that. Why do you think I'm so upset? All the time? About all the women that you bring into the winery, about the fact that my father gave it to you. About the fact that we're stuck together, but will never actually be together. And that's why I had to leave. I'm not an idiot, Jericho, I know that you and I are never going to… We're not going to fall in love and get married. We can hardly stand to be in the same room as each other. But I have wanted you since I understood what that meant. And I don't know what to do about it. Short of running away and having sex with someone else. That was my game plan. My game plan was to go off and have sex with another man. And that got thwarted. You were the one that picked me up. You're the one that I'm stuck here with in the snow. And I'm not going to claim that it's fate. Because I can feel myself twisting every single element of this except for the weather. The blizzard isn't my fault. But I'm making the choice to go ahead and offer… Me."

"I…"

"If you're going to reject me, just don't do it horribly."

And then suddenly, she found herself being tugged into his arms, the heat from his body more intense than the heat from the sauna, the roughness of his clothes a shock against her skin. And then his mouth crashed down on hers.

Seven

He was being an idiot. He was being a damned idiot. There were so many women out there in the world that he could sleep with and suffer no consequences for doing so. She was not one of them. She was in fact one of the few women who wasn't in that number. The only others were his friends' wives. And then there was Honey. And she was clinging to him like she wanted him. Like she wanted him and needed him. Like he was air.

He'd tried to resist. He'd told himself to.

But she wanted him.

That changed everything.

And she was so damn soft. And he was powerless not to rub his hands up and down her curves. From her rib cage just beneath her breasts, down her slender waist, to cup her ass, which was the most delightful handful he could've imagined.

And back up again. She was divine. And sweet. Just like her name suggested.

She might be vinegar when she talked, but when she kissed…

She shivered in his hold, her response to his kisses so intense it floored him. She was trembling with need. And it was… It was intoxicating. And maybe because she was a woman that he shouldn't want, he wanted her all the more. Maybe that's what made her skin so soft. Maybe that's what made her cries of pleasure so sweet. Maybe that was what made her so damned irresistible.

He moved both hands down to her ass and squeezed her tight, pulling her up against him so that she could feel how hard he was. And he knew it was too late. Knew that it was too late for better judgment and smarter decisions. There was no decision to be made. She was naked, she was in his arms and he wanted her.

He lifted her up off the ground, sat down on the wooden bench there in the sauna with her legs parted wide, her thighs on either side of his. He tilted his head back and looked at her, as best he could in the steamy room. Her breasts were small and round, beautiful, her nipples the same color as her name.

Tight and begging for his attention. Her stomach was flat, muscled from all the hard labor that she did, her thighs just the same. And that thatch of curls between her legs… It was all he could have ever asked for.

He gripped her hips, stared at the way his hands looked against her skin, moved them up beneath her breasts and slid his thumb across her nipples. She was beautiful. Delicious. He leaned forward and kissed her, right between her breasts, and she arched.

"Tell me if you want me to stop," he said, his voice rough.

"Don't stop," she whispered. "Please don't stop."

He lowered his head and sucked one bud into his mouth, flooded with relief. Because all this tension that had existed inside of him had suddenly unwound, tension he had known was there.

The denial that he wanted this. The denial that he wanted her. He did. And there was no denying it or hiding it. He had tried. He had put it down to a few errant moments of looking at her ass, but it was a hell of a lot more than that.

It had been building. And he knew it. It was why he'd been so furious when she said she was going to sleep with someone. It was why he'd been so obsessed when he'd found out that she hadn't.

Because he was full of this. This deep, dark, forbidden desire for a woman that he knew he wasn't supposed to touch.

But he was touching her now. Tasting her.

And it was a hell of a thing.

He moved his head from her first breast and then paid equal attention to the other, where she was just as sweet, just as filled with desire for him. She let her head fall back, and a cry of need escaped her mouth.

He didn't have a condom in here, so it wasn't going to go all the way. But he could take her there.

He curved his forearms up beneath her knees, pressed his hands to her lower back and lifted her from his lap as he slowly laid her down across the bench, parting her thighs and gazing at all of her feminine beauty.

"Jericho," she whispered.

She said his name. She said that she wanted him.

This seemed to prove it. Beautifully.

This was insanity. But he was neck-deep in it and feeling fine. Feeling ready to be submersed. He kissed her inner thigh, and she shuddered. Then he lowered his head, flicking his tongue over the source of her pleasure.

She gasped, arching against his mouth.

And she tasted sweet, and he knew that he had overdone it on the references to Honey, but it kept being true.

And he didn't know how he had ever thought of her as simply Creed and Jackson's younger sister. She was Honey and herself. And right now, she felt a whole lot like his. Right now, he didn't want to think of what moment followed this one, where she was so perfectly sweet and aroused for him. Only for him. All for him.

So he kissed her there, and teased her, until she was writhing against him, until she was begging.

Until she was crying out her pleasure, and he could feel it. Deep down inside. He could feel it.

"Jericho," she gasped.

The scene was all around them, between them. And she sat up. She looked dazed, filled with wonder. Her skin was dewy from the heat and the steam, and he wanted to lick every inch of her. And he had never seen a more beautiful sight.

Forbidden fruit. Pleasure deferred. Whatever you wanted to call it. It was damn sweet.

"Jericho…" And then suddenly she basically flung herself at him, kissing him, touching his chest, and he was so hard it hurt. She settled herself on his lap, the slick, wet heat of her hot against his denim-covered arousal.

He moved his hands over her curves, over her softness. And he knew that he would never get enough. Not of her. Not of this. Ever.

It was a scary thought, considering he shouldn't even have another bite, let alone gorge himself on the feast like he wanted to.

"I don't have a condom," he said.

"I have tons of condoms," she said.

"I meant I don't have a condom in here."

"Right," she said. "Oh… Oh. But we should get one."

"We should go back to the house."

"To get a condom."

"Maybe to take a breath," he said. But he would rather have a condom.

"I don't want to take a breath."

And she was looking at him expectantly, and he realized if he stopped now it would be… Well, it would be because of something other than her.

Sure, some of it was because of him. Some of it was because he was the last man who should be taking someone's virginity. He didn't have the sensitivity for that. He didn't have the sensitivity or the emotional… Anything. To be the person who should be handling something like this. But a lot of it was about Creed and Jackson, and at the end of the day, that wasn't fair. Because Honey was her own person, and the fact that her family seemed dedicated to not treating her like her own person, capable of making her own decisions, not even bothering to check with her before her dad sold the winery… All of that… That was… Well, it wasn't fair. She deserved to be treated like she knew her own mind.

Right. And that's the thing that will get you laid.

He wasn't going to claim he was being altruistic

about it. But he was looking at it from a different angle. That was all.

The angle that let him have an orgasm.

But no. It would never just be that. She would never just be that. She was Honey Cooper, and he wasn't going to pretend otherwise. If he wanted to get laid, he could get laid. But she said she'd always wanted him. She'd said...

Well. You're a little bit sad.

Because the fact that she'd always wanted him, that meant something to *him*. This girl, this beautiful woman, who was part of the best family he'd ever known, wanted him. He couldn't deny that did something to him. Made something inside of him that had previously felt shattered feel fixed. And the fact that he wanted to chase some feeling of redemption in her arms was messed up as hell. The fact that he seemed to believe on some level that the gift of her body was going to wash away a world of hurt... Yeah, well, he had never claimed to be the most emotionally well-balanced person. Quite the opposite. He knew that he was a mess. He'd always known.

The kid who'd never really been a kid. The kid who'd been rejected by his father. Who'd lost his mother. Yeah, he never claimed to be real balanced. So he might as well just embrace it. Because hell, they were snowed in. What else could they do? And he could turn away from it now, but the odds of them resisting were low. Unless they were going to be rescued in the next ten minutes, and the way the snow continued to come down didn't make it seem likely—well, he might as well just go with it.

So he wrapped her in the robe, scooped her up in

his arms, realized that she had never taken those boots off and pushed open the door to the sauna. It was still freezing cold outside. The snow was continuing to dump down in buckets, and he didn't know how long they would be stuck here.

"This is an extraordinary circumstance," he said, carrying them both through the snow. "And when we get rescued…"

"Right," she said. "I get it. Only during the snowstorm."

"Only during the snowstorm."

"What if we end up here for Christmas?"

"I don't know. I guess we'll cross that bridge when we come to it."

"I would like to cross this other bridge first."

"Seems like a good idea to me."

He kicked open the door to the cabin, then closed it behind him with his heel. They would need to get a fire going again in the bedroom.

He carried her up the stairs, and she clung to him, her arms around his neck, and her eyes took on a strange, soft look.

"What?"

"Well," she said. "No one has ever… I mean… No one has ever treated me like this. I had to be tough pretty much this whole time."

She had been. Tough, mouthy Honey, and everybody did treat her that way. He knew that was so. Even he was guilty of it. But did nobody really treat her with any softness? That was all he wanted to do. Wrap her in furs and make sure she was warm. Well, that was not all he wanted to do, but it was definitely the more gentlemanly thing he wanted to do.

He hadn't felt compelled to care for anyone in years. He'd been burned out on it. But Honey always seemed so invulnerable. And he knew she wasn't. That much had become clear on this little trip together.

It brought out tenderness in him he'd thought long gone.

He didn't say anything. Instead, he just kissed her. He kissed her because she was beautiful. He kissed her because he wanted her to feel that.

He kissed her because there weren't words to say that he was sorry for all the softness she'd missed out on because her mother had died. Because she had then been surrounded by people who were as wounded and hard and hurt as she was.

That was the truth of it. They had taken him in, but they were all in the same boat. Grieving and wretched and in general some of the least emotionally conversant people around.

And they'd all been there for each other, but clearly something was missing. For her.

Something no one had realized.

He would make it his mission for her to feel it here. For her to feel it this week. *Week. You don't know how long it's going to be.*

No. He didn't.

Someone could come knocking on the door right now—which he found he really didn't want—someone could find them in a week. Two weeks. They might be able to get the car out in the next couple of days. They didn't know.

But right now, it didn't matter. Right now, he was determined to dedicate everything in his power to making Honey feel all the things that she hadn't before.

That's a power trip.

Maybe. Maybe it was a power trip. Because he was a kid who—at the end of the day—felt like he had never really been able to offer much to anyone. He had tried, but his mother had still died. His father hadn't been there. The Coopers had given to him. And in the end, he felt like, to an extent, he had given back by buying the winery. Except he had still hurt Honey. And that did matter.

Sure, his own success was important. But so was her happiness.

And for the first time, he felt like he might be giving more than he was taking, and that was a pretty good feeling. Even if it was trumped up, all things considered. Since he was also getting sex and it wasn't like this was a mission of charity.

He was hardly the Mother Teresa of orgasms.

The bedroom was cold, and he laid her out gingerly on the bed and wrapped her up in the furs there.

She burrowed beneath them happily and kept her eyes on him as he began to build the fire.

The urge that he had to suddenly just…give her everything that he could think of… It was almost overpowering. He wanted her to have…every good thing. Every good thing. He got the fire going, nice and big, and when it was done, he straightened. "Okay. So tell me where the condoms are."

Eight

Honey fought the urge to burrow deeper beneath the covers. She was… She was so desperately aroused, so desperately excited that she could barely breathe. Jericho had kissed her. Well, she had kissed him. After stripping naked. And then he had… Hell. He had kissed her. And places that she hadn't even got around to fantasizing he might kiss her.

It had been transformative. And now this. This realization of her deepest fantasy. She wanted this man. She wanted this man in ways that defied her experience. That far outstripped anything she'd ever done, anything she'd ever fantasized about in a concrete fashion.

It was real. But it was ephemeral and unformed. A mass of feelings that made her breath quicken and made her heart beat faster.

He was beautiful. She had always thought so. But it

was the way he looked at her. That was what truly left her in awe. That was what made it so she couldn't think.

Because he wasn't looking at her like she was just Honey, the same woman that he'd seen every day for the past who knew how many years. He was looking at her like he'd never really seen her before. And that made her feel new. The kind of new that she had wanted. The kind of new that she had believed might be out there for her, but it was better than finding it with a man she had never met before. She had found it with him.

She had found it with him, and she hadn't been expecting that.

Oh, how she wanted this man, this man who looked at her as if he had never seen her before, all the while he was a man who saw her all the time.

It was the fulfillment of her deepest need. Her deepest fantasy.

He was everything.

But she was nervous. And she found herself shrinking into those furs and that soft mattress.

They had shared this bed last night, but they had kept a healthy amount of space between them. Just a few moments ago in the sauna there had been nothing between them at all. And now…

"Are you okay?"

"Yes," she said, doing her best to sound emphatic.

It came out with just a little more tremble than she would've liked.

"Are you sure?"

"I am absolutely sure. I did say."

"You can always change your mind."

In those words, coming from the strongest, hottest man she had ever known, who was essentially sex and cowboy boots, did something to fire up her arousal even more.

He was strong enough to take what he wanted, to do whatever he wanted. He was strong enough to break her if he wanted to, but he didn't want that. He wanted to use his hands to give her pleasure, and only the pleasure that she wanted.

He was more than any fantasy she'd ever had. And she was so unbearably aware, not of his strength then, but of the way that he kept it leashed.

That was power. And the intensity of it was enough to make her combust.

"I am 100 percent sure that I want to have sex with you, Jericho. I have been 100 percent sure of that for a very long time."

"And yet you're so mean to me."

"It didn't stop you from wanting to have sex with me," she pointed out. And then she suddenly became very afraid that he didn't actually want to have sex with her. What if she was just a charity case? What if this was just pity? Or worse, some misguided overprotective instinct because he didn't want her to have sex with a man she didn't know, a man that she was going to go work for. What if this was…him using his penis as a protective shield. Like parents who wanted their kids to drink at home if they were going to drink. Maybe he wanted her to have sex with him if she was going to have sex with anyone.

That would just be a whole lot of a hot mess. And she did not want that.

Except she didn't really want to question him either. Because she wanted him. But of course, him not really wanting her would be unbearable…

"Is this about me? I mean, at all? Do you... Are you attracted to me?"

He huffed a laugh. "I have spent the last little bit trying not to notice just how beautiful you were. Because the fact of the matter is, there's a lot of women that I could be with who don't present as much of a complication as you do."

"That is not very flattering," she said, wrinkling her nose.

"I'm not trying to flatter you. I'm trying to be honest with you. And honestly? This is a terrible idea. If your brothers find out, they're going to kick my ass. Your dad's gonna kick my ass. Hell, maybe when I come to my senses, I'm going to want to kick my own ass. But I want you more than I care about that."

He hesitated for a second. As if there was something else he wanted to say, but then he didn't.

"All this is insulting, and deeply flattering at the same time. I'll take it." Because her chest burned. With satisfaction. With triumph. With the knowledge and desire that whether or not she was a terrible idea, Jericho Smith wanted her. He could have any woman. Fundamentally, he often did.

But right now he wanted her. Right now, she was the thing that he craved. Right now, she wanted to luxuriate in that more than just about anything. "The condoms are in my suitcase."

"The lingerie suitcase."

"Yes. I have several boxes, and I bought different kinds. Because I didn't know... You know, they say ribbed on some of them. And I didn't really know what that meant, so I got that. But I got regular kinds too." She felt silly all of a sudden.

"As long as they're not hot pink, I'm fine."

"What if they are? Would that be a deal breaker?"

He shifted. "At this point, nothing is a deal breaker. I'm too far gone."

The fact that he couldn't reject her over a hot pink condom was another spurious compliment, but another one that she would gladly take.

He got up close to the suitcase and bent down in front of it, taking out a couple of boxes. "Did you choose the ribbed?"

"No."

"Why not?"

"Because I think I can manage your pleasure just fine without them." His lips hitched upward into a grin that made her stomach flip. "In fact. I know I can."

"You are very confident. Has anyone ever told you that before?"

"Yeah. Though, usually the word is *arrogant*."

"You don't sound bothered by it."

"The question I always have about arrogance is why is it a problem if you can back all your claims up?" He grinned. "Am I arrogant? Or am I just telling the truth."

"I feel that I will not be able to comment upon that until after... After."

"If you're still able to comment after, I'll consider it a personal failure."

He took a whole strip of the condoms from the box, dropped it back into the suitcase, then deposited the protection on the end of the bed. Then he stood there, pitched his cowboy hat up off his head and pulled his shirt up directly after.

Her mouth went dry. She knew that he was beautiful. She had known. But the last time she had seen him shirtless, it had been all fruitless longing and furtive, embarrassed attempts to keep herself from staring too intently. And now she just looked her fill. Because why not? Why not just look? His dark brown skin, with hard ridged muscles and just the right amount of dark hair was the perfect representation of all things masculine. And it called to everything feminine in her. To her softness. A softness that she'd had to deny more than indulge, because she had been dropped into a world that was hard. A world she knew was hard.

And all of her soft feelings had always felt twisted around that reality. Around the truth that there was no reward for being sad or grieving, and there was no special prize for having lost much in life. She'd made the mistake of getting lost in all that once, and she'd only caused other people grief.

So she had just done her best to cover it up, to get along.

And it had all come to a head in an explosion of anger when her father had sold him the winery, but there was just so much more to her than that. So much more to her than anger. And she didn't often let herself explore that or feel that. And maybe that was partly why her attraction to him had often come out as an expression of anger or aggression. Because it was easier. Because if it wasn't that, it was softness. And it was the softness she had always feared. But there was something about him, and all that masculine hardness that made her want to luxuriate in everything about herself that was different.

And she found herself slipping out from under the covers. Not quite so embarrassed now to show herself. She kicked the boots off beneath the blankets and shoved them down off the edge of the mattress, then slipped out from beneath the furs, parting her robe as she did. Exposing her breasts on a rush of air. She had done the same thing in the sauna, but she had felt insulated by the steam then. But there was nothing concealing her now. The firelight glowed over his skin and hers. And it added to the intimacy of it. To the mood. To the magic of the moment.

She climbed out from beneath the covers completely, slipping the robe away, showing him her.

He sucked in a harsh breath through his teeth. "You are so damn sexy."

He saw *her*.

Not what she had been able to show the world up until this point. Not the things her brothers wanted other people to see, or that her father thought. He saw her. A piece of herself that she wasn't even fully comfortable with. Because even when she had made the decision to go up north and sleep with Donovan, she hadn't been driven by an overwhelming surge of attraction. Or by being in touch with her sexuality. Rather it had been anger. Just more anger, fueling her and firing her on. And right now she wasn't angry. Right now, she was soft and she was vulnerable, and if he said something pointed, she had a feeling that he could rent her in two.

But he wasn't. Instead, he had said just the right thing. Just the perfect thing. Instead, he had made her feel like more, not less.

She was very unbearably conscious just then of all the things that she had missed in her life because she hadn't had a mother.

The conversations, the shopping trips. She wondered

if her mother would've shifted her focus just enough so that this feminine piece of herself didn't feel quite so foreign.

So that her focus hadn't been so squarely on simply fitting in with her family. Because there would've been someone else like her. Someone else who was different. And maybe she would've still been the same her, but maybe the feminine mystique wouldn't have been quite so...mystical.

It didn't feel mystical now. It felt simple.

But she was safe with him. The stranger who was also familiar.

He put his hands on his belt, while he kicked his boots off and shrugged off his jeans and underwear in one fluid motion. Her mouth went dry.

Because in his entirety, he was the most gorgeous thing she had ever seen.

A friend of hers in high school—just a casual friend—had once said that she had seen a penis in person and was not going to rush to buy artistic renderings of it for her room.

She really thought that she might buy some art if it was fashioned to look like him.

He was art all on his own. Thick and strong and large.

His thighs were muscular, his waist lean, every ounce of hard work that man did etched deep into his muscles.

He was a sculpture come to life, every loving detail on his body seemingly handcrafted into an ideal human form.

She had done a bit of time on the internet, trying to prepare herself for what was going to happen. Not with porn, obviously—she knew better than to try to consult male fantasies for what she should expect out of sex. But she had done a bit of reading on how sometimes the first time hurt—but probably not if the woman was a little older and had ridden a lot of horses—she qualified as an older virgin, and she had certainly done her fair share of horse riding.

She also knew—because she wasn't a child—that a man would fit.

But right now, inexplicably, she felt a bit nervous about that. Just a bit skeptical. But then he came down on the bed beside her, and he was kissing her, the length of his naked body pressed against hers, and she forgot to be nervous. She forgot everything but the way that it felt to be touched by him. Kissed by him.

And suddenly, ridiculously, her eyes filled with tears. Because this was… It was different than she had imagined it would be. He was different. There was no fighting, no banter, no ridiculousness. None of the things that they threw out between each other to keep the other distant. That was what she did. All the time. Throwing down gauntlets and throwing out outrageous statements to keep him standing back. So that she wasn't challenged. So that he didn't see.

But he could see now. And he knew. He knew that she wanted him. And the world hadn't collapsed in on itself. Rather, a whole new world had opened up to her. Rather, everything had become brighter and brilliant and more beautiful.

And, oh, how she wanted him.

She was on fire with it. That heat between her legs slick and hot and ready.

As if on cue, he put his hand there, between her thighs, rubbing at the sensitive bundle of nerves there. And she arched against him. He pushed a finger inside of her tight channel, and she winced.

Okay. Maybe the horse riding wasn't going to make this as easy as she'd hoped.

But then he pushed another finger in and kept on kissing her. And she got wetter and hotter, and if there was still pain, it didn't matter quite so much. If there was still pain, it didn't surpass the deep, throbbing need inside of her. She burned.

And he was the only thing that could possibly put out the fire. Or maybe he would simply be gasoline on a lit match. Maybe he would still get higher, and maybe that was what she wanted. To burn out of control with no end in sight.

He teased her and toyed with her until the pleasure built to unbearable heights. Until her entire world reduced to his mouth on hers and his fingers inside her.

And then she shattered. Her climax rolling over her like a wave. And when she came back to herself, he was positioned between her thighs, the protection firmly in place.

"I'm ready," she said.

And he thrust home. Deep and hard. She gasped, arching against him. She was overwhelmed by the sensation of fullness, but it wasn't bad.

No. It wasn't bad. It was him. Overwhelming and far too much, but the alternative was not having him, and that was simply something that she couldn't take. A reality that she wouldn't be happy with at all.

And then, he began to move, the fullness becoming

essential rather than unbearable, the weight of him a gift that she wanted to hang on to forever. Impossibly, she felt another climax begin to build. This went deeper, more intense than the previous two. Her body tightened around his, and she arched her back, throwing her head back against the pillows, crying out her pleasure. And that was when he gave himself over to it. Lost himself in his own desire. And all the while she was still riding out the aftershocks of her desire, she was flooded by the overwhelming satisfaction of his.

She had never been with a man before. And he had been with plenty of women. But they were shaking just the same. She was clinging to him, his body sweat slicked, his desire so apparent, and she felt...

She felt more herself than she ever had in her life.

She had done it. She was no longer a virgin. But she realized that wasn't even what mattered. What mattered was him.

She pushed that realization aside as quickly as it occurred, because of all the things that could potentially ruin this, that was the worst.

This was just for the blizzard.

It was great that it could be him. Because she had always wanted him, but she didn't need him to be essential. In fact she needed him to very much not be. He was hot, and she liked him. And without feeling the need to distance him because of her attraction to him, they would probably feel like they liked each other even more.

But it could only ever be this. This cold weather thing. That would melt along with the snow.

She chose not to think about that. Instead, she snuggled against him beneath the furs. She thought about saying something. There was nothing to say. And sleep was dragging her under.

So she gave in to it. For the first time in memory Honey Cooper just didn't bother to fight. Instead, she just rested.

Nine

"I told you," Jericho said when Honey's eyes finally fluttered open. "If you still had something to say then I wasn't worthy of my arrogance."

She gazed at him out of her narrowed eyes. "That is really the first thing on your mind?"

"Yes, ma'am. I'm always on hand for the 'I told you so.'"

"That is deeply, deeply petty."

"I never said I wasn't." And all right, it wasn't the most romantic thing. But they weren't romantic.

Except… She had been amazing, and he was getting impatient watching her sleep. It was the middle of the day, after all.

And you want her again.

Not that he could afford to. Not that either of them could afford this.

But hey, they were stuck here until the weather

cleared, which it still hadn't done. And as long as they could make the most of it, why shouldn't they? As long as they were here...

"Well, fine. You have earned your arrogance."

"Happy to hear it."

Her stomach growled. Audibly. "I'm hungry."

He was too. But not particularly for food.

"You can have some food. After you have a bath."

"Hey," she said, as he picked her up out of the bed. "I can walk, you know. You seem to have forgotten that."

"I didn't forget. I just like carrying you."

It was true.

He liked the feeling of the soft weight in his arms. He liked feeling her in general.

"I'll get you your bird book if you want."

"I don't want the bird book."

He chuckled. "How about I take a bath with you?"

A flush covered her skin, and he was ridiculously pleased by it. That she was affected by them. By this.

You've lost your mind.

Maybe. But it didn't seem so crazy that what he wanted was to stay here, not face what was out there. Not deal with the fact that he had a long-lost family he was supposed to be spending Christmas with. Yeah, spending time with Honey was a hell of a lot nicer.

He had run the bath already, because he hadn't been totally sure that they would have enough hot water, and it had been pretty close. He'd warmed a couple pots up on the stove and added them to the deep claw-foot tub in the bathroom.

He deposited her in the warm water and watched the way the firelight sparkled over her damp skin. She was so damned pretty. So perfect. It made him feel... Well, it made him feel a damn sight too much. "Good," he said. But she didn't move at all, and he laughed as he got into the tub and lifted her, setting her back down so that she was on his lap.

She sighed, letting her head fall back against his chest. Then she tilted her head. Looking at him as best she could. "This is very strange."

"How so?" But it made his chest tight.

"Well, just a few hours ago we were fully clothed and sitting across the room from each other talking about birds..."

"I never really talked about birds. It was mostly you talking about birds."

"Whatever," she said. "It's just that... It's very strange to now be sitting with you like this. Without clothes."

And perhaps the strangest part of all was it didn't feel strange. Because they were still them. She was still talking about birds.

"Right."

He lifted his hand from the water, let the droplets fall over her skin. Her breasts.

He was transfixed by the sight of her. By her beauty. And he hadn't gotten to where he was marinating in the strangeness of it, because he wanted her for as long as he had and now he finally had her.

She was as beautiful as he'd imagined that she might be. And that was... Well, his imagination had been pretty thorough, but it still hadn't quite managed to get the particulars. Every dip and hollow and facet of beauty that was unique to Honey.

It was strange. The rightness of it.

"Yeah. I guess," he said, even though he didn't feel

the same disquiet he imagined she did. Perhaps it was experience.

Except he knew it wasn't that. Maybe it was just the way they were cocooned in this moment. The entire thing had been a little bit surreal. Maybe he had just sunk into it. Maybe he'd been sinking into it for the last month, finding out the Daltons didn't know about him—or at least Hank hadn't. That he actually wanted to get to know him.

"It's only a few days before Christmas," he said.

What was supposed to have been his first Christmas with his father.

A father. What does that even mean when you find out when you are thirty-four years old?

What did it mean at all? He hadn't been there for anything. He hadn't been there to help Jericho when everything had fallen apart.

Whether or not it was his choice didn't really matter, because the end result was the same.

And joining the family now... It was kind of the ninth inning. He didn't need their support. Not anymore.

He figured out how to get along. He figured it out on his own. That he felt compelled to go... Well, maybe it was a good thing that he hit a snowstorm.

After all, he was here, naked with Honey, rather than dealing with the awkwardness of the family situation.

"We need a Christmas tree," she whispered.

"A Christmas tree?" There was weight that came with that, baggage and pain that he didn't want to think about now.

But Honey wanted a Christmas tree, and he found that he wanted to please her. It was such a strange sensation. One lost way back in time.

"Yes, Jericho," she said, oblivious to his inner turmoil. "So that we can have a Merry Christmas."

"I didn't get you anything," he said.

She laughed. "I think you did."

"Well, I'm not the kind of man who would say that a couple of orgasms for me were a gift."

That made her howl, slapping the surface of the water. "Since when?"

"All right, I am." Something sincere rose up inside of him, and he didn't quite know what to do with it. It was just that… For her that didn't seem like enough. He wanted there to be more. He wanted to give her something, and the impulse felt strange and foreign. The impulse felt undeniable.

It was the strangest damn thing.

"All right, how about a Christmas tree then? And maybe I can find a really pretty rock to wrap up for you."

"And what will you wrap it in?" she asked, smiling sweetly.

He smiled back, but it was wicked. "Maybe some of those lace panties that you brought."

She snickered, readjusting herself, her bottom moving over his growing arousal. He really needed to give her a break. She had been a virgin. And it was very likely that she could be sore.

If you had gotten her a nice enough gift, you might not have felt so guilty about her being sore.

Well, damn. That didn't say great things about them, but it was true. Because he wanted her again, soreness or not.

"All right," he said. "I'd rather see you in the panties. Though, I'd also rather see you out of them."

"That is something I don't really understand about lingerie," she said. "Are you supposed to dress up in another room and make a grand entrance? And then you just put it on so it gets taken off thirty seconds later."

"You could put it on in front of me right now, take it off fifteen seconds later, and I would still think the whole thing was worth it, because it was just all staring at you."

Her cheeks went red. "Really?"

"Yes. Because you're so damn hot I can hardly deal with myself."

"Wow."

"What?"

"Nothing. Just…" She looked up at him with wide, sincere eyes that damn near broke his heart. "You really *do* think I'm hot?"

That question, so artless, sat like a weight in his chest, along with Christmas trees. "I really do. I wouldn't say it if I didn't think it."

"How long?"

"Why do you need to know how long?"

She turned over, a slippery mermaid in his arms, then rested her forearms against his chest and looked up at him. "I need to know because I have had the biggest crush on you for most of my life, all the while wanting to hit you over the head with the nearest blunt object. You are both my favorite and least favorite person to be around, often during the same conversation. And I have felt like a fool for feeling that way this whole time."

That admission stole his breath. He was older, and he might not have felt that way about her back when she did, but it wasn't because she wasn't…wonderful.

It was because of their age gap. "Why did you feel that way? Like you were foolish for wanting me?"

"Because I just never thought that I was all that interesting or pretty or anything of the kind. I always felt a little bit on the outside in school. And I tried not to, but... I did. Beatrix Leighton gave me a mouse once. When we were in kindergarten. I kept him as a pet for three years. I thought that was one of the nicest things anyone ever did for me. I think she was about the closest I ever got to feeling like somebody might understand me. But she was usually nursing animals back to health and not doing anything social. But I just always felt like I didn't really fit. And..."

"I think everybody feels that way sometimes."

"Yeah?"

He smiled. "There aren't a whole lot of people who look like me around here."

"No, I know," she said. She looked away.

"Hey, don't be embarrassed. It's fine that you don't just think of it. But it is true. I get it. I know what it's like to feel different. But I also know what it's like to find people who get you. Who see past the obvious surface things and know you. Understand you."

"I don't know if anyone's ever actually understood me. I mean, my dad, Creed and Jackson, they all lost my mother, just like I did. And you lost your mother. You're about the closest anyone could ever come to understanding exactly what I've been through. But I think the thing that gets me is that... Or maybe I'm not very good at making myself understood. I'm just... I'm upset at how much this is my fault, I guess. I was mad at my dad, I am mad at him, but you're right. He wouldn't hurt me on purpose. I feel all these things and no one seems to know, and I don't know how to fix it. Except…you I just talk to."

"I'm glad, Honey," he said. "Your dad does care about you though. He knew I wouldn't get rid of you." He slid his hand down her arm. "I was never going to throw you out on the street or take your job away."

He was callous sometimes, and he knew that. His life had made him that way. But he'd never do anything to intentionally hurt Honey.

"But working for you isn't exactly the same as having a real career, is it? It's not the same as what I thought I was working toward. I guess that I somehow managed to never really… That he never considered it… I don't know. I just feel so desperately like maybe no one's ever known me, and maybe I don't show who I am enough. I've always felt like I was really honest. About who I was and what I wanted, but you know, I hid wanting you the whole time. Really well. Maybe I'm just hiding. Maybe it's a whole lot of hiding."

"Hey," he said. "We're all hiding. The fact of the matter is… We've been almost like family this whole time."

She wrinkled her nose. "Gross."

"Well, it's true. And for family you put on a little bit of a performance. Because there's parts of yourself that you gotta keep quiet. It's just…what you do. It's just how you navigate things. At least… That's my experience of family. I never wanted my mom to know how difficult it was for me when she was sick. So I hid that. Because I had to be strong."

He wanted to talk to her, and he didn't much ever want to talk to anyone. But maybe it was what she'd said. About being misunderstood. Maybe that was why.

Maybe he wanted to find ways they could understand each other.

She nodded. "Maybe that's it. I'm so used to hiding what I want, because I wanted a lot of things that my dad couldn't give me. And I never wanted to make him sad. So I just… I kind of bump along and pretend everything is great. Even when it isn't."

"It is not too late," he said. "Obviously, there's no question of you going to see Donavan now."

"I took a job from him, Jericho. He needs at least time to find a replacement."

"You aren't touching him."

She looked shocked. "No, of course I wouldn't."

He didn't have the right to make that statement, not when they were supposed to just be…for the blizzard. But still. He couldn't stand the thought. It made him see red.

"I'm willing to sell you part of the winery."

And hell, there were layers of complications now. But this… This thing between them, it was only for the blizzard. It was only for the blizzard.

"You will?"

"Yeah," he said.

Because somewhere along the way the reason that he had wanted the winery, that desperate desire to claim his place in the valley, in the family… It had faded a little bit. Because he could see now that Honey wanted the same thing. And he didn't want to take it from her.

He would have, before this. Because what he wanted had felt more important, but it just didn't anymore.

"I'd like that. I mean, I have money. From the sale. We're just kind of passing it back and forth."

"You can make payments on a bigger part of the winery, if you want. Because otherwise you're only getting a fifth."

"I'll consider it. I'll buy a fifth, and then we'll see. If I want to pursue a bigger share, I will after that."

"That sounds a good plan."

"Can we get the Christmas tree now?"

"Yes," he said. "Bundle up. We'll go get a Christmas tree now."

By the time they got out of the tub and dressed, twilight had fallen. This single day had felt like four days. And Honey felt a little bit like she was in a daze. But the good kind.

Being with him had been… Transformative. She felt transformed.

She wasn't going to tell him that, because his ego was healthy enough without her stoking the flames, but it was true.

They didn't have to go far into the woods to find a decent tree, and Jericho chopped it down, then slung it over his shoulder to carry back. As he walked, icy little droplets fell from the tree and hit Honey in the face, but she didn't mind. She felt…renewed.

She was going to be able to buy a piece of the winery. She and Jericho were…

Something twisted in her stomach. *Nothing, you're nothing.*

Right. Of course. They weren't anything. They were just… For the blizzard.

The snow had eased up, no longer falling in large fat flakes and piling up higher and higher. Still, it was so cold it wouldn't be going anywhere for a while.

Before they went back to the cabin, Jericho walked to the truck and confirmed that it was still blocked in.

She laughed as he shook the tree out when they got to the porch, and then leaned it up against the wall in the living room, because there was no tree stand.

Honey found string and some popcorn kernels, which she popped on the stovetop in a big Dutch oven, and the two of them worked at making popcorn strings by lantern light, which then led to a contest to see who could make the most innocuous household object into a tree decoration.

In the end, their monstrous masterpiece included several ceramic figurines, a tinfoil star up on the very top and, possibly silliest of all, some perfume bottles hung from the branches by string, which ended up twinkling merrily in the lantern light and giving the entire thing a cheerfully strange effect.

"Without a doubt, the weirdest ass Christmas tree I have ever seen," Jericho said, taking a step back and putting his arm around her. The casual touch was so strange. How odd to have gone from existing in a space where it felt like there was a wall between them physically, to this moment, where they had now bathed together, and he was touching her like she was his...

She wasn't anything. She was just Honey.

She looked up at him, at his sculpted face, the firelight illuminating his brown skin. His dark eyes glittered there, his square jaw rough with black stubble, his lips... Well, now she knew what they tasted like. And what they felt like when they tasted her.

How could she ever go back to a time when she didn't know that? Where he wasn't hers anymore? To touch and do with as she pleased. How could she ever bear it?

You've borne a lot of things. You'll just have to bear this too.

She had more than she had when she'd first set out on this trip. She lost her virginity and she secured a job. It just wasn't what she'd been planning.

It was better.

She'd gotten what she wanted.

She wanted him physically, and nothing more.

And if the thought of that made her ache now... That was her own problem. It certainly wasn't his.

"It is indeed. But it's nice."

They lit a fire in the hearth there, and Jericho brought furs down from upstairs and spread them over the floor while Honey gathered together some cheeses, cured meats and crackers for a cheese board. There was even a glass of wine, and all up, the entire thing felt nearly sophisticated.

"I didn't imagine that being off-grid could be so glamorous."

"Helped very much by the fact that the generator runs some indoor plumbing," he pointed out.

"Well. There is that." She wrinkled her nose. "Not much glamour to be had with an outhouse."

"No indeed."

They settled into each other, into the moment. The furs soft and warm, the fire crackling in the hearth. It felt safe, right. She felt safe. To say what she needed to. To feel what she needed to.

The thought made her heart feel pierced, because her emotions had felt too big and wrong from the time she was a girl.

From back when her father had been so upset with her grief, and she had nearly drowned in it. And she'd learned to put it away because she'd had to.

"I never knew what to do about you," she said, her chest feeling tender. She shouldn't talk about this. Except, maybe it would help. Maybe it would explain things. Because she wasn't foolish enough to believe that she had a future with Jericho, and she never had been. It was just that… She knew him. And there was something about desiring him that had felt both dangerous and safe at the same time. And maybe that was it. Maybe that was all it was. Because she hadn't had a mother to talk to her about those things…

"You were this…teenage boy that came into the house and you weren't my brother. And you made me feel all kinds of things and they were scary. I've never really had anyone I could talk to about this. Some casual friends at school when I was kind of on the outskirts of a couple of different groups. But I never really felt like I could share with them. I never really wanted to. It felt too… Precarious, I guess. I didn't know how I was going to explain to the girls in my class that I was more interested in a boy in his twenties than a boy my age. And I didn't really want to… I don't know. Maybe it's just that you've always felt safe."

"Safe?" he questioned, lifting his brows.

"You know. Not in a beige kind of way, but in a… I've always had a lot of feelings, and I've always been around men. And the way that men do feelings. And so I've always had to be really careful… Or I felt like I did. Because I wanted to fit in and I wanted to be understood, but at the same time I didn't want my brothers or my dad to think that I was dramatic. And I didn't… I dunno, maybe keeping my sexual attraction type feelings down to somebody like you was… Because I could talk to you, always. Even with all of that. Because our relationship has always been… Sure, we fight and things like that, but it's always been important. And kinda special. And…"

"You've been lonely for a long time, haven't you?"

The words were far too incisive, and they hit Honey right where she lived.

"Yeah," she said. "I guess so."

"Well, we can talk."

"We've always been able to talk," she said. "I mean, that's what I'm saying."

"You did not tell me about the way you felt about the winery."

"Yes, I did. I just waited too long to do it. But you were still the first person that I told."

He shook his head. "Honey, you should've talked to me sooner."

"And what would you have said?"

He looked at her, long and hard. "That I was buying it. And you were out of luck."

"Yeah, I thought so."

"I feel differently about it now though."

"Oh please don't… Please don't be trading my virginity for a fifth of the winery."

He recoiled. "No," he said. "That's not it. It's talking to you. It's talking to you and understanding where you're coming from. What you want. It's actually listening. Which, I'm embarrassed to say, hasn't always been my strong point."

"Well, mine either. Which you know."

"Here we are. Listening."

She looked up at him, and her happiness suddenly felt so big that it threatened to overflow, and with that came a sense of wonder so big it threatened to burst

from her mouth in the form of a song or a laugh or…
Declarations that she wouldn't even really mean.

She didn't know if it was the wine making her a little
bit tipsy or if it was just…him.

"This is the Maxfield label," she said. She shook her
head. "So basic."

"The wine or the fact that they have it?"

"Regrettably, the wine is complex and lovely," she
said.

"It is," Jericho said. "Not like my wine. Our wine."
He shook his head. "This is some surreal stuff."

"What is?"

"I guess it's the same moment that you had up in the
tub earlier. Us. Sitting here together. Drinking wine. I
own a winery. Same as I don't know how I got from
that boy to here."

"I do," she said. "You worked hard. I mean, you more
than worked hard. You worked like there was a demon
on your back."

"Yeah. I guess I did."

"And this is what you've earned. You know, less
my fifth."

"True."

And suddenly, this wasn't enough. The joy that she
had felt a moment ago was still there, but it had taken
on a strange, sharp sensation. It made her feel like she
was suffocating. Like she couldn't breathe.

There was a desperation with it. A hunger. And she
didn't know how to satisfy it. Because it wasn't enough
just to sit here with him. Wasn't enough just to talk to
him. Suddenly, they weren't close enough. And much
like what he'd said just a moment ago, she couldn't rec-
oncile where they were right now with where they had

been two days ago. The Honey and Jericho that had walked through the snow to this cabin were not the same two people that sat here now.

Or maybe they were. And that was the strangest part. That the transformation was so real. That it had actually just reshaped everything that she had believed about him, about herself. About her feelings. Or perhaps it had simply exposed what was already there. He had wanted her before. And she wanted him. It was just that they hadn't been able to be honest enough about it because their worries about what other people might think got in the way.

And there was none of that here.

This was like a snow globe, its own separate world with a beautiful glass dome that kept the bad parts away. Their trauma, their pasts. All the people they might disappoint, the future, and what they could or couldn't have in it. All of that. It was as if only they and this moment truly existed. Encircled by snow and magic and firelight. By an improbable Christmas tree and an improbable desire. Because outside of the space they were both…too them to ever make something work. That was just a fact. But here… Here it all seemed possible. And she wanted to seize hold of it. Wanted to grab it and hold it to her chest, claim it for herself, only for herself.

She felt wild with it. Selfish. And utterly and completely at peace with it.

Because he was hers. And this moment was hers.

And she wanted it to be naked.

She wanted him skin to skin. She wanted him inside of her.

She wrapped her arms around his neck and kissed

him then. The flavor of the wine lingering on his lips, and the desperation of her desire creating a palpable need that drove her. Made her feel wild.

She clung to him, and she didn't know if she wanted him to feel what was inside of her, or if she never wanted him to know. If she didn't even want him to get a peek at the profound, forever changing sensations that were rolling through her. Her desire was so deep. So raw and real that it touched places in her own soul that she had never seen before, and the idea of sharing it was terrifying. So all she did was kiss him. All she did was kiss him, because it was all that could be done. Because everything else felt uncertain. Because she didn't even know what she wanted. Because she didn't have names for the feelings that ebbed and flowed and grew and snaked themselves around her like vines or glitter, magic or a curse, she didn't know. She took her shirt off and cast it to the side, then pushed her hand beneath the waist of his. His body was solid, hard and well muscled, and her heart nearly leaped out of her chest when her fingertips grazed over his abs.

Because she had spent a lot of years fantasizing about this. About him, and emotion aside, there was just so much pent-up desire there.

No. There was no emotion aside, there never could be. And that had been her biggest mistake. Thinking that desire and emotion did not have to exist together. Thinking that she could simply ignore emotion. That she did not have to take it on board. Believing that she could have sex and go back to seeing him as she had done before, or maybe even with her attraction to him neatly removed, having been explored.

No. Instead, everything had gotten tangled together,

and there was no going back to seeing him any other way besides this. Because it wasn't separate.

This need inside of her, the ache in her chest, the man that he was. It wasn't separate. And it never could be.

She had been a fool for thinking so. For thinking that common sense and bird field guides and a hard limit on time could fix this thing. Could help them make sense of it and be sensible with it.

But there was no sense to be found here. It was only need.

It was only this.

But she tried to focus on the feel of him beneath her hands, tried to focus on his body, because at least while that overwhelmed, it was not as sharp as the rest.

She pushed his shirt up and off, moving her hands over his chest, down his stomach and back up again. Then she wrapped her arms around his neck and kissed him. Ran her hands over his short hair, down his muscled back as she tasted him. As she angled her head and took a deep breath, meeting the thrust of his tongue with enthusiasm.

He had taken her bra off and she hadn't even noticed, not until one large hand came up to palm her naked breasts.

She shivered.

And she arched into him, wanting more. Craving more.

She found herself laid back against the soft furs, and he was over her, and she loved the feel of his body against hers. Luxuriating in it as he removed the rest of their clothes. And then suddenly, she got that feeling of being overwhelmed again. Of deep need that demolished her sanity. All the energy building inside of her propelled her forward, and she sat up, pressing her hands against his shoulders and pushing him back.

She moved so that she was over him, leaning over and kissing him hard, her heart hammering, threatening to beat right outside her chest. She ached between her legs. Felt hollow with her need for him. She reached over for his jeans and happily found his wallet and a condom inside.

She tore it open, then with shaking and uncertain fingers, wrapped her hand around the base of his arousal as she rolled the protection over him with deep concentration.

Then she positioned herself over his body, taking him in slowly, a moan of satisfaction rising in her throat as she did.

"Jericho," she whispered.

His hands came up and gripped her hips, his hold bruising, but she loved it.

She began to ride him. Establishing a rhythm that pleased them both, watching as the cords in his neck went tight with his need for her. She shivered. And nearly came right then, just from watching his pleasure.

From watching the effect that she had on him. He arched up into her, thrusting up, changing the tempo, the pace and the strength of it. She bowed over, grabbing hold of his face and kissing him on the mouth, shattering as her orgasm overtook her, wave after wave of pleasure that blended into his as he shouted his release, the two of them shaking and trembling in the aftermath.

Then he gathered her close, swept the cheese platter to the side and wrapped them up in the furs.

She reached out and grabbed a cracker, chewing on the end as he held her close.

Because hopefully focusing on that would keep the tears at bay. Would keep her from dissolving completely.

How could they ever go back?

There was no going back, that much she knew. But maybe they could go forward and find a new shape. A new evolution. That was what this was, after all. A different sort of shape than what they'd been before. So no, they would never be able to be the exact thing they had been previously. But maybe they could find what Honey and Jericho after sex looked like. After baths and cheese platters and sharing secrets.

They had to. There was no other choice. She owned part of the winery now.

She had what she wanted.

Yet she felt hollow. A winery and a saltine cracker were not going to fix that.

Ten

When Jericho woke up the next morning, he could see that the sky was clear outside the window.

He was lying on the floor wrapped up in fur and Honey, still feeling the aftereffects of the night before. But he was going to have to check the weather.

He got up and put his pants on, then went out for his coat. He did his best to get out of the house without disturbing Honey. Outside it was completely quiet. Still. The sun was shining now, making it look like diamonds had been scattered across the surface of the undisturbed snow. The only dents had been made by their footprints last night when they went to get the Christmas tree.

It was bright today, and likely it would bring a little bit of snowmelt along with it.

It was Christmas Eve. He wondered if that meant there would be people coming to plow the roads or not.

He hiked out to the road, and there was a snowplow. There were also a few ODOT workers standing around.

"Hey," Jericho said to the first man, who was wearing a heavy coat and a bright yellow vest. "This is my truck," he said. "What are the odds that he gets out today?"

"We'll have this cleared within a couple of hours," the guy said.

"Thanks. It doesn't start well. Would I be able to get a tow truck out here you think?"

"Everything is eased up so much, and we're expecting highs to hit the fifties today. So this should be your window."

"Thanks," Jericho said.

He hiked back over to the house, where Honey was just beginning to stir.

"Looks like we'll be leaving today," he said.

She looked… Well, she looked stricken. But she didn't say anything. They started the task of putting everything in the house back the way they'd found it.

Jericho wrote a note with his contact information, asking that the owners tabulate the cost of what they had used and send him a bill. Plus charge whatever occupancy fees they normally did.

They looked at the tree.

"I guess we have to take it down. And put everything back."

It was a lot less festive than putting it up had been.

But they had everything restored to its rightful place, and he walked back up to the road to find his truck had had the snow cleared out from around it.

They could go.

"You ready?"

She nodded slowly. "Jericho… I'm not going to Lake Oswego."

He froze.

"All right."

"I think you already knew that. You know, what with the offer of the winery and all."

"Well, yeah."

"But I would like to go to Christmas with you. For… For the Daltons and all that."

"Oh," he said. "Well, that's…good of you."

"It's not good of me. I want to go with you. This is going to be super… Super weird for you. Wouldn't you like to have a friend with you?"

"Yeah," he said. "A friend."

Honey was his friend. But the word felt limp in comparison to what they'd been here. Where they were snowbound and hot as fire anyway. Where they'd talked and made love and decorated the first Christmas tree he'd touched since he was sixteen.

A friend.

He supposed that's how it would have to be explained to Jackson and Creed when it came up. Because it would come up.

As soon as they hit civilization, their phones were going to go crazy.

They'd been out of communication for nearly three days.

It suddenly felt like longer, and a lot less time all at once. It would be like walking through a veil. Where everything changed when they got back to civilization. And she wanted to go with him to see the Daltons.

He helped her carry her bags through the woods, back to the truck.

And when they climbed inside, it all felt a little bit too modern.

She laughed. "I'm not going to know what to do when a heater just comes on."

It was funny the way her mind tracked with his. For a minute, he wondered if the engine would even turn over, but it did. And it was a strange little string of miracles, if he was honest. From the vacation rental down to this.

I mean, it made him question why they had to be caught in the snowstorm in the first place, but everything that had happened since had a strange sort of charmed feeling to it. He would've called it fate if he believed in things like that.

Hell, he couldn't actually fathom that fate had led him to cozy up with his friends' sister for a few nights of pleasure. Hell, one night. Hadn't been enough. But it was done now. It was done now because it had to be.

The heater got going and the only sound was the air, the tires on the newly plowed and graveled road and the engine.

They had talked easily at the vacation rental, but neither of them seemed to know what to say now.

Now it seemed like…

"When do you think we will have service?" She was looking down at her phone.

"I have no idea. I didn't know there was as big of a dead zone out here as there is."

"Oh," she said, tapping her fingers on the door.

"Right."

"So."

They said nothing for another whole minute.

"What if… What if we kept on doing it. You know, just while we're away," she continued.

He looked over at her, and she was staring fixedly out the window.

"Are you looking for birds out there?"

"No," she said, looking back at him. "I just... Yeah I... Maybe we should... Keep doing it. Yeah. Don't you think that would be fun?"

"Fun," he echoed.

"Yeah. Fun. Real fun."

"Look," she said. "If you don't want to do it."

"No. I don't want to make a bigger mess out of this than we already have. At least before we came to the cabin, we would fight when we were sitting together in a car. Now we can barely speak a sentence to each other."

"That's a very coherent sentence," she said.

"Thanks," he said.

"I mean... I just can't see being at the Dalton place and not doing it."

"We should have just gone back."

"No. Let's do this." She slapped her hand on her thighs. "We're survivalists."

"Right."

"We are. And... I still feel bad that I never really... That I didn't realize what a big thing it was. You finding out that Hank never knew about you. I didn't really think about it. And I'm embarrassed. And if I can help you through it any way, I want to do that."

"And you want to get laid," he said, unable to keep the smile from curving his lips, even though mostly the entire topic wasn't that amusing to him.

"Well, I'm not dead below the waist. Or anywhere, for that matter. So all right. Maybe I want more."

More.

More.

He tried not to let that word resonate too much inside of him. Because she meant more sex, and more sex was all it could be. More sex wasn't what it should be, but still.

More.

More people in his family. And with that, just more complication in general. Yeah, initially he thought he'd show up and flaunt his wealth. His success. And now he was…bringing a girl home to meet his folks. Well, his dad anyway. His father.

Tammy Dalton was not his mother. Tammy Dalton was the reason his life had gone the way that it had.

He wasn't going to let himself get too bitter about it. Mostly because, even though what Tammy had done was wrong, Hank had committed the first wrong, and he didn't know if a person was responsible for being perfect in response to something like that.

Still. She was just the woman who had paid his mother off and made her go away. Who had lied to her husband about the extent of his misdeeds for all those years.

"Looks like we'll make it in time for Christmas Eve dinner."

The rest… He wasn't going to think about.

It took another couple of hours to get up to the compound, and by the time they did, they had cell service. He could call and let the Daltons know he was coming, but the idea of speaking to them on the phone felt… wrong somehow. He didn't want to answer questions about where he'd been. He had directions to the cabin that was his for the next couple of days, and he went straight there.

"I guess dinner is kind of a formal affair," he said. "I don't think your lingerie is going to cut it."

"Oh, I have something," she said. "I was prepared for the fanciness of Lake Oswego."

She was a dark horse, was Honey Cooper. And that was for certain.

The cabin itself was small but luxurious compared to where they'd just been. It had all the modern amenities, hypermodern even. A steam shower, not a wood sauna, and towel warmers and lights. There were lights. He may have stopped and flipped the switch off and on a couple of times.

"What are you doing?" Honey asked.

"Aren't you amazed by the electricity?"

"I'm not that far gone," she said.

"Have you looked at your phone yet?"

"No," she said, wincing. "I was expecting to get chewed out by my dad and my brothers for my disappearing act, and that was when I just thought I was going up to Lake Oswego and would be able to contact them that same day. Though I guess… At least… At least I'm not moving."

"Should we get dressed for dinner?" he asked.

"Yeah," she replied.

She disappeared off into one of the other bedrooms, which he thought was interesting, considering she was the one who had suggested they keep things up. Not that he was complaining. And he couldn't stop himself from imagining her getting undressed now. Peeling her clothes off, revealing her beautiful body.

He gritted his teeth, then went to the other bedroom with his suitcase and took out the suit that he brought for the occasion. He dressed and put a black cowboy hat on his head. And he figured he probably looked more rodeo royalty than Hank Dalton did on a good day.

He went out to the living room, and Honey still hadn't appeared. He checked his watch, waiting.

And then she emerged, wearing a figure-hugging red dress, her hair spilling over her shoulders in a curled cascade. He couldn't remember ever seeing Honey in makeup, the effect dramatically highlighting all the things about her that were already beautiful.

"Damn," he said.

"Do I meet with your approval?"

"Hell yeah," he responded.

She smiled.

"Is that why you hid from me?"

"Well, yes. I wanted there to be a little bit of a surprise."

"You are a surprise, Honey. Every day. In a thousand different ways."

He linked arms with her, and led her out of the cabin. It was dark out, but it was easy to navigate their way from there to the main house, which he knew Hank and the rest of the family were in.

He had been told to just come in when they arrived, so he did. Pushing the door open and revealing a glittering Christmas scene. A huge tree that had to be eighteen feet high at least, stretching up to the top ceiling beam, casting a warm glow over the room. There were garlands and big velvet bows. On the big mezzanine floor that overlooked the living area. No one was here, but he could hear voices coming from what he assumed might be the dining room.

He took Honey's hand. Without even thinking.

They walked down the short hallway and went to

the left, and there it was. There everyone was. The table was massive, laden with food, huge candelabras in the center, along with tiered trays of meats and desserts. It was the gaudiest, tackiest thing he'd ever seen this side of the *Harry Potter* movies, and it was incredible.

And around that table was… Everyone.

Hank at the head, wearing a white cowboy hat and suit, along with a bolero tie. Tammy at the foot of the table with big hair and a big smile.

And filling in the middle part… His half siblings and their spouses. Everyone went around the table for a quick intro.

West, who he'd met, and his wife, Pansy. Gabe, Jacob and Caleb, with their wives and kids. Logan and his wife, and McKenna, the lone sister, and her husband.

He knew who they all were, but he hadn't… Had never really thought that he'd be part of the family. Not ever.

But here they were. And here he was.

At a crowded table, and he had the strangest ache at the center of his chest that he ever felt.

"Jericho," Hank said. "We thought you decided not to come."

"I got waylaid by the snowstorm. We had to wait it out in a cabin on the way here."

"No shit," Hank said, laughing. "That must be quite a story. Pull up a chair. Who is this?"

"Honey," he said. "She's a…a family friend."

"He's not calling me *honey*," she said. "My first name is Honey."

Hank laughed at that too. "I love it."

"My parents are…were…are eccentric," Honey said.

"Eccentric," he said. "I like it. I can definitely understand eccentric."

It was Tammy, though, who stood.

There was a strange, soft note in her eyes, and Jericho couldn't say that he liked it much.

It was too much like pity. Or sorrow.

"I'm glad you could come," she said, walking forward and reaching her hand out.

It was Honey took it. "Thank you," she said.

And he realized that Honey was protecting him. That she had sensed his hesitance and put herself right in Tammy's path.

"Have a seat," Hank said. "The food's getting cold."

"Thanks," Jericho said.

They added another chair for Honey quickly, and they sat down beside each other. Honey made quick work of putting her plate together, then jumped right into the chatting.

And he had never been more grateful to have someone he knew at his side than he was right at this moment.

Because she was covering the awkwardness with ease, and he had never really thought that Honey was the kind of person who would do that.

"So what is it you do?" This question came from Grant, who he supposed was his half brother-in-law.

"I own Cowboy Wines."

"Are you familiar with Grassroots Winery?"

"Yeah," Jericho said.

"That's my sister-in-law's. She's great. If you like to do any kind of collaborating, you should have a chat with Lindy."

The family connections just kept growing. But he supposed that was the nature of something like this.

He wasn't clear on everyone's stories or circumstances, but as the evening wore on, he began to get filled in with bits and pieces of conversation. Grant and McKenna had met and married several years ago when she had come to town looking for Hank. Grant had lost his wife several years before and had never really thought about getting married again.

West was an ex-convict, and as opposite to his wife—a good girl police officer—as it was possible to get.

But they seemed completely crazy about each other.

Gabe Dalton's wife was a total horse girl, and had plenty in common with Honey, who took up easy chatting with her over dessert.

Jacob and Caleb were married to teachers—who taught at the school for troubled kids that was apparently now on Dalton land. Logan and his wife were ranchers.

They were an interesting group, all with completely different stories. Though loss was something most of them had dealt with in one form or another. McKenna had been abandoned by her mother, while Logan's had died.

He felt an immediate kinship to him.

He vaguely remembered Logan from high school, though they weren't in the same year. And he'd been too caught up in his own grief to think about a kid younger than him dealing with anything similar.

The fact was, tragedy was more commonplace than anybody really liked to think.

It made your aches and pains feel like garden-variety stuff, when it felt absolutely significant to you.

He wasn't sure if it made it worse or better. He had

lived in a cloistered version of this experience for most of his life. What he wasn't used to was having casual conversations about things like this with people he didn't even really know all that well.

"So she's a friend?" West asked, looking at him pointedly, then over at Honey, who was chatting with Jamie and Rose.

"Yeah," he said. "Actually, my friends' sister…"

At that, Gabe and Logan laughed. They laughed.

"What?"

"Been there," Logan said.

"Married that," Gabe added.

"Well, I'm not getting married."

"Why not?" West asked. "I recommend the institution, actually, and I never did think that I would."

"Nice for you," Jericho said. "But…"

"Oh, have you had a hard life?" West asked.

"Too bad," Logan said.

"Are we talking about hard lives?" McKenna came over to them, hands on her hips. "I'd like to play. Who had ten homes in four years?"

"You win that game," West said. "I had way less. Well, not way less."

"But who has the most half siblings?"

"I wouldn't know," McKenna said. "Because I don't know my mom."

"I only have the one other half sibling that I know of." West looked at Jericho. "No relation to us. My mom's kid."

"Just you people," Gabe said.

"Same," Logan added.

"You all seem pretty…relaxed about this."

"No point getting wound up about it at this point,"

Gabe said. "Now, that wasn't true back when it all first… Back when it all first happened."

"Yeah, it was not the best when I showed up," McKenna said. "Everyone was trying to put all the unpleasantness of the past behind them, and there I was, a big reminder of the way things had been before."

"No one blames you for that," Gabe said.

"I know you don't," McKenna said. "And I'm glad that I came here. If I hadn't… I wouldn't have all of you. Or Grant."

"I think you like Grant best," Logan said.

"I do," McKenna said. And that made her brothers laugh.

Her brothers. He supposed they were his brothers. And he was her brother.

Growing up an only child, that was a strange thing to wrap his head around. Sure, he had been brought into the Cooper family, but it wasn't quite the same. And he'd been sixteen when he had been.

Of course, he was thirty-four now.

"I think you like her," McKenna said.

"Well, you don't know me," Jericho answered.

"Oh good," McKenna said, smiling. "You have a chip on your shoulder. You really will fit in nicely. I was feral when I first came here."

"I'm not exactly feral," he said.

"But not exactly not," McKenna said.

All right, that was a fair enough characterization of him in the entire situation. But he wasn't going to let her know.

"Well, it's getting late."

"You have to make sure you get back here bright and

early," McKenna said. "They take the present opening very seriously."

"We do," said his brother Caleb's wife, Ellie, holding a baby and hanging on to her seven-year-old, who was looking terribly sleepy.

"Yeah, and Amelia isn't going to wait," Caleb said, indicating the child.

He stood up, and Honey stiffened. She wasn't even looking at him, but she seemed to sense his move to leave. He couldn't begin to figure out how she was so in tune with him. It was just the strangest thing. The way she seemed to know what he felt. The fact that she was here at all.

"I'm going to head back to the cabin," Honey said. "I need to call my dad. I'll see you in, like, ten minutes."

That surprised him. Because he thought that she had sensed his readiness to leave. But then she was scampering out, saying good-night to everybody, and Hank was looking at him. And he realized she had done that on purpose.

She was sensing things, but she wasn't on his team.

"Hey there, son," Hank said. "I wanted to have a talk with you."

"You don't have to do that."

"I don't have to do what?"

"Call me *son*."

"Maybe I don't have to. But I want to."

Maybe I don't want you to. But he didn't say that. Because he was here to see Hank, after all, so what was the point of being hostile. At least overtly.

Hank stood, and he followed him out of the room, back into the grand dining room, which was now empty. "Thank you for coming," he said. "I didn't think you would. But you know… Whether you believe it or not, I've known you were out there for a while. I just didn't know your name. And her last name made it tricky to track you down. I had never gotten your first name, and your mother, Letty Smith, it was a common name. And when I finally did find her… And I found out she was gone…"

"Yeah. She died when I was sixteen."

"I'm sorry. I didn't know."

"I know you didn't, Hank."

"You thought I did though. For your whole life, didn't you?"

"Yeah. But you know… It's good to have an enemy. Good to have a bad object that you can fight against. It's probably why I have been so successful." There he was, giving him credit for something that he had been bound and determined not to give him credit for. Even if he had said it as a joke, it was closer to acknowledging the role that Hank had played in his life than he wanted.

"Sure," Hank said. "I know a little something about that. I ran from my demons for a long time. And they took me to dark places. I wasn't a good husband to Tammy. And I failed a lot of other women as a result too. McKenna is working on teaching me about feminism."

"Is she?" Jericho asked, and that was truly the funniest thing he'd ever heard.

"Yeah," he said. "Because of the patriarchy and power imbalances and things, what I did was especially wrong. But at the time it just felt like… I didn't feel particularly powerful. I felt like a dumb kid that was out of control. I felt like a fool. Someone who didn't deserve any of the things that he had. Who was just trying to feel alive. But at some point, you have to feel more than alive, and you have to work at feeling more than good. What you have to do is learn to sit on your bad feelings. That's a hell of a thing."

"Yeah, I've had enough bad feelings to get me through for a long time."

"I'm not meaning to lecture you. I'm just… I'm glad that you're here, I hope that I'll see you past Christmas. I hope that you give this family thing a chance."

"Then that would give you a happy ending, wouldn't it? It would make all of it seem like it had a meaning? If you could get all of your wayward kids here and happy to be with you. Everybody forgiving everybody else and getting along. I guess that would go a long way in soothing your guilt."

Guilt.

He was more familiar with the concept than he'd like. Especially in regards to Honey.

Not touching her. He couldn't feel guilty about that. But because of all he could never give her.

"Sure," he said. "But you know, it's a lot of guilt, Jericho. Because McKenna was in foster care for all of her life. And Logan lost his mother. And you lost yours. And you boys were alone. McKenna was alone. There's a lot of guilt with that. It's not easy to live with."

"Well, we'll see what happens. But whatever happens, I'm not making the decision for the purpose of saving your soul. I enjoyed tonight. But I have a life. I have family." The Coopers, whom he was drastically betraying with his dalliance with Honey. But he wasn't going to think about that.

"I wouldn't ask you to," Hank said. "I wouldn't ask

you to do anything for the purpose of appeasing me. But sure, the side effect is that it probably will. If that stops you then… Not much I can do about it."

"Sorry," Jericho said. "It's been a hell of a trip up here. It's been a hell of a few days. I don't know if I'm coming or going. But I'll be here for Christmas morning."

"Merry Christmas," Hank said. Then as Jericho turned to go, he added, "Son."

Hank was pushing. Jericho should be furious and yet…

He'd been a boy with no one. When he'd been sixteen and people had complained about annoying parents… He'd been nothing but jealous.

Something in him… Something in him wanted this and he couldn't deny it, even as the wounded part of him wanted to pull away from it.

Jericho turned. "You couldn't resist."

"I couldn't."

"You did it because I told you not to."

"Maybe. Look. I might've tried to better myself, but I'm still a no-good jackass. I just keep it managed now."

"Well, see that you do."

"Also, I'm going to have to build the bridge between us," Hank said, his voice full of gravity. "No matter how wide the valley is, I'm committed to it, Jericho, I promise you. But I'm the one that should have to work for it. I'm the one who messed up. I just hope you'll stick out waiting for me to get to the other side."

Jericho's throat went tight. "Yeah. Sure."

Which wasn't enough, but there were no other words.

He turned and walked down the long hall, out the front door, managing to slide by everybody without having to say a string of long messy good-nights.

He didn't think he could face that level of family.

Outside it was crisp and cold and the sky was clear, the stars twinkling above, the trees inky black with spots of white snow a shout in the dark.

He had a family back in that house. A family.

And a woman waiting for him at his cabin.

And suddenly, his life felt fuller than it ever had.

Eleven

"I'm okay, Dad," she said, pacing back and forth in the living room. It was a little bit dastardly that she had left Jericho to talk to Hank. She had realized at some point that Hank was itching to do it, and she knew that unless she did something like this, Jericho was going to come back to the cabin with her.

But, she needed to talk to her dad. He needed to talk to his.

"I wish you would've talked to me about leaving in the first place. By the time I found out you'd gone up north, you were already gone, and then I had no way of knowing that you were trapped in a snowstorm."

"Jericho found me," she said. "We found a vacation rental. We hunkered down there." And the less she said about it the better. "And then I decided to come up with him to support him while he met with his dad."

"You're not usually all that friendly with him."

"Well, he saved my life. I mean, really, if I hadn't been with him I don't know what would've happened. And I'm not moving. I changed my mind."

She'd left it all in her note. Well, nothing about her virginity of course.

"Really?" her dad said.

"Yeah. Really. I talked to Jericho, and he said that he's going to sell me a portion of the vineyard back."

"Did you… Did you want some of the vineyard?"

"Yes, Dad. I wanted it desperately. It's why I've been furious for the last few months."

"You've been furious?"

She'd been so honest with Jericho. And the walls she'd always felt existed between herself and the world felt thinner now. And she liked it that way.

So why not speak?

Why not now?

She'd been ready to leave. Which was so extreme in hindsight. More ready to run than have a conversation.

But being with him had changed her.

And this was her moment to live in that change.

"Yes. Furious. Absolutely incensed that you would do that to me. That you would sell the winery out from under me without talking to me first. It's why I decided to move away. But, Jericho saved me from the snowstorm, and we talked about my future."

There. Now Jericho sounded like a hero.

She heard female voices in the background. "Are you at the Maxfields'?"

"Yes," he said.

"Are you and…"

"I really do love her, Honey."

"Right. You love her and… I guess you're going

to marry her and close this big strange circle of our families?"

"Well, that depends. She ended up getting so much of the winery. She's a very rich woman. I'm not sure that she's interested in getting hitched. We might just live in sin."

"Oh, for heaven's sake, Dad. I don't want to know that."

"You should be happy for me. I've been miserable for a long time."

"I am happy for you. Only if you can be happy for me too. And realize that for me the winery is happiness."

"Of course, Honey. I only want what's best for you. I'm sorry if I didn't see it. I just… I was never very good at having a daughter."

"I don't know, sometimes I wonder if I was any good at being one. I just wanted to be like the boys. But I'm not. They're outspoken and they know how to tell you what they want. And they do it without emotions. But I have feelings. A lot of them, and I just spent a lot of time shoving them down deep. I didn't want to cause trouble. I know how much it upset you… The way I was at Mom's funeral."

It was a memory that lodged deep inside of her. One that she didn't like to talk about.

"It was an upsetting time."

"I just didn't want to upset you. Not again."

"I love you, Honey. You don't upset me. I think sometimes I just don't look at you and know immediately what you want."

She thought of Jackson and Creed and the different things they'd been through, and honestly, she didn't think her dad knew anymore what they wanted. Hell, they hadn't known what they wanted until they'd gotten with Wren and Cricket. So maybe that was just it. Maybe everybody was always learning, and they needed to do a better job of talking.

"I love you, Dad," she said. "I'll be home in a couple of days."

"Tell Jericho no funny business."

And then her dad laughed, as her heart shimmered down into her stomach. And she realized he thought it was a hilarious joke.

"I think I'll let him have his way with me," she said.

"You do that," her dad said.

"Merry Christmas," she said.

And then got off the phone, happy that the idea of Jericho touching her was just such a joke.

She frowned furiously, and was still frowning at the front door when it opened and Jericho came in.

"Hey," he said. "What's up?"

"I told my dad I was going to let you have your way with me, and he literally laughed."

"Oh, don't take offense to that," Jericho said, shrugging out of his jacket. And she couldn't help but admire the muscles in his body as he moved. In fact, she just went ahead and ogled him, because she was out of sorts, and she felt owed.

"Why should I not take offense?"

"Because it's to do with it being you and me. It's not you."

"Well, why do people think we're so incompatible?"

"Because we bicker."

"So what?"

"Well, we bicker quite a bit."

"Clearly unresolved sexual tension. Haven't they ever seen a romantic comedy?"

He crossed the room, wrapped his arm around her waist and drew her up against him. He gripped her chin between his thumb and forefinger, his dark eyes intense. "Honey, we are not a romantic comedy." And she could feel the evidence of his desire pressing against her body. And no. They were not a comedy. There was nothing funny about this.

"Okay," she said.

And what she meant was, *I trust you*. What she meant was, *you matter to me*.

And he seemed to know that, because he leaned in and kissed her on the lips.

"It's Christmas Eve," she said.

"It's Christmas Eve."

"Did you like Christmas when you were a kid?"

"No," he said, his voice hoarse. "I hated it. I always had to figure out ways to get Christmas decorations up. Get a tree. Get a meal from the local church, so that we had something nice, even though in the end my mom didn't want to eat. But somebody had to make Christmas happen. And she didn't have the energy to do it. So I always did. After she died, I just didn't do it. I mean, I would go be with your family, but I haven't put up a decoration in my own house... Ever."

"Jericho," she whispered. "I'm so sorry." Because for all that she had felt like she had to do something to hide her emotions, there had always been people there taking care of her. It might not have been perfect, but she wasn't alone. She might've had moments of loneliness, but that was different than being alone. It was different than being a child who was expected to be an adult. Different than being forced to be the one that brought the Christmas magic into the house when people should've been making it happen for you.

"You never believed in Santa Claus, did you?"

He shook his head. "No. Because I figured I was about as good as a kid could be. So if I was going to magically get gifts... No. I didn't. I wanted to believe in Jesus though. Because that made me feel less alone. So that was about...the only point of Christmas as far as I could see. Well, and Christmas dinners made by church ladies."

"I'm so sorry."

"It's okay. I've made it okay."

But when he smiled, it didn't reach his eyes, and she wondered how she hadn't realized that before.

And she knew what it was like. To carry things that were absolutely not okay, but to also realize there was no point mourning what you should've had, because none of it was going to bring it back to you. But her heart ached for the little boy who had made sure there was Christmas for his mother. Who probably needed there to be Christmas so that she didn't feel quite like she was failing him so badly, but it had rebounded and turned into something he had to perform. And it made her feel so... So desperately sad.

And for the first time, she wanted to tell the story of what happened at her mother's funeral. She had never talked about it with anyone. Until she had mentioned it with her dad a few moments ago, they had never even brought it up to each other.

"I was so sad when my mother died," she said. "I couldn't stop crying. I thought I was going to die myself. I was gasping for air, gulping. It lasted...days, Jericho.

Days. Then I stopped. And it was just sort of a horrible silence. But then at the funeral it all came back. And I just… I screamed. And I cried. My father was so distressed, he didn't know what to do with me. He was stoic, and the boys were stoic. And…"

"You were a little girl."

"I know," she said. "I was a little girl who really really missed her mother. And… My father found it so upsetting. He didn't know what to do with me. He told me to be quiet. And he told me to stop crying. He told me to wait outside the church until I could get my emotions together."

"Honey…"

"So I just sat there and I bit my tongue through the whole thing. And eventually, the pain did something to block out my sadness. The tears. I just tried after that. Every day. To be a little bit stronger. Because I realized that…on top of everything else my dad couldn't handle my sorrow."

"Dammit," Jericho said. He put his hand up to her cheek. "That's wrong."

"He was just trying his best. It's like Christmases that you have to throw yourself when you're a child. Yeah, it's sad. But… There's nothing you can do about it. We just got stronger. We just did the best we could."

"You don't have to hide yourself. Not now."

She could tell he hadn't meant to say it.

"You don't have to hide yourself either."

And then he was kissing her. When she thought they might both be consumed by it. By the flames of their desire. The fire of this need between them that could no longer be controlled. And she couldn't quite wrap her mind around this Jericho. Vulnerable, strong. Sexy. So much more than the man she'd always seen. The man she'd wanted, but the man she hadn't really known.

He was… He was brilliant and wonderful and everything. And so strong, so amazingly resilient, having been through so much.

And she wondered how she had ever believed that it was a crush. How she had ever thought that all that they were could be reduced to something so basic, so… juvenile.

Because it was easier. Because it was then. But all it had taken was a few honest conversations, and it was different. She was different. And she saw the ways that he was different.

And that they were the same. All the ways that he was able to fill the gaps in who she was, and who they both were. And the way that she was able to do the same for him.

And she kissed him. Because she wanted him. Because he was the man she'd always known, and this man she had gotten to know over the past few days. Because he was her brothers' friend, but most importantly he was her friend. Because they were business partners and they had known each other half their lives. Because… Well, quite simply because she loved him.

And it was a truth that rang out as clear and lovely inside of her as anything ever could have. It was a truth that reverberated across her soul. She loved him. And she was in love with him. It was every layer, every piece of all the ways she'd seen him bonded together in one strong undeniable feeling. Because she saw the truth of who he was now. The whole of him. All of him. And because of that she saw the whole of herself, as well. The woman that she was. The woman that she wanted to be.

The ways that she had been hurt and the way that she had overcome. And the way that she wanted him. The way that she loved him. She was no longer protecting herself, because that was what it had been. Telling herself it was a crush. Pushing herself to find a way to get over him. To be with someone else, because of course being with someone else would've been easy. The easiest thing.

Because Donovan might have taken her clothes off her, but he would never have stripped her bare. And Jericho had brought her down to the truth of who she was.

Jericho was... He was the only man for her. The only one that she could ever love. And she did. She had told him... Oh, foolish her, she had told him that she didn't expect them to get married or be in a relationship, or be anything. And she had been wrong. She had lied, even though she hadn't meant to. Because she had hoped. She had always hoped. And in a life that had given her so few reasons to hope, this one last bit of light had existed in the very corner of her soul, reserved for him, reserved for this. For all that she wished they could be.

And she kissed him with that truth. All of it, resonating inside of her.

And when he picked her up and carried her to his bedroom, she didn't make any comments about his carrying her, didn't try to defuse the tension with a joke. No. She was there. Completely. Doing nothing to block out the intensity of her need for him. The intensity of their desire for one another.

It was raw and real, and she would do nothing to make it less.

She wrenched his black tie loose, slid it through the

collar of his shirt and cast it down to the floor. Pushed his jacket from his shoulders and unbuttoned his white shirt, revealing a wedge of tan skin. He was so beautiful.

Utterly brilliant in all of his glory. Whether he was in a T-shirt and jeans or a suit. Naked, which was how she preferred him most of all.

She stripped him bare, like it might give her access to the deepest parts of him. Like it might give her a part of his soul, that part of him that she so desperately craved.

She stripped him bare, as if she was dependent upon it.

And then he was naked before her, his eyes shining with the light of intensity that ignited her from within.

She reached behind her back and grabbed the zipper pull on her dress and let it fall free, let it pool at her feet. She was wearing some of the lingerie. Lacy and white, bridal, it could be said.

And the way that he looked at her, as if he wanted to devour her, satisfied her. Made her feel utterly and completely captured. By a look. By the promise of his touch. By the desperate hope of his love.

And when they were finally joined together, laid out on the bed, she wrapped her arms around his neck and kissed him. Poured out every ounce of her love—her love because she would name it now—into that kiss.

She had been afraid before, of all the things rising up inside of her.

Because she had been afraid of her feelings for so long. For too long.

But they were here, and they were big. Bigger than she was. Maybe bigger than the both of them. Maybe they would consume her. Maybe they would swallow them both. Maybe it would leave her with desperate, sad scars, but she could no longer live a life where she denied all that she was for the sake of safety. For the sake of making everyone else comfortable.

She had to do this. She had to step into who she was. Into who she hoped to be. Because the only reason she had ever been unhappy was because of her own self. Because she had kept too many things to herself. Whether it be her feelings about the winery or her feelings about Jericho. The way that she felt disconnected from her family sometimes… She was the one that had chosen to keep them locked down deep, and it might've been for other people, but no one had ever outright asked for it. And even if they had… Why did she have to give everybody what they wanted?

Couldn't she have something for herself?

Perhaps this was growth, and other people needed to grow right along with her.

Perhaps, she wasn't the one who was broken.

"I love you," she whispered.

And then they both went over the edge together.

Jericho was shaking. The aftermath of the pleasure he just experienced roared in his blood, in his head, along with Honey's words.

"I love you."

His chest felt like it had been rent. With sharp claws and sweet words, and everything Honey.

"Honey… Don't do this."

"Don't do what?"

She rolled away from him, all soft and naked, and he wanted to bring her back into his arms, because what he wanted to do was hold her all night. He didn't want her to do this. They were supposed to have this thing until they all went back to their real lives. It was still Christmas. He was still supposed to get to have this.

"Don't do what?" she repeated.

"Don't make this into something that it isn't supposed to be," he said.

"Who gets to say?"

"We already said."

"Yeah. Things change. Life is not fair. You and I both know that. Why are you acting like just because we decided on something doesn't mean we can't change our minds."

"Because I can't," he said, looking at her earnest face, feeling his heart beating so hard he thought it might tear through his chest and land bloody on the bed in front of them.

"So I was just supposed to keep my feelings to myself again. How is that any different than what my dad wanted me to do when he made me sit outside of my mother's funeral."

"Because that was real," he said. "Those feelings were real. But this… This is just you having your first sex partner."

He felt like he was standing on the edge of a dark, endless well and all that was down there was…grief.

All-consuming, terrifying.

It was the only path love led to.

It took and took and took, until in the end, love took itself away too and you were cut off at the knees.

He couldn't.

He *couldn't*.

"Don't do that to me," she said. "Do not be condescending to me. I am not a child. I am a woman. And what life has thrown at you it's thrown at me too. I know what it's like to lose somebody that I love. I know it. Deep in my soul. To miss someone all the time that you can never see again. To feel so isolated in your grief, even though there are people around you who should understand. To feel the way that it burns when you just need this person who's gone forever. I know. I had to grow up early too. I get it."

"You didn't have to throw your own Christmas."

"No. I'm not saying I had every hardship you did, but I am not a baby. Don't treat me like one. Don't you dare."

"I'm not treating you like a baby, but I am treating you like what you are. A woman with vastly less experience than I have. And I think you want to listen to me when I tell you that you're probably just putting too much weight on this."

"As if you don't put any weight on it," she said. "As if it doesn't matter to you at all that we had sex."

"I'm not saying it doesn't matter."

"What are you saying then?"

"I don't want love. Not yours, not anyone's. It is too much work, Honey. And I am not worth the struggle."

"That isn't true."

"Fine then. I don't think it's worth the struggle. I don't want it. I don't want to do it. I don't want your love. I don't want to love you back. I just wanted to fuck. That's it. I think you're hot—I have for a long time. You told me you were going to go give your virginity to some other guy, and it pissed me off. Because I'm a guy. But that's it. It's the beginning and end of the story."

Tears were running down her face, and he felt like…

He was the worst. He was the absolute worst person. He hated himself just then. But all he could think of was that horrific, weighted feeling when Christmas rolled around. When he had to do everything and make things merry and bright and pretend that he wasn't living in some damned horror show in his heart, where he knew that the end of his mother's life was coming, and he knew that he was facing a future by himself, and it was just spinning out slowly and terribly, and he was putting on a grim performance in the meantime. He couldn't stand it. He simply couldn't stand it. The expectation. The certain feeling that no matter what, no matter how much he loved, no matter what he did, he was hurtling toward an inevitable end, something that would never be fixed or satisfied.

And he couldn't. He just couldn't.

"Honey… No. We can't do this."

And her face crumpled. And he felt like an absolute ass.

But there was nothing he could do about it. Sitting there, lost in every bad feeling that he'd ever had in his life, every grief that he never contended with, he simply couldn't do it. She got up, and she walked out of the room.

And it took him a few minutes to realize that she wasn't just leaving the room. She was leaving.

A car pulled up to get her some fifteen minutes later. And then she was gone. And he was left. Crushed beneath the weight of damn near everything.

He looked outside the cabin window and he saw the Christmas tree shining through the window of the main house. And he nearly choked.

Merry Christmas.

This was what Christmas was all about. At least what it always had been for him.

Being given a taste of something, something brilliant and beautiful and hopeful, the light of the damned world.

Knowing that darkness hovered around the edges, knowing that this feeling could never really be his.

That was what Christmas was to him.

Apparently, it was what it always would be.

Twelve

Honey didn't collapse until she got home and climbed into bed.

Then she wept like she was dying.

It was two o'clock in the morning by the time she got back to Gold Valley, and she was a whole disaster mess.

She cried and cried, and then slept for about two hours before climbing out of bed and putting on clothes to go to the Maxfields. Because even though she didn't want to see anybody, she figured she had to go do it. Because it was Christmas.

But she felt devastated. Horrendously.

And she hoped that she could pull it together for the celebrations.

But what if you didn't? What if you let them know that you were hurt?

The idea made her shiver slightly.

But still, she got dressed and went into the house.

"Honey," Emerson said. "We weren't expecting you."

"I'm here," she said, looking around the Tuscan-style villa, feeling as hideously out of place there as she always did.

The Maxfields were fancy. Fancy fancy, and she had never really felt comfortable with it.

But why? She supposed it was because she was afraid of what they might think. That she might not blend.

That she might stand out.

Well, who cared.

She wasn't fancy.

Neither was Cricket.

And all the worries that she had about connecting with Cricket were based around what Cricket might think too. Because she was just so... She was so consumed by that. By making everybody comfortable, and not exposing them to her weirdness.

Except Jericho. She had been 100 percent herself with him, and it had not gone well.

But who cared.

She was done. She was tired.

"I figured I should spend Christmas with all of you. So here I am."

"You don't have any presents here," her dad said. "I was planning on mailing them."

"It's fine, Dad. I don't really need any presents. And you won't have to mail them, because I'm not leaving."

"Well, that's a good thing."

She looked awkwardly at her dad's girlfriend.

Lucinda Maxfield was supernaturally beautiful. But smooth like a doll, and a bit unapproachable in Honey's opinion. Though the other woman had warmed a lot recently.

"It's good to have you here, Honey," she said.

"Thanks."

She still didn't really know how to interact with her.

It was Jackson who looked at her with the hardest eyes.

And she chose to ignore him.

Instead, she helped herself to the pastries that were set out and took her position around the tree while the others began to open gifts.

"And do you care to give a full accounting for your whereabouts?" Jackson said, succumbing to sit beside her.

"No," she said.

"You were going to leave?"

"I was," she said.

But you didn't. "I didn't."

"But you've been gone."

"Well, I got stuck in the snow."

"Dad mentioned something about that. He mentioned that you and Jericho stayed in…a cabin?"

"I mean, it was a massive vacation rental. But yes."

"I see," he said.

"But I also heard that you were staying with Jericho while he dealt with the Daltons."

"Things change." She sniffed.

"What exactly changed?"

"I didn't want to stay with him anymore?"

"Why?"

"I don't see how that's any of your business," she said.

"You have had the biggest crush on him for as long as I can remember," Jackson said.

Honey's mouth dropped open as a mortified blush spread over her face. She had been prepared to own this and shock them all, and they'd known she had feelings for him! "Now that's not fair…"

"Look, just tell me if I have to go kill him or not."

"I don't want you to kill him," she said, stamping her foot.

"Who are we killing?" Creed asked.

That seemed to get her father's attention too.

"I'm trying to find out about killing Jericho."

"You are not killing him," Honey said.

"Why?" Creed asked.

"Because she's upset about something," Jackson said.

"And?" Creed asked, his tone getting dangerous.

Cricket punched Jackson in the arm. "What is your problem? If you're going to interrogate your sister, at least do it privately. Don't make a dick out of yourself in public."

It was especially funny coming from a woman who was roundly pregnant.

"I'm not being a dick," Jackson said. "I'm trying to figure out if my best friend did something to her. Because I will kill him."

"On what grounds?" Cricket asked, eyeing him closely.

"She's twenty-two."

"And?" Cricket asked, squarely in the same age bracket.

"She's…inexperienced."

Cricket narrowed her eyes. "And?"

"He's my best friend," Jackson said, pointing at Cricket as if that ended things completely.

"Fine. Something happened between myself and Jericho."

That earned her a shocked gasp, and she decided that was pretty satisfying. "And I'm upset about it. But so what? I'm allowed to be upset. You can't protect me from every bad feeling, any more than you can just order me not to have them. I'm going to live life."

"He didn't need to help you do it," Creed said.

"I wanted him to," Honey said. "Because I love him. Okay?" She was saying it. Saying it all. If she'd gotten one gift from Jericho over this time, it hadn't been losing her virginity or the winery. It had been this. This path to honesty. To figuring out that she wanted to share her emotions, whether it made others comfortable or not. To having the confidence to be true to herself, no matter what.

"I don't have a crush on him. I am in love with him. And he can't handle it. That's fine, it wouldn't be my problem, except that I'm in love with him, so it de facto becomes my problem, because he hasn't sorted his shit out yet. But I love him. And that's just… It's the way it is. I don't need any of you getting up in my grill and meddling. I don't need any of you to tell me not to be upset. Because I am. I'm upset. And I'm just… I'm going to be upset for a while. That's how it is."

"Honey, he should never have…"

"He should never what? No, I'm part of this. It wasn't him. It was me too. I wanted it. I want him. And everybody needs to listen to me and to what I want for a minute. Because I have done a pretty terrible job of making myself seen these last few years of my life, and I'm over it. I want him. I want to own the winery. I'm not a kid. I'm a woman. And I want to be treated like one."

"Nobody means to treat you like a kid…"

"No, you do. Because it makes you more comfortable. And I have been all about making sure that you guys are as comfortable as possible. And I'm done with it. So yeah, I'm hurt. And I'm going to be hurt for a little while. And maybe I'm going to have to navigate working with Jericho while I also sort through dealing with the fact that he broke my heart. But I have to deal with it. Not you. You don't get to go and punch him in the face just to make yourselves feel better. Because that's all it would be."

"I aim to kill him," Jackson said, which earned him another slug from his wife.

"Your sister just told you not to. So who would you be doing it for?"

"Me," Creed and Jackson said together.

"I am sorry," her dad said slowly, shaking his head. "I haven't stopped thinking about what you said about your mother's funeral. Not since you mentioned that to me last night. I knew I'd handled that badly, but honestly... I had not been able to remember it. So much of those days are a blur."

"It affected us all," Creed said, taking a step closer to her. "We should have recognized you needed more."

"No, you were grieving too," Honey said.

"Yeah, of course we were," Jackson said. "None of us were ready to lose her. But you were thirteen."

"I didn't handle it well, Honey, and I'm just so sorry," her dad said.

"Dad, I don't need you to apologize to me."

"But I need to," he said. "Your tears hurt me, Honey. And I couldn't stand them. I tried to make myself comfortable, you're right. And I never meant to teach you to do that for the whole rest of your life. That's not what I wanted. I don't want you to be hurt by Jericho. It makes me angry enough to go ask him how the hell he could betray me after I did so much for him. But you're right. It was your choice. And it's your choice what you do going forward. Because heartbreak happens. It just does. And there's nothing anyone can do to shield us from it. I wish I could, but I didn't protect you when it mattered most, so I have no right to go meddling in your business now."

"But you did protect me, Dad. You loved me, and you gave me a place to live. You didn't fail me across the board just because I have some issues. We all have issues."

At this, Lucinda laughed. "Yes, we really do."

Emerson raised her glass, and next to her, so did her husband Holden. "Amen," Emerson said.

"I don't know what any of you are talking about," Wren said. "I am a shining example of being perfectly adjusted."

"Yeah, your choice of husband says otherwise," Emerson pointed out.

"What's wrong with Creed?"

"It's not Creed himself," Emerson said. "It's the fact that you literally thought you hated him so much you wanted to tear his throat out with your teeth before you hooked up with him."

Creed shrugged. "She does have a point. That's not exactly the act of a well-balanced person."

"You're all terrible."

But they weren't. They were her family. And it was a little bit of a strange mess. And so was she. And she wasn't entirely comfortable here still. But… She would be. Because she would figure it out. She wasn't afraid of trying and failing. She wasn't afraid to ask for what she wanted.

She had done it, and it had backfired spectacularly. But now there was basically nowhere left to go.

She was just going to survive it, because she had to.

And that was—in the middle of a very bad Christmas—perhaps the brightest revelation of all.

When he arrived at Christmas breakfast without Honey, he got a lot of follow-up questions.

"She had to go back home," he said.

And that was how he fended off every single one of them.

They had only been his family for two seconds. They didn't get to ask questions. They didn't get to pass judgment on him. Even though he was neck-deep in passing judgment on himself. He just kept seeing Honey's face in his mind's eye. The way that she was crying.

Yeah. He was a total dick.

"How are you finding the family?"

McKenna sidled up beside him, a big gooey cinnamon roll in hand.

"Just fine."

"You seem…like you aren't sure about all this."

"I'm not," he said.

She nodded. "I get that. I do. You know, I was just going to try to get money out of Hank." She tore a strip off the cinnamon roll and took a bite of it.

"I don't need his money."

"Well, nice for you. I sure did. I was homeless when I came here. Pretty much hated everyone and everything. I did a lot of rough living. I was just… I was really angry at the world. And it was really something meeting Grant, who experienced… Just such a sad loss. And yet he was him. Just unfailingly him. He's a really good man. I don't know that I was a good person when I showed up. I just wanted to get what I felt like Hank owed me. And go on my way. But in the end I got something a lot more."

"You sound like a holiday commercial for plastic wrap."

"Are they particularly sappy?"

"Every holiday commercial is particularly sappy."

"Well, sorry I sound like an ad. I don't intend to. But I don't want you to just never come back."

"Why?"

"Because we all need somebody. I really needed this family. I didn't know it. And I really needed Grant."

"And why mention that?"

"Because I don't want you to let Honey get away either. I think you love her."

"Yeah, because you've known me for twelve hours?"

"Maybe that's how being your sister works. I don't know. Maybe I just sense it."

"So, you're psychic?"

"Maybe I'm just not a dumbass."

"Right. Okay." He started to move away from her, but she followed him. Was this what having a little sister was like? He couldn't say that he loved it.

"I think you love her, and I think you're letting your baggage get in the way. I don't think she just randomly left."

"So what? So what if something happened?"

"I think it's sad. Because I think she's a sweetheart.

And I think you're probably a decent guy underneath all your rage at the unfairness of life."

"Look, you've been through some stuff," he said. "Haven't you ever just felt like love was too hard? Like it was too much work?" He shouldn't have asked for that. Because it pushed at tender places inside of his soul that he didn't want to acknowledge. Things he never wanted to deal with.

"Sure," she said. "And loving Grant wasn't simple. Because he had to make room in his heart for me, because he... He'd been in love with someone else before. And she was a really neat woman. She changed him. Into the man who I needed. The man who could love me. Always be grateful to her for that. But that didn't make our road easy, and yeah, I wondered if it was worth it. And why I had to work so hard for love. But you know... In the end, it's worth it. In the end it gives more than it takes."

"Unless it takes everything."

"Are you really afraid of love being hard work? Or are you afraid of losing it? Because I have to tell you, I'm pretty sure it's the second one. And it seems to me that you've already lost her."

"I…"

"The fact that it's on your terms doesn't make it any different."

And he didn't know how to argue with that. Didn't know what to say. Because yeah, he was sitting there, and he didn't have Honey.

He didn't have her.

The realization hit him with the force of a ton of bricks.

She had said that she loved him and he chased her away.

And she was…

He never wanted that. That domestic life, because it reminded him of dark houses and struggle. Of illness.

But not Honey.

She was something else. She was a generic imagining of what marriage might be like. Of what love might be like. She was her. Utterly and uniquely her, and she had been brave enough to tell him how she felt and he had pushed her away.

Did he love her?

Yeah, he already did. He had for a long time, and he hadn't known what to do about it. And he could see himself suddenly, clearly. A man at the top of his game, at the top of the world. Rich as fuck, but poor where it counted. He had come to his family to prove how together he was, but he wasn't together. He just happened to own a lot of shit. That wasn't the same as being successful. He didn't know how to love.

He didn't know how to accept the love of the beautiful woman he had taken to bed last night. He didn't know… You know how. You just got too selfish. Too scared to do it.

The truth stretched before him, undeniable, like the clear harsh light of the sun. And he didn't want to look directly at it. Because it burned him, that truth. That he was nothing. That he had nothing. That he would trade every ounce of success for a week in a cabin with her. No electricity, just Honey to keep him warm.

Right then he felt bankrupt. As rich and successful as he'd ever been, and useless with it.

"Are you having a revelation?" McKenna asked.

"You know," he said. "Having a sister really is overrated."

"It's a weird thing, to go from looking out for yourself to having a whole bunch of people look out for you. Believe me, I get it. But in the end it's worth it."

"So what do I do?"

"It's not easy. But something my husband did… All those years ago and we were working out our stuff, it has stuck with me ever since. It's informed a lot of what I've done, and the ways that I worked out my own issues. Because it's ongoing. I love Grant more than anything in the world, but I'm still scarred from the way that I grew up. And sometimes I lash out. Sometimes I'm not the best to be around. Sometimes I'm insecure. He used to wear this wedding ring. Around his neck. And it was a symbol. Of his grief more than anything else. And one that he chose to set down. He left it at her grave. And it doesn't mean that all the feelings went away. But it's just that… The act of it. Putting it down. Rather than carrying it. That has stuck with me. So every time an issue from my past comes up, I ask myself… McKenna are you just carrying this around? Are you still holding on to it? Why don't you put it down?"

"And that works?"

"Like I said. Not perfectly. But I can picture myself doing it. And walking away. And being happier for it. Just because the world gave you grief doesn't mean you're obligated to carry it on your back forever."

"I don't want to."

"Then don't. I choose to carry around love in the greater measure. And my arms aren't big enough to hold everything. So, mostly, I try to make room to hold that."

"Still sounds like it's work."

She shrugged. "So is being miserable."

And she had a damn good point. She really did.

"What do I do?"

She smiled and took another bite of that cinnamon roll. "Grovel."

Thirteen

By the time Honey got back to the winery that night, she felt gritty. Tired. She was glad she had persevered through the entire holiday, but she hadn't always been the best company, and… She hadn't minded.

She had spoken her piece. And she had been honest about how she felt, and from her perspective that was some pretty decent growth.

Good for her. She had emotional growth. She did not, however, have the love of her life.

She saw headlights, and her heart stopped. She looked out the window of her little house, and she stared.

Was it Jericho?

It was a big ass truck.

He would go to the house. He wouldn't come talk to her.

Except he pulled right up out front, and he turned the engine off.

Like he intended to stay a bit.

She paced back and forth for a second, and then she decided to take action.

She flung the door open. "Have you come to cause more damage? Because I warn you, I am not in a space to make stupid men comfortable by minimizing my feelings."

"You sound like my sister," he said.

"Your sister?"

"Yeah. McKenna."

That made something in her chest tighten. "Oh. So that went well."

"Yeah. I'm going to have to see them again another time. Because I realized that I needed to get back here."

"Why?"

"I realized I needed to get back to you."

"Back to me?"

"Yeah," he said. "Because I realized that I was being a coward. You said that you love me and I couldn't handle it. Because it reminded me of grief. You know why I hated Christmas so much? Because it almost made me feel happy. And it gave me this terrible sense that there was joy out there in the world, and all these people were feeling it. And I felt like I was standing on the outside of it. Able to feel just the edges of it. But never the whole thing. Like I could see the light in this dark winter, but I could never really... I can never really stand in it. It reminded me of that. You offering me your love. Like I was standing on the edge of something beautiful but I didn't know how to take it."

"Jericho..."

"I want it. I want all of it. I want you and me and I want to love you. And I want you to show me. And I need you to have all your emotions, Honey. I need them to be as big and bright as Christmas Day. I need them to be bigger and brighter than the sun, because I need to feel them. Because I need… I need that joy. I need more than the darkness."

Her heart expanded, full to bursting. "I need it too," she said, flinging herself into his arms. "I love you."

"You're not even going to make me suffer?"

"We've both suffered enough," she said.

And that was the damned truth. It truly was. They had both suffered enough.

And what he found was that even though it filled his chest, love wasn't heavy. Not really. It wasn't light, but it didn't weigh them down. And it lit up the dark corners of his soul with all the brilliance of midday.

With the promise of Christmas. And joy to the world. But most especially and finally, to him.

They had been caught in the storm, but the biggest storm had been raging inside of him all this time. And now it was like the sun had come out from behind the clouds. And everything was gold.

Gold like Honey.

"I love you," he said. And while he did, he imagined himself setting his fear down on the floor and leaving it there. Dropping bits and pieces of grief, of doubt. Because all he wanted to carry was her. He wanted to fill his arms with her, fill his chest with her. Forever.

"I love you too," she said. "I'm really glad I didn't burn this place to the ground."

"What?"

"You know, just something I considered. When I was furious at you and convinced that I couldn't have everything that I wanted."

"And what do you think now?"

"That I'll take everything I want and then some. Because why should we settle? That's what we've been doing. Deciding that people like us—who have experienced a measure of tragedy—that we don't get to have the full measure of happiness. But I say we do it. I say we claim it."

"That sounds like a great idea."

And he kissed her. With no doubt or shame, and a whole lot of love.

And he knew that he would be doing it for the rest of his life.

Epilogue

Their whole family was practically a town gathering. Between the Daltons, the Maxfields and the Coopers, Cowboy Wines was absolutely full tonight for Christmas. They had decided in the end to rotate around the Christmas festivities, because it allowed everybody to have the kind of Christmas they loved the most. And no, they didn't do it once a year, they had three Christmases. And everyone was invited.

And when the Daltons hosted, the festivities included the Dodges, Luke and Olivia Hollister, and hell, they might as well just have invited the whole town.

If there was one thing Honey had learned, really learned in the last few years, it was that love grew to accommodate. To expand around all your joy, all your sorrow. And she was sure that their joy was only going to expand more as they added to their family. She hadn't told Jericho yet.

But she would. Christmas morning.

She smiled thinking of the onesie wrapped beneath the tree.

And she felt tears sting her eyes. Just for a moment.

As she thought of the ones they wouldn't have with them for the birth of their first child.

And then she realized, with absolute certainty. But they did have them. In their hearts. Always. Because all the people they'd lost, whether it was her and Jericho or even the members of the Dalton family... Their losses had brought them to this place. Of loving with fierce abandon. Of loving as if it was the most important thing on earth. The only thing on earth.

Because it was.

She looked over at her husband, and she smiled.

She was quite certain that their love was the biggest and brightest of all.

And the next morning when he took that small box from beneath the tree and unwrapped it, it was a moment shared just between the two of them.

"You're kidding me," he said, his eyes filled with wonder. Joy. And she realized that all those years before, she had never seen him look quite like that.

"I'm very serious. And very happy. I hope you are too."

"I didn't have a father growing up," he said, his voice sounding strangled. "And I never imagined I'd be one. I didn't think that I would ever get to be so damned blessed."

"We both are. We both are."

And he kissed her. In that way that she had grown to love so very much. That way that meant forever. That way that always reminded her of Christmas and field guides to birds and love.

Always and forever love.

* * * * *

BIDDING ON
A TEXAN

BARBARA DUNLOP

For Mom and Dad,
who packed up four kids to vacation
on a cattle ranch.

One

Rafe Cortez-Williams opened RCW Steakhouse in Royal, Texas, against his father's wishes. He was expected to carry on the family legacy, running the cattle ranch that had been in Mustang County for multiple generations. But Rafe had four brothers, all of them highly skilled cowboys, and the ranch felt crowded at times.

So three years ago he made the break.

His brick-fronted steakhouse in the heart of downtown was a local hit from the start. It served tender steaks and juicy burgers charred to perfection along with seafood sides and a few Asian fusion specialties. RCW was considered a prime venue for celebrations and special events, which meant patrons were open to higher-priced indulgences.

Despite his father's doubts, things had worked out exceptionally well for Rafe—at least they had up to now.

"Decent lunch crowd today?" RCW head chef JJ Yeoh was working at the long gas stove top in the center of the big kitchen. He spoke over the sizzle of steaks and sautéing vegetables, and the clatter of pans and dishes as the kitchen staff efficiently prepared dozens of meals.

"We're completely full out there," Rafe replied, swiftly stepping to one side as a waitress passed by carrying two sizzling T-bones with all the trimmings. "I don't think the brand's been tainted...at least not yet."

"None of the scandal is on you," JJ said. He glanced up from where he was spicing a skillet of shrimp. "All you did was invest in a good cause—generously."

"Our name was strongly attached to Soiree on the Bay. There'll be blowback. Don't you doubt it."

JJ, always an optimist, gave a shrug. "People still like to eat."

"People can eat at other places."

"Ahhh, but not like they can eat here." The chef turned his attention back to his cooking, stirring the mixture in the hot skillet, releasing a spicy aroma that made Rafe's stomach growl.

JJ was right about that. But in the end, it might not matter.

Because if Rafe couldn't pay the second mortgage, not even his top chef's signature sambal shrimp dish was going to save him. But he didn't have the heart to tell JJ about the company's true financial peril.

The noise level ebbed and flowed as waitstaff came and went with meals and baskets of homemade sourdough bread. A busboy entered through the far door to deposit a load of dishes with the washing staff. On a busy day like this, it was important to get the tables bused quickly and set up for the next party. Rafe hated to leave people waiting in the foyer.

"I'm going to take a walk around. See you in a bit."

JJ gave a nod, most of his focus on his cooking as he started on the next order.

Rafe like to do a circuit of the dining room every half hour or so. He wasn't the kind of owner who intruded on the customers' dining experience. He liked to think he had an innate sense of who wanted a hello, who coveted a brief chat and who wanted to be left alone to enjoy the company at their own table. The clues were in people's expressions and their body language, but mostly in their eye contact.

He was particularly cautious with couples. The last thing he wanted to do was interrupt a romantic evening for two. Those were sacrosanct. Not that he'd had one himself in the past while.

Rafe made his way down the short kitchen hallway and into the main dining room. His restaurant was set up in three separate sections, and the sections were further divided by strategically placed wooden pillars and narrow, glass-fronted carved wood cabinets. The layout cut down on the ambient noise and gave diners additional privacy.

He checked the front dining room first with its muted lighting, rich wood panels and open wine racks.

He approached a party of six. It looked like a multigenerational group, and he guessed the older man at the head of the table was the host.

"Good afternoon," he said, taking in the whole table. "I'm Rafe Cortez-Williams, owner of the RCW. How are you enjoying your meals?"

The party looked to be about halfway through dining.

"Delicious," the older man said with a grin, gesturing to his plate that held a thick rib eye steak. "What's the secret to your baked potato?"

"A touch of cayenne," Rafe answered. "Gives it a little zing."

"I liked that little zing," the man responded.

Rafe looked around at the other diners to see if they had anything to say.

A pretty blonde woman who looked to be in her twenties lifted her blown crystal goblet and gave it a rock. "These are deliciously dangerous," she said.

"Is that the guava cranberry or the raspberry?" Rafe asked.

"Guava cranberry."

"That's one of my favorites," he said. "Would you like another?" As he asked the question, he discreetly signaled behind his back for the waitress.

The blonde woman looked to the man sitting next to her.

"Go for it." The man answered the question in her eyes with good humor. "I'm driving."

"It's a family reunion," a woman to the right of the older man said.

Rafe assumed she was his wife.

Their waitress, Shirley, arrived by Rafe's side.

"I believe this woman might like another guava cranberry blend," he stated, raising his brow at the woman in a question.

"Yes, please," she laughed.

"Enjoy your meal and the rest of the reunion," he said to them all, leaving them in Shirley's hands.

Smiling to himself, he moved on, stopping at a few more tables before he entered the southern dining room at the back of the restaurant.

Rafe swiftly scanned the vicinity from the doorway, barely believing what he was seeing. Gina Edmond, the only daughter of oil magnate Rusty Edmond, had graced RCW *in person*.

Though Rafe had never met Gina, he knew the gorgeous and glamorous heiress on sight. She was Royal's most pampered princess, and RCW was definitely not her usual haunt.

It hit Rafe then why she was here. She couldn't exactly show her face at the Texas Cattleman's Club right now. Not after that colossal scandal that had rocked the town.

At the center of that scandal was Billy Holmes, the man who was at the very least a close friend of the Edmonds, and possibly Gina's secret half-brother. Billy had disappeared with millions of dollars of investment in the Soiree on the Bay festival. And by all accounts, the Edmond houseguest had not only doomed the festival to failure but was directly responsible for bringing some of the local businesses to bankruptcy.

The last person Rafe wanted to chat with was Gina Edmond and…his attention moved to her dining companion. It was Sarabeth, Gina's estranged mother. Well, not so estranged anymore since Sarabeth had returned to Royal and was planning her wedding, a very *expensive* yacht-board wedding, proving the Edmonds weren't suffering in the slightest from the financial ruin of Soiree on the Bay.

A waitress slipped past Rafe, and he reminded himself to get on with business. Gina was here. She was a customer, and he'd be professional if it killed him.

Gina Edmond was aware she'd spent her whole life on the gilded social glide path that came with being Rusty Edmond's only daughter. Rusty was a legend in the Texas oil business, a prominent member of the Texas Cattleman's Club, and a mover and shaker in the Royal Chamber of Commerce. For twenty-six years, Gina had been treated with automatic respect and had enjoyed the advantages of her family's position.

But her glide path had come to an abrupt halt.

The family was no longer venerated by their fellow citizens and TCC members. Instead, the Edmonds were *all* treated with suspicion, even though they'd had nothing to do with Billy's crimes. Her family had been duped along with everyone else, and they'd suffered for it.

"After the false accusation about Asher..." her mother, Sarabeth, was saying from across the dining table. "And now Billy and the missing money on top of it all. You kids have way too much on your plates. I wonder if we should postpone the wedding."

"Don't you dare postpone!" Gina countered. Her stepbrother, Asher, had been exonerated of the embezzlement charge and was out of jail now.

Gina was looking forward to the wedding. She'd been estranged from her mother since she was eight years old. She'd been angry for most of those years, but she'd since learned about her mother's troubled past. And after getting to know her mother these past few months, the rift between them was healing. Sarabeth deserved her hard-won happiness with local rancher Brett Harston.

"It seems…" Sarabeth was clearly searching for the right word.

"It seems wonderful, exhilarating and inspirational," Gina finished for her. "It's just what the community needs to take their minds off the disaster. Everyone loves a happy ending."

"I feel selfish," Sarabeth admitted, looking unconvinced.

"You'd be selfish to cancel," Gina countered.

She wanted her mother to be happy, but she honestly believed the rest of her sales pitch as well. Royal needed a distraction, and the wedding would provide it for the four hundred guests on the invitation list, covering many of the TCC members and most of the families and businesses that had been hurt by the cancellation of Soiree on the Bay.

"You think so?" Sarabeth asked.

"I *know* so." Gina reached out to pat her mother's hand. "And if you're going to worry about anything," she joked, attempting to lighten the mood, "worry about me getting a date for the wedding."

Sarabeth waved away Gina's concern. "You can get all the dates you want and then some. Look at you!"

Gina knew her looks were fine. She wasn't exactly the life of the party, but she thought she had a decent sense of humor. And if her grades were anything to go by, she was reasonably intelligent. She'd earned a bachelor's degree in business administration from Texas Southern. Still, she'd never truly clicked with a boyfriend, and she already knew most of the men in Royal.

"You can't stick to such a strict list of attributes," Sarabeth said, taking a thoughtful sip of her chardonnay.

Gina leaned forward to lower her voice. "I don't have a list of attributes." That said, she supposed she did have a few general criteria she'd look for in a man. Honesty, for starters, as well as someone who was honorable, funny, successful or, she supposed, more like happy in their chosen career. She wasn't a snob about money.

"Who would be perfect?" Sarabeth asked. "Toss out a name."

Gina didn't have a name.

Just then she caught sight of a tall, dark, broad-shouldered man in a finely cut jacket chatting with the diners at another table. His smile was bright white and beautiful. His dark eyes were warm and friendly. And judging by the laughter from the four people sitting at the table, he had a good sense of humor.

"What about him?" Gina asked, giving a discreet nod.

Her mother looked over her shoulder. She stared for a moment then turned back, a worried expression on her face. "Uh… Gina…"

"Shhh. He's coming over."

The man strode their way, looking self-assured and in his element. But as his gaze met hers his brown eyes hardened. His beautiful smile disappeared, and his jaw went taut.

"Ms. Edmond," he said, giving her a curt nod. "Mrs. Edmond," he said to Sarabeth.

"Hello," Gina murmured in return, puzzled by his attitude.

"I'm Rafe Cortez-Williams, owner of the RCW."

Recognition jolted Gina like a splash of ice water.

RCW was a major sponsor of Soiree on the Bay. Rafe had been among the biggest financial losers in the festival debacle. And he blamed her. Or at least he blamed her *family* for his loss.

"I hope you're having an enjoyable lunch." His friendly scripted words were at odds with his hostile demeanor.

"Everything is delicious," Sarabeth said in a perfectly amicable tone.

Gina shot her mother a look of confusion. Why was she kissing up to the guy?

"I'm very glad to hear that. Please, enjoy." And then he was gone, off to the next table where he smiled and treated them to the compelling glow in his gorgeous eyes.

"Unfortunately, not the guy for you," Sarabeth said.

"Why were you so nice?"

"Rafe lost a big chunk of money. He deserves to be angry."

"It wasn't *our* fault. It was Billy's fault…maybe." They didn't even know that much for sure.

"And if Billy's your half-brother?"

"We don't know he did it, and we don't know for sure he's Dad's son."

Sarabeth lifted her glass again, gazing contemplatively at the pale wine. "Remember, I was married to your father back then."

Gina took a drink of her merlot, needing it. She'd gotten past the squirming discomfort at discussing her father's infidelity with her mother, but it was far from her favorite subject. "Antoinette Holmes admits she also slept with other men."

"Maybe," Sarabeth said, looking unconvinced by that detail.

"Back to your wedding," Gina said, wanting to move her thoughts past Billy and *well past* Rafe Cortez-Williams, since he was obviously *far* from her perfect man. "Let's talk about your hair…"

Sarabeth easily switched topics. "What do you think? Up or down?" She gathered her blond hair at the back of her neck and pulled it up to demonstrate.

As they delved into an in-depth discussion about hairdos, veils and age-appropriate wedding gowns, from the corner of her eye, Gina caught another glimpse of Rafe. She tried to ignore it, but he snagged her attention—his square shoulders, confident walk, that thick head of lustrous dark hair...

He might be all wrong for her, but he sure was smoking hot.

"Gina?" Sarabeth prompted her.

"Hmm?" She gave herself a little shake.

"I like the idea of tea-length. I don't want to dress up all frothy like some dewy-eyed ingenue."

"Do they even use that term anymore?"

Sarabeth chuckled. "Ingenues? Maybe not. But you know what I mean."

"We need to go talk to Natalie Valentine," Gina said, referring to the owner of a local bridal shop.

It might not be her own wedding, but she was excited about planning her mom's. Maybe someday it would be hers. Her thoughts went back to Rafe for a split second before she banished him. Sure, he'd look good in a tux at the front of church, but there was a whole lot more to a marriage than a guy who could rock the wedding.

"I *am* marrying a rancher," Sarabeth mused. "What about country rustic?"

"But you're marrying him on a yacht. Maybe go for a classic or elegant style?"

Sarabeth closed her eyes.

Gina couldn't seem to stop herself from glancing to the archway that led to the front dining room. Rafe was on the other side of it in the distance, and she gazed at him for a minute longer, thinking there was no law against looking.

"I'm thinking tea-length, slightly A-line," Sarabeth said, opening her eyes. "Ivory silk, maybe a thin organza overlay and flat lace on a sweetheart neckline with cap sleeves?"

"That's a very detailed picture."

"Can you see it?"

Gina *could* see it, and it was beautiful. She smiled. "Yes.

Not too froufrou, but formal enough for the opulent surroundings."

"That's it!" her mother said, sitting back. "Next, we do you."

Sarabeth left to meet her fiancé, Brett, while Gina stayed behind to take care of the RCW tab. She hesitated over the tip amount. She wanted to be generous to their waitress, but she was afraid Rafe might see a large tip as flaunting the family wealth, especially in light of the collective losses of Royal businesses from Soiree on the Bay.

Then she laughed at her own foolishness, realizing Rafe would never even see the tip. What were the chances he went through a day's credit card receipts? Slim to none. She tipped big and punched in her PIN.

There. Done.

She came to her feet, smoothing the front of her sleeveless black-and-white dress and slipping her olive green handbag over her shoulder. She walked with confidence in her jungle-patterned pumps. The spike-heeled shoes weren't made for long walks, but they did great things for her calves, and they'd get her as far as her Jaguar convertible.

As she rounded a polished wood pillar near the front foyer, a man stepped unexpectedly out in front of her. She stumbled, nearly falling into his chest.

His hands came out, grasping her upper arms to steady her, and she looked up to find it was Rafe. Strong hands, handsome face, sinfully sexy lips…

Gina told her brain to shut up already.

"Sorry," he said, then obviously registered who she was. He let go of her like she was contagious, that frown reappearing on his face.

"My fault," she said, because it was, and she didn't have to like him to tell the truth. "I was in a hurry."

He glanced into the dining area behind her. "Your mother?"

"Left to meet with her fiancé."

"Ah, yes, Brett Harston."

"Right. You would know Brett."

"Ranching fraternity."

Rafe didn't look much like a rancher. His face was tanned a deep brown. His hands were broad and strong, but she hadn't felt thick calluses on his fingertips like most ranchers'.

She wondered how long it had been since he rode the range on his huge family ranch.

"I haven't seen you in here before now," Rafe drawled, his watchful gaze betraying his assumption. He'd concluded she was persona non grata at the TCC. He was right, but that didn't excuse his rudeness.

"Are you trying to start an argument?" she asked bluntly.

"No...yes...maybe." There was a hint of amusement in his expression along with what seemed like a flare of admiration for her grit.

She might have laughed at the comeback if he wasn't being such a jerk. "We were victims, too, you know. Just like everyone else."

His dark brows went up in obvious amazement. *"You?"*

"Yes, me."

"The Edmond princess, a victim of financial misfortune?" He made a show of peering out the front window to the parking lot. "Let me guess which car you're driving."

"Well, that's irrelevant."

He took his time looking over her designer outfit. "Where, exactly, are you going to have to cut back, Princess?"

Her clothes were expensive, sure. But, again, *irrelevant*. "Don't call me that."

"It fits." He waited a moment. "You don't have an answer, do you?"

"An answer for what? For you being so rude?"

"On where you're personally cutting back. Give me one concrete example of the festival embezzlement impacting your exclusive lifestyle, and I'll apologize unreservedly."

She didn't have a quick answer for that.

"That's none of your business," she huffed.

He laughed at that, a full, rich sound.

"Well, clearly nothing's changed around *here* yet," Gina pointed out, glancing around at the bustling staff and the upscale decor.

Rafe sobered. "You can't see what's happening under the surface."

"You can't see what's happening under my surface, either." The Edmonds might not be in an immediate cash crisis, but their reputation had been savaged, starting with Asher's arrest and then with Billy's disappearance. And the fallout from that was just beginning.

Never mind that she and her brothers felt honor bound to try to fix the mess. She'd never admit it to someone like Rafe, but she did feel some responsibility for the catastrophe since it was her family that brought Billy into the community.

Rafe considered her for a minute. Up close, her initial attraction to his looks, his powerful presence and his graceful movements grew even more potent. She felt hot and prickly with awareness of him as a man.

"You want to show me?" he asked, his low, deep voice reverberating around her.

She was taken aback by the question. It could be interpreted in a whole host of different ways, some of them extremely seductive. Her face and neck warmed with her reckless thoughts.

"Hang on," he said. "I didn't mean it that way..."

She didn't know what she hated more, that he seemed to be able to read her mind or that she seemed to be able to read his.

"I didn't think you did," she answered tartly, willing her hormones to calm the heck down.

"Then why the blush?"

"I don't blush."

"You're blushing now." He was making it worse.

"I'm *angry* now," she said.

"Why?"

She didn't have a quick answer for that either, but she tried her best. "Because…because, you're being so rude!"

"Me?" He feigned surprise.

"Yes, you."

"I only asked about the more subtle impacts of the embezzlement situation on your family."

She narrowed her eyes, not buying his innocent act for a moment. "Yeah, right."

He shook his head pityingly. "Oh, Gina. You're so used to men falling at your feet in abject adoration that you don't recognize anything else."

She wasn't. She didn't. She hadn't just done that…

Had she?

Two

Rafe was nothing more than an ordinary guy.

Sadly, that meant he was cursed like all the rest with an undeniable urge to fall at Gina Edmond's feet in abject adoration. But he'd never do it. He was far too smart for that. But he wasn't immune to the unmistakable sex appeal that oozed from her very pores. It was in every move she made, every expression she gave, in her deep, sultry, sexy voice. He hadn't cared what she said to him, so long as she was talking.

"I said borrow money from Dad." His brother Matias spoke up from where he sat on a padded chair on the deck of Rafe's house, overlooking Pine Valley.

The sun was setting now on the western horizon, yellow, pink and wild-rose red painting the distant storm clouds. The temperature was August-hot, but an evening breeze brought some relief as Rafe arrived back from his beer run to the kitchen.

"You know I'm never going to do that." He set an icy bottle of beer down for his brother on the small round table, then took the chair on the opposite side, his own cold beer slick from condensation in his hand.

"Too proud?" Matias asked.

"Too practical." Rafe was also too proud, but that wasn't the most salient reason for his decision. "I promised myself RCW would make it on its own. I'm not liquidating my assets to prop it up, and I'm not asking anyone in the family for money, either."

"The embezzlement is just a temporary setback," Matias said.

"Maybe so. But I made the decision to invest in Soiree on the Bay."

"You and half the businesses in town."

Rafe took a pull on his beer. "It's like being in Vegas."

"Huh?"

"You set your limit going in, and you don't deviate from it even if the losses mount up."

Matias shot him a puzzled look. "You set a limit in Vegas? How is that any fun?"

Rafe chuckled. His brother might be the most reckless of the Cortez-Williams brothers, but he'd never let himself lose big in Vegas.

"Seriously," Matias said. "If you're going to gamble, gamble. It's not gambling if nothing meaningful is at stake."

"You're telling me you've lost real money in Vegas?"

Now Matias looked affronted. "Of course not." He snorted out a laugh. "I *win* in Vegas. But sad to say, I haven't been to Sin City in months."

"You betting on anything locally?"

"I'd bet on you," his brother said with all sincerity.

Rafe shook his head. "I don't need your money."

"You just said RCW is in serious financial trouble."

"It is. But we'll work it out with corporate resources. That's the deal I made with myself when I walked away from the ranch. Maybe we'll find Billy and get the money back."

"Given what I've heard about the scheme? Doubtful. That's a guy who's been thinking about this for a long time."

"I suppose," Rafe said. "What do you think does that to a man?"

"Sucks his conscience from his soul?"

"Yeah." That was pretty much what Rafe meant.

"Well, it looks like he's probably an Edmond."

Rafe chuckled at that, taking another drink, the effervescent liquid feeling good on his throat in the sultry evening. "You're saying the flaw is in the genetics?"

"Rusty's a cutthroat. Look what he did to his son Ross when he went against him."

Rafe gave his brother a mocking look. "You watched me walk out on Dad. Are you saying we're genetically tainted?"

"You and Dad didn't have *that* kind of a fight."

"It took us a while." Rafe's father considered the ranch his sons' heritage and their obligation, all five of them.

"But you got there," Matias said, gesturing again with his beer bottle for emphasis.

"We got there." Rafe's relationship with his father was a bit of an armed truce, but they were working on it. Still, he couldn't help but wonder what he'd be in for if RCW failed. The *I-told-you-so*s from his father would be unrelenting.

"You were too cocky," Matias said.

"I was younger. No. Scratch that. I'd do the same today."

"Even knowing how it ends?"

"It hasn't ended."

"Especially if you let me lend you some money. Or buy in. I could be your partner. Sell me half of RCW."

Rafe burst out laughing at that. "You're not cut out for the restaurant business. Besides, can you imagine Dad coming unglued if you announced you were throwing in with me? Your horse breeding sideline is bad enough." Rafe shook his head. "Plus, you're a rancher, Matias, you and Lorenzo both."

"And you're not?" His brother looked disappointed as he asked.

"I'm not. I mean, I can rope and ride, run a herd, and pick cattle at auction. But I don't love it like you guys do."

"You love the restaurant business?" It was clear Matias couldn't understand that.

"I do." At least Rafe relished the day-to-day running of RCW, the enthusiasm of the staff, the joy of the customers having celebrations, the creativity of JJ and the other chefs.

He wasn't so wild about the Royal business community. They seemed to prefer the Cortez-Williams brothers as ranchers, slightly on the outskirts, not smack-dab in the middle of their corporate world. The ostracism was subtle, but he was still struggling to be accepted as a fully functioning member of the business community.

"To each his own," Matias said. "Hope you can hang on to it."

"I do, too."

There was a meeting of the Royal Chamber of Commerce this week to discuss a way out of the financial debacle for the chamber, the TCC and the whole town. Rafe was going to be there, and he was going to put his shoulder to the collective solution, whatever it was.

Gina came early to the Royal Chamber of Commerce meeting. She wanted to get seated before too many people arrived—ideally somewhere near the back, where the accusatory gazes of her fellow community members couldn't easily find her. It was no fun being a pariah.

For as long as she could remember, she'd been greeted warmly at TCC events and other happenings in Royal, first as a child and a teenager accompanying her father and other family members, but in recent years on her own, acknowledged as an Edmond in her own right.

However, today, she was slinking quietly in and trying to hide in the background.

Lila Jones was at the front of the room leaning over a rectangular table, the only person there so far. She looked up as Gina entered through the double doors at the back.

"Hi, Gina." Lila's expression was welcoming, her voice friendly. Then again, she had always been a decent person.

A little understated maybe, before her recent makeover, but a solid, hardworking, respected member of the Royal business community.

Gina tried to imagine Lila being treated as a pariah. She couldn't. No matter what Lila's family did or didn't do, she would be respected for herself and her own accomplishments.

Gina wanted that for herself.

Her footsteps were muted on the carpet as she decided to make her way forward. "Can I help?" she asked the other woman.

"Help?"

"Anything to get ready?" It was a small offer, an insignificant offer really.

Normally, she would pour herself a coffee at the refreshment table or help herself to a bottle of water, sit down with friends and have a nice chat while the meeting got under way. This was the first time she'd considered the work that went into convening a chamber gathering.

Gina supposed it was Lila's job to put the meetings together. But the Royal Chamber of Commerce was primarily a volunteer organization, and it had never occurred to her to volunteer.

Lila glanced around, seemingly puzzled by Gina's offer. "I…uh…guess you could put out the agenda packages. I mean, if you don't mind."

"Not at all." Gina spotted a stack of agendas on the table. She tucked her purse snugly under her arm and picked up the stack.

"Thanks," Lila said.

"It's nice to have something to do."

Lila gave Gina a sympathetic smile, and started to say something, but then shut her mouth.

"What?"

"Nothing." Lila shook her head.

"Go ahead." Gina was curious.

"I'm just…sorry for what you're going through."

"It's been hard on the family."

"Not the family," Lila said. "You. Personally. It can't be fun having everyone staring and whispering behind your back."

Gina looked down at the agendas for a second. She wasn't used to pity. There'd never been a need for it in her life.

"I'm learning to cope," she admitted.

"That which doesn't kill us…" Lila let the famous quote fall away.

"Oh, I hope this makes me stronger," Gina said.

"Do you want it to make you stronger?" The other woman seemed sincere.

"I do."

"How're you going to do that?" Mere moments into the conversation, Lila had hit on the crux of the problem.

"Honestly? I have no idea. I usually just go along for the ride." As Gina said the words, she realized how very true they were. "How can that be?"

"You are who you are." Lila looked intelligent now, insightful, reminding Gina how she had always excelled in school. A grade ahead, while Gina and her friends were fussing about clothes and makeup and boys, Lila had been busy pulling in top marks, working hard, like she still seemed to be doing even after making a splash on social media.

Gina had never envied Lila. But she did now. Lila pulled her own weight in the world. It obviously gave her her independence and self-worth.

"I don't want to be who I am," Gina impulsively admitted.

"Who do you want to be?"

Gina almost said *you*. "Someone who helps." She looked

down at the agendas and laughed at herself, because she was standing here talking instead of getting to work. "But you've given me something to think about. Thank you." She began to step away to put the pamphlets on the tables, but then stopped and looked back. "Can I ask you something?"

"Sure."

Gina heard voices behind her and realized the other attendees were starting to arrive. She had to talk fast. "This thing you did."

"The *thing*?"

"Changing from studious to glam."

"I wouldn't say—"

"I want to do the opposite. I'm all glam all the time. I want to undo some of it. I want people to take me seriously. *You* are such a great balance."

There were more voices now, chatting together, calling to one another, chairs moving, people settling. Gina hated the thought of turning around to face them, but she was determined to pass out the agendas. It was a tiny thing, but it felt like a turning point.

"How about we chat over lunch?" Lila suggested. "One day this week?"

"That would be great." Gina took a bracing breath and turned to the room.

She kept everyone in her soft focus as she moved, not meeting any of the stares she knew were following her, ignoring the indistinct conversations that were probably about her and her family, focusing instead on the royal blue tabletops where she was depositing the agendas.

Finally, she finished, ending in a back corner of the room. She quickly sat down in a chair against the wall.

"Hello, Gina."

She didn't have to look over to recognize Rafe's voice. She'd definitely picked the wrong table.

* * *

Rafe couldn't help but admire Gina's moxie as she sat down next to him and his brother Lorenzo. But one look at her stricken expression told him it was an accident.

He waited to see what she'd do. Would she get up and flee, or would she stick it out?

"Hello, Rafe," she said. "Lorenzo." Her lips thinned and her posture straightened, but she made no move to switch to another table.

Her brother Ross Edmond walked in then. He scanned the room like he owned the place, which he practically did, the Edmond family being founding members of both the TCC and the Royal Chamber of Commerce.

When Ross spotted Gina, he was clearly confused by her choice of location. The Edmonds were front-and-center kind of people. He was probably puzzled by her table companions as well. He scanned Rafe and Lorenzo for a moment, then walked over to sit next to his sister.

"Hi, Lorenzo, Rafe. Hey, Gina." He gave her a half hug where she sat.

Asher Edmond entered the room and reacted the same way as his stepbrother, Ross, doing a double take of where his family was sitting.

Rafe could only imagine what was going to happen when patriarch Rusty Edmond walked in. He'd probably move the whole family to some better real estate near the front of the room, as was their due. The family might be persona non grata in the eyes of many business owners, but Rusty was unlikely to let that slow him down.

For now, Asher sauntered over. There were only four chairs at each table, set over half the round so everyone was facing front. Asher commandeered a chair from the next table, dragging it over next to Ross.

"Lorenzo, Rafe. How you guys doing?"

"Fine," Rafe said, although he was anything but, and these three people were at least in part to blame for that.

"Hey, Asher," Lorenzo said. "Welcome back to the world."

Asher gave a half smile at the joke. "Good to be back. Valencia didn't come out?"

Lorenzo shook his head. "She's with the horses. She's shorthanded right now."

Rafe knew Valencia Donovan had been counting on a share of the ticket sales from Soiree on the Bay. Her charitable horse rescue organization was strapped for cash now that the event had fallen through.

"Hopefully something good will come out of tonight," Asher said with a gaze around the filling room. "Heaven knows we all need it."

Lorenzo nodded his agreement.

"Can I have your attention, please?" Lila asked over the microphone.

The stragglers finished picking up cups of coffee and moved to their seats, while the conversation in the room settled down. Rafe couldn't help a surreptitious glance in Gina's direction. But when he met Ross's gaze, he looked away. The other man had to be used to guys eyeballing his sister, and Rafe wasn't about to be one of them, even if it *was* tempting.

"I'll officially call the meeting to order," Lila continued. "As you can see, there's only one item under new business tonight. And the minutes from the last meeting are attached. Will someone move to approve the minutes?"

A voice came from the far side of the room. "I'll move."

"Thank you. Anyone second?"

Ross closed his package and put up his hand. "Second."

"The minutes are so approved. Now on to new business. As you all know, the Royal Chamber of Commerce was a supporter of Soiree on the Bay rather than an investor.

And while we can't be involved in any criminal probes or investigations, what we can do is facilitate a discussion on ideas for recouping some of your losses. We've been made aware that local businesses are struggling, and we hope this will be an opportunity for everyone to work collaboratively on viable solutions."

"What are the Edmonds going to do about it?" someone shouted out.

"Where are they?" said another.

"Hiding in the back corner."

There was swiveling in seats and turning of heads until all gazes were focused their way.

Gina shifted in her own seat, and Rafe felt sorry for her. Clearly, she'd chosen to sit back here to stay out of the fray. That clearly hadn't worked out for her.

"Where's Rusty?" someone called out as sidebar conversations arose around the room.

"Shouting isn't going to help," Lila broke in. "We're looking for *constructive* solutions."

Ross came to his feet, and people quieted down, clearly curious.

"My brother, sister and I—" Ross began.

Rafe scanned the room, monitoring the expressions of the crowd as Ross spoke.

"—will be donating to a relief fund set up through the Chamber of Commerce for local businesses impacted by the festival cancellation."

"Cancellation?" someone bellowed out incredulously.

"How much?" another person demanded.

Rafe could see the crowd wasn't softening toward the Edmonds. They were still suspicious and hostile. He didn't blame them. Because he felt the same way himself. In fact, he hoped nobody interpreted him and Lorenzo sitting at this table as being an implicit endorsement of the Edmonds.

"Together, we lost millions," someone else pointed out. "You gonna donate millions?"

"We can't cover it all," Ross admitted gruffly.

Everyone started talking at once.

"Please," Lila tried again through the microphone. She was doing a valiant job of trying to keep order.

"We're not saying it's the complete solution." Ross's voice rose. "We're just saying we want to do our part."

The crowd kept shouting out.

"I'm about to lose my business."

"Forget your business, my house is at stake."

"I've lost a year's worth of profits."

"I don't know if I can recover from this!"

Gina shifted in her seat, and Rafe checked out her expression, thinking she had to feel like she was under attack along with her brother. Protective instincts welled up inside him, even though it was none of his concern.

To his surprise, she didn't look intimidated. In fact, she looked determined. She put her hand on Ross's arm.

He glanced down at her, clearly taken aback when she rose to her feet.

"Let me," she whispered to him.

It was easy to see he was about to refuse.

"Please," she implored.

After a moment, he sat down.

The move surprised the crowd enough to quiet them down.

Her voice was slightly shaky as she started talking. "I'm not going to say I understand," she began. "But I will say that the best thing we can do here tonight is brainstorm some fundraising ideas. I get that it's satisfying to complain, and I know you're all looking for someone to blame."

Rafe could see that statement was a mistake even if she couldn't. The expressions of the crowd changed, and they looked like they were about to start shouting again.

"And maybe we are," Gina said in a clear, ringing voice. "But that won't help tonight. It won't help any of you get your money back. We need fundraising ideas."

Surprisingly the crowd settled again.

"That's a very productive suggestion," Lila said. "What about standard things, a walkathon, bowl-athon or read-athon."

"We could sell T-shirts," someone shouted.

"A white elephant sale?"

"Those are all local," Gina said. "We can't depend on local dollars this time."

There were nods around the room on that point.

"What about a talent show?" Lexi suggested.

"You mean a festival lite?" someone scoffed.

"We'd need a really big name to get any traction at all on social media," Abby Carmichael pointed out.

Lila spoke up again, sounding disheartened. "Big names won't want to be associated with Soiree on the Bay."

"What about services?" Gina asked. "What do we do here in Royal that's unique and valuable?"

"A bake sale?" someone asked.

"Too small-time," another person answered.

Rafe had an industrial kitchen, but he didn't see a bake sale—or any other fundraising suggestions that had been brought up so far—providing the kind of cash they needed.

Lexi's idea had been the best of the bunch, but only if they could get a big name, which they couldn't. No way, no how was any A-list performer going to touch Royal and Soiree on the Bay.

"We have beautiful scenery," someone said.

"Wide-open space."

"Cattle."

"Horses."

"Ranches!" Gina said, a thread of excitement in her voice.

"Sell a ranch?" someone asked incredulously.

"No. Not exactly." She started talking faster, her voice growing more animated. "Just raffle the ranch experience. Better still, a cowboy experience. The entire South, no the entire *country* is full of big-city dwellers who have no idea what it's like to spend a day on a working ranch with a real cowboy." She glanced at Lorenzo and Rafe.

Uh-oh. Rafe didn't like where this was going.

"We do the auction online. We go national. Maybe the cowboys give a little video spiel to entice bidders. We could get some stills of the ranches, show them off. Make it sound fun. Make it sound exciting. Lila, you're the social media expert." Gina paused.

Everyone shifted their attention to the front of the room where Lila stood at the microphone. "It's an…idea," she said, clearly trying to organize her thoughts. "Maybe it could work…"

"Who's going to volunteer for *that*?" a male voice asked. It was Tucker McCoy, sixty-eight years old and still riding his own range. "Video myself yapping about heifers and hog-tying, then take some city slicker onto the range and maybe get them hurt or killed?"

"There'd be liability," someone noted.

"We'd cover the insurance," Gina said.

Both her brothers swung their heads to gape at her.

"A rider on the Edmond corporate policy," she said. "We could donate that. And the flights to get here. We'd donate those, too." She glanced at both her brothers, who were staring at her in stunned surprise.

"The Edmond family was already planning to donate to the cause. This could be part of the package. We add a high-end dinner to each experience, an outdoorsy day followed by a five-star evening." She put some cajoling humor into her voice. "If the cowboys are handsome, all the better."

"You still need willing cowboys," someone observed.

From the podium, Lila looked expectantly around the room. "Any volunteers?" she asked.

Nobody spoke up.

Rafe had to hand it to Lila, she was willing to make them all sweat it out. He had to give Gina props, too, for standing there with her idea crashing and burning in front of the whole town. Turning, he took a quick glance at her face, and saw her brave smile but also the trepidation in her eyes. He felt a spike of pity.

Aw, hell.

He came to his feet. "I'll do it," he said.

Lorenzo looked astonished.

Rafe motioned to his brother with his head, *get up*, being the clear message.

Lorenzo gave an imperceptible shake.

Rafe came back with a glare.

But before Lorenzo could stand, Tucker McCoy stood. "I'll do it, too," he said. "Don't see why a pretty gal wouldn't want to spend a day with me. I got more exciting stories than any of you young cowpokes."

"I'll volunteer Matias," Lorenzo called out.

More men stood, and the joking began.

Gina's shoulders drooped in obvious relief.

Three

Gina's brothers stayed silent until they were halfway across the chamber parking lot and out of earshot of the other meeting attendees.

"*What* was that?" Asher demanded.

"We *had* a plan," Ross added.

"Our plan wasn't working." Gina knew she'd gone way off script, but the crowd was turning on Ross, and she'd felt like she had to do something to help.

Ross stopped next to his car. "I can't imagine what Dad's going to say about this."

The three of them formed a small circle to continue the conversation.

Gina couldn't imagine what her father was going to say, either. "If he cares so much, he should have come out to the meeting," she boldly stated.

"Is *that* what you're going to tell him?" Asher asked.

Gina had hoped they'd talk to him together about the auction and their financial pledges to the cause. She wasn't afraid of Rusty, but she was intimidated by him. She always had been. "I'll tell him we're hoping to recoup some of the town's losses. That's a positive."

"I'm not sure he's in the mood for a positive," Ross ventured as vehicles started up around them, headlights sweeping as people pulled out for home, a few curiously craning their necks to look at the Edmonds as they passed.

"Rusty's not thinking straight on any front," Asher added. "He's raging at everyone right now."

"He has a right to be mad at Billy," Ross said.

"Maybe," Gina offered, not feeling a whole lot of sympathy or respect for her father given the revelations about his infidelity. "But you also have a right to be mad at him," she said to Ross.

Ross nodded. "I know. But it's hard to stay angry and be so happy at the same time."

"I admire your capacity for forgiveness." She wasn't sure she'd have done the same.

Ross had almost lost his child and the love of his life because of Rusty's machinations.

"Charlotte's the forgiving one," he said. "Dad has her to thank for that—Mom, too." He gave his head a shake. "After all she went through."

Gina understood the reconciliation with their mother more easily, since Sarabeth had been wronged by Rusty, too. "Has Dad thanked her?"

"In his way," Ross said.

"That man," she said through gritted teeth. "He almost sent Asher to jail."

"I did go to jail," Asher said ruefully. "But I got out again."

"We should have trusted you from the start," Gina said more softly, regretting that she'd ever doubted her stepbrother's innocence.

"Billy did a damn good job of framing me," Asher said. Then he gave Gina a playful bump with his shoulder. "If I didn't know for sure it wasn't me, I might have been swayed by the evidence."

"We were wrong about you," Ross said with regret.

"Water under the bridge," Asher stated. "And besides, we've got bigger problems than regret right now."

Ross shook his head, his attention going back to Gina. "I can't believe you went rogue on us back there."

"I think it's going to work," she said, feigning a confidence she wasn't feeling. They'd have to ramp up interest in the cowboy experience auction, get some attention on social media, and hope and pray that city people with deep pockets would be excited to fly to Texas.

Ross's tone was fatalistic. "I guess we'll all find out together."

"Thanks for the vote of confidence," she deadpanned, taking out her key as she prepared to head for her car on the other side of the parking lot.

There was a glass of brandy at home with her name on it. If she could make it through the mansion undetected by her father and whatever industry or political VIPs he was collaborating with tonight, she might just wrangle an hour of peace and quiet on her balcony overlooking the pool.

"I better get home to Lani," Asher said.

"Night," Gina murmured to her brothers, before turning to make the walk to her metallic blue convertible.

As she approached with her fob, the lock on her car clicked open automatically. She then caught sight of Rafe angling his way to an SUV two stalls down. Gina knew she should thank him for supporting her on the auction, so she stopped and waited.

He slowed as he came up to her.

"Thanks," she said. "You didn't have to do that." In fact, she was still surprised that he had.

He wasn't even a rancher anymore, but he'd stepped up when nobody else was willing, getting the ball rolling instead of leaving her standing there.

His broad shoulders came up in a shrug beneath his nicely cut business suit. "Somebody had to do something."

"To help with the fundraising." That made sense.

"To save the princess from public humiliation."

His words shocked her to silence. What an appalling thing to say when she was trying to be polite.

"You're too accustomed to the free ride," he elaborated.

"Excuse me?" If he was so resentful of her, why had he even offered to help?

"You're used to people loving you unconditionally, so you go boldly forward wherever the muse takes you."

"I am *not*." Sure, she'd grown up in privilege, but she wasn't naive. She thought about her actions before she took them—all the time.

"Ah, Princess." He shook his head.

"Quit calling me that."

"Then quit being one."

"You act like I'm spoiled when I'm stepping up. I'm taking the lead to solve the problem," she pointed out.

"You call that taking the lead?"

"What else would you call it?"

"Suggesting an elaborate idea off the cuff."

"It was a *good* idea." She regretted stopping to thank him for his help. The big jerk sure didn't deserve it.

"It wasn't a *terrible* idea," he conceded.

"Well, I didn't hear you suggest anything better."

When he didn't answer, she felt emboldened.

"And *my* idea turned out to be the best."

He gave a slow smile at her declaration. "Were you also teacher's pet?"

She tensed. "Why are you criticizing me?"

"Because no one ever has. It was an idea, Gina. It's a decent idea. But it's going to take a whole lot more than the flicker inside your brain to pull this off."

"I never said I was finished." She got that there was more to do. She wasn't exactly sure how that more would happen, but that was step two.

"Yeah?" he said, widening his stance. "What are you going to do next?"

"I'm going…" Her mind started to work. They'd need liability insurance. A venue to hold the auction. And they'd need—

"Yes?" he prompted.

"Cowboys," she said, confident in her decision. "We

need more cowboys to increase the profits." Only ten had volunteered tonight.

"Where are you going to get them?"

Ha. She had an answer for that. "The TCC."

"Your daddy's out of favor with the members right now."

She was insulted again. "I'm not running to my father for help."

"You've lost your sheen at the TCC, too. Your whole family has. And a lot of those TCC guys don't even have working ranches anymore."

She leaned in, challenging him. "Are you going to stand there and shoot down all of my ideas?"

"I'm trying to help."

"Is *that* what you call it?"

He shifted slightly closer, and she picked up his woodsy scent. His big, tall form was imposing, his face ruggedly handsome, with that chiseled chin and the shadow of a beard, and those deep dark eyes that made his mood a mystery.

She would have guessed he was angry, but an energy also lurked in their depths. It looked more like excitement than ire. But maybe she was projecting. Because she was excited—no, *aroused*. And that wasn't good.

"I want you to succeed," he said, pulling her off the emotional tangent. It was frighteningly easy to get lost in Rafe's magnetism.

"By insulting me?" she asked.

"By grounding you in the real world."

"I'm grounded."

He chuckled at that. The rich sound cascaded around her, amplifying her attraction and threatening to distract her from the argument again.

She caught herself just in time. "Have you paid *any* attention for the last few weeks?"

His expression hardened, shadowed by the overhead light. "Believe me, Princess, I've paid plenty of attention."

"Then you know what I've been through."

"This isn't about you."

She stumbled over that. Gina knew his business was in trouble, and she hadn't meant to imply it was about her. She was trying to fix the problem, for all of them.

Rafe stepped even closer. "Take *that* as a lesson."

While she didn't exactly understand, she didn't want to admit it. So instead, she stood her ground while her brain struggled for a cogent response and her hormones galloped off with unbridled attraction.

He had a confident tilt to his chin, a hungry gleam in his eyes, but a softness to his full lips—especially the lower one—that made them kissable, *highly* kissable.

He bent slightly forward, then stopped. A heartbeat went by, and she could almost feel his hot lips graze hers. But then he straightened instead. He stepped back, and his words sounded far away. "Let me know if I can help some more."

She shook herself back to reality and to the unmistakable feeling she'd been bested at something. She couldn't quite put her finger on what.

"Uh…okay." It was the best she could come up with on the fly, her hormones still clouding her brain.

He seemed to focus on her forehead as he took another step away. "Night, Gina."

"Good night."

He turned for his vehicle then, long strides taking him effortlessly away.

She watched his smooth gait, firming her own legs beneath her, struggling to ascertain how he'd so easily hijacked her hormones and used them against her.

Then he paused at the driver's door and turned, looking back at her one more time as the night wind brushed her heated skin.

* * *

Rafe couldn't put his finger on what had happened last night. One minute he was teasing Gina Edmond about her ineptitude and inexperience, the next he was headed in for a kiss and fighting a sudden startling desire to haul her into the back seat of his SUV and—

"So, you just stood there and *let* him?" Matias's question brought Rafe back to the present as the two men crossed the RCW Steakhouse patio.

Rafe set the two Tex-Mex omelets he'd cooked up in the RCW kitchen on a dining table by the rail that bordered one of the town's greenbelts. The restaurant didn't open for another three hours, and it was still comfortably cool outside. Maples and oak trees dotted the lush grass and would shade the tables once afternoon rolled around.

Rafe sat on a padded chair, settling in. "He didn't stop to ask me before he did it."

Matias sat across from him, dropping utensils in the middle of the table and setting a steaming cup of coffee in front of each of them. "He had no right to just up and volunteer me."

"You got something better to do?" Rafe told himself he didn't care if his brother participated in the auction or not.

Gina would be disappointed, sure. But it wasn't up to Rafe to keep Gina Edmond happy, even if she did have the greatest smile west of New Orleans, or maybe it was west of Miami, probably even Rome.

"Yes," Matias said.

"Like what?"

Matias cut into his omelet. "Plenty of things—horse training, irrigation, tractor maintenance."

"We haven't even picked a date."

"It doesn't matter the date. I'm busy. Tell her no."

"Me? You tell her no." Not that Rafe wanted to give up a chance to see Gina again.

"I'm not good around pretty women." Matias took a bite of the omelet.

For some reason, Rafe was hit with a jolt of jealousy. "Pretty?"

Matias swallowed, then lifted his tall black coffee mug with the stylized RCW logo. "We *are* talking about Gina Edmond, right?"

"Yes." There was no other.

Matias gave a gesture with the cup that clearly said *then what are you talking about?*

His brother was right.

"You're fine around pretty women," Rafe said instead.

"If I'm making them happy, sure." A sly gleam came into Matias's eyes. "It's when I'm disappointing them—"

"And I *know* you've had plenty practice at that." With a satisfied grin, Rafe put a bite of the spicy omelet in his mouth, enjoying the results of his efforts. He was nowhere near JJ's caliber, but he could whip up a mean omelet.

"You'd know more about disappointing them than me," Matias retorted.

"No complaints," Rafe said. "Well, maybe a few complaints." With a self-deprecating grin, he took a swig of his hot coffee.

Matias chuckled.

"Just do it," Rafe said. "It'll take a day. Make a little money for the town. Show some community spirit."

His brother watched him for a moment. "You still feel it, don't you?"

"Feel what?"

"That you're not really one of them, not good enough, don't fit into the business leaders' clique in the chamber."

"I fit in fine," Rafe lied. "RCW is one of the top-rated, most successful restaurants in Royal. People come from Dallas for our T-bones, never mind the sambal shrimp. We had a write-up in *Southwestern Gourmet* just last month. They featured our cranberry apple pastry."

"Methinks the cowboy protests too much."

Rafe realized he had. "I was only making a point."

Matias's expression turned thoughtful, and he sobered. "Is that what you're so scared of losing?"

"I'm not scared." *Worried* was a better word.

But Matias kept following his line of thinking. "If the restaurant closes, you know you won't go personally bankrupt. And I don't think you care about Dad's opinion as much as you pretend you do."

"Would you want an I-told-you-so from Dad?"

"Nobody wants that." He was watching Rafe closely now. "But you can take it."

Rafe didn't like where this was leading, mostly because it was hitting close to home. He raised his voice for emphasis. "It's simple. I've put my heart and soul into this place. I don't want to lose my restaurant to bankruptcy."

Rafe caught a movement in the corner of his eye. He twisted his head to see JJ standing there.

"Sorry, boss," the chef said, turning to go. But there was no way he could have missed Rafe's statement.

"You heard that," Rafe said.

JJ looked back, disheartened. He nodded.

Rafe gave in to the inevitable. "Come and join us. Grab a coffee."

Matias exchanged a look with Rafe while JJ got himself a cup of coffee.

"He didn't know?" Matias asked unnecessarily.

"I was going to have to tell him sometime."

"Man," Matias said on the whoosh of a breath. He knew JJ was one of the foundational staff members at RCW. He'd worked almost as hard as Rafe to ensure its success. And unlike Rafe, JJ relied on a regular paycheck to support his mother and his extended family.

"I'm not going to let it happen," Rafe said to JJ as he sat down between them.

"But it's possible?" JJ asked, twisting his cup back and forth.

Matias took another bite of his omelet.

"Yes," Rafe admitted. "But the whole town's trying to dig everyone out of the financial hole."

"Even the Edmonds?" JJ asked, knowing as everyone else did that the Edmonds' fortune was legendary. "Will they take an equity stake in RCW?" He frowned at that. "It's none of my business, Rafe, but I don't think you want to get tangled up with that family."

"I'd listen to JJ," Matias chimed in.

"I'm not going into business with the Edmonds," Rafe stated firmly. Giving up a piece of RCW would be his very last choice of a solution. And Rusty Edmond was reputed to be cutthroat in business. "They're fundraising and donating to the cause. To start, there's an auction coming up."

"And that's where I came in," Matias said, setting down his fork, clearly preparing to leave.

"An auction?" JJ asked.

"It might be workable, and it might not." Rafe didn't really trust Gina to pull it off on her own, never mind turn it into the kind of marquee event they'd need to raise a serious amount of money. "A *cowboy experience* auction."

"With genuine ranchers," Matias put in with disgust. He pointed to himself and to Rafe. "Local sacrificial lamb cowboys who are apparently required to humiliate themselves on the auction block."

JJ ventured a little grin as he glanced between the two men. "Luckily, my Malaysian heritage is in fishing."

"You grew up in Maverick County," Matias said.

"Not on horseback," JJ countered.

"You're worrying way too much about doing it," Rafe said to his brother. "Chill. It'll take one day, tops."

"Will it help recoup our losses?" JJ asked.

"Yes," Rafe said, silently hoping so.

"Then saddle up, cowboy," JJ told Matias. "We've got a business to save."

Gina was pondering Rafe's advice, even though he'd given it sarcastically. She'd sat out on her bedroom balcony and thought through the mechanics of pulling off an auction. And to her consternation, she'd come up with about a hundred moving parts.

Her degree was in business administration with a major in marketing. But she'd never had to put any of her skills to use. She came home from college to a guaranteed job in the family oil company with an executive assistant, a spacious office and very little work to do. She'd eventually fallen into the habit of reading company reports, attending board meetings, taking long lunches and asking very few questions, since her father kept an iron grip on operations, they had excellent employees, and the company was thriving without her participation.

Since she'd never managed a real project before, she'd spent this entire morning strategizing a plan of action and then formulating a task list that had eventually frightened her, since about ten different things had to happen right away.

Resisting an urge to throw a dart to choose her starting point, she settled on Mandee Meriweather. The host of the celebrity gossip show, *Royal Tonight!*, was far from Gina's favorite TV personality, but she was popular and could bring the event some much-needed publicity.

She drove directly to the studio and approached the reception counter on the ground floor, giving the middle-aged woman sitting there a bright smile. "Good morning. I wanted to talk to someone about *Royal Tonight!*"

The receptionist gave her a critical up-and-down look.

Gina was wearing a lightweight sleeveless dress, pure white on top, snug in the bodice, with a kicky flared skirt in a flowing autumn leaf pattern that grew denser and bolder toward the hem. She'd paired it with classic cream-colored heeled sandals and a few pieces of plain gold jewelry, except for her earrings, which were a cascade of jade beads set in gold, nicely balancing the highlights of the leaves. Her brunette hair was left free and flowing, and she'd tucked her sunglasses on top of her head.

She had no idea why the woman was frowning.

"We don't directly hire talent," the receptionist said.

"I'm not here—"

"Do you have an appointment?" the receptionist asked.

"No. I have a proposal for—"

"I'm sorry, you'll have to call for an appointment."

"Call?" Gina was standing right here.

"Or you can go to our website royaltonight-dot-com."

"To make an appointment?" Did the process need to be that convoluted?

"To submit your portfolio."

Gina calmed her annoyance. "I'm not here looking for a job. I'd like to make an appointment with whoever schedules shows for *Royal Tonight!*"

The woman heaved a heavy sigh. Then she extracted a business card and pushed it across the reception counter to Gina. "If you don't want to use the website, then call this number."

Gina heard the door open behind her. "You can't book me an appointment now?"

"All appointments are done through central booking." The receptionist's attention moved past Gina. "Can I help you with something?" She put on a welcoming smile to greet the new arrival.

Gina looked sideways to see a crisply dressed, serious-looking thirtysomething woman.

The woman handed the receptionist a business card. "I'm Taylor Millen from Kuntz and Walker. I was wondering if one of the marketing reps had time for a quick chat."

The receptionist picked up her phone and pressed a few buttons.

Ms. Millen gave Gina a nod, and Gina nodded back.

"Do you have time for a walk-in?" the receptionist asked into the phone. She waited a minute. "Thank you, Peter." She put down the phone and pointed to a hallway to the right of the reception area. "You can go right in. Third door on the left."

"Thank you so much," Taylor said before moving on her way.

The receptionist looked back at Gina, her expression making it clear she wondered why Gina was still there.

She wondered that, too. Why was she still cooling her heels in the reception area? Was she not a walk-in? Maybe she needed a business card. Better still, she should get herself a no-nonsense navy blue suit and a pair of glasses.

She pocketed the card with the phone number and headed out to the sidewalk, deciding to give up on the receptionist and just call. Hopefully, she could book an appointment for today or tomorrow.

Three voice mail messages later, with no idea when they'd call back, Gina sat in her car, tapping her thumbs on the steering wheel. She'd blown most of her first morning on the auction project, and she had practically nothing to show for it.

She thought about cowboys. But that made her think about Rafe. She didn't want to think about Rafe, especially after their near-kiss last night...

She shook the image of him from her mind, backing further up in the evening to her conversation with Ross and Asher. But thinking of Ross and Asher made her think about her father and how she hadn't yet told him about the auction. She promised herself she'd do that tonight, after dinner, after he'd had a bourbon or two. Then she moved on.

Her next thought was of Lila, and she knew she was onto something useful. The woman would be her next stop. Gina pushed the button to start her car.

Ten blocks and one pit stop at Angelo's Pizzeria later, she was pulling into the Chamber of Commerce parking lot. She went through the main entrance to reception, hoping to find Lila in her office.

It was nearing one o'clock and the admin area was empty, but she found Lila's open office door and knocked.

Lila looked up from her computer and seemed surprised. "Gina?"

Gina gave an apologetic smile and held up the large pizza box and two soft drinks. "Lunch?" she asked.

Lila pushed back from her computer, beaming then. "A woman after my own heart."

"I'm here to pick your brain," she admitted. "I hope you don't mind."

"Does that pizza have pepperoni on it?"

"The works, plus extra cheese."

"Then my brain is all yours." Lila gestured to a small round table in the corner of her office. She cleared away a few files and put them on her desk. "Smells amazing."

Gina set the pizza box in the middle of the table and peeled back the lid.

Lila helped herself to a slice and they each opened a soda. "So, what's up?"

"Two questions," Gina said while Lila took a bite, then made a comical face of ecstasy.

Her phone rang, but she waved it off and swallowed. "It'll go to voice mail. Go ahead."

"First, what would my authority be to organize and execute the auction?"

"Good question. I mean, nobody really said at the meeting. But it *was* your idea. And you're arranging the liability insurance." Lila shrugged. "I'd say, go for it."

"You're saying nobody'll stop me if I take the helm?"

"I don't see why they would."

Gina chalked that one up as a win. She lifted a slice of the gooey pizza, looking forward to diving in. "Then, second, I need people to take me seriously."

"Who's not taking you seriously?"

Voices sounded in the reception area as people obviously returned from lunch.

"Hang on a second." Lila rose to close the door. Then she returned to sit back down.

The two women ate and drank in silence for a few minutes before they got down to business.

"So, who needs to take you seriously?" Lila asked as she went in for a second slice.

"I went down to the *Royal Tonight!* studio this morning. I thought we could get Mandee Meriweather to MC the auction."

"That's a really good idea."

"I couldn't get past the receptionist." Gina rolled her eyes. "She thought I was an actress looking for a job."

Lila took in Gina's outfit. "That's because you're so pretty."

Gina knew it was more than that. "You're pretty, maybe prettier than me. *Lots* of women are pretty. But everyone respects you."

Lila seemed to consider. "Maybe it's a glam thing. You've got a flare, a style."

"So do you."

"My glam look is really new." Gina recalled how Lila had undergone a transformation this summer as she became active on social media.

"I was thinking I should get a pair of glasses."

"You need glasses?" the other woman asked.

"No. They'd be clear, but they'd give me, you know, an intellectual look."

"Maybe," Lila said, tilting her head sideways as she considered Gina. "But I think it's more of an attitude."

"Could you teach me that? The attitude?" Gina wiped her glistening fingertips on her paper napkin.

"Okay…here's the thing." Lila rocked her head, like she was thinking hard. "Am I going to insult you?"

Gina braced herself. "Go ahead…give it to me with both barrels. No, wait!" She took another slice of pizza. "Okay. Now."

Lila laughed. "It's not how you look. Okay, it's a little bit how you look. I wouldn't get glasses. I might rethink the dress and the earrings—for the purpose of business, that's all. They look *great* on you. But maybe separates? Or solid colors?"

Gina nodded. She could do that…and wouldn't even need to go shopping. Her closet was full of all kinds of different pieces, some she'd never worn.

"Attitude, too. How do I say this? Don't depend on… guys wanting to buy you a drink."

Gina drew back, a little bit insulted. "I don't try to get men to buy me drinks."

"But they do."

Yeah, Gina would admit that, always of their own volition. But she nodded again.

"You've spent your whole life being charming."

"And nothing else?" Gina guessed that's how the sentence ended.

Lila gave a grimace. "Yeah, here's the part where I might insult you."

"Wait. We haven't gotten there yet?" Now Gina really braced herself.

"It's more what you do."

"I haven't done anything."

Lila grimaced again.

Oh, ouch. "And it shows."

"Not so much shows in that people can see it on you, but you don't have a reputation for getting things done. You haven't built up credibility, made connections, gained people's trust."

"Too busy being charming, huh?"

Lila shrugged. "Too busy doing what's worked for you your whole life. Nobody blames you for that."

"It sounds like you do."

Now it was Lila who looked like she was bracing herself.

"No," Gina said. "I'm not mad. I'm…disappointed, in *me*. Because you're right."

"You succeeded in your world, probably because you're smart. But if you want to succeed in a different world—and that's what I'm hearing—you need to be smart in a different way. Stop depending on your charm and your looks and your family connections. Hone some of your other tools."

Gina considered what those tools might be. "I took a project management course in college. I can write a critical path."

"That's good. But there's one particular best-in-class, beats-everything tool you'll need."

Gina was all ears. "What's that?"

"Hard work."

"But, I do—" Gina cut herself off. If she was already working hard, she wouldn't have this problem. And that was Lila's point. "Wow."

"You took that better than I thought," Lila said.

"I won't say it didn't pinch."

"You barely flinched."

"Hard work," Gina repeated, thinking the theory was so simple, but the execution would take work, and that work would be hard. She almost laughed at herself for the circular thinking.

"You just look around and pick up whatever needs doing."

"*Cowboys* are what needs doing." Gina grimaced. "Wait, that didn't come out right."

Lila laughed.

Gina elaborated. "First steps are to find enough cowboys for the auction. Also, to get Mandee Meriweather to agree to MC."

"You're off to the races," Lila said, giving a mock air toast with her slice of pizza. "Or, in this case, more like off to the roundup."

Four

Rafe heard Gina was failing miserably with the local cowboys. He got wind of the rumor from Lorenzo, then from Matias. Same story, two sources, only difference was that Matias was happy about the potential cancellation of the auction.

Rafe understood the business community was in trouble, and the ranchers were being asked to step up—again. He didn't think it was up to him to save Gina Edmond. But then he spotted her coming out of the *Royal Tonight!* studios looking dejected, like she'd just had something else go off the rails.

Questioning his own sanity, he swung his SUV into a parking spot at the sidewalk next to her shiny sports car.

She didn't look up, so he opened the driver's door and stepped outside to get her attention.

Gina saw him then and froze like a deer in the headlights.

He couldn't imagine why. Their last interaction had been spirited, sure, but it had also been fun, at least for him. He'd found himself attracted to her beyond her looks, which were obviously spectacular. But he also liked her spunk, her buoyant style, her intelligence and her ability to spar with him.

He'd wanted to kiss her that night, to kiss her and so much more, and he'd wanted it pretty bad. But she didn't know that. She wasn't a mind reader.

"Hey, Gina," he said, giving her a casual nod in greeting.

"Hi." She didn't move, so he shut his door and approached her, stepping up on the sidewalk.

"How's the auction coming along?" He knew the answer was "terrible," but he didn't want to let on that he'd been listening to gossip.

"I'm working hard," she said defensively.

He was sure she thought she was. And maybe that was the truth. She'd certainly approached a whole lot of ranchers the past couple of days.

He nodded to the *Royal Tonight!* studio. "Are they on board?"

She followed the direction of his gaze with her own. Her answer was subdued. "Not yet."

"Why not?"

She squared her shoulders like she was gearing up for battle dressed in her slim gray dress and fitted jacket. The outfit was adorned with matte silver buttons, giving it a slightly military air. Her hair was swept back in a loose knot revealing a pair of tiny twister-silver hoop earrings.

She tossed her head. "The small size of the event. At least that's what they claim."

"You need more cowboys to auction?" he guessed, going with logic as well as what he'd learned from his brothers.

"I've talked to most of the ranchers in Maverick County, even went over to Colonial. They're not willing to volunteer their property or their cowboys."

"Did you go dressed like that?" he asked.

She looked down at herself. "No. Not exactly. And what's wrong with this?"

"You look…"

"Professional?"

"Staid, uptight."

"No. I look *professional*," she told him archly. "I already went over this with Lila."

Rafe let the Lila comment slide, since it wasn't his central point, even though he was curious about what the other woman might have said. "They're ranchers, not bankers."

"I don't care who they are, looking competent and capable is important."

"So is looking approachable, respectful, like an actual human being."

Gina scowled at him. "Did you stop me just to insult me?"

"No. I stopped you to help you."

She let out a strangled laugh.

"When in Rome, Gina." He raised his eyebrow to drive home his point.

"I'm not going to pretend to be a rancher. Do you not think they'd see right through that?"

"I'm not saying fake anything. But with your pedigree, your…" He paused to frame the right words. "Bearing and attitude, when you march up to a rancher's front door looking like *this*, you can't expect them to give you the time of day." He realized his voice had grown louder and glanced around the quiet sidewalk to make sure no one had overheard.

She didn't respond, but she looked even more miserable.

"Gina."

"Is this you gloating?"

"No. It's me helping," he answered.

"You have a ridiculous way of helping."

"I'm being honest."

"You're being *insulting*."

He could see this was getting them nowhere. "What about this? Let me pick your wardrobe."

She opened her mouth to speak, but he bowled right over her. "And I'll come with you to see the ranchers, and we'll try again."

She shut her mouth, peering at him with suspicion.

"No trick," he assured her, holding his palms up. "I want this to work." He *did* want it to work—for him, for the other businesses, for Royal itself, and even for Gina.

"Why?" she asked.

"For the sake of Royal. Come on." He gestured to his SUV. "Let's find you a pair of blue jeans that cost something less than an average mortgage payment."

"My jeans don't cost—" She stopped mid-sentence, and her expression turned perplexed.

"You don't know the amount." It was both funny and sad at the same time. Rafe rounded to the passenger side of the vehicle and opened the door, gesturing her in.

"I…"

"Which of them eludes you?" He genuinely wanted to know. "The cost of an average mortgage payment or the price of your blue jeans?"

She lifted her chin and marched his way. "Neither."

"Oh, Gina."

She paused beside him and looked up. "Don't *oh, Gina* me. I know things. They're just different things. And I'm still learning…"

She was too delightful for him to stay frustrated with for long. It was her superpower. Plus, he believed she truly was trying. A guy had to give her points for that.

Inside the SUV, he doubled back along Cedar Street and turned onto Silversmith Road.

"We're not going to the Courtyard Shops?"

"No, Princess."

"You want me to start calling you Cowpoke?"

Rafe shrugged. "Call me whatever you want."

"Okay, *Cowpoke*. I don't even know what you expect to find for clothes at this end of town."

Rafe knew exactly where he was going.

A few miles later, he pulled into the parking lot of a strip mall.

"Mama's Subs?" Gina read one of the signs. "Black Peak Appliance Repair? Sheila's Dog Grooming?" She turned to him. "Is there a joke in this somewhere?"

Rafe nodded directly in front of them.

Gina looked. "Second Chance Shelf?" The name sank in and her eyes went wide. *"What?"*

"You can't stagger up to a ranch house in a pair of brand-new blue jeans. They have to look lived-in."

"I'm not wearing someone else's clothes."

"Relax. They wash them before they resell them."

"No, Rafe. No freaking way. This is a showstopper for me."

He shut off the engine anyway. "You're *seriously* going to stop the show over this?"

"Yes."

"It's not like I'm asking you to ride a bull or eat a bug."

She slid her gaze his way. "Eat a bug?"

"The clothes are clean. They're fine. And you're wearing underwear." He paused then, taking in the flinch in her expression. "You are wearing underwear, right?"

"Yes, I'm wearing underwear." But the look on her face made him wonder just how flimsy that underwear might be.

He was forced to shake off several enticing images. "We don't have time for this."

"Good. Let's go."

"I mean, we don't have time to mess around. Businesses are getting more stressed by the day, and I can't see you keeping up the enthusiasm for this project forever. You need to sign up participants, nail Mandee down and find yourself a venue."

"We're using the Elegance Ranch."

That answer caught him off guard. "Does Rusty know?"

Gina's father was an intensely elitist and private person. Rafe couldn't see him agreeing to let his ranch be used for an auction that would be broadcast across the country, especially now with his family under such intense scrutiny.

"Not yet," she said.

"You are bold. And you're brave. And I can't believe

you're going to let a little thing like wearing used blue jeans stop you from making this work." He had her with that argument. He *knew* he had her.

She gave him a glare, and he opened the driver's door, sliding out with the certainty that she'd follow.

She did.

Gina stared in the cracked and pitted sliver of a mirror inside the tiny changing cubicle of Second Chance Shelf.

"The red plaid is way too much," she called through the thin curtain.

"Show me," Rafe called back.

She whipped open the curtain to make her point. In the faded boyfriend-style blue jeans, the scuffed, tooled leather cowboy boots and the bright red plaid flannel shirt, she looked like someone from a sitcom.

She stepped out and spread her arms wide. "See?"

Rafe grinned. "It's not that bad."

"It's comical, satirical, mortifying."

"The shirt is a bit of overkill."

"A *bit*?"

"The jeans are okay." He walked around to look at her from other angles. "And the boots work."

The light brown leather boots were surprisingly comfortable, worn but not shabby, with low, blocky heels. It had been a while since she'd worn shoes that had this much stability. They'd be good for crossing gravel driveways and uneven pastures. The jeans were faded an attractive pale blue with white top stitching. They were loose in the calves, low-waisted, soft against her thighs even though she'd bet they didn't have a stitch of Lycra fabric to give them stretch.

"Try the one with the flowers," Rafe suggested. He'd sent her into the changing room with four different shirts.

"The appliqué? No, thanks."

"It's cute."

"I'm not going for cute."

"Yes, you are."

She gave him a look that was half frown, half glare.

"They're cowboys, Gina, not critics at Fashion Week."

"What do you know about Fashion Week?"

"Enough to know it doesn't have Western wear."

"Fine." She'd decided humoring Rafe was her best move forward, so she gritted her teeth and did just that.

It was easy to see she wouldn't get any more local cowboys on board by herself. For better or worse, Rafe was her best bet to change their minds. And if she could recruit a few more cowboys, then she could get Mandee on board, and then she'd have a fighting chance of pulling this whole thing off.

She flounced back into the cubicle, pulled the curtain and stripped off the red shirt.

The flowered shirt felt like it was almost new. But the style was outrageous.

He gazed at her critically for a moment. "Let's call that plan B."

"Let's call it plan H."

"The snake print?" he suggested.

"I wasn't even going to try that one on."

"Come on. Be a sport."

"Fine. If only to prove you wrong."

"Go ahead. Prove me wrong. I dare you."

Back in the cubicle again, she stripped down to her cream-colored lace bra and slipped into the slinky fabric of the silver-and-blue snakeskin shirt. It felt embarrassingly supple against her skin, whisper-thin without being at all translucent.

She moved, twisting from one side to the other, watching the light play off the subtle pattern. She didn't *hate* it. She'd give it that.

"Come on out," Rafe called.

She pulled back the curtain.

He gazed for a moment. "Now all you need is a ponytail and we can have a little fun."

"Hard work," she muttered to herself as she turned in the mirrored, checking over her shoulder to see how it looked from behind. "But a critical path is a critical path."

"Did you just say I was on your critical path?" He was suddenly closer, and the timbre of his voice rumbled through her.

She turned and they came face-to-face. Her chest tightened as a now-familiar surge of desire rose within her.

"I said…" She lost her train of thought.

"Yeah?" he prompted. There was no denying the heat in his dark eyes.

She searched her brain for logic. "Cowboys." She landed on it. "Cowboys are on my critical path."

"I'm a cowboy." He quirked a half smile, and her desire ramped up further.

Did the man have to look so kissable?

"*New* cowboys…for the auction." She felt like she was subtly swaying his way, but she couldn't tell if it was an illusion.

"So, not me," he said. "At least not here. Not right now."

She didn't really understand the question. If it even *was* a question.

He touched the fabric at her shoulder, rubbing it between his fingertips. "Soft." Then his fingers rested lightly on her shoulder, warm through the fabric. "I want to kiss you, you know."

Gina had no response for that. She didn't want to say no, but she was afraid to say yes.

He brushed her cheek with the pad of his thumb. Then he glanced around at the other shoppers. "But that's going to have to wait."

Wait? As in, later? As in, he was planning to kiss her at some point in the future?

It seemed like something she should shut down right away, refuse to be drawn into. She should tell him a kiss between them wasn't going to happen now—or ever. But her focus was on his dark lips, imagining them against her own, hot, tender, probing.

Oh, man. This was going to be—

"So, we're agreed?" he asked.

"On the kiss?"

His grin went wide, flashing white with obvious amusement. "On the shirt."

Mortification suffused her. "Right." She swallowed then stepped back and turned away. "I'll go change."

His hand shot out to cup her shoulder.

She paused and looked back, and the air crackled between them.

"The kiss, too," he said with a meaningful lift of his brow.

Fourteen ranches and twenty cowboys later, Gina was beaming in the passenger seat as they whizzed back down the highway. Their windows were open and fresh wheatgrass-scented air billowed through the SUV.

Rafe was happy to be done and heading back to Royal. The sun was setting, and he had kissing Gina on his mind.

"That's thirty in all," she said, satisfaction in her voice.

It was odd, but she seemed to have grown into the casual clothes over the course of the day. She looked sexier than ever slouched down in the seat, wisps of her brunette hair blowing loose around her face.

"That sounds good," he said.

"It's the perfect number. There's some duplication in the ranches, sure. The Nester Ranch has three cowboys participating. But that place is huge. We'll be able to get a ton of different still shots to sell it on the website."

Rafe knew his presence had helped the effort. His family was familiar with everyone in the community. At some point in his life, he'd either worked with or partied with every rancher in both Maverick and Colonial Counties. The fact that he was enthusiastically participating in the auction had gone a long way toward boosting their confidence in the project.

But that didn't detract from Gina's effort. Once she'd calmed down a little and taken some of the intensity out of her pitch, she'd done well with the ranchers. They were great people, and invariably ready to step up for their neighbors.

"Two Cortez-Williams cowboys, too," he noted.

"I'll never forget that you were first."

He glanced momentarily her way. "I wasn't looking for gratitude."

"I know. But none of this would have happened without you. On both fronts."

"You did good back there," he told her honestly. "Once you relaxed."

"I was nervous. Some of those guys had already turned me down."

"But you got right back on the horse."

"I did." She gave a nod. "Mandee Meriweather will *have* to admit it's worthwhile now."

"That can wait until tomorrow." It was coming up on eight o'clock in the evening. "You hungry? We could stop in Joplin."

She sat up straight. "Ooh. Have you ever been to Custom Creekside?"

He gave her a sidelong look of incredulity. "You're asking a restaurant owner if he's checked out the competition?"

"When you put it that way… I guess you have."

"That's right. So you want to hop in the back seat and turn yourself into the real Gina?" He wasn't anxious for her to do that, but her dress and jacket were in the back of the SUV if she wanted to change for the upscale restaurant.

She seemed to hesitate.

"Or we could stop at the Twin Bears instead," he said.

"I've never been there."

Her answer didn't surprise him. "Burgers and milk-shakes. All homemade, great stuff."

She pulled down the sun visor and checked out her face in the little mirror. "I'm definitely beyond repair."

She looked gorgeous to him.

"Twin Bears it is," she said, flipping the mirror back up.

Rafe was glad to hear that, because he wanted Gina to stay exactly the way she was.

Five miles down the road, he swung onto Blackbird Boulevard. The Twin Bears was on the edge of town, well away from the upscale shops and restaurants. It had a big parking lot with wide spaces to accommodate pickup trucks and family-friendly SUVs.

Gina recombed and refastened her ponytail before they left the vehicle.

They crossed the lot to a covered porch and a set of wide wood-beamed doors that were the main entrance. He grasped the oversize handle to pull the door open and let Gina go in first.

The Twin Bears was a lively place with a big square bar in the center that had seating all around it. Polished wood tables with rounded burgundy leather chairs were nicely spaced throughout the rest of the big dining room. Two of the walls were dotted with windows, showcasing minia-ture palm tree gardens with little white lights that were just coming on in the dusk.

It was a seat yourself kind of place, and Rafe led them to a table against a brick feature wall.

A waitress immediately appeared to fill two red-tinted water glasses with a stream of ice water.

"Can I get y'all something to drink?" she asked.

Rafe looked to Gina.

"What should I try?" she surprised him by asking.

"I'm getting an Irish Freeze. It's a coffee, caramel, whiskey milkshake."

"Our most popular," the young waitress said. She handed Gina a slim drink menu. "But we've got Guinness and Baileys, peach bourbon, coconut chocolate rum, and boozy banana cream."

"Think I'll go with the favorite," Gina said with a smile and handed back the menu. "When in Rome." Her gaze turned to Rafe and went warm.

Which had him thinking about their kiss again.

The waitress handed them each a food menu and disappeared.

"Do I even need to look at this?" Gina asked him. "Or can I count on your expertise?"

"I'm getting a loaded Angus burger with wedge fries— messy sauce, but well worth it."

She didn't hesitate. "You haven't led me wrong so far today."

"You're having an Angus burger?" He couldn't hide his surprise.

She hadn't struck him as a messy burger kind of woman. Then again, she hadn't stuck him as a milkshake kind of gal, either. She was slender and, well, to be blunt, pretty fussy. He'd have expected her to look for a kale and responsibly harvested seafood salad.

"Sure," she said, a challenge in her expression.

"Is this the clothes?" he asked with a thread of humor. "Did they magically change Gina Edmond from a princess to a cowgirl?"

"This princess has a lot of layers to her."

The waitress arrived with their drinks, and Rafe placed

their dinner order. Afterward, Gina took a sip of her milk-shake, and her eyes went wide.

"Good?" he asked.

"*Amazing.* I don't usually indulge in things like this."

"Imagine my surprise."

"Hey."

"I took you for a cabernet sauvignon hundred-point grand cru kind of woman."

"Now you're just baiting me," she accused.

"A little," he admitted. "But tell me it's not true. Tell me your daddy's wine cellar isn't full of old-world wines from the very best years of overpriced vineyards."

"I wouldn't know."

"Not a wine person?" That surprised him.

"I drink whatever the chef pours."

Rafe couldn't help but laugh. "The was the snobbiest defense of snobbery I've ever heard."

"I meant I don't spend any time in *Daddy's* wine cellar."

"I know. But you have to admit…"

She took another sip of her milkshake. "I don't have to admit anything to you. I think you have wine envy."

"Me?" He hated that it came out like a weak question instead of a strong denial. He hated it more that she was right. He'd kill for Rusty Edmond's wine cellar.

"No restaurant can compete with a private collection," she allowed. "Unless you've got nothing but millionaires as your clientele."

"We've been increasing and improving our selection."

She looked guilty. "I shouldn't have picked on you."

Great. Now he had her pity. How had *that* happened?

"I have plenty of fine wines at RCW."

"And I have a terrific milkshake." She stirred it with her straw.

Their burgers arrived then, hot and fragrant on huge wooden platters.

She looked the half-pound monstrosity up and down. It was layered with tomatoes, lettuce, mushrooms and Twin Bears' famous sauce.

Rafe could see she was overwhelmed.

He lifted the sharp wood-handled knife from his cutlery selection. "Want me to cut it in half for you?"

"Yes, please."

He reached across the table and sliced through her burger.

"I don't depend on my dad for everything," she said as she wrapped a paper napkin over the rounded edge of a burger half.

"Who said you did?"

"You implied it."

He lifted his burger from the sides, knowing the sauce would drip onto his plate. "You're the precious daughter of a town legend. Everybody thinks you've had an easy ride."

"In some ways I suppose I have," she agreed.

"Current situation notwithstanding," Rafe concurred. "But even with the embezzlement, your family's in better shape than most." He took a first bite of the juicy burger. It was as delicious as he'd remembered.

"And I'm trying to do my part to help the town."

Rafe nodded his agreement with that.

Gina took a first bite. Like she had with the milkshake, her eyes lit up with appreciation. "Mmm."

"Right? And you don't even have to dress up for it." He looked around at the other patrons, all casually dressed, many of them families. And then turned to take in the cheerful waitstaff moving efficiently from table to table amid the hum of friendly conversation.

"It's a nice place," Gina agreed. "Laid-back, relaxed."

"You don't do this often?" Rafe couldn't help but ask.

"Eat hamburgers?"

"Relax."

The question seemed to stump her. "How do you mean?"

"Take time for yourself...enjoy some peace and quiet, a little comfort food, maybe read a book."

"You do know where I live, right?" It was a rhetorical question.

He answered anyway. "The infamous Elegance Ranch."

"Not exactly a hotbed of casual peace and quiet," she told him, taking another draw on her milkshake. "Wow. This is sinfully tasty."

He thought about warning her that it packed a punch but decided against it. At the same time, he flagged the waitress for a cup of coffee so he could switch to a nonalcoholic beverage. "No privacy?" he prompted her.

"CEOs of major oil companies don't punch out at five o'clock."

"You're not a CEO of a major oil company."

"I live with one, and I work for one."

"It bleeds into your homelife?"

"It's no secret that my dad isn't one for big social gatherings. But he does his share of schmoozing."

"You'd have to at his level," Rafe reasoned. He himself made sure to stay in touch with industry organizations and his fellow restaurateurs, also with suppliers and marketing influencers.

Locking eyes with him, she took another drink. She'd made it about halfway through her burger and eaten quite a few of the fries.

He was surprised she'd done that well, given the size of the meal and the size of her. "Can I ask you something?"

"Go for it." She picked up another crispy fry. "These things are addictive."

"What do you do in the evenings when your father is entertaining business associates?"

"Smile," she said.

"And?"

"Nod. I nod a lot."

"I thought you had a job with the company."

"I do."

"What's your title?"

She hesitated a moment before answering. "Senior vice president of corporate relations."

"Relations with who?"

Her lighthearted mood abruptly disappeared. "Are you done? Should we get going?"

Five

Gina might be on the move now, but it was hardly smooth sailing.

Mandee Meriweather and *Royal Tonight!* were now on board for the auction, and Gina had thirty-two cowboys signed up—since two more had called after the recruitment drive. She also had her full project plan mapped out on her laptop. But she had a long way to go on plan implementation, and a very tough sales pitch to make to her father.

As she entered the reception hall of the Elegance Ranch, with its cool marble floor and twin curving wrought iron staircases leading to the second floor, she could hear her father's voice from the library through the carved wooden archway. She hoped whoever was with him this evening wouldn't stay long. Their conversation was going to be difficult, and she wanted to get it over with.

"That is *not* what I wanted to hear," her father complained.

Great. He was in a mood. Then again, when wasn't he in a mood lately?

Nobody answered, but that didn't stop him from continuing. "He didn't just disappear into thin air. Can we not get the FBI involved?" Rusty went silent for a minute. "That's what I'm paying you *top* dollar for. To get me results."

Gina guessed he was on the phone, presumably talking to the private investigation firm he'd hired to look for Billy. Rusty wasn't ready to admit Billy was his son from a long-ago affair with Antoinette Holmes. But Billy's social media posts were getting increasingly darker.

He claimed to have become Ross's college roommate

and confidant to use what he learned about the Edmond family to worm his way in. It was a revenge plot years in the making and a thousand lies in its execution, and Gina felt sick every time she discovered something new.

She considered going up to her room and talking to her father later. But she'd steeled herself for this conversation, and she wanted to get it over with. She dropped her purse on a side table and waited for the phone call to end.

"See that you do," Rusty all but shouted into the phone. "I'll be waiting on an answer."

Silence reigned until the library's grandfather clocked bonged the hour. Gina waited a minute longer before walking briskly into the richly furnished wood-paneled room to find her father standing in front of the main bookshelf, next to the spotless cherrywood desk.

"Hello, Dad."

"You're home." He seemed surprised to see her and not particularly happy.

She didn't seek him out often these days. Not that he'd ever been her favorite conversational partner or had ever paid much attention to her one way or the other.

"There's something I'd like to talk to you about," she said.

His gaze narrowed. "I don't need any more bad news."

"It's not bad news. It's good news." She plowed forward before he had a chance to react. "Ross told you we were planning a fundraising auction for the business community?"

Rusty frowned at her. "He certainly told me you'd pledged Edmond money for it."

"Some," she said. "The three of us all agreed."

"I don't remember agreeing."

"Dad."

"Don't *Dad* me."

"Billy was—"

"*Not* my son, that's what Billy is," her father snapped.
"Billy was our responsibility."

"And how do you figure that?"

Gina realized she'd made a tactical error. Talk of Billy was only going to infuriate her father.

She quickly backtracked. "I wanted to talk some more about the auction."

His glare would ordinarily have stopped her.

"Yes, we pledged some family money," she continued. "And it was the right thing to do. The Edmond family has always been a huge part of the local business community. I was always told, by you, that we prided ourselves on our participation. As far back as I can remember, you said we were pivotal to the success of the town."

He waved a dismissive hand, but he didn't outright disagree.

"The auction is a good idea. Lots of people are buying in. Thirty-two cowboys have stepped up, and *Royal Tonight!* is going to broadcast the program. Mandee Meriweather has even agreed to host." Gina could tell she had her father's interest.

Mandee was flamboyant and attention-seeking, but Gina always had the impression her father admired the on-air host. She'd assumed it was because the woman could be influential. The three things Rusty admired most were money, power and influence.

"We expect to make good money on it," Gina said. "But we need a location for the live broadcast."

"They have a studio."

"That's way too small and not nearly enough pizzazz."

"*Pizzazz?*"

"We need thousands, tens of thousands of people to tune in to watch the broadcast and log in online. We need an interesting location, a magnificent location to help draw them in."

"Did you have a specific place in mind?"

"Yes," she murmured.

"And where would that be?"

"The Elegance Ranch."

Her father stared at her, looking more perplexed than angry. But then her meaning seemed to sink in. *"What!?"*

The force of his question nearly made her step back.

"Have you lost your mind?" he demanded.

She stood her ground. "It would be perfect. We could use the back patio, the lawn for seating, the pool gazebos as a balancing feature…"

"No! Absolutely not. TV cameras? In the house? What are you even *thinking*?"

The reaction was pretty much what Gina had expected, but she wasn't done yet. "It's not like we'd film in your bedroom."

Rusty's mouth moved, but no sounds came out. At the same time, his face turned a comical red color.

"And it's not as if the family secrets are just lying out there on the coffee tables for anyone to see," she said.

He found his voice. "We don't have secrets."

"Great. Then there's no reason not to let the world see a little bit of life behind the scenes." She made a small space between her thumb and forefinger. "Just a little bit of our magnificent house."

"No."

"It's for a good cause."

"Do it at the Cattleman's Club."

"Nobody's going to tune in to see the Cattleman's Club, but the Elegance Ranch…now that would be an audience draw."

"Ghoulish curiosity," Rusty said with disgust.

"Take away a little of the mystery," she said. "Show them we're a normal, functional, happy family."

He tilted his head in obvious incomprehension.

"We can pull it off," she cajoled. "People will be too busy looking at the furniture, the sculptures and the paintings to pay much attention to the people. And if we show them the wine cellar?"

"The *wine* cellar?"

"Okay, maybe not the wine cellar. It's so big, we'd look like we overindulged in liquor every night. But the reception hall, the great room, the patio and yard, and here." She gestured around the library. "The most personal we'd get is the kitchen and dining room. It'll make us look more ordinary. It might tone down some of the gossip."

He didn't respond for a minute, and she grew hopeful. Had her reasoning worked on him? "Just think about it."

"Where did you even come up with such an asinine—"

"Dad?" Ross appeared in the archway.

The tension remained between father and son, but it was diminishing as the weeks went past.

Ross glanced between Gina and Rusty, taking in their posture and expressions. "What's going on?"

Rusty rounded on his son. "Will you talk some sense into your sister?"

Ross looked to Gina.

"I'm asking about holding the auction here," she said.

Comprehension came into his eyes.

Gina put a pleading look into her own. She needed her brother's support on this. "We have everyone on board. It's going to work, Ross. I *know* it is. We just have to have a stellar location to bring it all together."

"Elegance Ranch is not some tacky Hollywood film location," Rusty groused.

Gina bit her tongue. "We need a big audience," she said, spreading her arms wide. "The bigger the better. That's how we get the bidding up high. That's how we make real money. That's how we save Royal businesses."

"But does it have to be here?" Ross asked. "Surely another venue besides our family home can—"

"No!" Gina cut in. "No. I don't ask for much around here.

I show up when the rest of you need me. I smile. I nod. I don't push my ideas in the company. Even when I think of something—even when I see opportunities—I keep my mouth shut because that seems to be the way everyone wants it. But *I* want this. I *need* this. This is *my* project, and last time I checked, this was my house, too."

She stopped talking, and the room went dead silent.

The grandfather clock chimed the quarter hour, a single bong. It seemed significant somehow.

Ross stared at her as if he couldn't believe what he'd just heard.

She couldn't really believe it, either. Confrontation was not her strong suit.

Rusty cleared his throat. "Well. You sounded a little bit like your mother there."

Gina didn't imagine that could be good. She tensed, waiting for him to reject her idea again, wondering if she should argue back one more time or simply give up and accept inevitable defeat.

"I suppose if you stuck to the main floor," her father said.

It took Gina a moment to absorb what she'd heard. Even then, she didn't quite believe it. "So...*yes?*"

Rusty nodded, but he also frowned. "But I don't want to be tripping over these people. You hear me?"

"Loud and clear. We'll stick to one day, maybe two if they need some setup time." She hoped she wasn't making a promise she couldn't keep.

"I can always take a drive down to Mustang Point," Rusty grumbled. "Got some things to do there anyway."

It was all Gina could do not to cheer out loud. She couldn't wait to call Lila and give her the good news.

It was Sunday, so Rafe's mother, Carmen, was happily bustling around the yard of the ranch house making sure everyone at the cookout had a drink and was sampling her

grilled peppers and empanadas. The family was all here—
Rafe's father and grandfather, Lorenzo and Valencia, along
with Matias who was entertaining the ranch hands' kids by
throwing a lasso, plus Rafe's two younger brothers, Tomas
and Diego. About twenty assorted hands and staff members
from the Cortez-Williams Ranch were also in attendance.
Diego was currently strumming his guitar for a small ap-
preciative audience.

The only person who looked happier than Carmen was
Gina, and Rafe settled back to watch her from a distance.
He was gratified to see her again after their dinner at the
Twin Bears had ended so disappointingly. He took responsibility for that, for letting the conversation go in a negative
direction. He liked teasing her too much, and he'd ended
up annoying her.

She was working with a photographer now at his family ranch. Apparently she'd decided the fun of the cookout
would make a nice addition to the auction website photo
array. The photographer had taken landscapes this morning and was focused on Matias and his lasso right now.

Rafe figured his turn would come next. He wasn't crazy
about being a model for the website advertising, but he'd
suck it up and let them take a few shots of him dressed in
blue jeans and a Stetson, especially if it gave him a chance
to spend more time with Gina.

Her mood had soured so abruptly at the Twin Bears that
he hadn't found a way to work the conversation back around
to the kiss. He felt like she owed him one, or he owed *her*
one, assuming she was still willing.

He watched from a distance, thinking she hadn't exactly
dressed the part of cowgirl today. Her black pants were
snug to the ankles, showing off her toned legs. She wore a
white tank top layered under a filmy sapphire blouse that
flashed bright in the sunshine. Her heels were low, but her
boots were a pale cream color, a risk on a ranch for sure. She

also wore a gold pendant necklace, a matching bracelet that jangled enough to scare a horse, and a pair of long earrings below a messy knot of hair up high on the top of her head.

He was also thinking she was stunningly beautiful, and he couldn't stop staring at her, remembering their dinner, her expressions and gestures, how much she'd loved the milkshake and how he'd wished they were on a real date. He *needed* to find a new reason to kiss her. And quick. Because she looked absolutely ravishing in the late-afternoon sun.

His mother approached Gina, clearly offering her an empanada. Gina tried to say no, but Rafe knew that was a losing proposition. His mother had raised five boys on a working ranch. In her mind, there was no such thing as being too full since you'd likely burn off the excess calories in the following twenty minutes.

Carmen's determination worked yet again, and Rafe smiled to himself as Gina accepted one of the little empanadas. She took a bite, and her eyes went wide. He guessed it was spicier than she'd anticipated. But she smiled and nodded, obviously telling his mom it was delicious.

But when Carmen turned away, Gina wiped her eyes with the back of her hand.

Rafe took pity on her and started across the lawn, weaving his way through groups of people who were laughing and drinking punch, past the five picnic tables and around the grill where his dad, Lorenzo Jr., was grilling under a billow of smoke and surrounded by the tasty aroma of beef.

"What'll you take on your burger?" his dad asked as he drew close.

"In a minute, Papa."

"What do you mean *in a minute*? They're ready now."

"The works, then," he said over his shoulder. "I'll be right back." A few steps later, he was beside Gina.

"Hi," he said.

She looked up from cautiously eyeing the empanada. "Oh, hi."

He couldn't help but smile at the flush in her cheeks.

He leaned close. "When I say…"

"When you say what?"

"When I say *now*, hand it over."

She looked confused. "Hand what over?"

"The empanada. My mom makes the best ones in three counties, but you need to work up a tolerance for the habaneros."

A wave of relief crossed Gina's face as she glanced around and lowered her voice. "I don't think I've done that yet."

"Now," he said, seeing his mother's back was turned.

Gina surreptitiously handed it over, and he popped it into his mouth.

"Thanks," she said. "You saved me."

"No hardship. I love these things."

"I'm impressed with the strength of your palate."

Rafe didn't recognize the photographer taking the unscripted shots of Matias and wondered if he was associated with *Royal Tonight!* "Who's that guy?"

"Quentin Waters," Gina said. "He's part of our marketing department."

"At the Edmond Organization?"

Gina nodded.

"You got Rusty on board?" Rafe was surprised by that. He'd taken the oil tycoon's absence from the Chamber of Commerce meeting to mean he'd wanted nothing to do with the fundraising effort.

"I wouldn't exactly say *on board*. But he did agree to us hosting the auction at Elegance Ranch."

That shocked Rafe even more. "How'd you ever pull that off?"

"Smiled and batted my princess eyelashes."

"Daddy's little girl?"

"That was sarcasm, Rafe."

"Oh." He'd taken her literally, earning himself an irritated frown.

She continued with exaggerated patience. "If you must know, I explained the merits of a compelling location in growing the audience size and therefore forcing the bidding higher so more Royal businesses could benefit from the funding raised."

Rafe felt bad for making the quip. "That sounds very logical."

"I wish you wouldn't sound so surprised that I'm logical."

"I'm not surprised." He wasn't, exactly. It simply hadn't occurred to him that logic and reason would be her go-to strategy for persuading her father.

"Rafe?" his own father called out from behind him.

"You want a burger?" He was more than happy to change the subject.

She shook her head. "I'm working. I don't expect your family to feed me."

"Don't let the spicy empanada scare you. The burgers are quite tame." He called out to the photographer. "Hey, Quentin. Come and get a burger. Matias, bring the man along and feed him." To Gina, he said, "When in Rome, remember?"

She capitulated with a look of surrender, and Rafe squelched an urge to take her hand.

After collecting their burgers, they got settled at one end of a picnic table, Rafe and Gina across from Matias and Quentin.

"Turn sideways," Quentin said to Rafe.

Rafe swallowed and did as the other man asked. "Why?" He didn't see anything untoward, just a bunch of kids climbing a fence and a couple of dogs rushing around beneath them.

"I want to check out your profile," Quentin said.

Rafe used it as an excuse to turn Gina's way.

She turned to meet his gaze.

He'd thought all this time that her eyes were rich mocha, bordering on hazel. But he'd been wrong. In the sunlight he could see they were much more complex, with spikes of green radiating from the pupils and a blue-gray ring at the edge of the iris. They were exotically beautiful. He'd never seen anything quite like them.

He was about to say something when Quentin interrupted.

"Little more," the photographer said.

Rafe didn't want to move. He wanted to stay right here in this position and stare into Gina's eyes forever.

"Toward the back," Quentin instructed.

Rafe moved his head but kept looking at Gina.

Her expression smoothed out, and her lips seemed to soften as she gazed back.

"With a Stetson," Quentin said. "Can you see it?"

Rafe realized the man was talking to Matias.

"See what?" Matias asked. "Rafe's ugly mug?" He took a bite of his burger.

Gina's face broke into an amused smile.

"At sunset," Quentin said. "Maybe leaning on a fence post, that profile, hat pulled down, little bend to the head. Oh, yeah. We gotta get that."

Matias was staring openly at Quentin now, clearly confounded by his level of enthusiasm.

For that matter, so was Rafe. "I'm not—"

"He's saying you'll look rugged," Gina said. "Outdoorsy, über cowboy."

Matias made a sound of disgust. "I'm more cowboy than he is. I ride bucking horses. Heck, I breed bucking horses. Rafe waits snooty tables."

Rafe chuckled while Gina turned back his way, looking

shocked that Matias would insult him and clearly bracing herself for his reaction.

"I do wait tables sometimes," Rafe said easily. "And Matias means he used to ride broncs when he was young and fit."

This time his brother grinned at the comeback.

Gina looked equally worried, like the good-natured ribbing might turn into an actual fight.

"Relax," Rafe told her. "We're just joking around."

"I know just the spot," Quentin broke in, his mind obviously firmly on his photography. "The split-rail fence beside that old windmill where the river bends into the shallows. We can get those oak trees in the background. But we have to hurry."

Rafe checked the sky and agreed they had to hurry if they wanted to catch the sunset. It was a twenty-minute drive then a fifteen-minute walk to the old windmill—and that wasn't even accounting for Gina's fashion boots.

He couldn't say he was happy about Quentin going all artistic-vision on this, but mostly he wanted to get it over with. So he dug into his burger, and soon they were all traipsing into a pickup truck.

When Matias started to hop into the pickup box, Rafe handed him the keys and told him to drive. Before Matias could ask why, Rafe ushered Quentin into the middle of the bench seat, then Rafe climbed in and gestured for Gina to sit on his knee. It was an obvious trick, and he could tell by the amused expression on his brother's face that he knew exactly what Rafe was doing. But Rafe didn't care.

Gina hesitated for a second, but then gamely climbed in.

He shut the door and left his arm circled around her.

Matias was a speedy driver, leaving Gina with little choice but to brace herself against Rafe's shoulder as they skimmed along the gravel road. He loved the feel of her in his lap, her soft buttocks and firm thighs pressing down

on his, her warm shoulder tucked against his, and the side
of her breast just grazing his chest.

Arm on the rest, he let his fingertips brush the side
of her thigh. Her pants were thin and taut, and he imagined he could feel the satin of her skin beneath the fabric.
Loose wisps of her hair fanned his cheek, and he inhaled
the light citrus scent, thinking he'd never look at oranges
the same way again.

Matias rocked the truck to a stop at the trailhead, and
Rafe opened the passenger-side door. He was gratified
when Gina didn't jump straight out. She seemed to take a
little time, accepting the arm he offered and slipping down
to the ground.

The path to the old windmill was wide and scenic as it
wound toward the river.

Gina was keeping up, even though her boots seemed far
from ideal for the dusty walk.

"That's the spot," Quentin said as they came out on the
flat grassy meadow.

He felt like a prize heifer being posed for a money shot.
But then Gina smiled encouragingly, and he thought about
the return trip with her on his lap.

"Put on the hat and lean your elbow on the post," Quentin instructed, lining up his camera and adjusting his position. "Now look to the south. This light is amazing. Magic
hour."

The photographer had Rafe move around for a dozen
more shots.

"What are you going to do with all these pictures?" he
asked Gina once he was finished.

"A montage for each of you. I've got the tech team at
Edmond putting together the website."

"Whatever works." He loved watching her face in the
soft light, listening to her sweet voice.

"We'll also do a behind-the-scenes house tour as a teaser and an opener to the program."

"Rusty agreed to that?"

"I figure it counts as part of the auction."

"I'm not the one you have to convince."

She frowned at that. "But you think it's a good idea, right?"

Given the chance, Rafe would watch a video on where Gina lived—too bad it wouldn't include her bedroom.

He pictured her surrounded by pastels and florals, stretched out on a queen-size bed, dressed in silk and satin, or maybe lace. His fingers twitched with the need to touch her, and he subconsciously moved closer still.

A breeze blew the strands of her hair over her pink cheeks. His gaze dropped to her full lips, and he suddenly realized the silence had stretched between them. She was waiting for him to react. Too bad he couldn't remember what she'd said.

Matias's and Quentin's voices grew more distant as they worked their way along the riverbank.

"I'm impressed," Rafe answered, meaning it on a whole bunch of levels.

"It's really coming together."

The breeze picked up again, and her hair fluttered across her face. Without thinking, he brushed it back. His fingertips fanned her cheek, and they both stilled.

"I still want to kiss you." He said the thing that was most on his mind, easing closer. "We got sidetracked the other night."

Her gaze flickered to Matias and Quentin beside the river. "That's a bad idea."

Rafe glanced over his shoulder. "They're not paying any attention."

"We're out in the open."

He crossed the final inches between them. "That seems kind of exciting to me."

"Rafe." She put her palm to his chest.

"What? Don't tell me no, Princess. It's just a kiss."

She glanced worriedly over her shoulder again. But then she looked back. "Make it quick."

Rafe wasn't sure he could comply with that directive, but he was willing to do his best. He touched her chin, tipping it gently toward him while he shifted to block her from Matias's and Quentin's accidental view. Then he bent his head and brought his lips to hers. A wave of sweet tenderness bloomed between them. Driven by instinct, he firmed the kiss, parting his lips. His hand splayed into her hair while the other moved to the small of her back and drew her closer, pressing her tight against the apex of his thighs.

His mind screamed at him to do more, bring her fully into his arms, deepen the kiss, make it long and thorough, then kiss her over and over and over again.

A small moan vibrated from her lips, and her hands squeezed down on his shoulders.

He was struggling on the ragged edge of control.

"I don't *think so*," Matias called out.

Rafe jerked away.

Matias laughed, but when Rafe checked he was laughing at something Quentin had said. Neither of them had looked this way.

"Sorry," Rafe rasped, turning back to Gina. "They didn't see."

Her cheeks were fully flushed now, and her lips were deep red. Her eyes seemed to glow with an inner desire. "We can't."

"We didn't." At least they hadn't done anything that was anywhere near what Rafe had wanted to do.

Out of desperation, he forced an air of nonchalance. "It was nothing, just a simple kiss."

Six

After their explosive kiss, Gina avoided Rafe in the days leading up to the auction. It might have been nothing to him, but that "simple" kiss had rocked her world.

She'd been kissed in the past, had prior romances. Which amounted to fleeting relationships compared to most of her friends. She'd never been head over heels about a man, and maybe that's why her kissing track record was so lackluster. But not anymore. Rafe's lip-lock had shown her what was possible. It was embarrassing to admit how badly she wanted to do it again.

Luckily, she was busy, the busiest she'd ever been, taking care of the auction details. She was also energized by the work. It felt good to matter, to have what she did be important to other people.

All that effort was coming together on the morning of the auction. She was nervous, hadn't slept much the night before and got up early to run through the last-minute details. Now she was hovering in the entrance hall waiting for Mandee Meriweather to arrive for the behind-the-scenes house tour.

As he'd sworn he would, her father had left for Mustang Point yesterday as soon as the first technical crews showed up.

Today was a split-second operation. Mandee and the crew would film the tour of the main floor, then the cooking staff would start putting together all the fancy hors d'oeuvres they would serve to the in-person guests. The gardeners were setting out white folding chairs in perfect

rows on the lawn between the pool and the back terrace
that would serve as the stage.

For now, three SUVs drove into the roundabout, stopping at the front of the house. Gina opened the double
doors wide to welcome Mandee, her director, Sebastian,
and the film crew.

"Good morning," she called out cheerfully as they all
trooped inside, equipment in hand as they fanned out across
the marble floor of the hall.

Mandee removed her sunglasses and looked around with
interest.

"Let's start out in here," she said to Sebastian, before
sparing Gina a quick glance. "Hi, Gina."

Over the past two weeks, she had found the celebrity
reporter to be both brusque and demanding. She was the
queen of her domain and assumed everyone existed to cater
to her whims. Watching Mandee's behavior, Gina couldn't
help thinking about Rafe telling her she was a princess. She
hoped her attitude was better than Mandee's and hated to
think she came across as that entitled.

"Sweep through the front door." Mandee continued bark-
ing out orders to Sebastian. "And get a panoramic of the
staircase. After that, just follow along."

"You heard Mandee," he said to the camera crew. "We'll
upload footage on the fly to the editor's suite. We're on a
deadline, people."

Everyone started to move as if it were a choreographed
play.

Gina quickly stepped out of the way.

They followed Mandee from polished wood-paneled
rooms to artwork-accented spaces as she exclaimed over
the paintings, sculptures and furnishings. They paused in
the rotunda, then again in the dining room with Mandee
asking viewers to imagine themselves being invited to a
lavish party at the Elegance Ranch. Then they stopped in

the kitchen, taking note of the blue labradorite counter-tops before the cameras scanned to the family room where Mandee unexpectedly asked Gina what it was like to grow up in the mansion.

Caught off guard, she didn't want to sound like a spoiled princess in her castle. "I liked the stable best," she said on a little laugh. "Between the horses and the pool, it was hard to get me inside the house."

"Most kids make do with a front yard and a sprinkler," Mandee said. There was an edge to her voice that brought Gina's hackles up.

"Royal has some of the best junior horse riders in the state," Gina added, ignoring the jab. "And most of the cowboys in tonight's auction grew up on horseback right here in Maverick and Colonial Counties."

Mandee looked annoyed by the deflection, but she broadened her smile.

"On that note," she said into the closest camera, "please stay tuned to this special broadcast of *Royal Tonight!* and enjoy this exclusive invitation onto the Elegance Ranch. Better still, make a bid in the auction and come on out to visit us in person here in Royal, Texas."

"Cut!" Sebastian called out. Then he made a whirling motion. "Let's grab some B-roll to flesh it out."

The crew started to film various angles of the family room and the kitchen.

"Main floor only," Gina reminded them. The last thing she needed was to run afoul of her father.

"Where's my greenroom?" the TV host asked to no one in particular.

Sebastian looked to Gina. "Where can Mandee rest and freshen up?"

Gina quickly improvised. "Donna?" she called to the head housekeeper, who she knew was hovering off the kitchen waiting for the camera crews to finish.

Donna quickly appeared. "How can I help?"

"Can you show Mandee to the guesthouse?" To Sebastian, she said, "It's nice and private."

Nobody had used the guesthouse since Billy had so unceremoniously hightailed it out of Royal. On Rusty's orders, it had been cleaned top to bottom to erase any sign of his stay. It had two self-contained bedroom suites in case Queen Mandee needed a nap or a shower.

"Please follow me." Donna gestured the way toward a door to the back veranda.

"I'll have some refreshments sent over," Gina told Mandee as she left.

Several members of the cooking staff made their appearance as the camera crew finally trailed out of the kitchen, clearing the way.

When the last crew member left, Gina grinned at Horatio, the mansion's head chef. "It's go time!"

If Rafe had known then what he knew now, he never would have volunteered for the cowboy experience auction. Ever since his auction listing had gone up on the website, he'd been inundated with both questions and *questionable* offers. Some were about the ranch and the experience, but more were about him personally.

Quentin should have made clear what he was doing with that sunset profile photo. It had sounded innocuous enough at the time—make Rafe look like a rugged old-time cowboy who knew his way around horses and cattle. And sure, that made sense for the sake of the auction.

But what Quentin *hadn't* said was that he'd planned to make Rafe look like some Hollywood version of a cowboy. The filtered sunset, the tilt of his head, the warm light reflecting off his chin… It was all too much. At first, Rafe had accused Quentin of retouching the picture, misleading anyone who'd be bidding on his experience. But Quentin had sworn he hadn't retouched a thing.

Rafe had then tried to get him to take it down and replace it with something less personal, but the website marketing team gave him a flat-out no. And since Rafe hadn't set any restrictions on how they could use the photos, he couldn't convince them to change it. They'd also told him his listing was garnering more interest than any of the other cowboys'. Matias was a close second, and Tucker McCoy was a surprising third.

He walked through the open doors of the Edmond mansion. When he spotted Gina from afar, he admitted he'd do it all over again. To get up close and personal with her, especially to hold her in his arms and share that mind-blowing kiss beside the windmill, it was worth it.

"Champagne?" a formally dressed waiter asked him.

"No, thanks." Rafe wasn't in the mood for anything sweet and bubbly.

"If you'd prefer something else, there's a full bar service available beside the pool."

"Thanks," Rafe said, taking in the well-dressed crowd, feeling out of place in his gray-and-blue-plaid shirt, worn blue jeans and wide leather belt. He'd shaved, trimmed his hair and ironed the shirt, but he'd been forced to wear a pair of scuffed cowboy boots. All he had were the ones he'd worn while working on the ranch, and every pair had seen a whole lot of miles. But he'd promised Gina he'd come dressed like a cowboy.

Right now, he looked for a place to ditch his Stetson until the bidding started. There was an open room next to him in the entry hall, so he took a look inside. It was a library, and he found a desk in a corner to set his hat. When he turned, Gina was coming in through the archway.

"Oh, it's you," she said. "Glad you're on time."

A shaft of warmth pierced his chest, and he sucked in a tight breath as she came closer.

She looked sexy and sophisticated, hair up, makeup fresh and bright. Her dress was fitted flat lace, both structured and soft at the same time. The blazer gave her a no-nonsense air, while her pretty sandals accentuated her amazing legs.

"I'm punctual," he said for something to add to the conversation. What he really wanted to say was she was beautiful and could they please get out of here and go someplace private.

"Did you get some champagne?" she asked in full-on hostess mode. She came to a halt a couple feet away.

"I'm not crazy about champagne," he admitted.

"Something else then? A beer?" A sparkle came into her eyes. "I didn't think to plan for milkshakes."

He smiled at that. He liked that she referenced their dinner together. It felt like an in-joke, like they were more of a thing than they actually were. They weren't even close to being a thing. But he'd like it if they were. What guy wouldn't?

"I'm good," he said, easing as close as he dared.

"You should go mix and mingle a bit. It could bring up the bids from the local crowd. We had three hundred people register as in-person bidders." She leaned in and lowered her voice. "But I think there are some crashers here."

His hands twitched with the need to touch her. "They probably want to check out your mansion." He looked around the library. "Spectacular place you've got here."

Gina gave a cursory glance to the bookshelves, the opulent furniture, the rich rug and the chevron hardwood floor that on its own must have cost a fortune. "I can't take any credit. I didn't even decorate my own bedroom."

Rafe once again tried to picture her bedroom. "Is it like this room?" he asked.

"You know, Mandee asked me earlier what it was like to grow up here. I didn't have an answer for her."

Rafe squelched his disappointment at not getting any bedroom details. "Do you have an answer now?"

"Not really." Gina looked like she was thinking hard. "Maybe. Truth is, it was surreal, like I didn't have a real home. I had a place where I slept and where I ate, but other people decorated and cleaned them, other folks planned and cooked the meals. My clothes and toys simply appeared. I never needed to want anything. I never had time."

The Cortez-Williamses owned a big spread and had wealth and power in their own right, but they'd worked their tails off for every scrap of it, every generation from his three-times-great-grandfather to him and his brothers, and the next generation would do the same. The family money didn't go into children's toys, it went into buildings and equipment, feed and vet care, wages for the ranch hands and workers.

"I've done chores since I was seven years old." He gave a small chuckle of remembrance. "Probably before that, too, although I wouldn't have been much help."

"What kind of chores?"

"Typical ranch stuff—feeding the chickens, gathering eggs, mucking out the barn. It's a never-ending cycle of feed and manure."

Her expression turned thoughtful again. "I rode the horses, never fed them, though. Well, a handful of oats or a carrot as a treat after riding, but a little girl wouldn't have been trusted to manage the hay and water."

"Tossing out vegetable scraps for the chickens isn't exactly a complex undertaking. I didn't have any sisters, so I don't know what girls would have done growing up. Baking bread, maybe."

"Wow. That was sexist."

He shrugged. "I only know my own experience. My

mom and nana loved the kitchen, and my dad and grandfather spend their lives outdoors. But I suppose you could
have made a case for shoveling manure along with the rest
of us."

"Didn't ever do that either," she looked embarrassed
to admit.

"What did you do besides riding?" He was curious now
about her life growing up.

"Piano, gymnastics, dance."

"You took dancing lessons?" He pictured himself dancing with her in a fancy ballroom, an orchestra playing.
She'd look stunning in his arms.

"A little ballet, modern dance, ballroom. I needed to
hold my own at parties."

"Ahhh, the parties. Couldn't have those go bad on you,"
he teased.

"They were business functions mostly. And those dancing skills come in handy to this day."

"I suppose they would."

She quirked a brow. "Are you saying you don't dance?"

"Sure, I dance. But we did it for fun, no lessons. Papa
and Diego play guitar, and everyone in the family would
sing or dance. Some Saturday nights, everyone who worked
on the ranch would be out on the patio whooping it up."

"That sounds like fun."

"It was fun, lots of fun." There were times when Rafe
missed the close-knit community he'd belonged to on the
ranch, seeing his mother, father and his brothers every day,
working alongside them and coming home at night with a
sense of satisfaction along with the exhaustion.

"What is it?" Gina asked, peering closely at him.

"I was just remembering," he admitted.

"Remembering what?"

"My roots." Not that he wanted to delve into his dust-
eating, manure-slinging roots with little miss ballet. He

didn't expect her to understand the satisfaction of sweaty work or the simple pleasure of warm chocolate-cinnamon cookies on a Sunday evening.

"Different worlds," she said, sounding almost sad. Then she unexpectedly touched his cheek. "I'm picturing you as a young boy on a horse."

He willed her to keep her soft fingertips exactly where they were. "And I'm picturing you in a pink tutu."

She smiled at that. "I did have a pink one, frilly tulle and all."

He took a chance and eased forward. "You must have been delightful."

"That was my job back then." Her expression turned pensive. "Still my job now, mostly."

"But not today." He knew she'd worked hard on the auction.

She was so much more than just decorative on this project.

"That's nice of you to say." Her hand fell away from his face.

He captured it and shifted closer still. "It's the truth, Gina."

The noise from the get-together faded into the background. They were around a corner in the library, out of casual sight to people passing in the entry hall.

"I…" She seemed to run out of words.

Still holding her hand, he framed her smooth cheek with his rough palm. "You look wonderful today, professional, efficient, intelligent. Not to mention absolutely gorgeous."

He was rewarded with her sweet smile.

"You look rugged," she said, her voice dropping to a husky whisper. "Perfect…so sexy."

Want and desire and need all rose within him, simultaneously clamoring for him to take action.

She was here, right *here*, practically in his arms. She

tipped her chin, slanting her lips, easing up enough to make it an invitation.

He took it, kissing her all over again, deeper this time, more amorously, as if his subconscious knew the way and had unleashed his passion. He framed her face, then he wrapped his arms around her as the kiss went on and on.

She seemed more than willing, pressing against his thighs and his chest, rocketing his desire up notch after notch. She braced her hands on his shoulders as if he was her anchor.

In that moment, he *wanted* to be her anchor, her rock, the person she depended on for…he didn't even know what.

Too soon, voices sounded outside the room.

Rafe drew back, gazing with wonder into Gina's astonished eyes. Her lips were parted, swollen dark red with passion. Her cheeks were flushed again. Man, she was so incredibly beautiful.

He raised her hand to his lips and kissed the back of her fingers, drinking in the scent of her skin.

"Rafe?" she asked, a small tremble in her voice.

"This," he said, keeping her hand in his, her fingers still lightly brushing his lips, "is getting really hard to ignore."

She gave a wide-eyed nod of agreement.

"You going to be okay out there?" With a slant of his head, he gestured to the library entrance.

She looked that way, seeming to remember for the first time she had a major event going on outside these walls.

"Yes," she said, blinking to clear the passion from her eyes.

He immediately missed it.

But then she stepped back, and he released her hand, missing so much more than just the expression in her eyes.

She gave a hand gesture toward the entry. "I have to… uh…you know…"

"I know. Let's get me auctioned off."

* * *

It was standing room only on the back lawn. The three hundred white folding chairs that faced the terrace had quickly filled. Shade trees and the building's shadow helped offset the eighty-plus-degree heat.

Mandee was on the terrace now and anticipation was building as the first cowboy on the docket appeared off to one side.

Gina moved to the morning room where technical had been set up. Half the equipment was devoted to the *Royal Tonight!* broadcast, the other half dedicated to the social media interface. Ten people sat at makeshift desks with workstations or laptop computers, and the floor was a maze of wiring and computer towers. She stepped carefully around the cables.

"All systems go?" she asked Kane, Edmond's head of technology, coming up beside him where he was watching over tech Cassie Norio's shoulder.

"Analytics look fantastic. Good thing we added the surge capacity, or else we'd be crashing the website by now."

Gina realized she should leave him alone and let him work.

He gave her a nod and a wave as she headed outside to the opposite end of the terrace from the on-deck cowboy. The auction staging area was in the formal dining room on the other side of the house. They were being organized there by Lila and personally thanked by some notable members of the Royal Chamber of Commerce for their contributions to the cause.

Gina couldn't help picturing Rafe and wondering how she'd feel when he walked out for his turn. His kiss was still a tingle on her lips, and his embrace felt like it had left a permanent imprint on her body. Her mind wandered as the bidding got underway.

Pricing on the first cowboy went up quickly, and Mandee gaveled him off with a bang to get things started.

She introduced the second cowboy and started the bidding higher this time. People jumped in, and a jovial rivalry developed between the online bidders and the in-person audience. Every time a live person upped the bid over a virtual bidder, a large cheer came up from the crowd.

Gina's brother Ross appeared beside her. "Very well executed."

She took in the crowd again, the waiters still circulating with drinks and hors d'oeuvres. Mandee, whatever Gina might think of her personally, was doing a highly professional job as MC.

"Thanks," she said to Ross.

"Dad's still gone?"

"Last I saw. I doubt he'll be back before tomorrow."

"Probably a good thing," her brother said, looking around. "He'd hate this. And someone would probably say something about Billy, and Dad would end up in an argument."

"Please, let's keep the drama to a minimum."

"So far, so good," he murmured.

Mandee brought the hammer down on the second cowboy. The experience went to an online bidder, and the crowd moaned in disappointment.

"They're really getting into this," Ross said on a chuckle. He took a sip of his champagne.

"Civic pride," Gina told him "But we want to sell as many experiences as possible outside Royal. We all agreed on that."

"The point being to bring in new money."

"Exactly," she replied. "Royal citizens are doing enough already. We need some Dallas or Chicago money, maybe LA or New York."

"You think big."

"I do," Gina answered with pride. She had thought big for this event, stretching and testing herself. She hoped she could find a way to keep doing that.

Tucker McCoy was up next, and he strutted out onto the terrace dressed in a bright red shirt, a leather vest with fringe and a pair of worn blue jeans covered in scuffed leather chaps. The online bidding turned fast and furious, with the bids mounting up at record speed.

The local audience seemed slightly stunned by the turn of events.

"I didn't expect that," Gina admitted.

"He's a character." Ross shook his head, taking another sip of his champagne. "You thirsty?"

She was. "I can go inside and grab something."

But her brother flagged down a waiter.

Tucker's experience went to an online bidder, setting a record by a wide margin.

While the cowboy held up his hands in victory, Ross handed Gina a glass of champagne.

She'd been avoiding alcohol as she managed the event. But then Rafe came out on the terrace to wait his turn, and she took a drink.

He took in the audience, then his attention went to Mandee.

Gina surreptitiously studied him, wondering how high his bids would go. What kind of women would like to spend a day with Rafe and—according to the outline on website—go horseback riding, move a cattle herd, meet foals and calves, and take a walk through the Cortez-Williams Ranch before enjoying a five-star steak dinner at RCW?

Gina, for one. She could easily picture herself doing all those things with Rafe.

Mandee enthusiastically called *sold* on the current cowboy, and Rafe walked across the makeshift stage. The crowd greeted him with energy and excitement, while Mandee gave him a glowing introduction.

Bids started from the crowd, and the internet quickly kicked in, the offers seeming to go up even faster than they had with Tucker.

"Well, I'm jumping in here myself," Mandee unexpectedly called out with glee, naming a number quite a bit higher than the last bid.

The move stunned Gina. "Can she do that?"

"She just did," Ross said on a laugh. "I guess if she's willing to shell out the cash…"

Gina didn't know the technicalities of formal auction rules, but Mandee jumping into the ring wasn't in the spirit of their overall plan.

"We all agreed we wanted sales from outside the city," Gina reminded Ross.

The bidding kept going up and up, and then Mandee called out another bid.

"This is *wild*," Ross said, sounding like he was having a jolly time.

Gina tried for another sip of champagne but discovered her glass was empty.

A local bidder upped the ante.

An online bidder came right back, then another, and another.

Mandee jumped in again.

Gina felt a surge of jealousy at the thought of the stunning TV host spending a full day with Rafe. Before she could think it through, she'd called out her own bid.

She could feel Ross's baffled gaze on her.

Mandee looked over her shoulder at Gina and frowned.

Gina didn't dare look at Rafe.

"I thought you wanted out-of-town bidders," he said.

"She's annoying me." Gina set her empty glass on a

side table and glanced around for a waiter, thinking she could use another.

"Looks like your ploy worked," her brother remarked, nodding to the readout board as it displayed more incoming bids.

Gina hadn't intended to get the online bidders to go higher, but she pretended she had.

Some live audience members added to the bidding, then two people online duked it out for a few minutes, each going up in healthy increments.

Mandee jumped in again with her own bid, bringing a cheer from the crowd.

Gina reflexively upped her.

"Better be careful," Ross said. "You don't want to win."

Mandee shot her a look of pure annoyance and bid higher.

Everyone's attention went to the readout board.

No new bids came up.

"Sold!" Mandee called out gleefully, bringing her hammer down.

"She should have waited," Ross said with a frown. "A couple of them would have jumped back in."

"She wanted it for herself." Gina was sure of that.

A waiter offered her more champagne, and she took it.

"Well, you dodged a bullet then," her brother said. "You might have been the one shelling out the money."

Gina took a swallow. "True." She tried to look relieved at the turn of events.

By the end of all thirty-two cowboys, the Chamber of Commerce had made an enormous sum of money.

Lila was the first to congratulate Gina, giving her an ecstatic hug and telling her she should do more project management, since she so obviously had a talent for it. Many in the audience stuck around to mix and mingle, and virtually all the business owners who stood to benefit from the fundraising congratulated Gina on the accomplishment.

There was one notable exception. Rafe didn't appear. By the time Gina broke free and went to look for him, he was gone, leaving her to wonder what their sexy interlude had meant to him.

Gina had bid on him.

Two mornings later, Rafe told himself not to read anything into it. He wouldn't be so conceited as to think their kiss had something to do with it.

She was just helping to amp up the crowd. After all, she'd let Mandee win in the end. She could have upped the celebrity reporter's bid if she'd been that interested in spending the day with him.

Rafe would have loved to spend the day with Gina, but instead he got Mandee. He was trying not to dread it.

Maybe he wasn't being fair. He didn't know Mandee, not really. Sure, he'd watched her a few times on *Royal Tonight!* and he didn't care for the way she badgered guests and tried to score cheap laughs by embarrassing them. But that was her television persona. She could be a perfectly nice woman.

JJ appeared in the empty RCW kitchen, seeming surprised to spot Rafe coming down the short staircase from his office.

"You're here early, boss."

Rafe entered the kitchen, meeting JJ over the long prep counter.

"I wanted to sign off on payroll," he said. "I've got a full day today."

"What's up?"

"Heading out to the ranch."

"Ahhh…" the chef said with a gleam in his eyes. "The date with the pretty TV woman. That explains your outfit."

"It's not a *date*. It's a day on the ranch. You think she's pretty?"

"Sure, she's pretty. Though I guess they can make anyone look pretty on television. I wonder what she looks like without all that makeup. Maybe you'll find out."

"I doubt it." He poured himself a cup of coffee then held the pot up to JJ as a question.

"Sure…thanks." JJ grinned. "You guys really raked it in on that auction."

"We did. More than I expected, that's for sure."

"Is it enough?"

"Enough for what?"

"Well, to pull RCW out of the fire for one."

Rafe paused. He'd been thinking about that, growing less and less comfortable with the idea of taking charity to save his restaurant.

"Boss?" JJ prompted, seeming confused by Rafe's silence.

"When I started this place—" he looked around the spotless kitchen "—I swore I would make or break it on my own merits."

"And you did."

"So far. But this…getting free money from a charity event. It doesn't sit right."

"You lost money because of a crime. That's not on merit. You deserve to get some of it back. That's just justice."

"I've been thinking…" Rafe didn't want to risk RCW's future. The very last thing he wanted to do was lose the restaurant and force his employees to find new jobs. But maybe there was some middle ground.

"You're making me nervous," JJ said.

"What are our options? I mean our *other* options. If we had to pull ourselves up by our bootstraps, get creative and use nothing but RCW resources, how might we do it?"

"Hmm." JJ leaned back against a wall and seemed to contemplate. "First place I'd look is unused capacity."

"We don't open until eleven," Rafe noted. "Breakfast?"

"That's one idea, the most obvious idea."

"What do you think of it?" he asked.

"We'd need a whole new shift of employees. Plus a new menu, marketing…competition's really stiff at the breakfast hour."

"People might not like such a formal place for breakfast." Rafe knew RCW was a destination, an experience. It wasn't necessarily someplace for a quick short stack and fried eggs.

"What if we focused on the kitchen only?" JJ asked.

"How so?"

"This might sound self-serving…but what about my mom and sisters?"

Rafe was confused.

"Mom's an amazing cook."

"Most moms are." He thought of his own mother and his nana's delicious homemade specialties.

"She bakes. She plays with her old family recipes to create fusion desserts, and they're in demand at the recreation center, at church, for my sisters' sports teams."

Rafe could guess where this was going. "Are you suggesting she's ready to go commercial?"

"I think she is. I'd have to ask her. But she could use the kitchen from, say, four a.m. to midmorning, try to get some contracts with local grocery retailers and do a split of the profits."

As Rafe thought his way through the idea, he caught sight of the wall clock and realized he was behind schedule.

"You don't like it," JJ said, obviously catching Rafe's frown. "Forget I suggested it."

"No," he corrected him. "I think it has merit. But I'm running late. I gotta go." He started for the door to the dining room where he could cut through to the parking lot, but then abruptly looked back over his shoulder. "Would your mom bake me some samples?"

"She'd love to. Business opportunity or not, she'd be thrilled to bake for you."

Rafe grinned and gave the chef a parting thumbs-up as he rushed to the parking lot.

He hopped in his SUV and headed for the highway. Given the amount of money Mandee had paid for her ranch day, Rafe was determined not to be late.

He swung into the ranch yard with five minutes to spare.

Mandee was already there, chatting with Matias on the shaded front porch. Her outfit was almost glaringly bright, but Rafe supposed it must look good on camera. In his worn blue jeans, steel-gray shirt and a battered brown Stetson, he was perfectly happy to fade into the background.

He strode up to them, pasting a smile on his face. "Good morning, Mandee. Welcome to the Cortez-Williams Ranch."

She grinned back, while Matias smirked at Rafe from behind her back.

Rafe gave his brother a look that told him he was going down next.

Matias's experience had been sold to an online bidder named Anastasia Kovell from Boston who was due to arrive in Royal in a few days. Rafe and his brothers had taken bets on her age. With a name like Anastasia, Rafe had put his money on her being sixty-seven. Matias was going to have to be careful she didn't break a bone or something.

"Mom's put out coffee and honey cornbread muffins," Matias said.

Rafe looked to Mandee. "Hungry?"

"That sounds great," she answered enthusiastically. "Will your family mind if I take pictures inside?"

Rafe shrugged. "Shouldn't be a problem." He couldn't see anyone caring if their dining room made the internet.

Seven

When Gina saw the first photo of Rafe and Mandee pop up on her phone at ten o'clock in the morning, she knew it was going to be a long day. The pair looked annoyingly happy, sipping coffee and eating muffins with melting butter.

"Try the lemon curd," Sarabeth said, waving her hand toward one of the half dozen little cakes on the table in front of them at Best Baked. The specialty bakery was conveniently located next door to Natalie Valentine's Bridal Shop, where they were headed next.

Gina told herself to set thoughts of Rafe and Mandee aside. She should be grateful for the distraction of wedding shopping with her mother today. "Are you sure eating cake before trying on dresses is a good idea?"

"It's the *best* idea," Sarabeth said, taking another bite of the vanilla lemon curd cake. "Yum. This one is definitely in the running." She pushed the mini cake and a knife in her daughter's direction. "That way, we can pick dresses that leave us room to eat at the reception."

Gina couldn't help but appreciate her mother's logic.

She cut herself a thin slice of the cake and transferred it to a small plate, taking up a dainty silver fork to have a taste. The cake was moist and sweet, while the lemon curd layer was creamy smooth with just enough tang for balance.

"Oh, yes," she sighed with approval, taking a second bite to confirm. "Do we even have to try the others?"

"Of course we have to try the others. All of them. How often does a woman get a free-for-all with cake?"

Gina's phone chimed. She'd set up an alert for posts from

Rafe and Mandee's experience. Gina told herself it was part of her job as project manager. She needed to ensure each of the cowboy experiences was a success.

Mandee's outing with Rafe was the first one on the calendar, since the reporter was local and also very eager. As far as Gina knew, nobody else was planning to live-share their day. But if they did, she'd told herself she'd keep tabs on them, too.

She picked up her phone to see what was happening on the ranch. Breakfast seemed to be over. They'd moved on to the horse barn and were tacking up. Mandee looked glorious in a pair of burgundy jeans and a patterned shirt of burgundy, silver and white that was fitted perfectly to her slim curves. Topping off the outfit was a pair of Western boots and a gleaming white Stetson. The crowning touch was a big silver belt buckle at her waist.

Gina wondered if *Royal Tonight!* had specifically coordinated the dramatic outfit.

"Not the carrot. No." Sarabeth's words brought Gina back to the present. She was wrinkling her lips and scowling.

Gina set down her phone. "I guess I can skip that one then."

"Have a bite to confirm my opinion."

"Sure." Gina reached for the carrot cake, determined to please the bride.

In Gina's opinion, everything about wedding planning ought to be fun. It wasn't just a day or a weekend, it was a whole experience leading up to the ceremony and the reception—the cake, the dress, the flowers. She looked forward to doing it herself one day, maybe…hopefully.

Until then, she was her mother's go-to gal for this wedding, and she was determined to do a fantastic job.

In the end, they settled on the vanilla lemon curd and chose a white chocolate frosting with a spray of butter yellow flowers cascading down the multitiered cake. It had to be large given the number of guests invited to the wedding. But it would be elegant without looking too fussy.

As they walked down the block to Natalie Valentine's, Gina surreptitiously checked her phone.

If the video clip Mandee had uploaded was any indication, the horseback ride was a hit. They were walking their horses along the banks of the river, lush green trees flanking the trail and giving them some shade. Rafe looked sexy and at home in the saddle. Mandee's form left something to be desired, but it obviously wasn't her first time on a horse.

Rafe was laughing, looking like he was having a great time. Maybe they were having a great conversation. Maybe he thought Mandee was beautiful dressed up like that. Maybe he was glad she had won the auction.

Gina hated the jealousy that surged within her. But *she* wanted to be the one Rafe rode horses with, talked with, laughed with. She should have bid higher.

"Have you thought about a color for your dress?" Sarabeth asked as she pulled open the door to the wedding shop.

Gina guiltily tucked her phone away. "I'm flexible. What did you decide for the flowers?"

"With an ivory dress, I thought cream and pale yellow, maybe a bit of green to set things off."

"I like it."

"Hello, Sarabeth." A smiling thirtyish woman—Mary, according to her name tag—came their way. "Your timing is perfect."

The shop was light and airy with a long row of wedding gowns on one wall and a rainbow of bridesmaid and flower-girl dresses. The back of the shop featured large opulent changing rooms and curved full-length mirrors.

"I've got a sketch all ready for you," Mary said, indicating a round table with four plush chairs. "Please, get comfortable."

"This is going to be fun," Sarabeth said, moving eagerly to the table.

"You can see the sweetheart neckline," Mary pointed with the tip of her pencil. "Cap sleeves, like we talked about. We can play with the length."

"I love it," Sarabeth said with a wide grin. "You got it just right."

In her handbag, Gina's phone chimed another subtle alert.

A younger woman appeared from the back of the shop, approaching them with glasses of white wine on a silver tray. "Can I offer you a chardonnay?"

"Yes, please," Sarabeth said.

"I'm in," Gina said.

Not a date, she reminded herself, even if it did look like they were totally into each other. It was a cowboy experience. She could only hope Mandee didn't experience too much of Rafe before it was all over.

Mary opened a book pointed to a swatch of lace. "I was thinking of this one." She pointed. "Or—" she turned two pages over "—this?"

Sarabeth leaned forward to study the two options, and Gina slipped her phone out of her purse for a peek.

On the little phone screen, Rafe and Mandee had dismounted and the horses were drinking from the river. Mandee was showing off a bouquet of wildflowers to the camera, bringing them to her face for a sniff. Since she was the focus of the video, it was hard to see Rafe's expression.

Next there was a photo of Rafe with a quirky smile. The old windmill was in the background, catapulting Gina back to her kiss with him there, the moment his lips had touched hers, and her world seemed to fill up with sunlight.

"Oh, that I like," Sarabeth enthused. "What do you think, Gina?"

Gina looked back up, quickly orienting herself to the

swatch book and seeing a delicate ivory lace pattern of leaves and vines. "Nice," she quickly agreed.

Annoyed with her wandering attention, she stuffed her phone back into her purse.

"Time for you to get to work," Sarabeth said to her, pointing with her wineglass to the array of bridesmaid dresses.

"I have some ideas." Mary came to her feet. "After I did your sketch, a few of our new styles jumped out at me." She marched over to the wall of dresses, swiftly choosing a peach, a mint green and a butter yellow dress.

Sarabeth got comfortable in her cushy chair. "Give me a fashion show."

Gina took a bracing drink of the chardonnay and came to her feet.

It took over an hour of changing, laughing, twirling and sipping wine to find the right dress. But when Gina walked out for the final time, she knew it was the one, and Sarabeth obviously knew that as well.

It was a strapless chiffon of pale seafoam, skewing blue in some lighting, green in others, with a sweetheart neckline and a snug wraparound bodice that flattered her waistline. The skirt fell softly to land four inches above her knee. She had no less than a dozen pairs of shoes that would work with it.

"Well, *there* you go," Sarabeth said with a smile.

"That'll work," Mary said with a nod. "And we can do other colors."

"I like it just like this." Her mom stood, walked closer and tilted her head. "It brings out the green in her eyes."

"I've got some jade-and-gold earrings," Gina said. "Or just some little diamond studs." She drew back her hair. "Half up, half down, you were saying?"

"You'll need just the right necklace," Sarabeth told her.

"Show me what you're wearing, and I'll find something that coordinates."

"Or we could go shopping." Her mom's eyes lit up. "I haven't bought you a bridesmaid gift yet."

"You don't need to—"

"Oh yes, I do," Sarabeth said firmly.

"Something delicate," Mary said. "Yellow gold would be better than platinum."

"You can't go wrong with diamonds," Sarabeth said.

"Mom, you *can't.*"

"I want you to have a keepsake, honey. I want you to remember this your whole life."

"I'm never going to forget your wedding." The unbridled love Gina had felt for her mother when she was a little girl came suddenly spilling back. All their trials and tribulations, and the separation that had kept them apart for so many years, fell away.

Her throat clogged. "I love you, Mom."

Sarabeth pulled her into a warm hug. "I love you, too, honey." Then she stood back, her eyes shining. "You'll knock 'em dead in that dress."

Gina gave a brave smile, wondering who exactly she'd knock dead since she didn't even have a date. Her traitorous mind turned to Rafe again, picturing him out on the range in his blue jeans, then at the restaurant in his finely fitted suit. He was definitely a guy you could take anywhere.

The Edmond Organization was covering the hard costs for each of the cowboy experiences.

Gina could have paid the RCW dinner tab tomorrow or the next day or even next week. But when a picture of a candlelit dinner for Rafe and Mandee at a cozy RCW table came up on her phone, Gina decided punctuality was more important.

She left home, driving across town to park in the RCW

lot. She had no way of knowing if both Rafe and Mandee were still inside laughing over dinner and their day. The photo had shown them finishing up a chocolate soufflé, but maybe they were lingering over brandy now.

On the other hand, maybe they'd already left RCW. If they had, she'd never know if they went together or separately. And wouldn't that just mess with her mind.

But she'd come this far. She braced herself and headed for the front entrance, passing through the double doorway into the dark, richly appointed lobby.

"Good evening," the hostess greeted her with a smile from behind a narrow desk.

Moving forward, Gina craned her neck to scan the main dining room. No Rafe there, only a few diners in the flickering firelight among some empty tables.

"Are you meeting someone tonight?" the hostess asked pleasantly, coming out from behind the little counter. "I'm afraid we can't seat a new party after ten."

"I was looking for Rafe."

"Mr. Cortez-Williams?"

"Yes," she answered.

"I'm not sure he's still here. Can you wait here a minute? I'll check."

"Thanks."

Gina waited a few minutes, considered leaving, then stuck around a few minutes more. She told herself she was here to pay the tab, nothing more, nothing less. If Rafe had already gone, she'd thank the hostess for her help. But if Rafe was still here, and Mandee was with him… Well, she would still hand over her credit card and slink home in disappointment, knowing the cowboy experience had turned into a real date.

"Gina?" Rafe appeared in the archway from the dining room, looking surprised to see her. His shirtsleeves were rolled up and his tie was loose. Whatever he was doing, it was a lot more casual than dinner.

"Sorry to disturb you," she said, trying to surreptitiously check behind him for signs of Mandee. "Are you busy?"

"No. What are you doing here?"

She swallowed, trying for an offhand look. "Edmond is paying the tab, remember?"

He looked confused. "You're here for the check?"

She nodded. "Yes. I'm…uh…trying to…you know."

"Be ridiculously punctual?"

She nodded. "I don't like to leave things hanging."

"Sure," he said, still looking confused, but also looking deliciously disheveled and oh so sexy.

They both went quiet. After a moment, she could feel the hostess's curious gaze.

"I can give you my credit card," Gina offered, going for her purse.

He canted his head into the dining room. "Come on in."

She hesitated, sorely tempted to follow him, but wanting to keep up the facade that she was only here to pay the bill.

He started to walk away, and she had only seconds to make her decision.

With a quick thank-you to the hostess, she followed. He led the way through the swinging kitchen door into a wave of fragrant warmth where the cooking staff was clearing and cleaning.

The two of them skirted the edge of the kitchen before climbing a short staircase.

Rafe pushed open a door and stood back to let her pass.

She walked into what was obviously his office. It was surprisingly large and airy, especially for a room accessed via the kitchen. But then she saw a second door and realized they'd taken a back route.

His desk was at one end of the rectangular room. It was honey oak with clean lines and a low-back chair. In front of the desk were two light brown leather armchairs that looked very comfortable. There was also a six-person meeting table in the inside corner and a small conversation group with four armchairs and a low square table next to windows that looked out on the lush greenbelt.

The door clicked shut behind Rafe.

"This is really nice," Gina said, glancing around.

"You bid on me," Rafe murmured without preamble, a thread of amusement in his tone.

He caught her off guard, and she turned back. "I was only making a point."

His brow went up in a challenge. "That point being?"

"Mandee wasn't supposed to bid. None of us were. We wanted as much money as possible to come from outside the community."

"Her money is as good as anyone's," he said easily.

Gina didn't have a counter to that. "How did today go?"

Rafe shrugged his wide shoulders. "It went. I don't believe you."

"Don't believe me about what?"

He eased closer, a glint of determination in his eyes. "Why you said you bid on me."

She felt herself rise to the challenge. "Oh, yeah? Why do *you* think I bid on your cowboy experience?"

"Because you wanted it."

"Aren't you full of yourself."

"I didn't say you wanted me." But his heated gaze moved to her lips.

She wasn't about to admit anything. "You're saying I wanted a horseback ride?"

"Yes."

"I have a stable of my own."

"I guess you also wanted to meet the foals and calves and walk through the Cortez-Williams Ranch."

"Don't forget the cattle herding."

"Or the dinner," he said, leaning in, his voice dropping lower. "Admit it, Gina. You wanted to experience *this* cowboy."

His deep tone and sensual words vibrated through her, bringing desire, want and passion to life.

"Good news," he said, brushing his hand against hers.

She shivered in reaction, barely getting the words out. "What news?"

"There's a second prize."

She desperately hoped second prize was another kiss in Rafe's arms. "What is it?" she managed, easing closer, waiting for a witty comeback.

"The muffins, the foals, the cattle drive, the whole experience."

She drew back far enough to focus on him. "Huh?"

"You pay the amount of your last bid, and I'll do it all over again."

She realized they were having two different conversations. Could she have misread him that badly? "You want my money?"

"I do."

"And you'll take me cattle-herding?"

"I will."

She squelched her disappointment, telling herself to get real, get grounded, and deal with the fact that her intense infatuation wasn't reciprocated.

He liked her, she assured herself. He at least *liked* her. So, maybe their kisses didn't blow his mind the way they blew hers, and maybe he wasn't as desperate to fall into each other's arms all over again, but he must at least like her a little bit.

"What if I want something else?" she asked, thinking that if she was going to bargain for his time, she might as well get what she really needed.

"What? You mean like a picnic or a swim in the river?"

"I need a date."

"Well…we'd do the dinner thing at the end."

She shook her head. "To my mother's wedding. I need a date to my mother's wedding."

He tilted his head, his eyes narrowing. "You want to pay me to escort you to your mother's wedding?"

"No! I want to pay the Chamber of Commerce fundraiser for a cowboy experience. I just happen to want a *different* cowboy experience."

A slow smile grew on his face. "Are you under the impression we can customize, ma'am?"

"You can if you want my money, sir."

He gave a chopped chuckle. "Sure."

"You'll do it?"

"For you, Gina, I'll do just about anything." The sensual gleam was back in his eyes, but she didn't trust it this time.

"In the meantime," he continued, his eyes darkening further as he brushed his fingertips over her cheek, bending his head, moving in. "Is there any *other* kind of cowboy experience that might interest you?"

"I—"

"Just say yes, Princess."

"Yes."

In an instant, he was kissing her, his hot, tender lips slanting over hers, opening, deepening.

She moaned in relief, her arms encircling his neck to anchor her while her blood sang with happiness and her bones all but melted.

Rafe wrapped his arms around her waist, firmly tugging her against his body, holding her strong and steady. He kissed her lips, then her neck, then her shoulder, pushing the cap sleeve of her dress out of the way so he could have better access.

She splayed her hands on his warm chest, sliding her palms from his pecs to his washboard stomach, frustrated by the thin barrier of his shirt. Needing *more*, she started on the buttons, and he muttered something under his breath. Then she heard the lock click on the door behind him.

He grasped the tails of his shirt and pulled, popping the buttons, sending them scattering as he tore the cotton garment from his shoulders.

She gazed at his magnificent body for a few moments, but then they were back in each other's arms with their kisses growing frenzied.

Rafe pressed his hands to her back, her rear, moving down her thighs, massaging his way to the hem of her dress. Then she gasped as his fingertips touched her bare skin. She came up on her toes, running her palms over his shoulders, reveling in the strength and definition she found there. Emboldened, she kissed her way across his pecs, leaving damp circles as she moved to his neck.

His hands came to her lacy silk panties and she shuddered with desire, her teeth biting gently down on him. He stripped off her panties, dropping them to the floor. Then he lifted her to his waist, her thighs wrapping around him, her body brushing erotically against his pants.

He moved then, carrying her, kissing her deeply as they crossed the few paces to his desk.

Perched on the edge, she stripped off her dress, meeting his eyes for a long, hot moment as she sat naked in front of him. He brushed back her hair, framed her face with his hands, kissed her tenderly, long and deep, then his hand moved to cup her breast.

Gina moaned again, arching backward, letting sharp sensations of pleasure race to her core. She wanted him, *badly*, and she reached for his pants, popping the button and sliding down the zipper.

"Gina," he groaned in her ear, dragging her close, producing a condom. "Yes. Oh, yes."

"Rafe," she moaned in return, gasping as he entered her.

His breathing went deeper as he thrust, becoming ragged as he sped up.

Hers did, too, lungs laboring as if there wasn't enough oxygen in the room.

She clung to him, passion coursing through her belly, her thighs, to the tips of her toes and roots of her hair. Her nipples hardened, grazing his chest, as his motion increased again. A roar came up in her ears and light glowed around the edges of her eyes.

Digging his fingertips into her hair, he kissed her deeper and harder. Then he scooped one hand beneath her, holding her fast against his rhythm.

She could feel the world falling away, night turning into day and back to night again as she floated free, stars sparkling all around. His breath brushed her ear, and he called out her name, lifting her up against him as the stars swirled against black sky, coalescing then bursting into wave after wave of bright energy.

Her pulse pounded in her ears.

Rafe held her close, cradling her head and her back as he gently set her back down on the desk.

Her heart rate settled, syncing with his.

"Wow," he muttered.

"Wow," she answered.

He drew back just far enough to focus on her face. "I didn't plan…"

She shook her head. "Me, either."

He paused. "Too soon for a cowboy experience joke?"

She cracked a smile.

He gathered her into a hug again. "I really didn't mean for this to happen. I mean, sure, I wanted to kiss you. I'm human, and you're spectacular. But I don't want you to think I lured you up here to take advantage."

He hadn't taken advantage of *anything*, but she didn't know for sure what he was saying. She found herself parsing his words again, worrying that the lovemaking had meant something different for her than for him.

"It's fine," she said, attempting an air of nonchalance.

He eased back and she reached for her dress, swiftly pulling it over her head to cover up. While she slipped off the desk, Rafe adjusted his pants.

Her purse was around here somewhere, and she tracked it down. Finding a comb, she fixed her hair before refreshing her lipstick, all of which made her feel somewhat more together.

Clearly, they weren't going to hang around and whisper secrets in the afterglow, so she dug out her credit card as reality crowded in. There were still staff and maybe even some customers outside in the restaurant and kitchen. She suddenly wanted to get that walk over with, get back in her car and get safely home.

She turned to find Rafe still shirtless, a sheen of sweat on his chest as he braced himself back against his desk. She focused on his forehead, wanting to avoid his sexy body and preferring not to look him straight in the eyes.

She held out her card. "Can you run this through?"

He looked confused.

"For the dinner," she clarified.

His confusion turned to indignation. "You still want to pay for the dinner?"

"That was the deal. Edmond will pay hard costs. You put in the sweat equity."

"It's my restaurant," he said.

"And you've lost a lot of money because of this whole thing." She pushed the credit card closer.

"I'm not taking it."

She didn't know why he was acting like this. "Don't be so proud."

"Don't *you* be so patronizing."

"Rafe." The last thing she wanted was for him to treat

her differently because they'd just had sex. And not just *any* sex. Wild and crazy, impulsive sex. She'd burned for him, and he'd given her what she craved, but now he just looked...angry.

"No," he said with finality.

"Fine," she said, putting the card away.

She turned.

"Wait." The anger in his voice was gone.

But she reached for the door anyway, needing this episode to be over.

"Gina." His footsteps sounded behind her.

She quickly pulled the door open and slipped out, counting on the fact that he'd have to put his shirt on before he could try to chase her down.

Eight

Rafe knew he'd messed up with Gina. But the last thing he needed in that moment—still reeling from their earth-shattering lovemaking—was a reminder of the stark differences between them. He couldn't bring himself to take her charity last night. And he still felt the same way today.

The businesses that invested in Soiree on the Bay were well represented in the Chamber of Commerce conference room this morning. Lila was at the lectern organizing her notes as the stragglers wandered in and took their seats. Rafe had caught a fleeting glimpse of Gina far across the room, causing his chest to hitch in regret. She hadn't seen him yet, and he knew it was better that way.

Someone pulled out a chair at his table, and he looked up to see Lorenzo.

"Hey," his brother said as he sat down, a cup of coffee in his hand.

Rafe pulled his thoughts from Gina. "How're you doing?"

"Did you hear?" Lorenzo sounded serious.

"What?" Rafe braced himself for family news, maybe an accident on the ranch.

"On top of everything else, Billy Holmes is trolling Rusty."

Rafe's initial relief that nobody had been hurt was quickly replaced by confusion. Why would a man on the run from the law post anything on social media? "Are they sure it's him?"

"They seem to think it's him. Valencia was talking to

Lila, who was talking to Lani Li. Lani's still following the case closely."

"What's he posting?" Rafe was beginning to think Billy wasn't the brightest guy in the world. Then again, maybe he was blinded by emotion right now, because he'd certainly been smart when he'd hidden the embezzled money.

"Taunts about Rusty, how all this could have been avoided if Rusty had only treated him fairly. He's got a bone to pick with the Edmonds, that's for sure."

"So all this was about getting back at his father?"

"Looks like."

"Disappointment in your family is no excuse for a crime spree."

Lorenzo gave a snort of derision. "If it was, that's all anybody'd have time for."

Rafe quirked a smile and shook his head at his brother's dark humor. "Billy's oh-poor-me victim crap is ridiculous. The guy should confront Rusty if that's what it takes, but give the innocent bystanders back their money."

"Valencia's horse rescue could sure use it. Billy knew all the good the proceeds were going to do. What kind of a man takes money away from troubled kids to…what…buy gold fixtures for his condo in the Maldives?"

Rafe shook his head at that, too. "I hope we never find him." He paused. "I mean, I hope the Cortez-Williams brothers never find themselves alone in a back alley with the guy. The money, I want back."

It was Lorenzo's turn to smile.

"Can I have your attention?" Lila asked from the front of the room. Her voice was strong but not overpowering through the microphone.

People settled. Everyone was interested in what she had to say about the results of the auction.

Rafe glanced at Gina again. He could see her profile, her glossy hair, neat now, not like it was after he'd run his fingers through it making love to her. She was wearing a shimmering peach blouse and a dark blazer over a pair of tan slacks. She looked professional, but somehow more comfortably so than in the past. He supposed her success had done that for her. She had to be feeling hugely confident in her capabilities right now.

"—owe a big thank-you to Gina Edmond."

The mention of her name rocked Rafe back to reality.

The room burst into enthusiastic applause, and Rafe quickly joined in.

Gina rose to her feet to give the crowd a wave of thanks. As her gaze swung around the room, it caught on Rafe's. She paused for a second and her smile faltered. But then she recovered, finished the turn and sat down.

His regret deepened.

"The auction was an amazing fundraiser, and while we're a long way from recouping all the losses, I'm happy to announce we can refund about fifteen percent of the initial investment to each of the impacted businesses."

There was a murmur of disappointment that turned into lukewarm applause. Rafe's heart went out to Gina. She'd worked so hard to make as much as she had. Nobody could have done better, no way.

"Well, that's that," Lorenzo muttered, sounding distinctly exasperated.

Rafe looked to his brother, intent on defending Gina. "Fifteen percent isn't nothing."

"Fifteen percent of the investment doesn't help Valencia."

Rafe understood his brother's disappointment. He was also reminded that organizations beyond the investors had lost out, too. Many people in Royal had been hit hard by Billy's crimes, harder even than Rafe himself had been hit.

He made a split-second decision and came to his feet.

Lila looked curiously his way.

"I'm donating my fifteen percent," he called out, hoping to inspire others. "RCW will recover on its own. People will keep dining, keep celebrating special occasions and continue to take special evenings out. It'll take some time, but we'll manage. Other organizations might not be so lucky. Others were counting on this event to do good and important work, more important than feeding sambal shrimp and cranberry apple pastry to people with disposable cash."

He saw the crowd was listening with curiosity, some of them more suspicious than curious, including both Ross and Asher Edmond. Rafe realized he should get to his point. "I'm donating RCW's fifteen percent to Donovan Horse Rescue."

He caught Lorenzo's shocked expression from the corner of his eye.

"That's very generous of you, Rafe," Lila said.

He sat down.

"What the heck, bro?" Lorenzo asked.

"She can use the money."

"But RCW…it's in trouble."

Rafe gave a shrug. "We've been brainstorming and have some ideas. We'll dig ourselves out of this hole."

"Take the money," Lorenzo said.

"You take the money. Valencia deserves it. I made a bad investment, and I'm paying the price. But I'm strong and smart and hardworking, and I don't need the Edmonds or anyone else to take pity on me." Rafe's voice had grown fiercer at the end of the statement.

Lorenzo drew back, looking more confused than ever. "You feel that strongly about it?"

"I do."

"Well, Valencia is sure going to be your best friend."

"Good." Rafe said. "I like Valencia." His brother's fiancée was one of the best people he'd ever met. They were lucky to have her joining the family.

Conversation had resumed in the room. Lila had left the lectern and was circulating, answering questions.

Rafe dared to glance Gina's way again and found her surrounded by business owners. It was clear they were congratulating her, and he was happy about that. She deserved their thanks.

Gina didn't know what Rafe had been thinking at this morning's Chamber of Commerce meeting, but he'd made a big mistake. She'd gone back to the Edmond offices after the meeting, but all day long she'd worried that his anger with her might have pushed him to make a bad decision—a decision detrimental to RCW's future.

Feeling responsible, she'd looked for him at the steakhouse, even though she dreaded the idea of going back into his office. But she needed to talk to him, to change his mind about taking the money.

He hadn't been there, so now she was trying his home.

Gina had never been to Rafe's house before, but she was familiar with the neighborhood. She knew it was exclusive, and that some houses had amazing views of Pine Valley. She pulled around the crescent, located his address and turned into the driveway. There was a garage directly in front of her and she could see that a set of rounded concrete steps led to an oversize wooden door with etched-glass windows on either side, cut in diamond panes with gold filler. The front yard was nicely sized and well-trimmed, landscaped in shrubs rather than flower beds.

Gina stepped out of her car and made her way through the hot, humid air toward the door, gathering her courage along the way. She rang the bell and stepped back to wait. Glancing behind her, she took note of the other nice houses along the street. They were well spaced and very well cared for. The crescent was bordered with sidewalks, the driveways finished with exposed aggregate. It was an overly civilized neighborhood—a far cry from the blowing fields, paddocks and hills of the Cortez-Williams Ranch.

The door opened, and Gina turned back, taking in the sight of Rafe in the middle of the doorway wearing faded jeans with an olive-green T-shirt stretched across his chest. She'd expected a suit. She didn't know why.

"Gina?" He was clearly confused by her appearance.

She shook herself back to her purpose. "Why did you do it?"

"Do what?"

"You know what! The money. You need the money."

He drew himself up. "*Will* you stop worrying about my finances?"

"I can't stop worrying about your finances. I'm the problem with your finances."

He crossed his arms over his chest. "You have nothing to do with my finances."

"See?" She pointed at him. "See that right there? *That's* the problem."

He cocked his head and stared at her for a moment. "Did that make sense inside your head?"

"Don't play dumb."

"I'm not playing anything."

"Rafe, you flipped out the other night when I tried to pay—"

"Is this going to be a long conversation?" he asked.

"I don't know. I didn't think it all the way through."

He stepped back and gestured her inside.

She decided that was a good idea, since the alternative was standing out here on the front porch. She was a long, long way from being a celebrity, but there were people in Royal who would recognize her, and she'd rather not get questions about why she'd been arguing with Rafe on his front porch.

She walked inside, and he closed the door behind her.

"Carry on," he said, making a sweeping gesture with one arm.

It took her a split second to remember what she'd been saying. "When I tried to pay for dinner the other night, you flipped out."

"Because I own the restaurant, and it was unnecessary."

She peered into his eyes. "You're lying. For some reason, you don't want my money. Then today…" It was her turn to make a sweeping arm gesture. "Today, you turned down tens of thousands of dollars! You can't afford to do that."

"You have absolutely no idea what I can and can't afford."

"Why, Rafe? Am I so tainted?"

"Don't be dramatic. Everything's not all about you, Princess."

"You're picking a fight." She couldn't help but interpret that as a defense mechanism.

"I don't need to *pick* a fight. You're having one all by yourself," he pointed out.

"Take the money, Rafe."

"I don't need the money, Gina."

"I know you took out a second mortgage," she told him. "Everyone knows that."

"Well, that's none of everyone's business."

"Are you that proud?" The jut of his chin told her he was. "It's not *my* money, Rafe. It's raised money, and you helped raise it."

"You and your brothers kicked in."

"Because the Edmonds brought Billy to town. That makes it partly our responsibility."

"Maybe." He shrugged. "But I chose to invest in Soiree on the Bay. I took a risk, and that part is my responsibility."

She dropped her purse on a side table. "Forget pride, that's just plain stubbornness." Then she found herself looking around.

He had a wonderful house, spacious and tastefully decorated but not ostentatious. It was lighter than she'd expected, with open beam ceilings in the living room and high peaked windows showing a view of the valley. She saw four modern taupe leather chairs around a glass coffee table. Knowing Rafe's background, she would have expected dark armchairs and heavy wood side tables. In the corners, he had large, leafy, free-standing plants.

She took an unconscious step forward, curious to see more. "This is really nice."

"I'm *not* stubborn," he said.

"You're impossible," she retorted, but she walked past him into the living room and took in the pot lighting and a pale mosaic glass-fronted fireplace. "You live here?"

"Is that a serious question?"

She took a few more steps and found a formal dining room that seated eight. "It doesn't look like you."

He had followed her along. "Maybe you don't know me very well."

She had to admit, she really didn't.

"Ask me," he said.

"Ask you what?"

"Ask me why I don't need the money."

There was an archway leading from the side of the dining room, and she couldn't resist walking through it to the kitchen. His counters were gray marble, the cupboards white, and a small dining nook had a table set with—

She paused. "Are you having a party?"

The kitchen table was covered in the most delicious-looking baked goods. Her nose perked up at the tantalizing smells—banana, brown sugar, coconut and peanut butter.

"I'm not having a party. Ask me why I don't need the money." He'd come up close behind her, closer than was comfortable but still too far away.

She wanted to lean back against him, wanted his arms

to come around her, wanted to turn in his arms and kiss his sexy mouth and—

"Want to help?" he asked.

The question threw her. She craned her neck to look back at him.

He nodded to the table. "JJ's mom made those."

"Did you decide on a bake sale?"

"No, we're not having a bake sale. Those are for me."

"To *eat*? No offense, Rafe, I mean you're trim now, but that won't last long if you dig into all this."

He chuckled. "I'm not going to eat *all* of them. They're for taste-testing. You could give me your opinion."

The invitation was beyond tempting.

"Come on," he said, gesturing to the bright little nook.

Who could say no to an offer like that?

They sat down opposite each other at the kitchen table, bathed in the long rays of the western sunlight. Rafe handed her a fork, a spoon and a little knife along with a dessert plate.

"Sarabeth and I did this earlier in the week with wedding cake," she said as he set a slice of banana raspberry cake on her plate and then his.

"So you're experienced."

"I'm half a pound heavier."

He grinned. "Did you find one?"

"We did. Vanilla cake with lemon curd filling and white chocolate frosting. And the design is gorgeous—classic white, pale yellow flowers with a little mint green."

He took a bite of the banana cake. "And how does this stack up?"

"Not quite as elaborate," Gina said before taking a taste. The flavors all but exploded in her mouth. The sweet banana was balanced by the tangy raspberries, and there was a light honey glaze that lingered delightfully on her tongue. "*Oh*, it's unique."

"Isn't it?"

She tried another bite.

"Pace yourself," Rafe warned with a little wave of his fork.

She grinned self-consciously. "I can't resist."

He took another bite himself, despite his advice to her. "How about something savory instead of sweet?"

She gazed around the table at the various dishes, spotting something that looked like an herb puff. "What about that one?"

He held out the bowl. "Help yourself."

She did, and so did he.

The puffs were light and airy with threads of tangy cheese, garden herbs, dried peppers and tomatoes. They moved on to a cheese tart, a rolled pastry layered with pistachio and lemon chutney. Everything was fresh, unique and wonderful.

As Gina used her fingertips to take a final nibble of the pastry layer, Rafe sat back, his voice going low and sultry. "Ask me."

The atmosphere suddenly shifted, and her attention moved from the baking to Rafe. Her chest tightened and her pulse sped up as her brain considered the possibilities. "Ask you what?"

"Why I don't need the money."

She ordered her fantasies back from the brink. They were still talking about money, nothing more, nothing else. She sucked the tiny crumbs from her fingers. "Why don't you need the money?"

He nodded to the table. "We're going to sell these."

"You're extending the menu?" She was puzzled. She'd liked everything, *loved* everything, really, even if some of the exotic flavors seemed slightly out of step with the traditional steakhouse. But she didn't see it changing the company's cash flow in any meaningful way.

He shook his head. "JJ's mom. She's going to use the kitchen in the off hours and start a whole new line of business."

Gina sat back in her chair. "That's…"

"Smart?"

"Innovative, really innovative. Smart, too."

"It was JJ's idea. He came at it from the perspective of unused capacity."

"You're not a storefront." Gina couldn't help considering the marketing possibilities.

"No." He looked like he already had an idea.

She considered what that idea might be. "You'll need contracts with local retailers and grocery stores."

"That's the general plan." He glanced down at the table. "It's stage two. Stage one was testing the products."

"They so passed." Gina felt a shimmer of excitement. "Can I help out?"

Rafe looked surprised by the offer.

"I could talk to Lila, get a chamber directory, start making some calls."

Quenching their thirst with sparkling water, Rafe and Gina stepped out on the deck where the evening breeze was beginning to cool the concrete. He wondered if she'd stay long enough to have some wine. He'd love to sit back on the outdoor love seat and watch the sunset with her by his side.

Rafe watched her walk to the rail and gaze out at the trees, the lush valley, all the way to the mountains where the sun would set in another hour. Her hair was loose over her bare shoulders, her dress pressing gently against her thighs. While her legs, her *long, sexy legs*, took him back to that explosive night in his office…

He opened his mouth to ask her to stay, but her phone jangled from the kitchen.

She turned from the rail and smiled at him as she passed.

His stomach sank in disappointment.

It was probably something important, *someone* important. Her family, her social circle and her business network were chock-full of important people.

He polished off his water and followed her back inside, feeling like he was leaving a fantasy behind him on the deck.

"Wait," she was saying. "Slow down." She looked at Rafe with amazement in her eyes.

She had his attention.

"I don't know if I can do that," she said. Then she covered the mouthpiece and whispered, "It's Matias."

"What?" Rafe whispered back, worried.

"How—" She stopped talking for a minute. "That would be unethical."

"What?" Rafe repeated, moving closer, ready to take the phone from her hand and ask his brother what the heck was going on.

Gina held up her hand to stop him. Then she made a one-minute sign with her index finger. "Seriously, you... *seriously?*" She put her hand to her forehead in a gesture of disbelief. "Okay. Yes."

"What on earth?" Rafe didn't even bother whispering this time. He couldn't for the life of him figure out what his brother would want with Gina, but it didn't sound good.

Gina gave him the wait-one-minute hand signal again, and Rafe sucked in a frustrated breath. "I said yes. I will." She paused. "As soon as I can." Another pause. "Okay, go!" She laughed then and ended the call.

"What was *that?*" Rafe demanded.

"It was Matias." She chuckled again, gazing at her phone.

"And what, *exactly*, did my brother want from you?" Rafe had never spoken to Matias about his attraction to Gina. He'd never spoken to anyone about it. But he couldn't bring himself to believe Gina would make love with Rafe and then…he didn't know what to call it…*chat* with Matias.

"He's with Anastasia."

"Who?"

Gina gave Rafe a baffled look. "His cowboy experience person."

"Oh. Is that today?"

"Yes."

"Is something wrong?" Rafe wondered if Matias had rudely asked the woman from Boston her age. Rafe had put his money on sixty-seven, while his brother Diego was the next closest at fifty-nine. Rafe still figured he had a good shot at taking the pot.

"No. Quite the opposite." Gina typed something into her phone.

"What are you doing?"

"It's a little embarrassing."

Rafe's guard went up again. "Embarrassing how?"

"He wants me to change her ticket. Reservations, please," Gina said into the phone.

It took Rafe a minute to process the sentence.

"Hi. I'd like to change a ticket if that's possible."

"Her *plane ticket*?" Rafe asked, earning himself the wait signal yet again.

"It's for tomorrow," Gina continued. "The name on the ticket is Anastasia Kovell, but the booking was made by the Edmond Organization." Gina looked to Rafe and moved the phone under her chin.

"How old is this woman?"

Looking puzzled by his question, Gina went back to the call. "Sure. Thursday will work. It's a direct flight?" She listened. "Yes, that's right. By text is fine. Thanks very much." She ended the call.

Rafe stared at her in silence for a moment as the questions piled up inside his head.

"It seems your brother is having a good time," she said.

"With *Anastasia*?" Rafe couldn't erase the original gray-haired image of the woman from his mind.

"They're at RCW right now, probably ordering cocktails before the appetizers. It sounds like your brother wants dinner to last as long as possible."

Rafe pointed to Gina's phone. "Did you just—"

"Put my ethics on hold to buy your brother some extra time with Anastasia? Yes. I'm not proud of it, but he assured me she had the rest of the week free."

"Well, well, well." Rafe took out his own phone and texted Matias, demanding a photo.

"Rafe, wait—"

Rafe hit Send and looked up at Gina.

"Now he knows we're together."

Rafe didn't see the problem. "So?"

"He might think we're *together*, together."

Rafe wasn't crazy about the implications of her concern. Did he embarrass her? "He won't. And even if he does, we have a perfect cover story."

She lifted her palms in a gesture of incomprehension.

"It's business. You're helping me with the new bakery line."

Her phone pinged, distracting her. "It's the new ticket."

While she keyed something in on her screen, Rafe's phone pinged, too.

Matias had sent a photo, no questions asked, of a beautiful blonde woman with wide blue eyes and a dazzling smile.

"Ahhh," Rafe said aloud.

"What?" Gina moved to his side, leaning her shoulder into his arm for a better view. "Oh. *Ahhh*. Well, that explains it." She tipped her head to Rafe, her eyes alight with humor. "I just texted her that her flight was rescheduled. I feel like your partner in crime."

Her bare shoulder was warm against his skin, her gaze riveting, her lips pink and slightly parted.

His voice turned husky as he spoke. "Let's crime away." He set his phone deliberately down on the table. Then he slipped hers from her hand and set it aside. He smoothed her thick hair back, cradled her face and slowly lowered his lips to hers.

As they finally kissed, his entire being sighed in pleasure and relief.

She turned, and he wrapped his arms around her, molding her slender body to his. "This," he whispered on a rasp of emotion, kissing her again. "This is what I need."

As she opened to his kisses, one thought crowded his brain. *His bed.* He needed her in his bed, naked against him, her limbs wrapped around him.

He lifted her into his arms. His hormones surging, she felt light as a feather. His bedroom was down a hallway. He knew the way blindfolded, so he kept kissing her as they passed through the family room, around the corner, down to the end and through a set of double doors.

The screened windows were open, a fresh breeze wafting through. The setting sun cast long shadows, softening the light as he set her on her feet next to his king-size bed.

Her fingers raked his short hair, and he let his hands roam the curve of her waist, the flare of her hips, the sides of her silken thighs.

"I've thought of you in here," he confessed.

"Nice room," she said, her gaze staying fixed on his.

"It's not exactly a palace." He almost said, "Princess."

She gave a little smile. "Who cares?"

He stripped off his shirt.

She leaned forward and kissed his chest. Her hands moved over him, exploring the contours of his shoulders and pecs, sending little shock waves of pleasure darting under his skin.

"Oh, man." He exhaled.

Her touches moved lower and lower still until he sucked in a breath.

Then she took a step back, reached behind her head, bringing her breasts to prominence against the fabric of her dress. The dress pooled at her feet, revealing a dusty blue bra and panties trimmed with lace.

He took her hands, giving in to an impulse to draw them aside, away from her body, to improve his view. "Oh, Gina."

For a moment he was too transfixed to move. He wanted to hang on to the moment. But then she freed her hands and reached for his jeans, popping the button, drawing down the zipper, igniting passion stronger than any he'd ever felt.

He shucked the rest of his clothes and drew her down on the bed. He wanted her naked, to feel her skin to skin, but couldn't give up the sexy lace.

He skimmed the smooth silk of her bra, kissed her mouth and her neck, nudged the pretty strap from her shoulder and kissed her there, too. Then he peeled off her bra and kissed her breasts. Her head tipped and her back arched and she moaned his name.

His passion crackled like a storm cloud breaking open in the sky. He hooked his thumbs under her panties and drew them down the length of her legs. He reached for the bedside drawer, then settled between her legs, reveling in her hands as they kneaded his back, moving lower, drawing him to her.

He pulled away to drink in her beauty, cradled her face in his hands, smiled at the flush of her cheeks and the swell of her bottom lip. He kissed her sweetness, drawing out the moment.

Then her hips tilted, legs wrapping around him, and with the barest of movements, they were one. He held still for as long as he could, but then she shifted and arched, and he moved with her, filling his heart and his mind with mindless pleasure.

Holding still was impossible. Slowing was impossible. A primal need drove his movements, sweat glistening on his skin, his lungs filling with oxygen, and his heart pumping furiously to keep up with his demands.

Gina's breath came in sweet puffs against his face. Her fingernails dug into his shoulders. And her legs held him locked tight as he moved to a new plane of life.

"Rafe!" she cried out, and a shudder ran through her.

He followed her over, hot and gasping, closing his eyes to drink in every last ounce of bliss. Then he held her close, kissed her hairline, her temple, her mouth.

As his breathing steadied, he rolled, easing her over on top of him, worried his weight would be uncomfortable.

She lifted her head, still breathless, and blinked down at him. "Hi."

He grinned. "Hi."

"So…" She looked uncertain.

"*Together*, together," he said. There was no question about it.

"Good thing we have a cover story."

Rafe didn't want a cover story. He wanted to shout it to the world. But he'd do whatever she wanted. So he smiled and tucked her hair behind her ears. "I won't tell if you don't."

"Deal," she whispered. A moment later she was sliding off to the side.

He wanted to hold her, stop her from leaving, but it wasn't his choice. He forced himself to keep his hands still.

But she didn't leave. Instead, she snuggled up next to him, tucking her head in the crook of his arm.

He smiled in deep satisfaction and settled into the most amazing fantasy.

Nine

Gina was dozing off in Rafe's arms when a sudden thought hit her.

"Oh, no." She sat straight up.

Rafe sat up with her. "What?"

"I forgot about the hotel." She swung her legs over the edge of the bed. "I need to extend Anastasia's stay at the Bellamy."

Rafe's forearm suddenly looped around her waist, holding her back.

"Hey," she protested.

"Let Matias worry about the hotel."

Gina shook her head. "I made it sound like the airline had canceled the flight. That means the Edmond Organization is responsible for her delay."

"I don't know how you figure that." Rafe gave a tug and pulled her onto her back on the soft bed, her head landing on a plump pillow. "This is Matias's master plan."

"But we're his collaborators. That comes with a certain responsibility."

"Fair point." His gaze seemed to drink her in. "But I *really* don't want to let you go."

"I'll come back. I will. I just need my phone."

He leaned slowly down, barely brushing his lips against hers.

Her stomach contracted. The insubstantial touch seemed somehow sexier than the lovemaking. And she'd have bet there was nothing in the world sexier than Rafe's lovemaking.

"Promise?" His whisper was a vibration.

"Promise."

"Okay." He sat up, then stood.

"You don't have to come with me." She wondered if she should put her dress on for the walk to the kitchen, but that seemed silly if she was coming straight back.

"I'll get your phone," he said, starting for the bedroom door.

"You will?" she asked, pleasantly surprised by his chivalry.

He waved at her behind his back. "Lie back down."

"Are you that afraid I won't come back?" she called in a teasing tone.

"No. I'm a gentleman." His voice echoed along the hall.

Smiling to herself, she resettled herself on the bed, drawing the sheet up over herself and gazing around Rafe's bedroom. The white leather headboard highlighted a rock feature wall bracketed by two windows. A pair of steel-blue leather armchairs shared an ottoman and sat on a cream, taupe and pale blue mottled rug. There was a large oil painting on an eggshell wall, a ranch scene, the Cortez-Williams Ranch—she recognized the old cabin and the windmill. In the opposite corner was a huge plant pot with several different species around a miniature palm.

Rafe returned and tossed her phone to her on the comforter.

"Did you decorate this yourself?" she asked as she picked it up.

"Yeah." He looked around. "Why? Do you like it?"

"It's nicely coordinated."

He climbed in next to her on the bed, pulling the sheet to his waist. "I don't strike you as coordinated?"

She took in the square-shaded wall lights on either side of the bed and the sleek-lined bedside tables. "This doesn't strike me as a rancher's design."

"What, you expected a set of longhorns over the bed?" He didn't seem annoyed, merely curious.

"Something like that."

"I bought it out of a showroom," he said.

She didn't understand.

"I went into Willenberg's downtown, saw this setup in the showroom and said I'd take the whole thing. Except for the painting. I commissioned the painting."

"I recognize it." She looked down at her phone, seeing a text message from Anastasia. "She doesn't seem upset."

"Who?" Rafe was focused on his own phone now.

"Anastasia. She's taking the delay in stride."

"Lucky Matias."

Gina smiled to herself. She could easily imagine the strapping, handsome Matias had something to do with Anastasia's blasé reaction.

She pulled up the hotel website, entering the Edmond account and password. With a few taps she'd extended the reservation two more nights. Then she forwarded the information to Anastasia.

When she set down her phone, Rafe was still working away. She watched him for a few minutes, the focus and concentration on his face. "Are you a workaholic?"

He glanced to her. "You're the one who insisted we get our phones."

"I'm done. You're still working."

"I let JJ know I loved the baking. He's excited to get started."

"That's all?" She didn't believe him.

"A couple other things, too."

"Ha! Caught. Workaholic."

"You know you're never really off the clock when you own your own business."

Gina didn't know that. She probably should have known that. She wondered if her brothers felt that way. The oil business was definitely all-consuming for her father, that was for sure.

"What are you thinking?" Rafe asked. He was looking at her now.

"It makes sense," she said. "That you'd never truly forget about work."

"Does that upset you?" He waved his phone like he was offering to put it down.

"Oh, no. It's not that."

"Then what?"

"It makes me wonder, is all." What it would be like to be needed at the office, to not have unlimited time for tennis dates or riding or lunching at the Cattleman's Club.

"About?"

"My own job."

He set his phone on the bedside table and slid down in the bed. "Tell me about it."

She was embarrassed.

"A vanity position?" he gently asked.

She nodded. "I never really worried about it. I mean, who wouldn't love a big office, an expense account and little responsibility? I can attend any meeting, read any report, I just—"

"Can't have any impact?"

She shook her head. "Exactly."

"Then they're wasting a valuable resource. I saw how you managed the auction. You could apply those skills to anything you wanted."

She wasn't so sure she could apply herself to the Edmond Organization. "There's already Rusty and Ross and Asher. They even listened to the things Billy had to say, but not me."

"Have you ever tried?"

"A few times. When I first got back from college. I'd learned some things, you know. I had some opinions."

He leaned his shoulder against hers, touched the side of his head to hers. "Nobody listened."

"Nobody listened. Are you pitying me?"

"I'm mocking you, Princess."

That wasn't the answer she'd expected. "What? Why?"

"Because it's your own fault."

She picked up the nearest pillow and bopped him in the stomach.

He laughed. "You're a member of the family, every bit as much as Ross or Asher."

"I can't force them to listen to me."

"You can try."

Gina put an exaggerated pout on her face.

He kissed her.

"Hey."

"That wasn't more mocking. It was just for fun."

She couldn't exactly argue with that. Kissing Rafe was a whole lot of fun.

"What would you do?" he asked.

"In the oil business?"

"Yes."

She did have one idea. It was something she'd wanted to bring up to Rusty for a while now. "Methane."

Rafe's brow went up.

"There are whole new ways to capture the off-gas methane from oil wells and convert it to energy—heat, even electrical. It protects the environment and provides a reduced-cost source of energy for the oil field operation."

He looked surprised. "Have you ever suggested it?"

She shook her head. "They won't even listen to my marketing ideas, never mind something operational."

He seemed to ponder. "Tie the idea to marketing."

"How?"

"I don't know. It's environmentally friendly—corporate reputation, maybe."

Gina's brain lit up with the suggestion. She came to her knees and faced him, ideas forming one after the other. She grinned. "I can do something with that."

"Good," he said.

"You're smart."

"You're sexy."

"You're off topic."

"No." He reached for her. "I'm exactly *on* topic."

His touch was distracting, his kisses more so, and it was only seconds before she was succumbing to the luxury of his embrace.

Rafe expected Gina to forget about her offer of help with Royal Chamber of Commerce contacts. She'd been excited about pressing her family on the methane technology, and he knew she was already busy with planning her mother's wedding. But even without her, RCW was pressing forward on his own.

They didn't want to spend a lot of money on the bakery launch, since that would defeat the whole purpose. But the staff members had enthusiastically stepped up to help control costs.

Janelle, one of the hostesses, was studying graphic art and had mocked up a logo, while Samuel's father had a wholesale line on display baskets. JJ's mother had taken a no-nonsense approach to sizing up the kitchen and planning supplies, while virtually everyone had volunteered to help package the sample baking baskets. All that was left to Rafe was to find the right contacts and deliver sample baskets in the hopes of getting them to agree to sell the baking products.

He was about to call Lila when JJ rapped twice and opened the office door.

"What's up?" Rafe asked from behind his desk.

"It's Matias. He's in the dining room."

"Is he looking for me?"

JJ shook his head. "He's with a gorgeous woman. So far, he's looking for two April Rain martinis."

Rafe immediately rose, curious to meet the woman, who had to be Anastasia.

"If you're doing a recon, report back," JJ said.

"Will do," Rafe said as he cut through the kitchen.

The couple was at a round table in a corner of the main dining room, a mini hurricane lamp flickering in the center of the white tablecloth.

Rafe smoothly approached, keeping his voice low and conversational. "Hi, Matias."

Matias didn't seem surprised to see him. "Anastasia, this is my brother Rafe."

Rafe turned his attention to the woman, offering his hand.

She was stunningly beautiful, with porcelain pale skin, bright blue eyes and long platinum blond hair. Her smile revealed perfect white teeth as she accepted his hand.

"Hello, Rafe." Her fingers were long and slender, with a delicate emerald ring on her right hand. It matched her stud earrings and a small pendant that hung above the neckline of her peach-toned dress. Everything about her said class and dignity, even her smooth, gentle voice. "Matias told me about you."

"Nothing bad, I hope."

"All good. He promised I'd love RCW, and I do."

Rafe looked at his brother, who gave him a beaming smile that clearly asked if Anastasia was not the most amazing woman on earth. Rafe had to respectfully disagree; beautiful as she was, Gina had her beat. But he could see why Matias had wanted to keep Anastasia around for a while longer.

"You're from Boston?" Rafe asked her, detecting only a slight accent.

"Born and raised, in Brookline to be precise."

"And you bid on this mangy cowboy?" She struck Rafe as much too refined for the daylong horseback riding adventure Matias had offered up.

"I've always been a rebel."

"Did you ride in Boston?"

"Some, English style mostly, but it translates."

"It translates perfectly," Matias said and reached across the table for her hand, his eyes glowing.

The waitress arrived with their lime-garnished glasses and frosted martini shakers, and Rafe moved to get out of the way. "Enjoy your meal."

"Thank you," Anastasia said.

"Can you stop by later?" Matias asked.

"Sure. No problem." Rafe was a little surprised Matias would want another interruption in his evening.

As he made his way through the dining room, he stopped at a few tables to welcome the guests and ask how they were enjoying their meals.

Laughing with one family foursome, he glanced up to see Gina standing in the entry lobby. His heart lifted at the sight of her, and he quickly wrapped up the conversation.

She watched as he rounded the last few tables, smiling as he approached.

"Hi," she said.

"Hi, yourself." He was ridiculously glad to see her.

"I made some calls," she told him. "I got a contact list from the chamber and reached out to grocery retailers. They're all excited about the new product line."

"You did all that?" He was stunned.

Now she looked puzzled. "I said I would."

"I know, but that was only Monday, and you've got other things on the go."

"Other things?"

"Your work for Edmond, your mother's wedding."

"I can multitask. And you'll be happy to know my bridesmaid dress still fits even after all those baking samples."

He brought up the fond memory. "Well, that's probably because we—" Rafe stopped himself before he could finish the sentence. He also had to stop himself from brushing back her hair, reminding himself they were standing in a crowd. "Come back to the office."

"Okay."

He wanted to take her hand, but instead he simply led the way, cutting through the corner of the kitchen to the quiet and privacy of his office.

As he shut the door, her gaze went to his desk and lingered there for a second. He hoped she was remembering their lovemaking. He'd never forget the feel of her body around his that night.

He gestured to the armchair grouping beside the window. "Can I get you anything to drink? A cocktail or perhaps a glass of wine?"

"Glass of wine, sure."

She sat down and crossed her long legs beneath her tidy steel blue dress as he called the front desk and asked for a bottle of his favorite merlot and two glasses. Then he joined her, sitting across the low coffee table.

"I've made a spreadsheet." She set a couple of pages in front of him. "It's got the business name, owner, manager and purchasing contact, phone number, email address, and a short description of their initial reaction to the pitch."

"You made a pitch?"

"I just reworded some of the stuff you said while we were sampling, plus a few of my own impressions of the quality to personalize it."

Rafe gazed at the pages in disbelief. "You did all this? For *me*?"

"I thought that was what we agreed?" She sounded worried, like maybe she'd done something wrong.

"Yes, yes, it was. I'm just astounded that you did such a great job."

"Don't start sounding like my family." There was a thread of annoyance in her voice.

He looked up at her. "What?"

"Don't act surprised that I can tie my shoes."

"Tie your *shoes*?"

"Correctly complete rudimentary tasks."

"*This* isn't a rudimentary task. It's fantastic. It's perfect. We've been working on sample baskets, a logo, and now you—" He gave his head a little shake, telling himself to stop rattling on and get to his point. "This is *exactly* what we needed. Thank you." He rose to give her a kiss of appreciation.

When he drew back, she looked guarded, and he feared he'd been too presumptuous with the kiss. Before she could ask, a knock came on the door.

It was Janelle with the wine and glasses on a tray.

Rafe invited her in, feeling honor bound to share her contribution with Gina.

"Janelle designed a logo for us," he told Gina as the young woman set up the glasses and opened the bottle.

"I'm using it as credit for a college course I'm taking." Janelle deftly pulled the cork, allowing the wine to breathe for a few minutes. Meanwhile, he brought up the logo on his laptop. His hostess had used the same basic elements as RCW but replaced the R for Rafe with a Y for Yeoh, creating the Yeoh-Cortez-Williams YCW Sweethouse brand. "Come take a look."

Both Gina and Janelle joined him at the screen.

"That's incredible," Gina said, smiling at Janelle. "You are so talented."

"Thanks. But I really can't take all the credit. Rafe

came up with the YCW idea, and Mrs. Yeoh suggested Sweethouse as a play on Steakhouse."

"This is totally going to work," Gina said with conviction.

"I couldn't agree more," Janelle replied. "And I can't wait for us to get going on this!"

Rafe would have preferred to get going on the bottle of wine with Gina, but he knew better than to interrupt this level of enthusiasm.

Squaring her shoulders, Gina marched into her father's Edmond Organization office, determined to force him to listen. Behind his big desk he was glaring at his computer screen, a deep scowl on his face.

"This is ridiculous!" he ground out before she could say a thing.

She was used to his outbursts, and it was usually best not to probe for details. "Dad, I have something important to—"

"Have you seen it?" he asked, voice elevated, eyes smoldering with rage.

"Seen what?"

He spun his screen. "Today, yesterday, the day before. *That liar just won't stop.*"

Gina scanned over a list of social media posts that had thousands of reactions and responses. Billy was still out there ranting about Rusty's dishonesty, about Ross's disloyalty, about Asher not even being a real Edmond and all about how unfair his life was now and had always been. There were also posts that said the Edmonds owed him everything, and he was going to get revenge on them all.

She'd seen some of these rants before, but it was definitely getting worse. "Can the police not track him down?"

Rusty's eyes were still ablaze. "You don't think I've *asked*?"

"So they can't." She realized this was a bad time to propose her business idea. Her father wasn't about to say yes to anything in this state.

Ross came into the office, focused on his cell phone screen, this thumb scrolling. "What about another private investigator?" He looked at Gina. "Did you read these?"

"Just now," she answered. "I don't understand how he can be that active and still stay hidden."

"He's smart enough to ping through a whole raft of countries. We should try a bigger firm," Ross said to Rusty. "Maybe go international. He could be in Mexico or Canada, or may have even chartered a jet overseas. He's probably got money hidden around the world."

"Yes!" Rusty said to Ross. "Do it now. I want this over and done with."

Gina wasn't convinced that finding Billy would end anything. Sure, the rat could end up in jail, and they might even get some of the money back. But fissures in the family had been revealed through Billy's crimes, and it was going to take them a very long time to recover from those.

And when they did, the family dynamics were going to be different. Rusty and Ross and Asher didn't know it yet, but she intended to be an active participant in running the Edmond Organization. She had an equal ownership position with her two brothers, and she wasn't going to sit on the sidelines and play nice anymore.

"I'll set it up," Ross said and turned to go.

Gina took the opportunity to follow him out the door into the executive reception area, out of the line of Rusty's fire. "Can I talk to you?"

"Sure," Ross said, tucking his phone away. "About the wedding?"

"No."

He looked puzzled. "Oh. I thought you and Mom were working on that."

"We are, and it's coming together."

"I hope so, since it's a week from Saturday."

"You did the tux fitting?" She followed him into his office.

"I did. I'll be perfectly dressed to escort Mom down the aisle. I heard you picked a cake."

"We did. The cake is going to be incredible." She shut the door behind herself. "But that's not why I'm here."

"Oh?" He took a seat at a table for four and pushed a stack of reports out of the way.

Gina sat next to him and turned her chair to better face him. "Ross."

He looked intently at her. "Gina."

"You know I work here, right?"

"Well, you have an office right across the hall, an expense account and we pay you every month. So, yeah, I know you work here."

"I want to *really* work here. And I have an idea…"

He looked a little wary. "Okay."

"Don't look like that."

"Like what?" he asked.

"You haven't even heard it yet."

He gave a shrug, but his phone buzzed in his pocket, and he glanced down. His expression told her she was already losing his attention.

"Tell me your idea," he said, reaching for the phone.

Her hand shot forward, stopping him from reaching into his pocket. "I want you to listen."

He let his hand drop. "Okay. I'm listening."

"Methane," she said.

"What about it?"

"You know there are new technologies out there, right? Techniques to capture methane from the wells and generate energy."

"I do know that."

"Good. I've been looking at ways we can make use of the methane energy for our field operations."

Ross blinked silently.

"I've written a report. It's good. It's solid. And I want your support when I take it to Dad."

It took Ross a moment longer to speak. "You're writing a report on the utilization of methane power conversion technologies for Edmond?"

"Exactly."

"You have an engineering degree I don't know about?"

"I can read, Ross. I talk to experts. I can understand complex systems."

He furrowed his brow. "Exactly what does this have to do with marketing? You are still in the marketing department, right?"

"Don't be condescending."

He held up his palms in surrender as his phone buzzed again.

"Don't touch that," she warned.

"Wouldn't dream of it."

"In two years, five years, ten years…it's going to matter. Dad might not be thinking of it right now, but oil companies that are more environmentally friendly are going to have an advantage in the future with both shareholders and customers for starters. Plus, it's the right thing to do, and ultimately, it will save us money."

"It's a miracle?" he asked with an edge of sarcasm.

"No. It's good technology and smart business."

His phone buzzed again.

"Gina," he said, pointing to the phone. "It might be important."

"*This* is important. All I want is your support. If I can't make the case, I can't make the case. But I need Dad and you and Asher to give it a fair look, a serious look. Just don't blow me off this time."

"We don't—"

"*Yes*, you do. You always have. I open my mouth in a meeting, and everyone goes for their phones." She looked pointedly at his pocket.

"Okay," he finally said. "Okay. I promise I'll give it a fair read."

"And?" she prompted.

"And I'll support you with Dad."

She couldn't help but smile in both relief and gratitude. "*Now* can I answer my cell?"

"Yes. Thanks, Ross." Her heart lifted with hope as she left his office.

Ten

Despite everything that had happened between them, Rafe felt awkward calling Gina for what was essentially a date. It was impossible to pin a description on their relationship, impossible to even *call* it a relationship, even though he would be her escort to her mother's wedding.

He did have a good excuse for this particular invitation, and it was more of a double date really. Staring at his phone, he decided he was probably overthinking this. He pulled her number from his contact list and placed the call.

"Rafe?" She didn't sound elated to hear from him. But she didn't sound annoyed, either. She sounded more puzzled than anything.

"Hi," he said, ridiculously happy to hear her voice.

"Hi. What's going on?" The background sound said she was on the move.

"Where are you?"

"On my way into the Edmond building, why?"

Rafe glanced at his watch to confirm it was barely nine. "On a Sunday morning?"

"I'm working on something."

"Yeah?" He was interested.

"Polishing up the methane proposal."

"You got right on that."

"I already had a bunch of the information indexed. And the industry contacts have been fantastic. They're really excited about their recent tech progress."

"I'm glad to hear that, Gina."

"It's going well." She sounded satisfied.

The background sounds changed, and he knew she was inside.

"Can you take a little time off?" he asked.

"When? Why?"

"Tonight. Matias wants me to have dinner with him and Anastasia, and I thought—"

"Anastasia's still in Royal?"

"Yes."

"But her ticket to Boston was for Thursday."

"She's still here. I suggested you—"

"I didn't change it." Gina was clearly baffled.

"Maybe Anastasia changed it."

"On the Edmond account?" she asked. "How would she do that?"

"Maybe she missed the flight. Maybe Matias bought her a new ticket."

"But that would be—"

"*Gina.* The plane ticket is not the point."

"And what is the point?"

"I suggested Anastasia might like to meet you, too."

She didn't respond.

"Tonight," Rafe said. "With me. At dinner."

There was another beat of silence. "I can't believe she's stayed this long."

"That's not an answer. Dinner?"

"Yes. Sure. Of course. I can wrap things up here whenever you like."

Rafe liked her reaction—a lot. Like it was no big deal and a foregone conclusion that they could casually do a dinner together.

"Can I pick you up at seven?"

"I should change."

"I meant from your house."

"Oh." There was a clear hesitation in her voice.

"Is that a problem?" Was she reluctant to have him show up at the Edmond home?

"No." She quickly backtracked. "Not a problem. I'll be ready."

Rafe ordered himself to quit scrutinizing his relationship with Gina, to quit looking for pitfalls. They might not have talked about themselves as a couple, and so far, they'd kept their personal life a secret. But she'd agreed to come out with him tonight. Sure, curiosity about Anastasia had to be part of the draw. But she was coming out as his *date*.

He was slightly early pulling into the ridiculously expensive tiled roundabout at the Elegance Ranch. Without the crowds this time, the place was beyond imposing. Its multistory peaked roof rose to the sky, while marble pillars bracketed two oversize glass-adorned front doors. It boasted huge bay windows on either side of the wide porch, with balconies above on the second floor overlooking the sweeping majesty of the front lawn.

He left his SUV in front, expecting to be in and out quickly.

His ring of the bell was answered by a neatly suited middle-aged man, obviously a staff member.

"May I help you, sir?"

Rafe was glad to be well dressed himself in a favorite steel-gray suit with a pressed white shirt and a burgundy tie. People didn't look down on him when he was dressed like this. "I'm here for Gina."

The older man moved back and widened the doorway. "Please come in."

"Thank you." Rafe stepped onto the gleaming marble floor for a second time. It was hushed inside today. The decor was impeccable, the airy hall spotless, and the two wrought iron railed staircases were impressively glorious. The Edmonds sure knew how to build an entrance.

"Your name, sir?"

"Rafe Cortez-Williams."

"I'll let Ms. Edmond know you've arrived. Feel free to wait here, or in the library if you'd be more comfortable."

"I'm fine here."

As the man disappeared up the stairs, Ross appeared at the far side of the hall, coming around the corner from what Rafe knew was the great room. He had a heavy-bottomed highball glass in his hand, half full of something amber. Rafe guessed bourbon but possibly whiskey or a single-malt scotch.

"Hey, Rafe." Ross walked forward. The curiosity in his eyes told him Gina hadn't talked to her family about their date.

"Hi," he answered.

Ross came to a halt. "You're here to…"

"Auction follow-up," Rafe said, in case Gina wanted to continue being completely circumspect. "We're having dinner with one of the winning bidders."

"You and Gina?"

"Yes."

The man's gaze narrowed for a second. He took a contemplative sip of his drink. "So, you gave up your Chamber of Commerce funding."

"I did."

"That's a lot of money. Any particular reason?"

Rafe tried to figure out where Ross was going with this. "Valencia will make good use of it."

"Simple as that?" Ross's skepticism was clear.

"Simple as—" Before Rafe could finish speaking, Gina appeared on the staircase, and his breath was momentarily taken away.

Her dress was shimmering black, a halter top with a beaded V-neck that showed off her shoulders and dipped between her breasts. It was snug over her slim waist, while the skirt was full and flirty. But the part that practically left him gasping was the bright red satin lining visible under the asymmetrical hemline.

Her shoes were black, too, open-toed with a criss-cross around her ankle and red sole that flashed as she walked. Sexy didn't begin to describe the outfit.

"Where exactly are you guys going?" Ross asked, taking another sip of his drink.

"The Bellamy," Rafe answered, his gaze not leaving Gina.

She smiled as she stepped off the staircase, and his chest went tight in reaction.

"The restaurant, right?" Ross asked.

"Very funny," Gina said, making a face at her brother. "We're meeting Matias and his auction purchaser. She's from Boston."

"Trying to impress the big-city folk?" Ross asked, taking in her outfit.

"Exactly," Gina answered. Then she linked her arm with Rafe's. "Ready?"

"Absolutely. Bye, Ross." They turned for the door, and Rafe could feel the other man's speculative gaze on him as they left.

"You look fantastic," Rafe said as he opened the SUV door for her.

She had to grip the handle and step on the running board to get into the high vehicle. For a moment he wished he had a sports car instead. Gina would look *incredible* in a Porsche.

"You okay?" he asked as she got settled.

She looked confused. "Fine, why?"

"The seat's a little high."

She waved away his concern. "Don't let the outfit throw you off. You know I'm a perfectly capable woman."

He couldn't help but grin. "I know that very well."

* * *

Gina immediately liked Anastasia.

They'd been seated at a white-draped table with a pretty flower centerpiece near the atrium and with a view of the gardens. Ballerina-thin, Anastasia wore a dusty-rose dress with a beaded mesh bodice, spaghetti straps over her creamy shoulders and a full chiffon skirt that accentuated her shapely legs.

When they'd walked in, her movements were smoothly graceful.

"Do you dance?" Gina asked her after they'd ordered cocktails.

"Ballet when I was a girl."

"I took a little ballet," Gina said. "Switched to modern pretty early."

"My parents were traditionalists. Classical ballet three times a week."

"You must be good."

She gave a little shrug. "It was more for them than me."

"Ahhh, parents."

"Yes." Anastasia's gaze wandered to Matias, who was talking with Rafe.

"You must like it here in Royal," Gina ventured, probing for a little information.

"I know you were part of the plot to keep me here."

"I…" She was embarrassed to be called out.

But Anastasia laughed. "Don't worry. I don't mind that Matias was a little crafty, and I admire that you and Rafe supported his brother."

Gina didn't know what to say to that.

"I'm an only child," Anastasia explained. "I always wanted siblings. They would have been a friend, and would have taken some of the parental intensity off me. Do you have brothers or sisters?"

"Two brothers. One's a stepbrother."

"It must be nice."

"It has its moments." Gina thought back to Ross's pledge of support with the methane report. But then there was the falling-out between Ross and Rusty over Ross's wife, Charlotte, the fact that Asher was arrested and that the family had doubted him, and Billy, who it seemed increasingly likely was Rusty's illegitimate son.

"There's discord, too," Gina was quick to add. "Don't let anybody tell you big families are happy families."

Anastasia nodded to Matias and Rafe, who were now chuckling about something. "To be honest, that there is what I picture in a big family."

"That's the best of it," Gina agreed, contemplating Rafe's relationship with Matias and Lorenzo. She thought back to the Sunday barbecue when they'd taken the auction pictures. The Cortez-Williams family seemed very close-knit, incredibly fun-loving and loyal.

Rafe saw them looking over and quickly included them in the conversation. "Anastasia, Matias tells me your father teaches at Harvard?"

Anastasia looked uncomfortable for a moment and hesitated over her answer. "It's more of an affiliation than an actual job. He does have a doctorate from Harvard, but he's not a teaching professor."

"Oh," Rafe asked conversationally. "What does he do?"

"He sits on a few boards." She paused. "Makes a few donations."

Matias seemed surprised. "I thought—"

"Any area in particular?" Gina asked, hoping Rafe's question hadn't inadvertently caused friction between the two.

Anastasia looked at Matias. "It's not on the Harvard campus, per se. It's a fine arts pavilion." An apology came into her eyes. "The Kovell Fine Arts Pavilion."

"Wait," Matias said.

"And Academy," she finished, cringing slightly.

Gina recognized the name of the institution. It was prestigious and huge, and owned by...

Matias was shaking his head now. Luckily the drinks arrived, because he looked like he could use one. He took a swallow of his martini as the waitress left.

"You really are slumming," he said to Anastasia.

"No. I'm *rebelling*."

"And that's different how?" Matias was clearly annoyed.

Gina looked to Rafe, thinking maybe they should leave for a minute and give the couple some privacy.

Rafe started to rise. "Gina and I will—"

"No," Matias said. His smile was brittle. "No. It's not the end of the world. She was only supposed to be in Texas for two days. We've had five. I'm grateful for that." He raised his glass. "Thank you, Anastasia, for buying me and for coming all the way to Royal for an experience."

"Matias..." she said.

He rocked his glass meaningfully, annoyance still in his eyes.

Gina quickly raised her Bordeaux, hoping to help defuse the situation and give Rafe's brother a moment to calm down. "Welcome to Royal, Anastasia."

"Hear, hear." Rafe raised his glass as well.

Looking none too happy, Anastasia joined the toast.

Afterward, she was quiet for a moment.

Gina searched her mind for a safe topic.

But Anastasia spoke up. "I'm not going back there."

All three of them looked at her.

"I like it here," she said airily. "And I'm staying. Date me if you want to, Matias. Dump me if you want to. But I'm sticking around. Maybe I'll buy some real estate." She turned to Gina. "Do you know a good agent?"

Gina opened her mouth, not knowing what to say.

"Don't be ridiculous," Matias said.

"Matias." Rafe's tone was warning.

Matias glared at his brother.

"*What* are you doing?" Rafe demanded. Matias started to speak, but Rafe cut him off. "So she's richer than you thought. So what?"

"She—"

"Didn't tell some random auction cowboy her family had more money than royalty? Right out of the gate? I wonder why?"

Matias paused, his expression going pensive.

"I wouldn't either," Gina put in. "If I was in a new city, meeting a new guy, I wouldn't tell him about my family."

She caught Rafe's amused expression out of the corner of her eye.

"Okay," she said in response. "So, my family is pretty much infamous now. But still, you get my point. Who wants to be judged by your family? I know I don't."

"I didn't mean to keep it from you," Anastasia said to Matias. "I didn't lie, I just didn't..."

"Bring full financial statements on a first date," Rafe finished for her. "Get a grip, Matias. She's obviously way out of your league, and you're being a jerk, and she's still willing to give you a second chance. Apologize, thank her very much and order an appetizer already."

Gina almost laughed.

Anastasia tried to hide it, but she was clearly amused.

Even Matias rolled his eyes, shook his head, but then he smiled. "Fine. I'm sorry. I don't know why I reacted that way."

A waiter, clearly one with impeccable timing, arrived with their dinner menus.

The rest of the evening passed in fine food, good drinks and a luscious crème brûlée that Gina shared with Rafe for dessert. Then they were saying a cheerful good-night and she was climbing back into Rafe's SUV.

"She seems great," Gina said, settling into the soft seat as Rafe started the vehicle.

"Matias is a lucky guy," Rafe agreed. He backed out of the parking spot and steered them toward the exit. "Tired?"

"A little, yeah. It was a fun night."

"So…what…now…?" His voice was a sexy rumble above the sound of the engine. "Do you want me to take you home?"

She turned, gazing at his profile in the strobing street-lights. "Is that what you want?"

He glanced sideways and slowly scanned his way to her toes. "What I want is to take you, those shoes and that sexy little dress straight back to my bedroom."

Her skin flushed with heat while anticipation constricted her chest. "That. Let's do that."

The day of Sarabeth's wedding, Rafe drove to Mustang Point alone. Gina had traveled there with her mother and the rest of the wedding party the night before in a private plane. He'd booked himself a room at the Trinity Grand Bayside Hotel, a short drive from the marina where the wedding yacht would be moored.

Lorenzo and Matias were also attending the wedding and planned to stay at the Grand.

Rafe checked in and pocketed his key card as his bag was whisked away by the bell captain.

"You made it." Lorenzo approached with Valencia by his side.

Rafe gave Valencia an affectionate hug. "Good drive down?" he asked them both.

"We're all checked in, nice view of the marina from our suite. We were about to have lunch. Want to join us?"

"Sounds good to me," Rafe said. "Did Matias make it yet?"

"Should be here anytime," Lorenzo said. "They flew straight into Houston."

"Flew?" It was an easy three-hour drive from Royal.

"He didn't tell you?"

"Tell me what?" Rafe had spent the past week working with JJ and Mrs. Yeoh on the baking launch—that was when he wasn't taking every spare hour to snatch a little sexy time with Gina.

"He went to Boston to meet the parents."

"*Anastasia's* parents?"

"Let's get a table," Valencia suggested. "I'm starving."

"Sure, sweetheart." Lorenzo gently touched the small of her back as the three of them started for the lobby restaurant.

They were shown to a table beside the picture windows with a view of Trinity Bay. The beach was filled with families and sunbathers. Swimmers bobbed out in the ocean and volleyball games were underway on the sand. The shouts and calls of it all were muted through the glass.

As he sat down, Rafe glimpsed the wedding party at a table on the far side of the restaurant. Ross caught his gaze and gave him a curt nod—not a welcoming expression by any means. But Ross didn't have to worry. Rafe wasn't going to intrude on their family time.

Both Gina and Sarabeth had their backs to Rafe, while Ross's wife, Charlotte, was in profile, as were Asher and Lani.

"I see our timing is perfect," Matias said as he and Anastasia arrived.

Lorenzo quickly hopped up to move his chair closer to Valencia, making room for Matias to add a fifth seat to the round table.

"How was the visit in Boston?" Rafe asked Matias, curious about what had happened there.

"Her father hates me."

"He doesn't hate you," Anastasia quickly put in.

Out of the corner of his eye, Rafe caught sight of Zach Benning and Lila Jones being shown to a table. They were dining with Carter Crane and Abby Carmichael, obviously all here for the wedding.

"Who can blame him?" Lorenzo asked on a note of amusement, earning him a warning touch on the arm from Valencia.

His brother's fiancée liked to keep things calm. It served her well in working with horses and troubled kids, but the rowdy banter among the Cortez-Williams brothers sometimes made her uncomfortable.

Lorenzo kept on talking. "If I had a daughter of Anastasia's caliber, I'd want to keep her far away from a cowboy like you."

Even Valencia laughed at the joke and seemed to relax again.

"Mother *loved* him," Anastasia said to the group. "She'll bring Daddy around."

"I don't think a rancher was what he had in mind for his baby girl," Matias said, looking around for a waiter. "Have you guys ordered yet? I'm starving."

"Thank you, Matias," Valencia said. "Maybe we can get some appetizers to get us going?"

Rafe caught the eye of a waiter and gave a quick nod of his head. The man came straight over.

He handed menus around and offered to take drink orders.

Iced tea seemed to be everyone's preferred beverage, while Valencia and Matias agreed on a large appetizer platter with fresh guacamole.

"What do you think he had in mind for his baby girl?" Rafe asked Matias, his gaze straying to the Edmond table again, wondering if they had specific aspirations for Gina.

"Someone refined," Matias answered. "Likes the symphony and all that, maybe with a PhD in literature and wearing tweed."

Anastasia was clearly trying not to laugh at Matias's description.

"You disagree?" Rafe asked her.

She shook her head. "No, I completely agree. I've been dating guys like that since high school." She put her perfectly manicured hand on Matias's arm. "I didn't know what I was missing."

Valencia rubbed Lorenzo's shoulder. "Can't do better than a Cortez-Williams man."

Rafe looked at Gina again.

Lorenzo leaned over to give Valencia a quick kiss of appreciation.

Rafe caught a glimpse of the smiles and laughter between the two couples at Zach and Carter's table. It made sense that everyone was in a good mood anticipating tonight's wedding and the lavish reception and harbor cruise to follow.

"You're here solo?" Lorenzo asked Rafe, and it occurred to him that he'd been more than circumspect about Gina.

Rafe nodded to the far table. "I'm Gina Edmond's plus one."

Both of his brothers looked surprised. "Seriously?"

Anastasia looked confused by their reaction. "Gina came to dinner with him last weekend."

"That was business," Rafe said, sticking to their cover story. "The wedding's business, too, her cowboy experience."

Everyone looked at him in confusion.

"A bit of an inside joke," he said, wishing he'd kept his mouth shut about that. "She donated to the auction, and I agreed to be her escort to the wedding."

"This is a paying gig?" Matias joked.

Rafe shot him a reflexive glare. "The donation was to the Chamber of Commerce fund."

"Which I very much appreciated," Valencia said. "We've used the money to add three horses to the new stable and make room for ten more kids this year."

"I would have done it anyway," Rafe told Matias. He wanted to be clear on that.

"Who wouldn't?" Lorenzo joked. Then he looked at Valencia. "I mean, not me or anything."

Everyone laughed again.

"Any single guy would," Rafe said, putting a thread of humor in his own voice. He wasn't annoyed with Matias. He was only annoyed with himself.

The waiter arrived with the iced tea and another one set the appetizer platter in the middle of the table while Rafe watched Gina's party rise to their feet. She was talking with Charlotte and smiling about something. Then her gaze caught Rafe's and he physically felt the punch.

She said something more to Charlotte, then something to her mother, then she started his way.

The two waiters finished their work just as Gina arrived at the table.

"Hi, all," she said, putting a hand on the back of Rafe's chair.

He stood.

There was a round of hellos to Gina.

"Thanks for coming," she said warmly to them all. "Nice to see you again, Anastasia."

"Anything you need?" Rafe asked her.

"Not just now." Their eyes met and held for a moment before she turned her attention back to the group. "The chaos seems to be somewhat under control. There were a few bad moments with the cake, and a minor flower emergency that we were able to resolve." She glanced at her watch. "But the afternoon is young."

They all chuckled.

She put her hand on Rafe's shoulder and looked at him again. "See you after the ceremony."

"You bet," he said, wishing with all his heart he dared to pull her into his arms.

She sent a smile all around. "See you tonight."

Rafe watched her for a moment before sitting down. Then he looked up to see everyone staring silently his way.

"What?"

"Just business?" Lorenzo asked.

"She's been helping with the bakery launch. You saw how she handled the auction. She does terrific work."

"You had a bit of dopey look on your face there," Matias said.

"Matias," Valencia admonished.

"She's a beautiful woman," Rafe said matter-of-factly, temporarily shaking off his longing. "We all agreed on that. And I get to dance with her later."

"Business doesn't get any better than that," Anastasia offered with a grin.

"Exactly." Rafe made a show of scanning the appetizer platter. "Who said they were hungry?"

Eleven

In the captain's stateroom of the *Azure Moon* yacht, Gina helped Sarabeth with her final preparations. It was thirty minutes to the ceremony and the weather and wind were both cooperating. The ceremony would be held outdoors at the bow, while the formal reception would spread out in the ballroom and the aft deck. Dinner would be on the main deck with dancing later on the lower deck and a mix-and-mingle bar outside on the upper sundeck around the pool.

This afternoon at the Grand hotel spa, she and Sarabeth had both indulged in facials, mani-pedis, and professional hair and makeup. Now the hairdresser was anchoring the pearl-and-rhinestone comb into the loose knot of Sarabeth's beautiful blond hair. She had romantic wisps around her face, sparse enough to show off her dangling diamond earrings.

Gina was wearing her favorite diamond studs and the little cluster diamond necklace her mother had bought her as a keepsake. The seafoam chiffon felt light and airy on her legs. She'd sprayed just a touch of sheen on her tanned shoulders, and her brunette hair was swept back in a simpler style than Sarabeth's.

Gina double-checked the cream-and-pale-yellow rose bouquets sitting out on the table. They were subtle and classy, with just a hint of greenery to set off the blooms. Their shoes were ready to be put on at the last minute—no point in wearing out their feet too early—although they'd both brought along dancing slippers for later in the evening.

A knock sounded on the cabin door.

Gina moved to get it while Sarabeth and the hairdresser perfected the comb's placement.

It was Ross. "Got a minute?" he asked in a low tone.

Asher was standing behind him in the narrow corridor.

"Now?" Gina whispered back.

"We need to give you a heads-up."

They both looked serious, so Gina moved into the passage and pulled the door mostly shut behind her. "What's wrong?"

"It's Billy."

"What about Billy?" Who cared about Billy Holmes twenty minutes before the wedding ceremony?

"The overseas private investigative firm sent Dad a report."

Gina rolled her eyes. "This is a Rusty emergency?" She looked back and forth between her two brothers. "You don't think Dad's just trying to mess with the wedding?"

"No. Rusty doesn't care about the wedding," Ross said.

"He doesn't want Sarabeth to be happy," Gina countered. "He doesn't want *anyone* to be happy."

Both men considered that for a second.

"True," Ross said. "But that's not what this is."

"Gina?" Sarabeth called from inside the cabin.

"Be right there, Mom," Gina called back.

"Who's out there?"

"It's just Ross and Asher."

"Tell Ross I'll be a few more minutes."

"Will do," Gina called back.

"Take your time," Ross called out.

"So, what is it?" Gina asked her brothers.

The yacht pitched a little under her feet.

"They've got a line on some of the money," Ross said. "They're following trails in the Caymans, Singapore and Belize."

"Well, that's good news." She didn't know why they'd have to warn her about that.

"It's the first significant movement in months," Asher said. "They're boxing him in, and they think he might react to it."

"He could get desperate," Ross said.

"Then maybe he'll make a mistake," she suggested.

"If he thinks the money's being threatened—"

Asher jumped in. "They think he might switch to blackmail."

Ross gave Gina a meaningful look, like he wanted her to fill in a blank. "So…"

Astonishment rose within her. "Are you asking if I can be blackmailed?"

"Can you?"

"No. What is this? Are you actually warning me to hide *the bodies*?"

"We don't know what you—"

She cut Ross off. "I can't be blackmailed, guys. There's nothing." She gave a little laugh. "No videotapes of me with married men. No hate-filled rants. No tax evasion. No criminal financial transactions."

"Good," Asher said.

"I can't believe you had to ask me."

"Gina," Ross said. "Have you been paying attention for the past year? This family has a whole crap-ton of secrets."

"Well, none of them are mine." She thought for a second about Rafe, but Billy could hardly blackmail her over him.

She'd admit to the world she was sleeping with Rafe before she'd pay out a dime to Billy or anyone else. She didn't care who knew about the two of them. For some reason, it had been a secret at the start, but she couldn't even remember why anymore.

The door opened behind her and Sarabeth appeared. "I'm ready," she said breathlessly.

Both men immediately smiled.

"You look wonderful, Mom," Ross said.

"You'll knock 'em dead, Sarabeth," Asher added. "I better get up there." With a wave, he headed down the corridor.

"The bouquets," Gina remembered. But behind Sarabeth, the hairdresser was already handing them over.

"You look perfect." She gave her mom a beaming smile. "I can't wait to see you come down the staircase." Then she left down the corridor like Asher.

"I guess this is it," Ross said, stepping back to look at them both. "Let's go wow the guests."

Some guests were seated, the rest clustered more casually around the edges for the short ceremony, filling the bow of the mega-yacht right to the rails. Rafe stood near the back edge of the crowd, making sure his height didn't block others from seeing the ceremony.

A curving staircase flowed down one side of the deck space. It was elegantly decorated with white roses, greenery and subtle lighting, creating a bridal pathway with the sun setting far across the bay.

The music came up and the crowd quieted as Gina appeared at the top of the staircase. She started gracefully down, a bouquet in her hands, her pale sea-blue dress caressing her thighs. Rafe's vision tunneled to her, and everything around him disappeared.

She looked happy as she took the crowd in from one end to the other. Then she spotted Rafe, and her gaze stopped moving. Her lips curved into the softest of smiles just for him. At least it felt like it was just for him.

He started to move toward her but stopped himself just in time.

She wasn't his, even if he wished with all his heart that she was.

She stepped off at the bottom of the stairs, and the music

changed. Everyone's attention moved from Gina back to the top of the staircase where Sarabeth was on Ross's arm.

Rafe gave the bride a glance, but then looked back at Gina. She was by far the most beautiful woman he'd ever seen, full red lips, rosy cheeks, shiny, thick hair that glowed in the waning rays of the sun. Her bare shoulders shone, and he longed to run his hands over them. He couldn't wait for the dancing to start so he could hold her in his arms.

The ceremony was brief, and then Brett was kissing Sarabeth. The guests responded with whoops and applause and calls of congratulations as the bride and groom made their way down a center aisle toward the ballroom. Gina followed on the arm of Brett's best man. Rafe knew it was ridiculous to be jealous. They were simply fulfilling their roles in the wedding. But he couldn't help himself.

Ross, Charlotte, Asher and Lani fell in behind, and the rest of the guests rose and began to move in a swell from the ceremony to the hall.

Rafe lingered. He knew Gina would have official duties, photographs first, then dining at the head table, maybe making a toast. He planned to wander up to the cocktail bar on the top deck where it was a little quieter and wait his way through the next hour or so. He'd join his brothers for dinner, which he was sure would be off-the-charts delicious, but all he really wanted was to dance with Gina.

As expected, a sensational staff served a cheese-and-candied-nuts starter, followed by a crisp melon salad, a seafood cocktail, and grilled wild salmon with mushroom risotto and baby vegetables, all followed by a tray of delicate mini chocolate truffles with gold filigree. Everything was accompanied by the perfect wine pairings.

Finally, the guests migrated to the lower deck, and it was time for the first dance. A grinning Brett led Sarabeth onto the dance floor. She was radiant and clearly waltzing on air. Rafe couldn't help but smile at their obvious happiness and the oohs and aahs of the watchers.

Gina joined in then in the best man's arms. Rafe gritted his teeth, but it was only for the obligatory dance, and partway through other couples took to the floor. He made his move then, easing his way to the edge of the dance floor, successfully timing his arrival to when the song changed and Gina separated from her partner.

She looked up, seeming surprised to see him so close.

"Dance?" he drawled.

"Where have you been?" she asked as she moved into his arms.

The song the band started was thankfully slow, and he drew her close. "Waiting for you."

"I was looking for you at dinner. I was afraid you might have left."

He was surprised to hear her say that. "Never. You look stunning, you know." He chuckled. "You have a mirror, so I guess you know."

"You like the dress?" she asked.

"I like you in it."

She drew back and pouted a little.

"And I like the dress."

"I had to try on about thirty of them."

"You made a great choice. Sarabeth looks very happy."

Gina turned to look at her mother. "She is. She so deserves it. They both do."

Rafe tucked Gina's head into the crook of his shoulder, lightly feathering his fingers where her upper back was left bare by the strapless dress. "I missed you," he whispered.

"I missed you, too," she said. "It's been a busy week…"

"I'm glad it's over." He didn't know what came next for them, but he desperately wanted it to be *something*.

"Tonight may go on for a while," she warned.

"That's okay. You're free now. That's all I care about."

She tipped back her head and smiled. "I have to help with the cake-cutting later."

"I suppose I can give you up for that long." He put on a mock earnest expression. "I mean, I hear tell it's a really great cake."

She laughed and bopped him in the arm at the same time.

"Vanilla lemon curd with white chocolate buttercream," he said.

"You remembered."

"I remember everything you say to me, Gina. Everything."

The song ended and Ross appeared at Rafe's elbow. "Gina?" he asked, offering his hand.

Rafe's grip subconsciously tightened, but he knew she could hardly say no to her brother.

He forced himself to let her go and stepped back.

Ross shot him a challenging look that might have made another man back off. But there was no way Rafe was backing off from Gina. Not a chance in hell.

He moved out of the way, but only temporarily, standing a little way back from the dance floor, as Ross and Gina seemed to have a fairly intense conversation.

Lorenzo appeared at his side and handed him a drink that looked like bourbon. "How's it going?"

"Great." Rafe didn't even try to camouflage the frustration in his tone as he tossed the drink back.

His brother nodded in Gina's direction. "It's not just business between you two, is it?"

"It's not just business," Rafe admitted.

"So, what's going on?"

"I don't know." That was the truth.

"Are you sleeping with her?"

"Yes." Rafe was through keeping his feelings for Gina a secret.

"Does her brother know that?"

"Nope."

"Think he's guessed by the way you look at her?"

"Maybe." Rafe had to admit it was a possibility.

"Never thought I'd see that day." There was a thread of humor in Lorenzo's voice.

"What day is that?"

"A romance between our two families."

"You think they're too good for us?" Rafe asked a question that had been in the back of his mind since that first night with Gina.

"No. I think we're too good for them." Lorenzo gave Rafe a clap on the back. "Be careful around her."

Valencia arrived next to Lorenzo. "Honey?"

Lorenzo immediately wrapped his arm around her waist. His tone went soft. "You want to dance?"

She smiled and nodded.

Rafe took Lorenzo's empty glass to free him up for the dance floor, then deposited both glasses on a nearby tray. As the band switched songs again, Rafe looked for Gina, only to discover she was dancing with Asher. He settled back to cool his heels, swooping in again just as soon as the song ended.

It was a relief to have her back. He didn't talk, didn't ask about either of her brothers, not wanting to break the sensual spell of being in each other's arms.

The song ended. He was determined not to give her up again. But the MC stepped up to the microphone, and with a flourish he announced the throwing of the bridal bouquet. Claps and cheers came up, and the crowd parted on the dance floor, making space for the single women.

Rafe had no choice but to step to the side with Gina as a cluster of mostly young women moved into the center of the hall, chatting and laughing at the time-honored tradition. Someone came by and grabbed Gina's hand. She resisted, but another young woman stopped as well, coaxing her to the join the growing crowd.

Rafe backed off to stay out of the way, watching Gina take a position at a far corner of the group. The drummer gave a dramatic roll on his snare drum. Turning her back to the ladies, Sarabeth laughed. Then she tossed the bouquet high in the air.

As it arced in slow motion, Gina's eyes went wide. She took a step back, almost as if she was trying to get out of the way. But the bouquet landed square in her chest and she seemed to reflexively trap it with her hands.

Rafe couldn't help but smile at her look of bewilderment.

A figure loomed up beside him—*Ross*.

"It took me a while," Ross said as the women clustered around Gina oohing and aahing and congratulating her.

She still looked disconcerted.

Rafe wasn't going to take the bait. He stayed silent, letting Ross say whatever it was he was here to say.

"To work out why you wouldn't take the money," Ross said.

"Didn't need it," Rafe responded.

"That's a lie."

Rafe shrugged. "Think whatever you like."

"I am. I do. Why take the scraps when you can latch onto the mother lode?"

Rafe turned to Ross, his eyes narrowing. "Is that supposed to be some kind of a joke?"

Ross nodded to Gina. "You've cleverly wormed your way into her life. She even caught the bouquet. You must think it's going to be smooth sailing to the altar." Ross's scowl deepened. "It won't be smooth. I'll make sure of that."

"Back *the hell* off," Rafe ground out. He couldn't believe Ross would accuse him of romancing Gina for her money.

"Sucks to get caught."

"Leave," Rafe said. "Now."

A smug expression on his face, Ross strode away.

"The family's been through a lot." It was Asher's voice on Rafe's other side.

He twisted his neck, shocked and annoyed to see Gina's other brother eyeing him up with the same suspicion.

"*She's* been through a lot," Asher continued. "You might want to keep that in mind when you're messing with her trust."

"I'm not—" Rafe started to defend himself but clamped his jaw instead. He could protest until he was blue in the face and the Edmond brothers would never listen. They thought they had him pegged.

Rafe glanced around the room, wondering what judgmental thoughts were behind the other smiling faces of the who's who of Royal.

His gaze came to Gina, and he felt a little better. The cluster of women around her had trickled to three, none that he recognized, so he started her way.

"You never know," one of the women said to her.

"Your turn next," another said.

"No, really, there's nobody, nobody at all," Gina responded.

"Tradition is tradition."

"That's superstition," Gina countered, then she saw Rafe standing close and guilt flashed across her face.

It didn't take a rocket scientist to conclude that he was the nobody. His chest suddenly felt like lead.

The women spotted him. "Ah, here's a likely candidate now," one of them sang out.

Gina's face flushed a little, and she stammered as she spoke. "He's...that's...just... Rafe."

"Business associate," Rafe offered to the curious women. He tried to give Gina a smile, but he couldn't quite pull it off. "Nice catch." His voice came out cold. "See you later." He turned away.

"Rafe!" she called behind him.

He didn't turn back, sped up instead, efficiently crossing the big room as the crowd closed behind him. Then he came out on the deck and headed straight for the closest gangplank, getting off the yacht to make his way down the dock.

He couldn't believe he'd been so blind. He and Gina were good together, sure. But it was a lark for her, a temporary, fun fling that wasn't leading anywhere near where he'd wanted it to go.

He might have had an epiphany watching her walk down that staircase with a bouquet in her hands, but that was his take, not hers. At best, she was skipping blithely through their relationship with no thought to the future. At worst, she thought the same thing as her brothers—that he had an interest in her wealth.

It was only a few blocks to the hotel, but he didn't want to go back there. Rafe didn't particularly want to *be* anywhere right now. He shucked his jacket and undid his tie, turning from the parking lot to the boardwalk and the yellow lights spilling out from the row of tourist shops and cafés.

Gina had rushed after Rafe, regretting her words and hating the way they had sounded. She'd made it sound like he was nothing special, that he wasn't the most amazing man in the world and that she wouldn't leap at an offer to spend the rest of her life with him.

Catching the bouquet had rocked her to her toes. As a young girl, she'd dreamed of catching the bouquet, of the big white wedding that was sure to follow. She'd fantasized of dressing up like a fairy princess and gliding down the aisle of a huge cathedral to meet her waiting groom. In her dreams, the groom had been faceless, a tall, dark man in a fine tux who would whisk her away on a fairy tale.

But the groom had a face now. It was *Rafe*. And it was

the rest of the fantasy that had fallen away. She didn't care about the gorgeous dress, the flowers or the five-tiered cake. She didn't care about the crowds of people in the pews wishing them well or about jetting off on a fabulous honeymoon. She wanted Rafe, only Rafe, but she had no idea if he felt the same way.

Gina had been embarrassed by the inference that he might be her future groom, worried he'd feel pushed and prodded into something he wasn't anywhere near ready to even think about. She'd been so worried that he'd be uncomfortable that she'd stumbled all over herself, protesting far too much.

And now he was gone, obviously gone since she'd checked the entire ship and couldn't find a single sign of him. Even his brothers didn't know where he was.

"Gina." Sarabeth called her name from where she was standing with Brett near the bandstand.

Gina looked over and her mother motioned her forward, pointing at the cake that was being wheeled out on a tray by two waiters. The MC was getting ready to announce the cake-cutting.

"No," Gina whispered to herself. It would take forever to help hand out cake to all these guests, and she needed to find Rafe.

Her mother motioned her again, looking puzzled by Gina's lack of response.

With a last look around, she started forward as the MC made the pronouncement and the photographer got into position. She told herself this was her last official act of the night. Next, Sarabeth and Brett would wave goodbye to their guests and leave by private jet on their honeymoon to the Florida Keys.

Still glancing around for Rafe, Gina stood back while the official ceremonial cut was made. Then she moved in and smiled for some pictures. At Sarabeth's insistence,

Ross moved into the frame, then Asher as well, followed by their fiancées. Gina felt like the photos would never end.

But finally, the waiters stepped in to help cut and set out the cake. While the bride and groom circulated through the guests, Gina handed out slice after slice, thanking person after person for coming to the wedding. The cake lineup finally ended with a good portion of the huge cake remaining.

After it was wheeled back to the kitchen, the MC announced the wedding couple was taking their leave from the main gangway. Everyone was invited to gather there and bid them farewell.

Gina hugged her mother and her new stepfather goodbye. The crowd cheered and waved them across the gangplank and into a waiting limousine that drove them off on their honeymoon. Many of the guests chose the moment to leave the party as well, crossing the gangplank in couples and groups, heading into their cars in the sprawling parking lot.

Gina moved to one side to keep herself out of the way, finding Ross and Charlotte with their son, Ben, balanced on her hip standing along the rail. "Have you seen Rafe?" she asked them.

"No," Ross answered. "Why?"

She didn't want to talk about the bridal bouquet debacle, or her fear that Rafe left the wedding reception hurt and angry. She settled on something straightforward. "He was my escort."

"I can get you whatever you need," Ross said.

"No, it's not that—"

A figure suddenly loomed up in front of them, and Gina was stunned to recognize Billy Holmes. He was dressed like a guest in an impeccable suit, and she wondered just when he'd infiltrated the crowd. His black hair was unruly. His lips were drawn in a thin line. And there was an unmistakable glitter of hatred in his pale green eyes.

"Well, well, well," he drawled. "My beloved sister and brother."

Ross quickly urged Charlotte and Ben to leave and go back inside. But when he tried to do the same with Gina, Billy stopped him.

"Not so fast," he said, menace in his tone.

Gina stilled, afraid of what Billy might do, wondering if he had become desperate. People were still streaming off the main gangplank. The party was breaking up, and Billy had obviously timed his appearance.

"You shouldn't be here," Ross growled in an undertone, shifting closer to Gina.

"Would I miss the big day?" Billy taunted, sounding chipper but brittle. "The big family day."

Asher materialized on Gina's other side. "This isn't your family, Billy."

Gina could sense the coiled tension in each of her two brothers. She knew they were sizing the other man up, deciding what they could do to subdue him.

"You sure got that right," Billy barked back. "It *should* have been my family. By blood this is my family." He raised his voice to the crowd. "Wedding's over! Everyone off the ship. Only Edmonds allowed now. This—" he stared pointedly at Ross and then Gina, then Asher "—is a family matter."

The guests looked over, some confused, some concerned. Mostly, they hurried more quickly over the gangplank.

As the crowd thinned to nothing, Ross and Asher shared a look. Their expressions said they were going to make a move against Billy.

"Uh-uh," Billy chided, taking a step back. He patted the breast pocket of his jacket meaningfully. "You don't want to see what I'm carrying under here. I came prepared."

Gina's blood turned to ice at the thought that Billy might

be armed and mean them harm. She was grateful Charlotte and Ben were safely inside; presumably, so was Lani. She hoped they stayed far away from this confrontation.

"What do you want?" Ross asked Billy.

Gina was wondering the same thing. It was a risk for him to show his face. One or more of the guests might have recognized him and called the police. His picture had been plastered all over the Texas news for months now. She desperately hoped someone would think to alert the authorities.

Another person crossed the gangplank, boarding the yacht. With the glare of the parking lot lights in her eyes, it took Gina a moment to recognize Rusty.

"Dad?" she asked in astonishment. He should have been back in Royal.

"The gang's all here," Billy said with satisfaction as Rusty halted, taking them in.

"I came," he said shortly to Billy. "Time for you to live up to your end."

"What's the hurry?" Billy asked, his voice laced with faux charm. "The party's just getting started."

"Where's the money?" Rusty asked.

"You know your big mistake?" Billy bit out. "Thinking this was about the money. It was *never* about the money."

"Then why'd you steal it?" Ross demanded.

"To hit you where it *hurts*!"

"In our bank account," Asher said.

It didn't make a whole lot of sense, since the Edmonds had plenty of money left.

"No," Billy barked, taking a couple of quick paces to the side and then pacing back again.

Gina glanced around the deck and saw nobody else was left.

"You Edmonds," Billy continued. "Always bigger than life, swaggering around town, looking down on the peasants."

"Peasants?" Gina asked, baffled by the description.

"Give back the money," Rusty said. "Like you promised. Return it all, and we can talk. We can approach the DA, work out a deal, make things right."

"Simple as that?" Billy asked sarcastically.

"It can be. No guarantees."

"You wouldn't press charges?"

"No," Rusty said.

"Why, pray tell, *not*?" Billy looked even angrier with Rusty now, and Gina couldn't stop thinking about the gun he claimed to have in his pocket.

"You know why not," her dad said quietly.

"Because I'm your son." There was a sharp challenge in Billy's voice.

"That's right," Rusty said.

Everyone, including Billy, looked shocked by the admission.

"It's all there," Rusty continued, sizing Billy up. "In your eyes, your voice, your determination and drive. You're more like me than any of the rest."

Gina, Ross and Asher all stared at their father in open astonishment.

"Dad?" Ross asked.

"Don't you dare interrupt!" Billy's anger swung to Ross. "He's talking to me now, *me*, not you. You had *everything*. Russell Jr., the namesake, the eldest, the golden child. The heir apparent who got everything while I got nothing." Billy glared at Asher. "Not even the family name. *You* got the family name, Asher. You just showed up with your mother, and Rusty took you right under his wing. You got the family name, the company, the money, the prestige and power. What did I get?" Billy's anger seemed to increase by the minute.

"You're not returning the money, are you?" Rusty took Billy's attention back on himself.

"To save your hide?" he sneered. "To save the lot of you the pain and humiliation of being the town pariahs?"

"To save yourself a long jail sentence," Ross said.

"It didn't have to *be* like this." Billy squeezed his eyes shut for a moment, sounding more and more unhinged. "I thought you'd take me in, give me my fair turn, treat me the way you treated your precious Ross, that upstart Asher, and your flawless princess Gina all those years while I was scrambling for pennies."

Ross jumped in. "You have no idea what you're talking about."

"Don't I?" Billy challenged.

"He *disowned* me," Ross pointed out.

Billy leaned toward Ross. "Welcome to the club."

"He didn't even know about you."

Billy didn't seem to hear Ross's response. Instead, he gave a cold chuckle. "Taste of your own medicine, huh? You should know that was me." He mimicked the sound of an explosion, dramatically spreading his fingers and pulling his hands apart. "Charlotte was like a grenade with the pin pulled. That was a masterstroke, that was."

"You sent Charlotte back to hurt Ross?" Gina's fear was being replaced by anger now. "What is *wrong* with you?"

"But it was Dad who tried to drive us apart," Ross said.

"I thought I'd have to work a lot harder," Billy admitted, still sporting a chilling smile. "But you Edmonds were a domino line of dysfunction just waiting to fall."

"*I* went to *jail* over this," Asher said, his voice laced with anger.

"All part of the plot," Billy stated with satisfaction. "Frame the interloper. Alienate the golden child."

"I underestimated you," Rusty told him.

"Damn straight you underestimated me."

Rusty spoke again. "I was wrong, and I'm sorry."

Gina had never in her life heard her father utter those

words. It was beyond jarring that he'd used them with Billy of all people.

"You're my son, Billy, my flesh and blood. You're smart, driven, tenacious." Rusty looked oddly proud of him. "I should have acknowledged you, welcomed you into the heart of our family."

"The *heart*?" Gina asked with incredulity. If they were coming clean here, then she was coming clean, too.

The tone of her voice got everyone's attention.

"There was no heart!" she cried out. "Like Billy just said, we're a row of dysfunctional dominoes waiting to fall." She pointed to her chest. "I'm a grown woman, an educated, intelligent woman. But I'm treated like a decoration, pampered with possessions but discounted, ignored, never given a chance to do anything or to be anyone. My world revolves around the male Edmond whims, smiling at business functions, chatting up company associates. Nobody ever asked me what I could contribute."

Rusty's jaw dropped slightly.

"I was bullied and undermined at every turn," Ross said to Rusty. "You belittled me. You hurt the woman I loved. Then you threw me away when I didn't fit your mold."

Rusty jerked back, staring at them as if he'd been hit.

"You sat back and *let* them frame me," Asher told him. "You had so little faith in me that you assumed I was a criminal on circumstantial evidence. You think Billy's like you? *Yeah*, Billy's like you. The rest of us are *not*."

Rusty stared straight ahead for a moment, a haunted expression in his eyes. "I deserved that."

"You're a conniving man," Ross said, clearly not finished yet. "In big ways and small, you schemed to make us what you wanted no matter what it did to our own lives."

There was a long silence after that.

"I'm sorry to you all," Rusty finally murmured, his voice so low and husky that Gina thought she'd misheard.

"I'm sorry," he said more firmly. "You're my children. You're all I have, and I'm going to do better. And Billy—"

Rusty turned, and Gina looked to where Billy had been standing just moments ago.

The deck was empty, and they all stared in stupefied silence until an engine revved loudly in the parking lot below. A pair of tires screeched and a black sports car zig-zagged toward the exit. It was obvious Billy was making a run for it.

"I don't get it," Gina said as the car sped away. "What did he want?"

"Acknowledgment?" Ross speculated. "Maybe he thinks he got it?"

"More like he knew he'd go to jail if he stayed," Asher noted.

"He's family," Rusty said.

"You're saying you'd *help* him get out of this?" Ross asked incredulously.

"I'd at least get him a good lawyer."

"I don't think he's returning the money," Gina observed, looking at the now-empty road.

"I hope it's brought him some peace," Rusty said sadly.

"He stole *millions of dollars*," Asher reminded him.

"He wanted to be part of the family."

"He went about it in the worst way possible." Gina looked at her brothers and her father then, wondering what happened next.

Was Rusty's apology to them a first step? Could they pull it together and salvage their family?

"We will," Rusty seemed to understand her unspoken question. "This is my doing. It's mine to fix, and I'm *going* to fix it."

Gina immediately thought of Rafe. The rift with Rafe was hers to fix, and she was determined to make amends. He might not love her, but she was head over heels for him. She was going to make that clear as soon as she got back to Royal.

She was laying her cards on the table. The two of them didn't have a business relationship. This wasn't a fling or friends with benefits or any temporary euphemism someone wanted to give it.

Gina wanted a *real* relationship. She wanted to be Rafe's significant other, the woman he spent his downtime with, plus family dinners, barbecues, everything other couples did together and more...

"I'm exhausted," she said to her father and brothers, feeling impatient to get going. "I'm getting my things and heading home."

Gina made her way toward the stern of the yacht where a little staircase would take her back to the captain's cabin for her purse.

"Gina?" Rafe's voice startled her as he stepped from the shadows.

She couldn't believe it was him silhouetted against the deck lights. "Rafe?" But he was here, and her heart sang with joy.

"Hi," he said, a hesitant expression on his face.

She took a step closer. "I'm so sorry."

"It's okay."

"It's not."

He canted his head back along the deck. "I overheard just now."

"Billy?" she asked in surprise.

"I stuck close in case he tried something stupid."

She shuddered. "I thought he had a gun."

"He might have had a gun. He's pretty desperate."

"I know." Her knees suddenly felt weak in reaction.

Rafe seemed to sense it and stepped forward, reaching out to her.

She gripped his forearms for support.

"I knew you struggled with your father," he said, searching her expression. "But I had no idea of all that you'd been through."

"It's not going to continue," she told him.

"It seemed like you cleared the air."

"I have ideas, and I'm pushing them forward."

"Good for you." His smile seemed sad, and she remembered how they'd left things after the bouquet toss.

Her shoulders drooped. "Back there. Inside, I mean. I... I didn't mean for you to think..."

Rafe shifted closer. "Think what?"

"That you were nobody to me. That you were a business associate or a friend or something run-of-the-mill like that."

"Ross and Asher think I'm after your money."

The statement shocked her to silence.

"You know I'm not after your money, right?" Rafe asked, an earnest expression in his eyes.

She was baffled by the question. "I keep trying to give you my money, and you keep turning it down."

He chuckled in what seemed like relief.

"And the chamber fund," she continued. "That was a *lot* of money you turned down."

"I don't want your money."

"I know."

"I won't take it."

"Okay." She didn't know why he was pressing the point.

"You should write up an iron-clad prenup so you and your brothers, your father, and anyone else who cares will know that I am definitely not after a single penny of Edmond money."

Gina's mind stuck on the word *prenup*. She swallowed. "A *what*?"

He eased her closer and smoothed her hair. "When I walked away from you, I was hurt and angry. But then I got lonely, and then I got *scared*. Scared that I'd never see you again, never hold you again, never make love with you again. After that, I got determined."

Was he working his way up to the part about a prenup? She couldn't tell. "Rafe, what are you saying?"

"I'm saying that I'm determined to stay with you forever. I love you, Gina. And I hope you love me back, because I don't ever want to feel that kind of loneliness again."

Joy rushed through her, making her sway with relief. "I love you," she whispered through her clogged throat.

Rafe instantly wrapped his arms around her, holding her flush against his strength.

"There's not a lot open on the boardwalk this time of night," he whispered in her ear. "But I did manage to find this."

He reached into his pocket and produced a little box.

Gina drew back to look, her heart skipping a beat as he opened the box to reveal a stylized platinum band inset with a small sapphire, an emerald and a diamond.

"We can get something nicer," he said. "Design whatever we want. But I was in a hurry to seal the deal."

"It's beautiful," she whispered. She absolutely loved it.

"Will you marry me, Gina?"

"Yes." She nodded, her eyes going misty. "Yes! I love you, Rafe. I love you so much."

Epilogue

Gina's wedding was a far cry from her mother's yacht-board gala and completely different from the frothy extravaganzas she'd imagined as a little girl.

Her decoration was the fall foliage, bright on the trees at the Cortez-Williams Ranch. The air was comfortably cool midafternoon. The guests seated on folding chairs in the backyard were family and close friends, many long-standing members of the TCC.

She waited with her father on the back porch of the ranch house while bridesmaids Valencia and Anastasia walked over the cobblestoned pool deck toward the makeshift aisle. Rusty was all smiles dressed in his finest tux. His shave was close, his hair neatly trimmed as music from Diego's scaled-down acoustic band wafted on the breeze.

Rusty looked more at peace than Gina had ever seen him.

"Did you get hold of Antoinette?" she asked him.

"We don't need to talk about her right now." He took another look at Gina's breezy white cocktail-length wedding dress.

It was flat lace, a V-neck with spaghetti straps, a wide waistband and a full skirt that fluttered over her knees. Her bouquet was a ribbon-tied bunch of wildflowers picked just this morning on the ranch. She wore little white flats on her feet, great for walking on the lush lawn, while her hair was a casual low ponytail with a few waves and twists, just loose enough to frame her face.

"I'm curious," Gina said. "What did she say? How did she react?"

"We had a long talk, and she accepted my apology."

Gina knew he would be relieved. "So that's everyone?"

After the blowout with Billy, Rusty had become determined to turn over a new leaf with his immediate family and also to make amends with his ex-wives and lovers, along with some other folks he'd wronged in the past.

"That's everyone. And this is your wedding. Today is all about you."

"All about me?"

"Yes."

"Then can we talk about the methane energy proposal?" she asked, judging that she had about one minute left before Anastasia arrived at the greenery-decorated archway and the music changed for the bridal procession.

"No. I only have one daughter, and she's only having one wedding, and we're *not* talking business."

"You can't say no to the bride, Dad."

"That's why we're not talking business today."

"Did you read the report?"

The music changed, and everyone rose from their chairs.

"It's time," he said.

"Did you read the report?"

"Yes, I read it." He tucked her hand into his elbow. "Walking, Gina. We're walking. You don't want Rafe to think you're having second thoughts."

She started to walk along the pool deck. "I'm not having second thoughts."

"I know. Rafe's a good man."

"He made me write a prenup."

"I know that, too. He showed it to me. He was crystal clear on not taking any Edmond money."

"He signed it. I didn't. I'm not going to."

Rusty smiled as they rounded the pool. "You are the chattiest bride in the world."

"Known a lot of brides, have you?" she asked slyly.

Rafe came into view then, and she met his eyes, drinking in the depths of his dark gaze, watching his lips curve into a bright smile. His love seemed to reach out the length of the lawn, and she sent hers back to meet it.

Rusty squeezed her hand as they walked between the two rows of their close family and friends.

Gina smiled for everyone, but her focus was on Rafe, the man she loved, the man who was about to become her husband for better or worse, forever and ever.

She made it to the archway where Rafe stood with Lorenzo and Matias.

Rusty gave her a hug and a quick kiss on the cheek, and then her groom took her hand.

She passed her bouquet to Valencia to take Rafe's other hand for the ceremony.

Their vows flew by quickly, and soon they were exchanging rings. Then the preacher was pronouncing them husband and wife, and Rafe lifted her off the ground for a long, smoldering kiss.

The guests cheered and tossed flower pedals, and they were immediately surrounded by well-wishers.

Charlotte and JJ had joined in with Rafe's parents to produce a backyard barbecue feast. Mrs. Yeoh had baked an amazing honey orange wedding cake with spicy chocolate ganache.

Matias's band set up their speakers, and the dinner quickly turned into a rollicking dance.

When Gina finally sat down for a rest, Lila handed her a glass of refreshing iced tea and joined her at the table. "Did you hear the good news?"

"That Rafe married me?" Gina joked, lifting her glass in a mock toast before taking a drink.

Lila grinned and drank along with her. "I mean they got the money back. Well, most of it, anyway. Enough that none of the Royal businesses are at risk anymore."

"And Billy?" Gina asked, so happy to hear the news.

He hadn't been seen since the night at Mustang Point when his sports car slid off the road and into deep water during his escape.

"No sign of him. Could be sharks, or he could be on a beach in the Maldives."

"I hope he's on a beach." Gina couldn't bring herself to wish him any ill, especially now that they had the money back, and especially understanding that he'd been yet another victim of her father's misadventures. Her gaze shifted to Rusty where he was down on the grass, tux and all, playing with his grandson, Ben.

"Lani says someone sent Antoinette a million dollars," Lila confided.

"You think it was Billy?" Gina asked. It was oddly encouraging to think a man like Billy might finally be taking care of his mother after all this.

"Or it could be Rusty," Lila said.

"Possibly." Gina watched her father a minute longer, thinking it was like getting to know a whole new person.

Valencia plunked down on a chair next to Gina, her feet bare against the grass, her sandals dangling from one hand. "You and Rafe thinking about babies?" she asked.

The question took Gina by surprise. "We haven't even finished the wedding cake."

"I see you looking."

"At?"

"Ben. Adorable little guy, isn't he?"

"He is," Gina agreed. "But I was looking at Rusty, thinking how much he'd changed."

"Oh." Valencia seemed disappointed.

Gina took in her expression. "Wait. Why are you asking…?"

Valencia grinned and touched her hand to her stomach.

"No way!" Gina laughed, delighted with the news. "Tito

and Tita are going to be thrilled!" Gina knew Rafe's parents would adore some grandchildren, the more the better as far as they were concerned.

"Lorenzo can't wait to tell them."

"Is it still a secret?" Gina whispered.

A grinning Lila squeezed Valencia on the shoulder. "That's fantastic!"

"We wanted to wait until after your wedding. But now we'll start telling people. You should think about it."

"Maybe," Gina said. "Not tonight, though."

"Well, *I'll* keep you company," Lila said.

Both Gina and Valencia swung their heads her way.

"You *are*?" Valencia asked.

"Mine *is* a secret," Lila said. "It's really early. I just told Zach a couple of days ago."

Gina and Valencia both mimed zipping their lips and tossing away the key.

Rafe strode their way, his gaze drinking in Gina as he approached. "What are you all talking about?"

"Babies," Valencia said.

He reached for Gina's hand and drew her to her feet, wrapping an arm around her waist and giving her a quick kiss on the lips. "I'm in." He looked at his watch. "Can we do it now?"

"I like your attitude," Valencia said on a laugh.

Lorenzo joined them then, along with Zach.

"Rafe wants to make a baby on their honeymoon," Valencia told Lorenzo.

His eyes lit up. "Did you tell them?"

She nodded.

"Tell them what?" Rafe asked.

"Not Rafe, just the gals."

"Better congratulate me, little brother. It might be your wedding, but I'm going to be a daddy next summer."

"No way." Rafe grinned in delight and gave Lorenzo a hug.

Zach cleared his throat, and everyone looked his way. "Not to be outdone, Lorenzo." He pointed to Lila's stomach. "You're not the only one increasing the TCC junior membership next year."

"Congratulations, Lila." Lorenzo reached out his arms to give her a hug.

"I sense a challenge," Rafe said.

Gina held up her palms to slow things down, laughing at the same time. "We need to talk about this."

"Oh, don't you worry, Princess," Rafe rumbled in her ear, pulling her closer. "We most definitely will."

* * * * *

COMING SOON!

We really hope you enjoyed reading this book.
If you're looking for more romance, be sure to
head to the shops when new books are
available on

Thursday 14th
October

To see which titles are coming soon, please visit
millsandboon.co.uk/nextmonth

MILLS & BOON

THE HEART OF ROMANCE

A ROMANCE FOR EVERY READER

MODERN

Prepare to be swept off your feet by sophisticated, sexy and seductive heroes, in some of the world's most glamourous and romantic locations, where power and passion collide.

HISTORICAL

Escape with historical heroes from time gone by. Whether your passion is for wicked Regency Rakes, muscled Vikings or rugged Highlanders, awak the romance of the past.

MEDICAL

Set your pulse racing with dedicated, delectable doctors in the high-pressure world of medicine, where emotions run high and passion, comfort a love are the best medicine.

True Love

Celebrate true love with tender stories of heartfelt romance, from the rush of falling in love to the joy a new baby can bring, and a focus on the emotional heart of a relationship.

Desire

Indulge in secrets and scandal, intense drama and plenty of sizzling hot action with powerful and passionate heroes who have it all: wealth, status good looks…everything but the right woman.

HEROES

Experience all the excitement of a gripping thriller, with an intense romance at its heart. Resourceful, true-to-life women and strong, fearless m face danger and desire - a killer combination!

To see which titles are coming soon, please visit

millsandboon.co.uk/nextmonth

JOIN THE
MILLS & BOON
BOOKCLUB

* **FREE** delivery direct to your door

* **EXCLUSIVE** offers every month

* **EXCITING** rewards programme

50% OFF
YOUR FIRST
PARCEL

Join today at
Millsandboon.co.uk/Bookclub